THE REVELATION RELIC

BOOK TWO OF THE HUNTER FILES

ROB JONES

B
Boldwood

First published in 2020. This edition published in Great Britain in 2025 by Boldwood Books Ltd.

Copyright © Rob Jones, 2020

Cover Design by Tom Sanderson

Cover Images: Alamy and Shutterstock

The moral right of Rob Jones to be identified as the author of this work has been asserted in accordance with the Copyright, Designs and Patents Act 1988.

Every effort has been made to obtain the necessary permissions with reference to copyright material, both illustrative and quoted. We apologise for any omissions in this respect and will be pleased to make the appropriate acknowledgements in any future edition.

A CIP catalogue record for this book is available from the British Library.

Paperback ISBN 978-1-80600-006-7

Large Print ISBN 978-1-80600-007-4

Hardback ISBN 978-1-80600-005-0

Ebook ISBN 978-1-80600-008-1

Kindle ISBN 978-1-80600-009-8

Audio CD ISBN 978-1-80600-000-5

MP3 CD ISBN 978-1-80600-001-2

Digital audio download ISBN 978-1-80600-004-3

This book is printed on certified sustainable paper. Boldwood Books is dedicated to putting sustainability at the heart of our business. For more information please visit https://www.boldwoodbooks.com/about-us/sustainability/

Boldwood Books Ltd, 23 Bowerdean Street, London, SW6 3TN

www.boldwoodbooks.com

For my son Tom, an adventurer at heart

1

SUMMER, 1988

They had driven through the day, crossing a large part of the Sinai Peninsula and not reaching their destination until sunset.

It was a hard, dangerous route, and Vladimir Neverov cursed in the back seat of the GAZ-69 as they bounded down yet another sand dune. The old Soviet-built four-wheel drive was a relic from the production line back in Gorky during the Khrushchev Thaw, but the journey had been hard-going and it felt like the rear suspension was about to give up the ghost.

The young KGB officer aligned his compass rose with their present position and rotated the scratched glass housing until the arrow was oriented to the north. Then he turned the map and compass together until he had the final bearing. Like the rest of the team, he was keen to reach the final destination before full dark. Back in the Moscow winter, serious men in dark suits were anxiously awaiting them to report back with their findings.

'Update.'

Neverov turned and saw his boss, Mikhael Grudinin. Another serious man in a dark suit, only this one was sitting beside him on the other side of the GAZ. He looked like he wanted to be anywhere but here.

'We're almost there, sir.'

Grudinin shook his bald head and stared out of the window at the endless sand. 'Damn this place. I could be at home now, sitting in front of a plate of kurnik.' His mind drifted to the heavenly smell in his kitchen when his wife prepared his favourite savoury dish, a delicious dome-shaped pie stuffed with chicken, eggs, onions, and kasha. 'Instead I am here. I hate these cursed missions.'

'Sir?'

'You think I joined the Committee to chase stupid superstitious shadows out in the deserts of Egypt?'

When he said Committee, he meant KGB, and

from the tone of his voice, Neverov guessed his boss had not joined it to search for holy relics.

'What makes you think we're chasing stupid shadows, sir?'

Grudinin huffed a bitter laugh, shaking his head at the poor naïve fool sitting next to him. 'You have a great deal to learn about this world, Volodya.'

Neverov was surprised to hear the old man suddenly use the shortened version of his name, but kept his shock concealed from the much older, jaded man.

'And what do I have to learn, sir?'

'The stories in the Bible are just that – stories. Scary stories designed to keep gullible people like you in line.'

Neverov wasn't so sure, but he kept his thoughts to himself.

In the front seat of the GAZ, beside the driver, the Greek archaeologist leading the mission laughed and shook his head.

'Is something amusing you, Professor Samaras?' Grudinin asked.

'Nothing at all, Colonel.'

A tense pause. At the steering wheel, Agent Medinsky reached the bottom of the dune and struggled to navigate a bend in the rocky track. As he dropped down into second for extra torque, the old engine growled and belched a cloud of dark blue diesel fumes into the air behind them.

'Please, Professor,' Grudinin said. 'You can speak freely in here.'

Samaras turned and propped his elbow up on the back of the worn leather seat. 'You really think God is just a fairy tale?'

Grudinin stared at him, inscrutable and cold. 'I am an atheist, Professor. So, yes.'

'Ah, a good Party Man.'

'It's a personal conviction.'

Samaras nodded and grinned. 'Of course. I apologise.'

'But you disagree with me?' asked the Russian.

'I am a true believer, Colonel. So, yes.'

Grudinin managed a smile. 'And you have every right to believe in whatever you choose.'

'But what if it's more than just belief?'

The young Agent Neverov watched the conversation going back and forth like a tennis match.

'Explain,' Grudinin said flatly.

'What if I have seen things and touched things that prove to me that the stories in the Bible are true?'

Grudinin thought for a moment, determined not to be caught out. 'The stories being true would not necessarily prove the existence of God.'

'What if I have seen things that prove to me God is real?'

The Russian colonel shook his head. 'No, no. You're just being provocative.'

'I think maybe when you see what's in the Tomb of the Disciple you will have to ask yourself some serious questions. Maybe even completely change the way you see the universe.'

'But what exactly do you think we are going to find out here?' Neverov asked. 'My briefing notes were vague.'

'Deliberately so,' Grudinin said with a knowing smile.

'But Professor Samaras seems to have an idea, sir.'

The Greek man laughed. 'I have searched for the Tomb of the Disciple my entire career, young man. If we find what I think we might find, then our lives are about to change forever.'

Neverov leaned forward like a curious child. 'But what might we find?'

Samaras nodded at Grudinin. 'Something he doesn't want the Americans to find.'

Grudinin laughed. 'If you mean something that will help us end the Cold War in our favour, once and for all, then perhaps, but I remain sceptical.'

'Some say we will lose this war,' Neverov said, earning a sharp look from his superior.

'How can we lose against the Americans?' said Grudinin, wagging a finger of admonishment in the young officer's face. 'And I wouldn't talk like that if I were you. Moscow has a way of hearing everything a man says.'

Samaras sighed. 'If we find what I think we're going to find, I would be less worried about the Americans and more worried about...' He pointed his finger up at the sky. The truck rocked them all back and forth as Medinsky pulled it around another bend, tyres slipping and skidding on loose scree.

Grudinin laughed, but this time it was laced with uncertainty. He changed the subject. 'Just because General Patrushev thinks the end of the world is out here somewhere, hiding in some crumbling scroll or inside a bottle, I end up spending three weeks away from my family. How much further is this damned place, Agent Neverov?'

Back to formal titles. Much better, Neverov thought. He turned back to the folded paper map in his lap. 'Not much further, Colonel. Two or three miles.'

As they moved further south, they gained elevation and the sand gave way to a rocky landscape of feldspar and volcanics. The military vehicle struggled to climb another hill. The driver shifted down to first gear to increase torque as the tyres slipped on the rock chips and orange sands. Spying a shallower gradient to the north, he spun the wheel to the right but they quickly hit a patch of much softer sand. The entire vehicle lurched violently to the right.

They almost tipped over, and Neverov gripped the back of the seat in front of him as Medinsky struggled to control the problem. The map slipped off the KGB officer's lap as he stared down the steep slope of the hill. If they tipped over, the roll to the bottom would be a brutal lesson in desert driving and would probably write off their vehicle, not to mention the possibility of killing someone.

For a terrifying moment, everyone on board was certain they were going over, but then Medinsky finally negotiated a safer passage and brought the GAZ back around to more level ground before finally cresting the peak of the hill.

Neverov breathed a silent prayer, but his gratitude for still being alive was cut short by a breathtaking view stretching out to the west as they drove down the slope on the other side of the hill. The Egyptian sun was a blood-red semi-circle, cut in half by the desert horizon, and its soft, hot light was streaking across the ancient sands and lighting this desolate world a mellow amber.

The bleak landscape grew dark fast, and Medinsky switched on the headlights as they drew closer to their goal and the end of their mission. Neverov pulled the map and compass from the footwell and brushed the sand and grit from the creased paper. Realigning the compass on the map, he was relieved to see they had arrived.

Relieved and terrified.

Still new to the KGB, he wondered if every mission would be as unnerving as this one. Even his boss, the hard-nosed Yury Grudinin, fresh off the plane from Moscow, had worked hard to hide his nerves as he gave the briefing to the select group of field agents. The file which was marked ОВ – Особой Важности – raised a few eyebrows when it landed on their desks. Russian for Particularly Important, this was their equivalent of Top Secret, and the highest level of secrecy in the Soviet Union. Most work that came their way was usually a classification or two below this level so they all knew something critical to their nation's security was at stake.

None of them could have guessed just how critical it was, and not just to their own nation but the entire world. Critical, and so bone-chilling that three of the men had begged to be transferred off the mission after reading Grudinin's vague outline of the task to come. Hints, nudges, and winks moved slowly along the dull, underheated corridors of the Lubyanka. Even young Neverov had considered walking away, but he knew success in such a terrifying task would please people at the very top of the Kremlin and all but guarantee his future in the Communist Party.

'We're here,' Neverov said. 'According to our briefing notes, we have reached the location of the tomb.'

Samaras's eyes lit up like lanterns. 'I see it – hidden in that crevasse over there!'

Neverov squinted into the gloom. 'It's barely visible.'

'But I know what I'm looking for,' the Greek man said.

Grudinin tapped Medinsky on the shoulder. 'Kill the engine and get the men to set explosives at the entrance to the tomb. I want this done as fast as possible. American satellites are due to pass over the area in less than thirty minutes.'

'Yes, Colonel.'

Neverov climbed out of the GAZ just in time to see the sunset lighting the peak of Mount Sinai. A desert valley wind whipped along and cooled the sweat on his brow. His skin prickled as he imagined Moses taking the Ten Commandments from God on that very peak. Not that he would ever tell Colonel Grudinin he'd had such a thought.

To his left, Agents Medinsky, Lugovoy, and Gubenko had set the explosives in a narrow gully at the base of what the briefing notes had described in technical Russian as an alluvial apron. It just looked like a crumbling ridge of loose rocks to him. The three men clambered back up over some boulders and reported back to Grudinin.

'Everyone behind the GAZ,' the colonel said.

When he gave the order, Gubenko triggered the explosives and blasted several tons of Egyptian granite out into the purple twilight. When the dust and rock chunks had settled back to earth, they all saw an oval-shaped aperture in the rock around five and a half feet high.

'Smaller than I thought it would be,' Lugovoy said.

Gubenko spat on the sand and sniffed. 'Who gives a damn how small it is?'

Samaras smiled. 'The average height of a man during the Bible age.'

Grudinin was already padding up to the entrance.

'We must hurry. I don't want the satellites seeing us here. Professor Samaras, you're up front with me.'

'Should I watch the truck?' Neverov said.

Grudinin laughed. 'You think the goats will take it somewhere? No, we can leave the truck.'

They entered the hole and followed a narrow passageway into the side of Mount Sinai. The evidence that it was manmade was everywhere – chisel marks in the rock and even some scuffs left behind by the sandals of those who had carved it out. There were no twists and turns, just a long, straight tunnel inclining deep down inside the mountain. After a ten-minute walk, they found a small room-size chamber filled with chests and stone idols.

Samaras blew out a deep breath. 'Look at these idols!'

Grudinin pushed a button on his digital watch and lit up the time. 'Forget about the idols and search the chests. Time is running out.'

His men got to work, roughly prising the chests' lids off with crowbars and quickly going through the contents. Gold coins, plates and goblets, and uncut gems spilled out onto the dusty floor, but none raised even a flicker of interest in Grudinin. Then, Neverov gasped. The Russian colonel walked over to him and looked down into the chest he had been searching.

'My God.'

'Literally,' Samaras said.

Neverov noticed Medinsky and Lugovoy each take a step back. Gubenko, on the other hand, moved closer, his eyes wild with untamed curiosity.

'But what does this mean?' Neverov asked.

'Yes, Dr Samaras,' the colonel said. 'Can you tell us what we have here? Have we found what General Patrushev is looking for? Only you are qualified to authenticate it.'

Samaras tottered closer in the chamber, his dark unblinking eyes fixed on the cache before the tomb raiders. As he drew nearer, he brushed past Medinsky's arm and knocked his flashlight onto the floor. The KGB man swore at him in Russian, but the archaeologist was too enthralled by the glittering haul that he didn't notice.

'Well?' barked Grudinin.

Samaras picked up an impressive statue of an ox and began to study the inscriptions and images painted on its surface. Carefully turning it in his hand and checking the reverse, his lips bent into a nervous smile. 'Yes, this is the work of John the Apostle.'

'You're certain?'

'I have spent the last thirty years studying for this

moment, Colonel.' He blew a cloud of powdery dust from the glaze to reveal a dull sheen and a little more of the inscription. 'It's magnificent.'

'And you're totally certain?'

A quick nod and then his eyes swivelled back to the statue. 'Yes, I am quite sure.'

Grudinin needed no further proof. 'Lugovoy, take the statue from Professor Samaras and get it back to the truck. Gubenko and Medinsky, go with him. Prepare us for the journey out of this hellhole.'

'Sir.'

Samaras's eyes sparkled in the yellow glow of the flashlights. 'What we have found here will change the world, Colonel. All of our lives have just changed forever. We are about to go on a wonderful journey into a new era of enlightenment and belief.'

'Perhaps so,' Grudinin said. 'But unfortunately, you will not be joining us on that journey.'

Samaras frowned. 'I don't understand.'

'My apologies, but I have my orders.'

When Grudinin drew his trusty Tokarev pistol from an appendix holster and aimed it at Samaras, the Greek archaeologist took a step back, horrified. His inherent trust had been betrayed. Neverov was even more shocked, raising his palms in a desperate plea to his superior not to do anything crazy.

'Sir!' he said. 'What's going on?'

'Orders from the Kremlin, Agent Neverov. Take a step back, please.'

'You can't kill a man in—'

The gun exploded in the small chamber, almost impossibly loud. The acrid smell of the smoke clawed at Neverov's nostrils as Professor Samaras clutched his bleeding stomach and tumbled to the sandy ground. Reaching out with one hand in a desperate attempt to stop another shot, the ageing KGB colonel fired twice more into his head, killing him instantly.

'Out to the truck, Volodya.'

'I can't believe you killed him.'

'As I said, you have a lot to learn about this world. You think we want an academic bragging about this and writing papers on it? As of two minutes ago, this is the most important state secret we have. Tell the men to set more explosives. I want no evidence there was ever a passageway here, understand?'

Neverov mumbled a response and staggered out of the tunnel, still unable to believe what he had just seen. Scrambling up the slope back to the GAZ, he called out to Gubenko to bring more explosives. When Gubenko walked past him with his hands full of dynamite, neither man said a word. At the top of the gully, Lugovoy and Medinsky were packing the ancient statue into a steel box in the back of the GAZ.

When Neverov reached them, he leaned against the side of the truck and took a deep breath. Swigging warm water from a tin canteen, he watched Grudinin exit the passageway and walk back up the slope with Gubenko at his side. Then, when they were all gathered together, Grudinin ordered the tomb to be closed and Gubenko detonated the explosives, hiding the entrance forever.

Neverov wasn't sure what he had witnessed here tonight, but he knew it was nothing good.

2

PRESENT DAY

Amy Fox awoke with a start.

Somewhere in the darkness, her telephone was ringing. She reached out for the small lamp on her bedside table and switched it on, blinking as her eyes adjusted to the new light. Next job was to grab the phone and find out what was going on. She already knew from the ringtone that the caller was her boss, the former US Navy officer James Gates.

'Hello?' She was so drowsy she sounded like she'd been drugged.

'Up with the lark I see.'

She yawned loudly. 'It's five o'clock in the morning, Jim.'

'And I've already run ten miles, had a healthy low-fat high-fibre breakfast, and got half the crap off my desk.'

'But what about when your family finds out your secret identity as Superman?'

'My family already loves that part of my life. My wife especially loves the red boots.'

Despite the early hour, Amy smiled and swung her legs out of bed. 'I'm guessing this call isn't about your wife's strange taste in footwear,' she said, and then under her breath, 'or men...'

'It certainly is not, Special Agent Fox. I'm calling to alert you to a possible situation we might have up in the Port of New York.'

A possible situation. That was Gates's way of saying a large amount of shit was about to hit the fan in the biggest, ugliest way possible. She sighed. Another day, another dollar, right?

'So what's up in New York, Jim?'

'You remember the briefing I gave you and the team when you finished the Atlantis mission?'

She felt her skin crawl as she recalled the image on the slide he had projected up onto the wall of the conference room. 'How could I ever forget?'

'I have an update.'

'And?'

A slight hesitation. 'Not over the phone. Can you get into the office?'

She checked her watch. 'Give me a half-hour.'

* * *

Gates was sipping a steaming black coffee when she walked into his office in FBI headquarters. He set it down on the desk and winced at her. 'Damn it, that's too hot. And thanks for getting in so fast.'

She threw her bag down on a spare chair. 'I was intrigued.'

'Me too.'

'So what's the story?'

He leaned back in his chair. 'When I got in this morning I had a message to call a contact of mine in Amsterdam. It's now half ten in the morning there. You know that time. It's when you usually get out of bed.'

'A superhero with a sense of humour. Somebody pinch me.'

Gates smiled but ignored the comment. 'Pieter Klaver – that's my Dutch contact, if you've been paying attention – told me that they just got some intel regarding a container ship called the *Goa Ex-*

press. It left the Port of Rotterdam six days ago, headed for New York City.'

'If you're thinking of taking your wife on a cruise, I think she'll be disappointed.'

'A junior employee with attitude. Somebody pinch me.'

'Hey, you're talking to the deputy director of HARPA.'

'And as my deputy, you need to know that the *Goa Express* isn't just bringing plastic junk into the United States. According to Pieter, the ship is being used by a gang of international smugglers to bring a small treasure trove of stolen relics into the country. Could be one of the biggest hauls we've seen.'

'And how is this connected to the slide you showed us?'

Gates paused before making his reply. 'The strange statue of the eagle?'

'And more specifically, the message on it.'

Amy's words were spoken softly, but they had stirred a deep emotion in the two old friends. A silence fell over the small room as they recalled the terrible message delivered to them by the keramos clay eagle statue. Gates had found it on an earlier mission in Mexico and it had immediately concerned him.

Painted so carefully onto the feathered belly of the bird of prey, the simple Koine Greek lettering and the image below it had chilled the blood in their veins.

And the last word of God will unleash the Apocalypse and strike terror into Man.

The letters were painted on the terracotta clay statue and protected behind a classic ancient Greek black glaze, just like the horrifying picture beneath it – a terrible explosion blasting out of a mountain and leaving a wasteland of burning olive trees and corpses in its devastating wake.

Gates broke the tense silence. 'The eagle statue is a priceless historical artifact but mostly remained a mystery until Pieter contacted me. That's when I decided to show you the slide and bring you inside the mission. I'm bringing this up now because vague chatter has turned into something real. Now, Pieter's work has paid off, and some of the information he gave me leads me to think we might find something similar in the haul. Specifically, he mentioned a statue of an ox. Made of painted terracotta clay just like the eagle, same size, same colours, same sort of horrific picture and with similar lettering.'

'Is that as specific as Pieter gets?'

'Yes, but the intel is good. I trust him. Tell me, do you know how long it takes a container ship like the *Goa Express* to cross the Atlantic?'

'I'm guessing six days.'

'Then you win a cigar. It's sailing into the Port of New York right now. That's the good news – the bad news is that he thinks there might be someone else tracking it. He thinks maybe more smugglers are trying to steal it before it gets to its final destination.'

'That makes things more interesting.'

'And dangerous, so stay on top of this one.'

He got up from behind his desk. Amy had known him long enough to know this meant the meeting was over and she should get on with the job. She took the hint, got up from her chair, and smiled. 'And what about Dr Hunter?'

He paused in front of her, with no smile. 'What about him?'

'Has he got the green light to join us on this mission or not?'

Gates shrugged. 'He hasn't formally requested to join HARPA, but then you already know that, right?'

'I know.'

'Then the answer is no.'

'But we could use him, Jim.'

Gates tipped his head to one side. 'Then he has to

climb down off his little high horse and request to join the team.'

She sighed. 'He's not like that at all.'

A smile finally appeared on the director's face. 'Wait a minute, are you two seeing each other?'

She rubbed the back of her neck and glanced away.

'Question asked, question answered.'

'As a matter of fact, we might have spent some time together off the clock. Some meals, maybe. Gone to a few bars together. Anything wrong with that, Director Gates?'

He raised his palms. 'Hey, what you choose to do in your spare time is your business. It still doesn't get him into HARPA.'

She held in the sigh of frustration she felt building. 'We need him.'

'Sounds like you need him, but the team is another thing. There are a lot of relic anoraks out there, Amy.'

'We wouldn't have gotten to Atlantis without him, and I probably wouldn't even be here today.'

Another long pause. 'All right, if it makes it easier for his fragile eggshell ego, you can tell him I want him on board the team.'

Amy stood on her tiptoes and pecked Gates on

the cheek. They went back a long way and were more like family than friends. 'Thanks, Jim. I knew I could count on you.'

He blew out a breath. 'It's tough being the bigger man, but I can rise to the challenge.' He walked back across to his desk and pulled open the top drawer. 'I have prepared a small briefing file on the *Goa Express* and what you can expect up there, including some possible detail on the artifacts. As I say, it looks like it might link up to the operation I did in Mexico, and I don't like it. I want you to read it and then gather the rest of the team. You can brief them on the plane on the way to New York.'

She hesitated.

'Is there a problem? Major Ego needs a separate briefing?'

She pursed her lips. 'Not at all. I'd like to run this past Sal before the others.'

'Why?'

'He mentioned something to me a few days ago – said he was worried about something. I want to make sure everything's okay.'

'Good call,' he said. 'And good luck.'

* * *

Amy arranged to meet Sal Blanco on the steps of the Jefferson Memorial because it was halfway between his DC apartment and the FBI headquarters building. When she rounded the western end of the path running to its north, she saw her old friend leaning against one of its famous pillars with his hands in his pockets. He was looking out across the water, lost in thought, the wind gently lifting the lock of silver hair above his forehead.

'Hey, stranger.'

He turned. 'Amy, sorry. I was miles away.'

'I saw. Anything you want to talk to me about before we get to business?'

He shrugged. 'Just the fears of an old man. Nothing for a young fighter like you to worry about.'

She paused, hoping he might say more. When the silence stretched, she knew any hopes she might have harboured regarding him opening up to her were dashed. She decided to change the subject.

'I just spoke to Jim an hour ago.'

'So your message said.' Blanco had returned his gaze to the tidal basin at the bottom of the steps. 'Do I need to start packing for somewhere exotic?'

'Not sure,' she said. 'He wants us to go to New York.'

'That's a no then,' said the man from Brooklyn. 'What's the gig?'

'He wants us to intercept a container ship coming in from Rotterdam. Says he has intel it's got a big haul of smuggled relics on board. One of the biggest ever, potentially.'

He whistled. 'That's quite a comment coming from the master of understatement.'

She laughed. 'Just what I was thinking.'

Blanco kicked at a small stone chip in front of his boot and watched some tourists making their way across the water. For a long time, he had felt old and used up, but since working for Gates he'd experienced a new lease of life. While just about all of his old friends were settling down to an easy life and enjoying the soft pleasures of retirement, Blanco felt like he'd been given a second chance to make a difference.

'Any more detail on what we're looking for?' he asked.

'A possible partner to the eagle statue we saw in the briefing room after the Atlantis mission.'

Blanco went quiet. 'Ah.'

'Exactly, but this time it's an ox. The relic may be Greek and Bible-era.'

'How do we know this?'

'It's the specialty of the smuggler who Jim's Dutch contact is tracking.'

'We have a name?'

She pulled out her phone and started thumbing through to her notes. 'Sure, hang on.'

Blanco's eyes crossed back to the water. A cold, grey vista and dark omen of the long, bitter winter to come. 'You know, who the hell wants to take a paddle-boat out when it's this cold?'

She smiled. 'Here – guy's name is Boris Markovich, a Serbian relic smuggler with a record as long as your arm. Served time for a number of antiq-uity-related offences in Turkey and Italy as well as his homeland. Former Serbian Army corporal and all-round tough guy.'

Blanco let out a weary laugh. 'Okay, thanks.'

Amy decided to have another go at prising the quiet man's mind open once again. 'Sal, a few days ago you mentioned to me that you were worried about something.'

His head slumped down for a second. 'Geez, not this. I shouldn't have said anything.'

'No, you were right to, but I can't help if you don't tell me. I hope that I'm more than your boss, Sal.'

'You are. You know you are.'

'So, speak to me. Is there something wrong?'

'Not with me, no. It's a family thing that I thought maybe might stop me from working for HARPA for a while, but it's not going to be a problem. I swear.'

She wasn't convinced. 'Are you sure you don't want to tell me what's going on?'

'I said it's no problem.'

'All right, fine.'

He smiled and the old, unworried Sal was back. 'So what now?'

'I call the rest of the team and we fly to New York.'

'I'll go pack.'

3

Scheduled to touch down at JFK International Airport just before midday, the HARPA jet was making good time on the short flight from the nation's capital to New York City. Twenty thousand feet over northern Maryland and still climbing, Amy popped open her seatbelt and unlocked her swivel chair. As she turned to face the rest of the small team, the first thing she saw was the question on Max Hunter's face.

'Max, go ahead.'

'Is it normal for things to move this fast for a simple smuggling operation?'

'No, but this time we're under pressure. Our intel about the *Goa Express* is worrying and there's a real danger the relics are being tracked by another group. They could intercept the ship and Markovich's haul before we get there.'

Hunter shrugged. 'So, have some local law enforcement step in and keep it safe in the meantime.'

'This has already been arranged,' she said patiently. 'We're not fools. New York FBI agents are already onsite and keeping the ship under surveillance until we arrive. If Markovich tries to leave the ship with the goods, he'll be stopped. If there's any attempt to raid the vessel and steal the artifacts before we can get to it, their orders are to do all they can to protect them. But it's our job and ultimately our responsibility, so that's why we're on a plane.'

'Seems fair enough.'

'Imagine my relief,' she said sarcastically.

Hunter gave her a wink and a wry smile. 'All right, all right. I was just saying.'

'He was just saying,' Lewis repeated. The former US Marine liked to banter with the team and had enjoyed working with them since finishing his history doctorate. Watching Amy and Hunter battle for supremacy was as good a pastime as any, even if they all knew who was going to win in the end.

Quinn glanced up from the glow of her laptop and scanned the faces of the team. Shrugging, the young goth repeated Lewis's words, deadpan. 'He was just saying.'

Before Jodie could add to it, Amy clapped her hands and brought her team to attention. 'All right, settle down with the gags, and let's get to the briefing. We have a lot to get through and you need to know much more detail about what's going on before we go in.'

'Sounds ominous,' Hunter said.

Amy returned his wink. 'Then listen up, soldier.'

Hunter gave a mock salute. 'Yes, ma'am.'

'As you all know, we're on our way to New York to intercept a container ship. What you don't know is that we think we might have an idea about one of the artifacts on board.'

'Ah,' Lewis said. 'Another reason for the urgency?'

Amy nodded. It was good to know his mind was on the job and not on his new family. 'Sure. What's concerning Jim is a series of photographs his Rotterdam contact provided as part of the Dutch intel on the *Goa Express* smuggling operation. Most of the images are nothing more than the usual snapshots of artifacts and relics taken for auction catalogues or museum books.'

'But?' asked Jodie.

'But one of them – a partial shot of the top of a

statue – has raised some concerns due to its similarity with an object already seized by Director Gates.'

'Don't tell me,' Quinn said. 'The object in question is the statue Jim showed us in the briefing after the Atlantis mission?'

'Got it in one,' Amy said. 'I know we were all shocked by the implications of the eagle statue he showed us and the reference to the apocalypse painted on it.'

'Um, yeah,' said Jodie. 'You might say that.'

'Where did the eagle ágalma come from exactly?' Hunter asked.

'The what?' said Jodie.

'*Ágalma*,' Hunter repeated. 'It's the correct word for a Greek votive offering – a statue representing some kind of divine being.'

'That's real interesting, Hunter,' Jodie said.

He leaned forward and smiled. 'The plural being *agálmata*, just in case you want some small talk for your next dinner party.'

'Yeah, right.'

Amy was enjoying the banter but moved things back to business. 'Several years ago, Jim's previous team infiltrated a team of relic smugglers. It was a long and expensive operation designed to bring down one of the biggest artifact smuggling rings on the black market. It worked, but at a cost. Two of his men were shot dead on board the smugglers' boat and dumped overboard in the Gulf of Mexico.'

The tension rose. Blanco tapped his pen on the arm of the chair. Jodie chewed her lip and stared into the middle distance. Quinn pretended not to have heard at all and simply gazed out of the window at the cloud tops. Lewis dipped his head and sighed.

'Despite the loss of the two men,' Hunter said, 'you said the operation was a success?'

'That's right.' With the hard part over, her voice was now rising in tone again. 'The entire network was brought down, from the smugglers on the boat all the way to the men in suits pulling their strings from their headquarters in Salzburg.'

'An expensive success,' Blanco said mindfully.

'Ain't cheap flying to Salzburg,' Quinn said.

The man from Brooklyn frowned. 'I wasn't talking about the money.'

After a pause, Amy said, 'We work in law enforcement, Sal.'

'I know.'

Amy continued. 'When his team was going through the haul on the boat and building an inventory for the trial, they numbered over two thousand stolen pieces of value, mostly taken from museum burglaries around the world and also some robberies of private collections. However, several of the pieces were completely new and uncatalogued.'

'The eagle ágalma with the apocalypse reference?' Hunter asked.

Amy nodded.

'Statue,' Jodie said quietly. 'Please just say statue. I'm begging you.'

'I'll consider it,' he said. 'Just for you.'

'And this is where the plot thickens, right?' Quinn said.

'You bet it is,' said Amy. 'Most of the pieces were of relatively little value or interest, except for the legendary Japanese sword, the Kusanagi, which was swiftly dispatched to a—'

'Secure location,' the team said together.

'Yes, very funny,' Amy said. 'The sword was taken to a secure location, and no, I don't know if it's the same site where the Atlantean fire lance went, so please don't ask.'

'Wouldn't even think of it,' Hunter said.

She raised a sceptical eyebrow. 'Moving on. Apart from the Kusanagi, the only other item of serious interest was the eagle statue.'

'Which represents the resurrection,' Lewis said.

'No kidding?' said Jodie.

Lewis said, 'In biblical times, various animals symbolised different things. The lamb, most famously, represented Christ. The dove was peace and purity. Dogs usually meant loyalty. Snakes and dragons were symbols of evil or the devil. The eagle represents the resurrection.'

Amy continued. 'So, Jim had the eagle statue studied by all the best experts in the field...'

'Not all of them,' Hunter said with a raised eyebrow. 'I never saw it.'

'This was nine years ago,' Amy said. 'When you were in grad school.'

'Ah.'

'Ah, exactly.'

Jodie sighed. 'Would you let her finish, Hunter? You're driving me nuts, man.'

He raised his palms. 'I won't say another word.'

Amy said, 'So the best experts in the field studied the statue and agreed it was totally unique because of its artwork and colouring. However, a Professor Dominic Barton of—'

'Cambridge,' Hunter said. 'He died two or three years ago. A brilliant archaeologist. Julian knew him.'

Another silence as the team thought back to Professor Julian Walters, Hunter's mentor who had been shot and killed by the Creed in Egypt during the hunt

for Atlantis. The mysterious organisation had revealed itself to be an ancient cult secretly controlling
much of the world, and its mere mention filled them
all with a deep sense of dread. To break the tension,
Jodie leaned forward, glared at him, and said, 'Not
one more word, or I swear to God I will throw you out
of this goddam plane.'

'Not one more word, I promise.' Hunter pretended to zip his lips shut and throw away the key.

Amy smiled. 'Anyway, Barton went a step further
than the other experts and claimed that the creator of
the statue was connected in some way to John of
Patmos.'

'Whoa,' Jodie said. 'Brake check – who's that?'

Lewis's face had changed. 'John of Patmos wrote
the last book of the Bible.'

'Revelation?' Blanco asked.

'That's right,' Lewis said. 'Some scholars claim he
and John the Apostle were one and the same, but
there's a debate about exactly who wrote the book.
Either way, we all saw the Apocalypse reference on
the statue during the briefing, but connecting it up to
John the Apostle is another whole thing altogether.
Amy, this is heavy stuff.'

'Right. Heavy.'

'Me no likey,' said Quinn.

Everyone on the team saw Lewis's historian mind was starting to whir like a well-oiled motor. He was already trying to put pieces of the puzzle together, trying to contribute to the brand-new team. 'What made them say there was a connection between the eagle statue and John of Patmos – besides the apocalypse reference?'

'Full details can only come from Jim, but in his briefing notes, I read that Professor Barton was adamant about the connection. He claimed the signing of the name John found on some of the original Revelation manuscripts was the same as the signature on the statue. He also thought the statue contained some kind of hidden code relating to a missing scroll.'

'An unknown chapter of Revelation?' Lewis asked.

Amy nodded. 'Exactly, and along with the reference on the statue to the apocalypse, you can see why we're so concerned. If Barton was right, the implications are huge. HARPA has to stay on top of this one.'

Mouth clamped shut and with a look of mock-fear at Jodie, Hunter raised his hand.

Jodie sighed and rolled her eyes. 'You can speak, Hunter, but I reserve the right to throw you out of the plane if you're annoying.'

'Got it. Barton never wrote about this, Amy. Trust

me, I'd know if he had. I know all the literature in the field. Was he bought off? Silenced by the government?'

'Uncle Sam asked him politely to keep it to himself, classified the statue and his findings Top Secret and hushed it up.'

'But he never found any missing scroll,' Hunter said. 'I'm sure I'd have heard about it.'

Amy shook her head and glanced at her watch. 'Read the briefing notes before we land – there's just time. Each of you has a separate copy. The quick answer is that Professor Barton said the information on the statue was incomplete, fragmentary. He needed more to go on and he never got it. As you said, he died three years ago without ever knowing the truth.'

'And Jim says a statue in the Dutch pictures was similar to the one Barton studied?' Blanco asked.

'Eerily similar,' she said. 'The form of the statue is different – an ox – but it looks like it's got the same signature on it.'

'If it gives us the missing information Barton was looking for,' Hunter said, 'this could lead to a serious archaeological find.'

'Tell me about it,' Amy said.

Jodie muttered, 'And lots of trouble.'

Then the silence was broken by a new voice.

'This is your pilot speaking.'

'The voice of God!' Blanco said, causing a gentle titter.

'We'll be landing in the next twenty minutes. Please ensure you are seated and buckled up.'

Amy looked at Max. 'You heard what God said. Buckle up, Max – this ride's about to get interesting.'

4

The HARPA team's short flight to the city touched down at JFK and now they were driving west through Brooklyn to reach their destination. Happy in his hometown, Blanco was at the wheel and boring everyone with stories of his wild teenage years in Bensonhurst and Bath Beach. Their journey came to an end in Sunset Park when he pulled to a stop in the South Brooklyn Marine Terminal.

'We're here,' he said. 'Sorry about the rain.'

Hunter stared out of the window and took it all in. The Port of New York and New Jersey was an industrial district on the east coast of the United States built around Upper Bay. Airports, railroads, and highways converged and created a major transportation hub where once the vast natural harbour had been dominated by tidal salt marshes and oyster banks.

At the heart of it all, a complex system of navigable waterways spilled out into Lower Bay and further out, the mighty Atlantic Ocean. Here, some of the world's biggest ships cruised upstream to specially built container terminals at Howland Hook and Port Jersey and unloaded millions of tons of imports every year.

Lewis was first to step out into the drizzle with a loud yawn. Behind him, Jodie emerged from the back of the SUV and patted him on the back. 'That baby keeping you up at night, Ben?'

'You could say that,' he said wearily. 'Not one decent night's sleep since he was born. It's like a horror movie – *The Man That Sleep Forgot*.'

'You love him really,' she said.

Amy stepped out. 'How's Meg?'

'She's doing fine, thanks,' a beaming Lewis replied. 'She's a great mom. It's great bringing a brand-new life into the world.'

'Sounds like a pain in the ass to me,' said Quinn.

Amy glowered at her. 'Hey, you were someone's baby once.'

She folded her arms in a sign of defiance. 'Wrong. Ghost never had parents.'

Lewis turned to her. 'That I can almost believe.'

The goth shrugged innocently while Amy walked past her and took in the busy harbour. Among a host of smaller vessels, two supersized container ships were moored up on the grey water. One was mostly empty of containers and quiet with no sign of anyone on deck or the bridge. The other was full and being unloaded by a colossal ship-to-shore gantry crane. She watched the giant machine hoist a faded red intermodal container off the portside deck and lower it down into a yard busy with forklift trucks and men in hardhats.

'That's where we want to go,' she said, pointing at the ship. 'The MV *Goa Express*.'

Blanco stared up at the giant vessel. 'I think I see our guys on deck, too.'

They walked up an aluminium beam brow gangway and were met by Special Agents Bradley Miller and Nate Brown. The two men were wearing black suits and gave Amy a cheery handshake and a smile when she reached the top of the gangway.

'Where's the artifact we spoke about?' she asked.

'In an office on the bridge deck,' Brown said.

'And you're sure it's what we're looking for?'

He nodded. 'Pretty damn sure. I'll take you there.'

They followed the two FBI agents along one of the ship's corridors and then up another metal staircase. The paint was white but chipped, and the stench of old bunker fuel lingered in the air as they made their way up to the bridge deck. The black molasses-thick fuel used by ships like the *Goa Express* was the dregs of the oil-refining process and loaded with sulphur, which when burnt filled the air with highly noxious emissions. Amy waved the smell away from her face as she climbed to the top of the stairs behind Agent Brown, who now turned and showed them into a small office on their left guarded by another agent.

'This is Special Agent Frank Guy.'

'Hey.'

'There it is,' Guy said. 'Knock yourselves out.'

Amy stepped over the door's lower bulkhead plate and went into the room. The smell of oil was thinner here, almost non-existent, and a cheap, laminate table was pushed up against a white-painted steel wall. Sitting on top of it was a vintage wooden tea chest full of straw stuffing, its lid prised off and resting beside it. In the corner, a man was sitting on a chair, his right hand cuffed to a bilge pipe.

'Good news, Markovich,' Miller said to the man.

'These nice people are here to put you in jail for the rest of your life.'

Markovich sneered. 'Why don't you improve the world and jump off the side of this ship?'

'Meet Boris Markovich,' said Brown.

'We'll have a chance to talk later,' Amy said, and then she and Hunter walked over to the chest and peered inside while Blanco checked the small adjoining office was empty. Lewis slipped his hands in his pockets and started to chew the fat with Miller while Jodie and Quinn stood quietly beside him, eyes all over the mysterious chest.

Amy reached inside and pulled out the statue. 'What do you make of this, Max?'

Hunter's eyes were already sparkling with curiosity as he took the eagle from her and started to turn it in his hands. 'It's definitely Bible-era.'

Blanco's eyebrows raised half an inch. 'It's beautiful.'

'And I'm not entirely sure because my Koine Greek isn't perfect, but the inscription looks fragmentary, like the one back in DC. It reads "They must ask the Lion..." and maybe this word here could be "man" but the rest is in pretty bad shape. I'll need longer to be more specific, but I'm going to bet this is not a complete sentence. This suggests a preceding sentence that doesn't fit with the one on the eagle – "And the last word of God will unleash the Apocalypse and strike terror into Man." Given that we have an eagle and now an ox, it looks like we could be looking for another statue – a lion.'

Lewis's face lit up. 'Of course! The Four Living Beings of the Revelation!'

Amy looked at him. 'Ben?'

'In the third section of *Revelation*, "Before the Throne of God", John wrote about what he called the four living creatures or beings of the Revelation. These were the Lion, the Ox, the Man, and the Eagle. Looks like he had four statues created to represent the beings he saw in his vision.'

'Vision?' Jodie asked.

'That's for a little later, I think,' Amy said with a glance at Markovich.

'Please don't stop,' Markovich said smugly. 'This all makes sense. There was another statue.'

Amy said, 'What did you just say?'

'I said there was another statue, just like that one. Back in Beirut.'

Special Agent Brown walked over and stared down at the cuffed man in the chair. 'Keep talking, Markovich.'

He shrugged. 'I said there was another statue just

like the one he is holding but in the form of a lion instead of an ox.'

'Say that again,' Amy said.

Markovich sneered. 'What are you all, deaf?'

'Don't get cute, Markovich,' Miller said. 'You're already looking at a long time behind bars for your role in relic-smuggling. Maybe you start talking and tell us something about this other statue and we might whisper something nice about you in the judge's ear at your trial.'

Markovich's laugh was dark. 'I think you have this deal the other way around, my American friend. You get me immunity from prosecution first, and then I tell you what I know.'

Miller's face started to redden with anger, but Brown stepped in. 'That only works if the information you have is worth the immunity.'

Another shrug. 'Maybe it is, maybe it isn't.'

'We don't have time for this,' Amy said. 'What is it you know, Markovich?'

'Yeah,' Miller said. 'Do you know where this other statue is?'

Markovich sighed. 'No, but I know where this one here is supposed to be going, and that information is in my head only. Nowhere else. Not even on the manifest. He is a very powerful man and perhaps he knows a little more about the other statue. I can give you his name and location, but only when I see a legal court document giving me full transactional immunity.'

'You seem to know a lot about it,' Guy said.

'When you are in my trade, you learn to look after yourself.'

'Trade...' Blanco said with a cynical laugh.

'And you won't talk without it?' Brown asked.

Markovich shook his head, slowly and deliberately. 'Not one word.'

Brown looked at Miller and shrugged. 'You know what I think about this kind of thing.'

Miller said, 'Agent Fox?'

'If there's another one of these statues, we need to know where it is,' she said without hesitation. 'And fast. Both this one and the one we already have contain only partial fragments of some kind of clue relating to something that may be a threat to the vital national security of the United States, and possibly the world.'

Brown nodded as he mulled it over. 'Give me an hour.'

* * *

When Brown returned, he had what they needed. Pulling his iPhone from a pocket, he flicked to a scanned copy of the Judicial Immunity of Suit and shoved it in Markovich's face. The man handcuffed to the pipe cast his eye over it and smirked. 'Looks official.'

'It is official, you asshole,' Brown said. 'I wouldn't have given it to you. I'd have beaten the information out of you.'

Markovich shrugged. 'I guess we know why you are at the bottom of the legal food chain then.'

Brown bristled, but Miller pulled him back.

'You tell us the location of the man receiving these stolen artifacts,' Brown said, wiggling the phone in front of his captive. 'You tell us right now, or you can forget about this. And be careful what you tell us, Markovich, because if we get there and find out you were lying, you can also forget about your immunity.'

'I'm not lying,' the man said. 'I have nothing to lose. The man's name is Alexios Kandarian.'

They all recognised the name. Kandarian was one of the richest men in the world, famed for his entrepreneurial exploits and love of the ancient world. His international cargo company was worth billions.

Brown laughed. 'I think I speak for us all when I say, you're shitting me.'

'I am not lying to you,' Markovich said. 'This statue was sold to Alexios Kandarian, along with everything else in this shipment. I can't tell you what he wants to do with it. Perhaps he plans on keeping it, or fencing it on; maybe he is just a middleman. Who knows? But I tell you the truth when I tell you that this shipment belongs to him and that I saw another similar statue, just like this one but a lion instead of an ox, back in Beirut.'

'And you don't know who bought that other statue?' Amy asked.

'No. It went with another smuggler.'

'You get that, Special Agent Fox?' Miller said.

Amy nodded. 'Yes, thanks.'

Brown leaned in closer to Markovich and jabbed his chest with his finger. 'I meant what I said, you little bastard. If you're lying to us, then you can forget about this immunity. If my colleagues here don't find what they want when they speak to Kandarian, you're going down for at least ten years.'

'I'm not lying. I'm only too happy to speak with Mr Kandarian and talk to him for you. Perhaps I could even get the lion statue for you. I have many skills and connections that would make the task only too easy. Just remove these cuffs.'

Brown shook his head, fighting back the urge to strike him. 'All right, take him away.'

As Guy dragged Markovich to his feet, Amy took a closer look at the ox statue with growing concern on her face. 'I think Jim is right. I think this is part of the same set like the one he found in Mexico. I have a very bad feeling this is one of these Revelation statues Ben is talking about.'

Markovich paused in the doorway. 'I think you're closer to the truth than you think, Agent Fox.'

'Keep moving, asshole,' Miller said.

'No, wait,' Amy said, looking at the condemned man. 'Why did you say that?'

'Kandarian,' he said. 'I thought everyone knew.'

'Knew what?'

'He is part of an ancient—'

The bullet tore through Markovich's throat and buried itself in Miller's temple. Both men slumped to the metal floor, dead with blood flowing from their wounds. The Bosnian's arm was twisting up to the pipe where it was still cuffed, and a look of surprise haunted his face. Brown drew his gun and slammed up against the bulkhead. Guy instantly reached for his phone and called for assistance.

'We're under attack!' he said. 'We need backup on the *Goa Express!*'

5

Amy stared over the side of the ship and saw half a dozen men in black combat fatigues making their way over the marina towards the bow gangway they had used earlier to board the vessel.

'Gates told you there was another team after this statue, right?' asked Quinn.

'Uh-huh.'

'Think it's the Creed?' Quinn took a step back into the compartment. An old, oil-reeking space full of smuggled artifacts was, for now, her safest bet. The words she had just uttered seemed to lower the temperature by several degrees.

'No way to tell,' Hunter said. 'But I doubt it. It's been less than a month since we trashed their castle and took out the Apostle. Something tells me they wouldn't have got themselves up and running again by now.'

'Max is right,' Amy said.

'Naturally.'

Jodie sighed. 'Did you guys know Max stands for Maximum Possible Ego?'

Lewis watched the armed men as they drew closer. 'I actually did not know that.'

'Maybe we could talk about Hunter's personality defects a little later?' Amy said. 'Because right now whoever the hell they are, they're already on the gangway! They're going to be right on top of us in about thirty seconds!'

'But what about Markovich's last words?' said Quinn. 'He said Kandarian is part of an ancient secret society.'

'He never said that,' Blanco said. 'He was killed at "ancient".'

Quinn rolled her eyes. 'What else ends that sentence, Sal? He's part of an ancient golf club? He's part of an ancient square dance society? Maybe Kandarian heard about this operation from a contact in the government and decided to come and collect his artifacts before we took them away. And the ancient reference still bothers me. Maybe he is part of the

Creed. We know they have connections everywhere and take a strong interest in the ancient world.'

'Talk about it later! Right now, you guys have to get off this ship!' Brown said. 'Get that statue to safety!' Behind him, Guy was taking pot shots at the men boarding the *Goa Express*.

Hunter scanned the deck of the container ship and counted at least a dozen men, all armed with guns. They were still at the far end of the ship, around four football fields away.

'Kandarian's provenance can wait,' Hunter said. 'Right now, we have a more pressing concern – namely the heavily armed men storming this ship. Agent Brown is right. We need to get this statue out of here in a hurry.'

Amy ran inside the room, took the ox, and put it on the table beside the chest. 'Quinn, photos, now. You can't be too careful.'

The young goth pulled out her computer and took a series of images of the statue, then Amy picked it up and put it inside her shoulder bag with a few fistfuls of the straw.

Hunter raised an eyebrow. 'Take it easy with that thing! It's priceless.'

'It's stuffed with straw and wrapped in cloth inside my bag. We have no other choice, Max. We can't exactly ask those gunmen to stop shooting while we carefully carry it down to the SUV in the original chest, can we now?'

Hunter sighed. 'Fine, but just be careful with it!'

Another shot struck the bulkhead beside them and ricocheted off in a shower of sparks.

'Damn it,' Quinn said, her breathing getting faster. 'We're in deep shit, again.'

'Take it easy,' Blanco said.

Hunter watched the men. Again, he doubted they were the Creed's disciples, this time from the clothes they wore. The disciples' sharp black suits and sombre, clean-cut faces were nowhere to be seen here. Instead, these men were unshaven and wore torn, faded army-surplus combat pants and olive-green long-sleeve field shirts with ammo belts over their shoulders.

Blanco had noticed, too. 'These guys smell more like military than the disciples.'

'Just what I was thinking,' Hunter said. 'And check out the crew cuts. I think the men Gates's Dutch contact warned us about have definitely turned up to the party.'

'Fifteen seconds,' Jodie said. 'Is anyone even listening to me?'

Senior Special Agent Brown reached for his

sidearm, a Glock 22. 'I am, Agent Priest, and as the ranking officer, I'm calling the shots. Agent Fox – you have the ox statue in your possession and a possible lead to the lion statue. You get your team off this ship and find Kandarian. Agent Guy will stay with me and give these guys hell.'

'Thanks, Nate,' she said, patting him on the shoulder. 'How long till the backup arrives?'

He shrugged. 'They're on their way and we can lock the bridge door to stop them getting in. Have you seen how thick that steel is? Get out of here!'

'They'll divide into two teams when they see us make a break for it,' Hunter said. 'You keep one of them busy and give us time to lose the others.'

'But they've got the bow gangway covered!' Jodie said.

Amy adjusted the shoulder strap of the bag containing the statue to bring it tighter into her body. 'We can reach the marina if we take the stern gangway, too. We're already nearly there from our current position here in the bridgehouse.'

'But the second we break cover we're coming under fire,' Hunter said. 'Is everyone ready for that?'

Quinn shook her head. 'I'm never ready for that.'

'We can do it,' Jodie said.

Amy looked at her team. 'So is everyone ready?'

'Sure thing,' said Lewis.

'Then we go on three, two, one...'

She scrambled out of their position and ran hard down the remaining length of the portside deck with the rest of her team following her lead. Close behind, they heard a man shouting in Russian. Bullets nipped at their heels. Then Brown and Guy returned fire and forced the men back into cover.

'Russians!' Blanco yelled. 'I think they're Russians!'

Amy was slipping through the gap in the rail and running down the stern gangway with the bag still over her shoulder. One of the Russians was leaning over the side of the ship and taking aim. He fired and a puff of smoke drifted into the air above his head. The bullet pinged off the rail inches from her elbow and she screamed.

'We can talk about that later, Sal!'

'Yeah,' he called back. 'That might be a good idea!'

Another scream behind them, and Hunter turned to see Special Agent Guy tumbling over the rail on the second deck. He hit the top of a steel intermodal container with a crunch and then fell out of view behind it.

'They got Guy!'

'Shit, Brown's on his own!' Blanco said. 'We have to go back.'

'Keep running!' Jodie yelled.

'I'm going back!' Blanco started to turn but stopped in his tracks a second later. Two of the men in black fatigues were raking Special Agent Brown full of holes just outside of the bridgehouse. His jerking body was thrust back against the blood-streaked bulkhead of the bridge by the impact of the rounds entering his chest, and then he slumped to the deck, dead.

'Holy crap!' Blanco said. 'They tore him apart!'

'They're checking the chest in the bridge,' Lewis said. 'And when they don't find the statue it's not going to take them long to work out we have it.'

Blanco readied his weapon. 'I'm going back to take those bastards out!'

'Get your head down and get out of there, Sal!' Amy yelled.

He turned and followed her. She was still in the lead, ten yards ahead of the rest of the team. They were following in a single file, crouching down to avoid rogue bullets and ricochets. Then he watched in horror as she approached the top of the stern gangway and a man in a black balaclava stepped out from behind a container and grabbed her.

'Amy!'

The team reacted fast, swinging their weapons around into the aim and preparing to fire on the man, but it was too late. He roughly pulled her into the shadows behind the container. Blanco feared the worst.

Hunter was already sprinting over to her. The others were a few steps behind. Bullets zipped and traced in the air as Blanco turned the corner to find Amy on the ground with Hunter crouched down beside her. She looked dazed and confused.

'What happened?'

'He took the bag,' Hunter said. 'And by the look of it, he must have hit her.'

Blanco's resolve to kill the man who had struck her was steel. Gripping his gun, he took off in the direction the Russian had fled, sprinting down the narrow gap between the towering containers, checking each time he approached a junction where new walkways stretched away across the vast deck.

'You son of a bitch!'

Movement in the corner of his eye. He spun around to his left just in time to see the Russian fifty yards away beside the portside stern rail. He was holding Amy's bag in his right hand and a Steyr submachine gun was over his shoulder. Blanco lifted his gun just as the man spun around and flung the bag over the side of the ship like a shotput.

'Hands in the air, asshole!'

The Russian bolted. It was instinct. Turning to flee from the American, he was about to pass out of sight when Blanco fired three times. Each round found its mark in the man's head and neck and blasted him over the rail. There was no scream; he was already dead by the time he went over the side. When Blanco reached the rail, the man had already smashed into the bay and his broken body was bobbing about in the water between the ship's hull and the bleached wooden anchoring poles on the shore.

'Damn it!' Blanco smacked the top rail with a curse as he watched another man in black fatigues sprinting towards a Humvee parked up outside a Costco warehouse. He had caught the bag and it was already over his shoulder. As he approached the Humvee, he blipped the locks, threw the bag inside, and spoke into a palm mic.

When Blanco got back to the team, Amy was on her feet. Her left eye was slightly bruised and swollen.

'That bastard hit you?' Blanco said.

'I'm fine,' she said, waving him off. 'He could have shot me, Sal. Where's the statue?'

'One of them threw it overboard.'

'Then we need to get off this ship!'

Ahead on the dock they saw the familiar sight of flashing blue lights and heard the sirens of at least a dozen police cars and a black truck, all screeching out of Sunset Park and swerving to a halt all over the marina. Police officers emerged from the cars and took up defensive positions while a team of counter-terror operatives jumped out of the truck and started to fan out and head towards the ship's bow.

To the south, the black Humvee containing the bag was already moving out of sight of the police. At the stern, Amy jumped from the bottom of the gangway and hit the concrete marina running. 'Back to the SUV!' she yelled. 'That's plan A.'

Plan A was ended when one of the Russians in the team still on the boat shouldered a rocket-propelled grenade launcher and fired it at their SUV. The team crouched down to protect themselves as the lethal projectile screeched through the drizzly air above their heads and ploughed into their vehicle. It punched a hole right through the windshield and detonated in the heart of the SUV, blasting an enormous white-hot fireball into the air.

6

The gasoline ignited and burned hard and heavy, spewing a dark black cloud of noxious smoke into the air, scratched by pieces of gnarled, burning metal shards as they rained back down to the concrete marina.

'I think we need a new ride,' Quinn said.

The backup force of FBI and anti-terror units was set up in a defensive perimeter on the marina and throwing some serious gunfire at the Russian unit still on board the *Goa Express*. This gave Amy and her team the time they needed to get after the team fleeing with the statue.

'This way!' she cried out, weaving around the

smouldering wreckage of their SUV. 'We can use Brad Miller's SUV.'

Hunter said, 'Without a key?'

'I'm the key,' said Jodie.

They followed the ex-thief from California over to the FBI officers' black Chevrolet Suburban. With the Russians and FBI exchanging heavy fire behind her, she approached the vehicle and pulled a small black device from her pocket.

'What's that?' Hunter asked.

'Think of it as an electronic skeleton key, Hunter.'

'No such thing.'

Her eyes fixed on his as she raised an eyebrow and pushed a small button on the box with her thumb. When the locks blipped open, he worked hard to hide how impressed he was.

'It hacks the OBD.'

'OBD?'

'Onboard diagnostics computer. All the very best thieves are using them these days.'

'But you're not a thief,' Amy said. 'Inside, everyone! We need to get that statue back!'

They jumped in. This time, Jodie was at the wheel and revving the car as they buckled up. She hit the throttle and took off with an ear-piercing squeal of tyres before Quinn had even closed her door.

'Hey!'

In the back, Blanco was breaking two pump-action shotguns out of Special Agent Brown's vertical gun rack and passing one to Hunter. 'Here.'

'Got it.'

Jodie floored the throttle and the Suburban surged forward, pushing Amy back into the seat and stopping Blanco from loading up the pump-action shotgun. Spinning the wheel, the young woman turned north and headed for Brooklyn.

Quinn spun around and looked through the rear window. 'I think we're going to make it!'

'Don't speak so soon,' Jodie said. 'We've got problems at six o'clock.'

Hunter turned and saw a black Humvee pulling onto the road behind them. 'That can't be the Russians from the ship. No way did they get past all those counter-terror guys! That was a small army.'

'Maybe the men on the *Goa Express* have more friends than we thought,' Lewis said. 'That's where my money is.'

'Great. We got assholes on two fronts,' Quinn said.

'Keep going, Jo!' Blanco said.

'I'm on it.'

The other Humvee was leading them into the industrial area of Red Hook. Blanco opened fire on it as it slowed for a corner, spraying his shots all over its rear panels but just missing the tyres. The driver of the Humvee spun the wheel to the right and pulled away from them as one of its rear doors swung open to reveal one of the terrorists. He was gripping another rocket-propelled grenade launcher in his hands.

Blanco saw it first and yelled at Jodie to take evasive action. 'It's locked and loaded, Jo!'

'Got it.'

Not a single sign of fear on Jodie's face as she spun the wheel to the left like a pro and stamped on the accelerator. The Suburban surged forward and took the next crossroads at such high speed the axles shuddered and shook everyone on board.

'Holy crap!' Quinn called out.

'It's all good, Q.' Jodie let the wheel slip around to the right and straightened up on the new road. Blanco was gripping onto a headrest for balance as he watched the grenade streak across the junction behind them and explode in a US Postal Service distribution centre. The weapon ripped through the front of the building and blasted a substantial chunk of the roof clean up in the air. Seconds later, it returned through a cloud of black smoke to the ground in burning matchwood, twisting little contrails of smoke and embers in their wake.

'Damn it all,' he said.

'It was closed.' Lewis stared at the carnage. 'It's okay. I saw the sign as we drove towards it.'

'Thank God for that.'

'Did we lose them?' Amy said.

'No, they're heading north,' said Jodie.

'And we're heading right after them!' Amy said. 'I love that bag, damn it.'

'I think the statue is more what we're going for right now, Amy,' Hunter said.

'Whatever we're chasing, we're not going to get it,' Blanco said.

Amy turned to him. 'Huh?'

'Incoming!'

The next RPG exploded a few short yards to their left, its powerful shockwave blasting the Suburban clean off the asphalt. It crashed down at speed on its side in a shower of sparks and shattered glass and crumpled window pillars. Everyone cradled their heads in their arms as the Chevy roared and growled and screeched to a steel-scraping stop, ploughing into a curb with a heavy crunch.

'Crap!' Amy said. 'Everyone all right?'

Silence.

'Is everyone okay?'

Mumbled replies, and then the sound of the second Humvee rumbling along the road behind them at speed. One of the Russians inside was laughing as they slowed and raked the bottom of the Chevy with rounds. Seconds later, Hunter smelt fuel.

'We have to get out of here before she blows!'

Shocked and shaking, the HARPA team crawled away from the wrecked Suburban just in time to see the Humvees swerving around the corner on their way into Brooklyn Heights. Behind them, a pool of highly flammable gasoline was trickling out of a line of bullet holes in their fuel tank and running out into the road.

'We need to get further away from the SUV,' Hunter said. 'Call the fire department.'

A long, miserable silence fell over the team like a wet blanket as they took in what had just happened. Shot at, beaten, robbed, and nearly killed in a car fire. And they had lost the ox statue.

'Damn it all!' Blanco growled. 'How could that have happened?'

'We were outgunned,' Hunter said, his voice hardening. 'It won't happen again, but we need to know who those men were.'

'But first we have to patch up our wounds,' Amy said. 'Any ideas?'

Blanco's eyebrows raised half an inch on his forehead. 'Anyone like pizza?'

'Sure,' Hunter said, confused. 'But wouldn't a seedy motel be more appropriate? That's what they always do in the movies.'

The others shared a glance, a private in-joke between old friends.

'C'mon, Hunter,' Jodie said. 'Let's get some pizza.'

7

Black clouds gathered over New York and the city prepared for a storm blowing in from the north. In Brooklyn Heights, Sal Blanco introduced the team to his brother, Angelo, and ordered some pizzas and sparkling water. For now, they were all patched up and safe, hidden away under the shadow of the Brooklyn Bridge with a view across the East River to Manhattan.

Hunter remembered the view well enough but from the other side of the water. He had been to Lower Manhattan during an academic conference years ago and seen the bridge from the other side. Then, he was delivering an archaeology paper. Today, he was hiding from unknown assassins who had just tried to kill him. He was also waiting for a search warrant to enter and go through Alexios Kandarian's Upper East Side apartment. Finding the address of one of the world's richest men had not been hard, and now he gazed across the water at the skyscraper they were waiting to raid, all lit up like a Christmas tree in the gloomy New York afternoon.

A peel of thunder roared and tumbled down the Hudson River. Sighing, he turned and walked back inside the restaurant.

'You think he'll just sit around and wait for us to turn his place over?' Jodie asked.

'Kandarian?' Amy answered with a shrug. 'Markovich is dead and if Jim's Dutch contact was right and the men who raided the *Goa Express* are another group, then there's no reason to suggest our billionaire friend has any reason to fly away. We'll know more in a minute when I've spoken to Jim. He told me he might have something more for us.'

'Wait a minute,' Quinn said. 'Wait just one damn minute. I have a question.'

Amy looked at her, unsettled by the grave expression on her face. 'What is it?'

'Where are our pizzas?'

Amy took her phone out of her pocket and made the call to Director Gates, turning to the young goth as she waited for him to answer. 'Damn it, Quinn! I thought something serious had happened.'

'It has! I haven't eaten for hours!'

'Then fear no more,' said a gravelly voice from behind them.

They turned to see Angelo walking towards them. The big round man's soft stomach and cheery red cheeks couldn't be more different from the fit and strong physique of his older brother, and when he talked, he talked through a genuine, warm smile.

'*Buon appetito!*'

Angelo delivered the freshly baked pizzas to the table with an honest smile and flour dust on his hands and apron. As they shared the pizza out, he turned and went back into the kitchen where he rearranged some logs at the back of a roaring pizza oven with his trusty ash shovel. Then he shared a joke with his brother, but all eyes were on Amy. She was standing on her own at the other end of the restaurant, talking to HARPA Director James Gates about who had opened fire on them back on the *Goa Express*.

As everyone tucked into the pizza, Amy ended the call and walked back over to the table of hungry team members. Jodie picked up a slice of mozzarella and basil pizza and took a bite. She crashed down into one of the wooden chairs and savoured the taste for a few moments, but when she saw the look on Amy's face, she stopped chewing.

'What happened?' Hunter asked.

Amy sighed. 'All right, it goes like this. First, as we know, the men who attacked us killed all three of the FBI agents on the ship. Special Agents Brown, Miller, and Guy were all found dead at the scene. So was Markovich, the smuggler, and any remaining crew who were still on board.'

'Damn,' Lewis said. 'Taking out the whole crew? Who the hell would do that?'

'It gets worse. When the FBI and counter-terror units at the scene finally boarded the ship, the raiders made their escape on a motorboat waiting off the stern. The last they saw of them, they were hot-tailing it across the bay to Staten Island. They're long gone.'

'Damn it,' Blanco said. 'Do we know who these assholes are?'

'That's the good news.' Amy sipped some of the water, trying to calm down after the attack on the container ship. 'We have a lead. Jim requisitioned all the CCTV footage in the area and ran it through the FBI facial recognition system. Most of the men in-volved in the assault remain unknown, but a camera in Bay Ridge picked up their vehicles as they approached the port and turned up one single positive result.'

'Better than nothing,' Quinn said.

'Right,' said Amy. 'The man we got a positive ID on is called Vladimir Neverov.'

'Means dick to me,' Jodie said.

Amy glowered at the expression but said nothing.

'And me,' Hunter said. 'Although I wouldn't have put it in such a crass way, of course.'

'Bite me, Hunter.'

'Perhaps later, if we have time.'

Jodie brought her pizza slice up to her mouth to hide the smile and took a bite while raising her middle finger in Hunter's face.

'What was Neverov on the system for?' Lewis asked.

'Two things,' Amy continued. 'First, artifact smuggling and terror-related offences. He's been known to buy stolen relics from terrorist groups in the Middle East, including ISIL, and sell them to collectors in North America, Europe, and the Far East. The terror-related activity comes from his habit of purchasing some of these relics and artifacts not with cash but with weapons and explosives.'

'Sounds like just the sort of guy you dream about marrying,' Jodie said.

'What's the second thing?' Blanco asked.

'That's where the story takes a turn. Neverov's new life as a relic racketeer started in early 1992.'

'Right after the USSR collapsed?' Lewis said.

'Exactly, and before that, he had an entirely different existence. Captain Neverov was a KGB agent working directly under the notorious KGB Colonel Mikhael Grudinin. And here's where we take another turn – Grudinin worked in a department focused on the acquisition of religious relics.'

'Sort of like the Nazi Ahnenerbe?' Hunter asked.

'You got it.'

Blanco gave a low whistle. 'Okay. I can handle this.'

'They called themselves Volchya Staya, which is Russian for Wolf Pack,' Amy continued. 'And they were headed up by a man named General Dmitry Patrushev. Back in the days of the Soviet Union, he was a very senior KGB officer whose specialist field was recruiting and running spies inside Israel's Knesset.' Seeing the blank look on Jodie's face, she added, 'That's their parliament.'

'Got it.'

'More interesting to us is that he had an interest in hidden history, ancient cultures, and Bible prophecies. That's why they put him in charge of the Wolves.'

'That's just great,' Quinn said, dropping her pizza slice back onto her plate. 'I always wanted to be hunted by a bunch of ex-KGB agents called the Wolf Pack. It's what every girl dreams of when she grows up.'

Jodie rolled her eyes and leaned back on her chair. Blanco said, 'Anything more on this Neverov guy?'

Amy nodded. 'Sure. He's getting on in years but still fighting fit and the experience he brings to any situation or fight is hefty and not to be ignored. He retired as a full colonel.'

'Who else is on his team?'

'There are three other old-timers like him. We have only surnames right now – Lugovoy, Medinsky, and Gubenko. There are a number of younger men, mostly drawn from the ranks of the FSB. Some other names floating around are Yahontov and Turgenev. They are backed up by several unidentified former Spetsnaz soldiers. Also not to be taken lightly.' In her usual style, she switched subjects without warning or pause, now turning to Hunter. 'What about the statue, Max? You get anything from the pictures Quinn took back on the ship?'

He shook his head and sighed. 'Sorry, but I just haven't had enough time to study them since the attack. There's also a fair amount of damage on some of the inscription which is going to take some unpicking, but as I say, it looks like it's only a fragment anyway. We need the other statues.'

'You might get some help if anything turns up at Kandarian's place during the raid,' she said.

'You know what's bothering me?' Blanco said.

Quinn gave him a sly look. 'That your brother makes better pizzas than you do?'

'That's always bothered me,' he said with a chuckle, but then his tone turned serious. 'But no, that's not what's bothering me right now.'

'It bothers you all the time, big brother,' Angelo shouted over from the kitchen.

'Maybe the same thing that's bothering all of us,' Amy said, steering the conversation back around to business. 'The biblical element to all of this?'

Blanco gave a shallow nod. 'Yeah. That part.'

'I don't see the problem,' Hunter said. 'I've spent much of my career as an archaeologist studying artifacts from the biblical canon. It's an interesting era but it's no scarier than any other.'

'We're not just chasing relic smugglers any more, Hunter,' Jodie said. 'If this has something to do with the Revelation and the Apocalypse, then sure, that scares me.'

'Revelation and Apocalypse are the same thing,' Lewis said, mouth full of ham and cheese.

Jodie sighed the correction away. 'Do I look like I give a shit about that, Ben? I just said I'm scared by this. It freaks me out.'

'Me too,' Quinn said.

'Why?' Lewis said.

'You disappoint me, Ben,' Quinn said. 'You talk like the sort of sorry individual who got through his entire childhood without seeing the end of *Raiders of the Lost Ark*.'

Lewis laughed. 'Right, so that's what you think is in store for us? The holy spirit of an enraged god bursting out of an ark and melting us all down?'

She shrugged. 'You said it.'

'Anyway, they were Nazis. We're trying to do the right thing. Just relax.'

'I'll relax when the mission is over, thanks.'

'Any way you want to play it, Quinn.'

Jodie looked at her phone and sighed.

'Jodie?' Amy asked.

'It's nothing, boss.'

Amy looked at her for a second and then lowered her eyes. As with Blanco, something was going on in

Jodie's life, and she wanted to help, but she knew there was a certain way to approach this wild young woman, and a straight-out attack was not the right way.

'Sure, just checking on my team.'

Jodie flashed a fast, fake smile and slipped the phone into her pocket. 'No need.'

Then Amy got an alert on her phone and when she checked the screen, a nervous smile spread on her lips. 'All right, it might have taken over two hours, but it looks like we got the warrant to search Kandarian's place. Apparently, tonight he's hosting some sort of event for the city's high society.'

'Not blue bloods?' Quinn said. 'Why weren't you invited?'

Amy ignored her with a scowl.

'What sort of event?' Jodie asked.

'An auction selling ancient relics, ostensibly to raise money for one of his charities. Jim has seen the guest list and there are some archaeology professors there from Cornell, too.'

'Auctioning smuggled relics?' Blanco laughed. 'You couldn't make it up.'

'Archaeologists, huh?' Lewis patted Hunter on the back. 'You'll be right at home!'

Amy smiled and turned to Hunter. 'I've never

been to a party full of archaeologists before. When they start telling dinosaur jokes, be sure and let me know when to laugh.'

* * *

Across the city, Alexios Kandarian stared south across Manhattan island but saw nothing. His mind was too crowded with the agony of thought. The burden of life-or-death decisions. Thousands of miles away in the ancient lands, the Ark was nearly ready, but he fought down his excitement and brought his focus closer.

And his duty.

His duty to obey the divine will.

The Ancient of Ancients.

To act, rather than pay mere lip service to the cause. He was stirred from his thoughts by the sound of the telephone ringing. Then, he heard a heavy footfall behind him in the thick cream plush pile. He turned and saw the towering giant of Belisarius walking to the antique white Bakelite phone. The giant exchanged low, murmured words for a few seconds then replaced the receiver down in the telephone cradle. 'That was building security down in the lobby, sir.'

Kandarian returned his eyes to the rain striking the surface of the water out in the bay. It was mesmerising. Almost like a flood. 'What do they want?'

'They say the FBI is here. They want to talk to you.'

'I'm sure they do. Send them away.'

'They're already on their way up to the suite, Eminence. They have a warrant.'

Kandarian sighed. 'This is most inconvenient, Belisarius. My guests have already arrived for the auction.' He turned and stared at the giant. Behind him, hanging on the wall on oak mountings, were authentic bas-reliefs and petroglyphs from ancient sites around the world. His life's work. 'Can we keep them out?'

'I doubt it.'

'Then stall them.'

'I'll speak to your personal security on this floor. Peterson is on the desk. I'll have them tell him to make things difficult.'

'Good work, old friend. You are my most loyal lieutenant, Belisarius,' he said. 'A warrior saint who has given his life to serving the Brotherhood.'

'Will I be rewarded in heaven, Eminence?'

'Undoubtedly, but you will also be rewarded long before that glorious day,' Kandarian said serenely.

'What we do, we do because it is God's will. The Ancient of Days willed it when he sent his glorious star to our world. It is up to us to bring the prophecy to fruition. To deliver the divine will unto mankind and make this world of sinners pure again.'

Belisarius noted a flash of wild madness in his leader's eyes and then it was gone again. Exactly what part of the divine will Kandarian planned to deliver to the world was unknown even to him, but knowing his leader's interest in the apocalyptic, he knew it would be something truly devastating.

8

Kandarian's penthouse apartment on Madison Avenue was one of the most expensive properties in the city. Situated on the sixty-fourth floor, the curved window wall to the south peered out over the Flatiron District like an imperious goddess surveying her worshippers. Further beyond, the breathtaking vista transformed into a jumble of skyscrapers in Lower Manhattan and then finally the shifting green waters of the Upper Bay.

Amy Fox did not care about any of this. She was at work, in the pursuit of her duties, and right now that meant breaking up a charity auction and arresting Alexios Kandarian. She hadn't told anyone, but the Armenian magnate's wealth and reach had intimidated her. This was a man with a speculated eighty billion dollars in the bank, and whose flagship logistics company's latest market capitalisation was nearly half of that alone.

He had wealth beyond measure and that meant power and influence. He rubbed shoulders with senators and congressmen and also had high-level connections with members of several European governments. Arresting him was no ordinary thing to do, but no one was above the law.

When the elevator pinged and its brushed steel doors slid open, she looked not to Max Hunter but Sal Blanco. Normally their modus operandi was to intercept and infiltrate criminal enterprises like this covertly, but there was no time for an operation like this now. This needed action, and fast. That was why they had recruited two more agents from the NY office in the shape of Karl Mitzner and Mike Barnes.

'You ready for this, Mr Blanco?'

'It's why I have my badge.'

A typically honest answer from an old friend. She said nothing, but gave a nod and made eye contact with the rest of the HARPA team. No one was expecting any violence or personal danger in here; that wasn't how men like Alexios Kandarian rolled. Their retaliation was subtler, invidious, litigious. He would name them in lawsuits and hound them for years. Go digging around looking for dirt. Lean on contacts in lobby groups and governments to fire Gates and shut down their department.

Amy turned to face the penthouse lobby, straightened her suit and lifted her chin. She took a deep breath and reminded herself she had joined the FBI for moments exactly like this one. She stepped out of the elevator and walked over the thick plush pile to a desk where a young man in a crisp suit and wayfarer glasses was now looking up at her. He looked officious but content. She was about to ruin all that.

'Can I help you?'

Amy caught a note of contempt in his tone.

'I'm here to speak with Alexios Kandarian.'

He tutted and looked at his watch. 'The event has already started and all doors are locked.'

'Nevertheless, I need to speak with him.'

He leaned back, smug with power. 'Do you even have an invitation?'

Mitzner sniffed, unimpressed by the attitude as Amy flipped open her ID wallet with the casual ease born of years of experience. She flashed the young man her gold FBI badge. 'I think this is my invitation.'

He hesitated and glanced down at the phone on his desk. 'Maybe I'd better speak with Alina Jahovic.'

'Who is Alina Jahovic?'

'Mr Kandarian's personal assistant. There's nothing goes on in the Kandarian Group without her knowing about it.'

Amy and Blanco exchanged a glance. 'That's too bad for her,' Amy said.

'She's also very busy,' the man said.

'Aren't we all?' Barnes said, shoving his hands into his pockets and sighing.

Blanco stepped forward. 'You think we should do this guy for obstruction of justice?'

Amy made a big show of weighing it up. She leaned forward and looked at the polished brass name plate on the young man's desk. 'I think maybe we do. Mr Peterson here is now fully aware there's a formal proceeding underway and clearly, he has specific intent to obstruct and interfere with my investigation.'

'I think we'd get a conviction,' Blanco said nonchalantly.

'I do too,' Amy said. 'I think he'd get five years.'

Peterson cleared his throat. 'Now, just wait a minute. I never said you couldn't speak to him at all. I merely said the doors were locked and asked to see your invitations.'

'And I showed you my invitation,' Amy said,

putting her ID badge back in her suit. 'Are you going to take us to Mr Kandarian or is your next phone call to the most expensive lawyer you'll ever need?'

Peterson sighed and picked up his phone. 'Please wait a moment while I try and get Ms Jahovic.'

Amy sighed. 'That's a start.'

'Sounds good to me,' Blanco said.

'Progress at last.' It was the first thing Hunter had said since entering the penthouse. Amy had silently appreciated the English archaeologist keeping his mouth shut while they were talking to Peterson. He knew nothing about US law enforcement and had wisely decided to let the experts handle the situation. If there was one thing a situation like this didn't need it was Hunter's unique brand of humour.

A wooden door clunked open and a tall, athletic woman with blonde hair and bright red lips stepped into sight. As she crossed the carpet in her stilettos, she instantly owned the room and everything in it. Without even acknowledging Peterson, she approached Amy and her team.

'Is it me or is it getting hot in here?' Blanco muttered, tugging at his collar.

'I heard that,' Amy said.

The woman in black stopped in front of them. 'I'm Alina Jahovic,' she said. 'I'm Mr Kandarian's personal assistant and I understand you wish to speak with him?'

Noticing the looks on Hunter, Blanco, and Lewis's faces as they took in the lithe six-foot frame of Jahovic and the silken blonde hair floating just above her shoulders, Amy rolled her eyes and stepped up to her.

'Yes, we do. I'm Special Agent Fox with HARPA.'

'HARPA?'

'The Heritage, Artifacts, and Relics Protection Agency. We're a rapid deployment team and part of the FBI.'

Jahovic suspiciously eyed the team standing behind Amy. 'And what might the FBI want to discuss with Mr Kandarian?'

Amy knew she was trying to intimidate them, and worse, stall for time.

'That's between Mr Kandarian and the FBI. I already had to threaten young Peterson over there with obstruction. You want the same?'

Jahovic smiled like a crocodile. 'If you're trying to apply obstruction to me you're not going to get very far, Special Agent Fox. Code 1503 defines that very clearly and there's been no threats or force here today. I majored in law at Stanford after leaving the Armenian Army.'

Amy kept her eyes fixed on the woman. Paraphrasing the code had been intended to put her on the back foot, but it had failed. 'If you were such a hotshot at Stanford you'd know the code's definition includes any act corruptly impeding the due administration of justice, which is what your attempt at stalling for time is doing right now. Take us to Alexios Kandarian now or you're in cuffs by the end of the current minute.'

Lewis leaned into their conversation. 'And that's a New York minute, naturally.'

Jahovic was unfazed, but the smile faded. 'Very well, please follow me.'

* * *

The woman in the black suit led the way through the wooden door and down a long wide corridor, resplendent with ancient classical statues and ornaments. Her heels clicked on the white marble tiles as she hurried past priceless sculptures, glancing at the Cartier watch on her slim wrist on the way. On their right, the wall turned into a long window. Amy glanced through it and saw a swimming pool covered in rose petals and floating candles.

'How the other half lives,' she muttered.

'I don't think 50 per cent live like this,' Hunter said. 'More like a hundredth of a per cent.'

Directly ahead was a sweeping glass and timber staircase leading up to an expansive galleried landing boasting works of art from the Renaissance period.

'Mr Kandarian is up on the second floor,' Jahovic said. 'Please follow me.'

'What else does she think we're going to do?' Jodie asked.

'Maybe steal the artwork?' said Quinn.

The Californian woman gave a rare smile. 'I'd settle for twenty minutes in that pool.'

At the top of the stairs, Jahovic pushed open a door to reveal a large two-storey room filled with an opulence Amy could barely comprehend. The FBI woman was inwardly taken aback by the surrounding luxury, but too professional to let anyone know it. The same sort of curved window wall she had seen behind Peterson's desk, only this time much grander, was arcing around the outside of a vast living space decorated with furniture fashioned out of black wood and glass and chrome. It was not homely or inviting, but cold and stark and surgical.

At least fifty men and women were sitting on chairs arranged to resemble an auction house, and at the front of the room, a man in a grey suit was standing behind an art deco lectern with a hand-crafted wooden gavel in his hand. Pointing at a man in the front row, he accepted a bid and raised the increment.

Jahovic stopped on a dime and turned to Amy. 'Wait here.'

Before Amy replied, the PA was walking across the room to the front of the gathering. Amy scanned the crowd for any sign of Kandarian.

'You see him?' Jodie asked.

'Not yet.'

'Cruella de Vil seems to be walking around to the left,' Quinn said.

Lewis suppressed a chuckle.

'I think I see him now,' Amy said, ignoring the banter. 'He's sitting on the far left in the grey suit. Black shirt, no tie.'

'Dude with the black hair?' Jodie asked.

'I think so.'

Jahovic and the man spoke for a few moments, then he turned and looked over at them with a look of irritation on his face. He was in his late fifties with a lean, chiselled jaw and the physique of a man who possessed a private gym and swimming pool in every home he owned.

He rose from the chair, made his apologies to

those around him, and walked over to them with Ja-hovic gliding in his wake.

'You wanted to see me?'

'That's right,' Amy said, showing him her badge.

'It's not every day a simple businessman such as me is honoured by the presence of such an esteemed organisation. How can I help you?'

Amy felt everything that had happened in her life distilling down into the next ten seconds.

'Alexios Kandarian, you're under arrest under Title 18 of the US Code, Section 659, theft from inter-state shipment, and Section 668, theft of major art-work. You have the right to remain silent. Anything you say can and will be used against you in a court of law.'

Dozens of eyes turned and crawled all over the awkward moment.

'This is outrageous!' Kandarian said.

'You have the right to an attorney. If you cannot afford an attorney, one will be provided for you.'

'For this, I will destroy your career!'

Amy ignored the threat. 'Do you understand the rights I have just read to you?'

'All of you will be crushed by my lawyers!'

'I'll take that as a yes,' Amy said, turning to Mitzner and Barnes. 'Take Mr Kandarian away, please, and then get everyone's details and let them go.'

* * *

In the silence of the now-empty penthouse and with Kandarian and Jahovic safely out of the way in FBI custody, the HARPA colleagues worked diligently for over an hour in search of anything that might further incriminate the billionaire. But the real prize was anything relating to the location of the lion statue Markovich had talked about.

'I think I got something here,' Quinn said.

Amy stopped her search of Kandarian's desk and looked over at her. 'On his personal laptop?'

'No, on the iPad I found in the bedroom. It wasn't hidden anywhere and neither is this conversation on Messenger. He's in conversation with a man named Giuseppe Gallo who, from what's written here, has the other statue that Markovich was talking about.'

'We have a name!' Amy dropped the paperwork she was holding and walked over to Quinn. 'That's great! What else is there?'

'Looks like he's no friend of Alexios Kandarian, that's for sure. Kandarian had originally struck a deal with the smuggler in Beirut to buy both of the statues, but then the smuggler reneged on the deal and sold one of them after a higher bid from Gallo. Kandarian tried to buy the statue from Gallo but he wouldn't budge.'

'Where is this Gallo?'

'Looks like he owns some sort of private museum in Rome, Italy.'

Hunter caught a sparkle in Amy's eye. 'It's a tough job, but someone's got to do it, right?'

Amy said nothing. She was thinking about what Gates might say – visas, travel budgets, connections at the US Consulate General in the city.

'So, what's next?' Lewis asked. 'Are we going to Rome?'

Amy and Blanco shared a mutual look of pity. 'You think we're going straight to Rome without running this past Mr James Gates?'

'Judging by the look on your face, I'd guess not.'

'Good guess,' Amy said. 'Not only will Jim want a full debriefing about the raid on the *Goa Express*, but he's also probably going to order some serious research into our findings so far, especially the detail on the statues. This isn't some crazy adventure novel where we just fly off all over the place whenever we feel like it. This is real life, with real lives and real bureaucracy.'

'Yeah, I get it.'

'And God, how I love bureaucracy,' Amy said sincerely.

'Weirdo,' Quinn said.

Jodie said, 'You love computer coding. I'd stop talking if I were you.'

Amy turned to Hunter. 'How much longer will you need to look at the photos Quinn took of the statue back on the *Goa Express*, Max?'

'Five or six hours.'

'You've got three, and that includes the flight time back to DC.'

'That clears that up then,' Hunter said. 'So we're heading back to HARPA HQ now, are we?'

'You bet your ass,' Amy said, taking out her phone. 'I'm calling the pilot.'

9

Back in DC, Lewis took another peek at the image of his newborn son on his phone and couldn't resist smiling. He replied to his wife's message, signed off with a kiss, and slipped the phone back into his pocket. They were both safe, inside the family home in the Southwest Waterfront, having just returned from the Maine Avenue Fish Market. Meg was going to attempt a smoked salmon and halibut fish pie with mashed Yukon Gold potatoes while simultaneously looking after their two-week-old child. He saluted her optimism.

'Earth to Dr Benedict Lewis.'

'Huh?' He turned and saw Amy looking across the briefing table at him.

'I'm judging from the goofy look on your face that message was from Meg.'

'Your judgement is good, Special Agent Fox. You will go far.'

'They both doing okay?'

He nodded, still unable to fight the grin on his face. 'I think so. It's all so new.'

'You'll get used to it, I guess.'

Gates stormed into the room and threw a folder down on the desk. 'He might, but as for me, I won't get used to all this talk about babies in my briefing room.'

'Sorry, sir,' Lewis said, still beaming.

Gates gave him a chunky pat on the shoulder as he walked past to the head of the table. 'How are they both, Ben?'

'All good.'

'That's good to hear, Special Agent Lewis. If you need anything, just ask. Anything at all. Anything except time off.'

Lewis laughed. 'You got it.'

'Or a raise.'

'Received loud and clear, sir.'

Hunter walked in with a laptop under his arm and took a seat at the table. By now, they were starting to accept the newest arrival on the team, and for his part, Hunter was slowly beginning to learn about them, too.

Blanco was the diplomat, bringing the younger members of the team together. Once-bitten-twice-shy Jodie was distant, and yet in the Atlantis debriefing, she had been the one to ask Gates if Hunter was on the team. That had surprised him and let him see her in a different light. When it came to Jodie, he was reminded of the old sixteenth-century English dramatist John Fletcher's saying – *Deeds, not words, shall speak me.*

Quinn liked to appear as an unknown quantity. Unpredictable and mysterious. The definition of enigmatic. And yet he saw through the smoke and mirrors and found an insecure young woman looking for a safe haven. Worse, her intelligence frightened him.

Lewis was straight enough – he spoke his mind and stepped up to the plate without being asked. He liked Lewis, and he respected the time he had served his country in the Marines as well as funding himself through a history doctorate while trying to start and support a young family.

And then there was Amy.

Amy was something else altogether. A complex

childhood. Old money. She'd had a demanding mother who had pressured her into making decisions against her will. If any of this had harmed her, he couldn't see any sign of it. She was solid, intelligent, funny and a great leader – not that he would ever tell her any of that. As for Gates, he was a former US Navy officer who took no shit and wouldn't give you an inch, but he was also the type who would take a bullet if it meant protecting his team.

How they saw him, he had no idea. An English interloper stumbling into the middle of their patch with a head full of ancient knowledge and a smart mouth, probably. What he wanted them to see was a reliable and valuable member of the team, which is why he'd worked so hard on the statues.

Earlier, he had taken his laptop into a quiet room and spent a few hours poring over Quinn's photos of the ox statue stolen by the Russians. Comparing it to the eagle statue already in HARPA custody and consulting extensive research notes from previous projects, he had made good progress but it was getting late in the day. As he walked in, Gates sighed and looked at his watch, then pushed a chair out for the Londoner with his shoe.

'Glad you could join us, Dr Hunter.'

'When I told Special Agent Fox I needed five or six hours, I wasn't just pulling a number out of my arse.'

Amy sighed. 'Ass.'

'Arse,' Hunter said. 'I don't even own a donkey.'

'What the hell?' said Jodie.

'Whatever you call it,' Blanco said, 'I think Max is trying to tell us he needed longer than six hours to analyse the statues.'

'Damn right I did,' Hunter said unapologetically. 'I always mean what I say and I meant five or six hours.'

Quinn glanced at the time on her phone. 'And yet you did it in four. You're my hero.'

'Gee, what a great responsibility.' Hunter took the seat Gates had pushed out for him and set the photos and his laptop on the table. 'Let me start by saying that the reason it took that amount of time is because of what I mentioned back on the *Goa Express*. The painted images are clear enough but the ancient Greek inscription has not fared so well over the intervening centuries. I had to use a magnifying glass to make out some of the lettering and ensure I had that right before I could even begin to think about translating it.'

'I expected nothing less of you,' Gates said. 'Please brief the rest of us on your findings.'

'Of course. First, as I said back on the ship, the ox statue is certainly Bible-era and the same age as the eagle statue. Specifically, it's Greek. Probably a little after the main Hellenistic era.'

'Hellenistic?' Jodie asked.

'We can break ancient Greek art into three broad periods – archaic, which is around 800 BC to 500 BC, classical, which is around 500 BC to 323 BC, and then Hellenistic, which dates from the close of the classical period to around the first century BC.'

Jodie gasped with mock amazement. 'Keep talking, Hunter. You're turning me on.'

He gave her a wry smile and returned his attention to the photos. 'So, I date this ox statue to around the very beginning of the first century, maybe as late as AD ten or fifteen.'

'Old,' Quinn said sarcastically.

'Yes,' Hunter said, turning to her with an arched eyebrow. 'Old – and very interesting. On the body, obverse, we can see three women mourning a dead man laid out on a bier.'

'Beer?' Jodie asked.

Hunter shook his head and spelled it out. 'It's a

kind of frame on which a corpse was laid out before its burial. They were sometimes carried to their graves or cremations on them. That picture is on the obverse.' He looked at Quinn and slowed down. 'That's the front.'

'You mean like the opposite of reverse?' she asked. 'Fascinating. Is there no end to your genius?'

'Maybe,' he said, his head wobbling slightly. 'But no one's ever found it.'

Amy rolled her eyes. 'All right, back to the statue.'

Hunter cleared his throat. 'On the reverse – that's the back – we have something even more interesting. We're looking at a depiction of a god who seems to be sitting in judgement of the corpse on the front.'

'I think you mean obverse,' Quinn said with a wink.

'Thanks, Special Agent Mosley,' he said, returning her smile.

Quinn said, 'And when you said the corpse was laid out, you meant the prothesis, right?'

Hunter turned to her. 'I'm impressed.'

'Easily, I'd imagine.'

Blanco and Lewis laughed as Quinn and Jodie shared a high-five. Hunter could see it would be a long time before he got the better of Quinn Mosley.

'Moving on rapidly...' he said with a good-natured smile. 'The curious thing here – aside from the insolent nature of some of the younger members of this team – is that this statue also has a verse written on it, but as I've already mentioned, it's only a partial fragment.'

'But you have a fuller translation now, right?' Amy said.

He turned his eyes to her, smiling. 'Of course. Would you like to hear it?'

'Well, duh,' Jodie said.

'Okay.' Hunter's voice grew even more serious. 'I'm an archaeologist, not a Bible scholar or any other type of historian. I know some Latin and some ancient Greek and I have a reasonably good knowledge of some older writing systems, most notably cuneiform and also some Assyrian and Egyptian hieroglyphs...'

'I wish someone told me it was Celebrate Max Hunter Day,' Quinn said. 'I would have worn my Max Hunter t-shirt and brought in cookies with your face frosted on them.'

'Why wait for the actual day?' Hunter said with a smirk.

Amy stepped in. 'Please continue, Max.'

'The point I was trying to make was that I'm not a

historian. My translation of this verse from the ancient Greek is good, but that's as far as I go.'

'Which is why we have a team,' Gates said. 'Including Dr Ben Lewis, who is a highly educated and experienced historian specialising in the ancient world.'

'All true,' Lewis said. 'And I'm also available for weddings and bar mitzvahs.'

'For now,' Gates said, frowning, 'just stick to the history.'

'Yes, sir.'

'Read what you have, Max,' Amy said.

'Certainly,' he said, peering down at his laptop screen. 'The verse is fragmentary but now I have the full translation of it, and it reads like this: "They must ask the Lion, the Ox, the Man, and the Eagle." Combined with the inscription on the eagle, "And the last word of God will unleash the Apocalypse and strike terror into Man," this is all we have.'

'What the hell does that mean?' Amy asked.

'As I've already speculated, it's definitely a reference to the *Book of Revelation*,' Lewis said. 'No doubt at all. Apocalypse is a Greek word, but it just means revelation, as in the last book of the Bible. The lion, ox, eagle, and man mentioned on the second statue

are references to the Four Living Beings of Revelation.'

All eyes turned to the young scholar and the
room grew quiet and tense. Gates broke the silence.
'So, two references to the *Book of Revelation*?'

'Yes, sir.'

'I think you'd better tell us more,' Gates said. 'This
gets more interesting by the second.'

10

With the team hanging on his every word, Lewis sat up straighter in his chair and cleared his throat. Thoughts of Meg and his newborn son were banished as work quickly became his sole focus.

He said, 'Both the statues are highly beautiful pieces with very few flaws, and now thanks to Max we have both verses translated. As I have said, the forms they take – an eagle and an ox – are a reference to some future apocalypse, which is concerning.'

'Care to expand?' Hunter said. 'I never went to Sunday school.'

'Yes.' Gates shifted in his seat. 'More detail, Dr Lewis.'

'The last book of the Bible is the *Book of Revelation*. It's written by John the Apostle.'

'As in one of the Twelve Apostles?' Jodie asked.

'Yes,' Lewis said. 'And he wrote *Revelation* after experiencing a vision of Jesus who told him about mankind's future. The Four Living Beings – the Lion, the Ox, the Man, and the Eagle – were part of that vision. My opinion is that there are two more statues – the Lion that Markovich talked about, which we now know is in Rome, and a Man.'

'Of which we have no knowledge,' Amy said.

'No,' Hunter said, stepping in. 'But I concur with Ben's analysis of there being two more statues, so at least we know what game we're playing.'

'And it could be a dangerous one,' said Gates. 'So far, we have two statues, which when put together make part of a verse heavily implying some sort of apocalypse is going to be unleashed on mankind.' He slipped on his glasses and peered down at his notes. '"And the last word of God will unleash the Apocalypse and strike terror into Man..." I'm not happy about heavily armed Russian terrorists being so keen to get hold of these statues.'

'And there's also the Kandarian angle,' Amy said, frowning. 'We don't know what he's doing in all this.'

'Not much now he's in custody,' Gates said. 'We're doing okay.'

'Sure,' Amy said, 'but we'd be doing a lot better if I hadn't let the Russians steal the statue in the raid on the ship. I feel like I let everyone down.'

'No, you didn't,' Gates said firmly. 'You were viciously attacked and whoever did it is going to pay. Before that, you had the foresight to ask Agent Mosley to photograph the statue and it's thanks to those photos Drs Hunter and Lewis have been able to study it. Please continue, Ben.'

'In my view, the other two statues are likely going to contain another line of this verse on each of them and when to put together, they will lead us to something John the Apostle was trying to hide from the world.'

The room quietened. 'So Professor Barton was right then,' Quinn said. 'There really is a missing chapter of the *Book of Revelation*. I wonder why he hid it?'

'We don't know that yet, Quinn,' Lewis said. 'I'm just flying a kite.'

'An impressive kite,' Hunter said. 'I take it you went to Sunday school?'

'I did,' Lewis said. 'And I studied theology as part of my undergrad degree.'

'That's why he's on the team, Hunter,' Jodie said. 'Quit giving him a hard time.'

'That's not what I'm doing.'

'Take it easy, people,' Gates said. 'You can save the chest-beating and territory marking for when you're on your own time. Go on, Ben.'

'I think we need to tread carefully here, sir. If we look at what John wrote in *Revelation* about the end of the world, we could be facing something much worse than the Creed. It's possible – and I stress this is just a theory – John had other visions he was too terrified to share with the world and decided to hide them in some sort of codex.'

'Sounds a bit far-fetched,' Amy said.

'I don't think so,' said Lewis. 'Maybe there's another whole chapter of the Bible out there that no one has ever seen. Revelation 23. Maybe that's what this is all about. Maybe that's why he made the statues – to mark the place he hid his secret writings.'

'C'mon, Ben!' Jodie said. 'You can't believe this stuff is real.'

'I'm just making the point that there's a lot of stuff in the Bible which we simply cannot accept at face value.'

'You don't know that,' Jodie said. 'No one knows that. Not today. It was too long ago.'

'If it's literal, then we have some real concerns,' Lewis said.

Gates took off his glasses and twiddled them around by one of the arms. 'And why does it give us concerns?'

'Because you do not want to mess with some of the stuff in the Bible.'

Amy broke the tension and changed the subject. 'Maybe Ben is right and it's more than that,' she said. 'Maybe John knew more than he wrote about in the main *Revelation* text and wanted to keep what he knew hidden from the world. Perhaps it was just too frightening.'

'More frightening than the rest of *Revelation*?' Hunter said. 'Good luck with that.'

'Wait for just a second,' Quinn said. 'Isn't the real question why we're trying to unearth something that might trigger the Apocalypse?'

'That is a very good question,' Jodie said.

Deep in thought, Amy ignored her. 'But why would John of Patmos be leaving hidden messages on statues?'

'He wasn't always John of Patmos,' Lewis said. 'He was originally from Galilee and spent much of his time in Rome. He was boiled in oil in the Colosseum but survived and as a result, he was exiled to Patmos by the Roman authorities.'

'Wait a minute,' Quinn said. 'Didn't you say the Bible was not literal?'

'Sure.'

'Then how can you believe he survived being boiled in oil?'

'I don't,' Lewis said coolly. 'This story has to be allegorical.'

'Why was he boiled in oil?' Gates asked. 'Allegorically.'

'He forgot his tax return,' said Blanco, raising a gentle laugh.

'Heresy,' Lewis said. 'He was dangerous. What he was writing was dangerous. Remember, the *Book of Revelation* was prophetic, meaning he was writing about things still to come and predicting events, including ones with political implications. This was against the law of Rome during the period when he lived there. Hiding the information somewhere and then leaving cryptic clues on the four statues might have been the safest thing to do.'

Gates blew out a long breath as he calculated everything he had heard. 'All right. We have two statues. One I found in Mexico nine years ago that refers obliquely to the Apocalypse, and one uncovered this morning on a raid in New York which gives us a similar reference. We have the verses and some kind of cryptic clue, but it's only a fragment and we know another of the set, a lion, went to an Italian collector named Gallo. All good so far?'

Amy nodded. 'All good so far.'

'We also know there is a group of hostile Russians with a serious interest in these statues. Half-terrorists, half-relic smugglers, they're called the Wolf Pack and they already shot up my team, assaulted my deputy, stole one of the statues, and killed several FBI agents and counter-terror operatives in the raid this morning.'

'They were lethal, all right,' Blanco said.

Hunter nodded. 'I'll say. Those men were very highly trained. As part of my old life with the Guards, I worked with special ops teams in the past and there's something about the way they do business. You can tell, often just by watching the way they talk and their body language. They're a special type of person. Under fire, they react differently to regular soldiers, and it's my opinion that the men who stormed the *Goa Express* were without a doubt very highly trained special ops men. Our intel is right.'

'That's also my view,' Blanco said. 'Like Max, I collided with special ops guys from time to time back when I was in the army. That might have been several hundred years ago, but special ops guys don't change.'

The team chuckled at Blanco's self-effacing comment, but Hunter saw he was clearly aware of his older age and slightly uncomfortable with it.

'Ben?' Gates asked. 'Is that your view, too?'

'Yes, sir,' Lewis said. 'Was a Marine and know the drill. These men were very highly trained and totally ruthless. We can't take any risks with them.'

Gates nodded pensively. 'Okay, thanks. As we know, we already have a positive ID on Neverov and most of his team and they're not going to get away with what they did today. No one pisses in my yard and gets away with it.' In his customary manner, he changed the subject without warning, his mind working ahead of everyone else's by several seconds. 'Now I want to brief you about this Gallo character in Rome before you leave the States.'

Amy started making notes. 'What did you find on him?'

'Not much. Full name is Giuseppe Gallo. On the surface he is an Italian philanthropist, using money made from a highly successful fund management company based in Singapore.'

'And under the surface?' Blanco asked.

'It gets murky.'

'I thought it might.'

'You don't have to dig very deep around Gallo until you start finding evidence of the active role he plays in several esoteric secret societies, including the Knights of Rome and the Crucifanomen.'

Amy made a note. 'Never heard of either.'

'Most haven't,' the director went on. 'But that doesn't mean they're not out there, and Gallo is a key player in both. Considering many of these secret societies are no more than subsidiary branches of the Creed, the obvious deduction is he is also a part of them.'

'But he might not be?' Hunter said.

'No,' Gates said. 'But he might be.'

A tense silence fell over the meeting room. No one on the team would ever forget their first mission together, fighting against the Creed in the search for Atlantis. Driven by something deeper than any normal lust for money or power, which they had in abundance, the world's most secret society had fought like animals to secure a long-forgotten Atlantean weapon called the fire lance. The HARPA team had won the fight and secured both the lance and the Atlantean site, but at a heavy cost.

Jodie broke the silence. 'Like Hunter just said,

Gallo's membership in the Creed is just speculation, right?'

'At this time,' Gates confirmed. 'But like normal, we're going to proceed on the precautionary principle. Take it easy, review what little evidence we have in-depth, and presume the worst.'

'Sounds like my love life,' Quinn said, deadpan.

It raised a light laugh, but the tension soon returned when Lewis said, 'The last thing we need is to bring the Creed into this. Seems to me if we're not careful we could be fighting on two fronts on this one.'

Gates nodded. 'Possible, but so is the chance the Creed are already involved. Maybe they're out-sourcing the heavy lifting to some better trained military hands after their defeat in Atlantis.'

Lewis absent-mindedly scratched his forehead. 'Not liking the sound of that, Jim.'

Gates looked at him with sympathy, fully aware that the young man was thinking about the two people in the picture in his wallet. 'It's what it is, Ben.'

'Just speculation, is what it is,' said Amy. 'Just as Jodie said.'

'Okay, people,' Gates said. 'You fly first thing tomorrow morning.'

'Why the delay? We need to go right now,' Hunter

said. 'If Neverov and his team have translated this, they're probably already on their way to Gallo.'

'They need to know about him first,' Gates said. 'So just take it easy. We got Gallo's name from Kandarian and now he's in custody.'

'But there was another black-market relic trader in Beirut,' Hunter said. 'Markovich mentioned him. Neverov was former KGB and he's been relic-smuggling for thirty years! We have to presume he already knows about Gallo.'

'We're not in some James Bond movie, Dr Hunter,' Gates said. 'When on official business, FBI agents travel on official passports, and visas must be obtained. As it happens, US citizens may enter Italy for up to ninety days without a visa, but I still want to discuss the matter with my counterpart in Rome. I also have to arrange two pilots, have an aircraft fuelled and a flight plan filed with the proper authorities. This is law enforcement, not a spy movie.'

Hunter raised his palms. 'I'm just saying the Russians have a head start.'

Gates looked at his watch. 'You'll be airborne before dawn, so take some time out to take a shower and get prepared for trouble. Dismissed.'

Outside the briefing room, Amy grabbed hold of

Hunter's elbow and waited until Gates and the rest of the team had moved out of sight.

'What is it?' Hunter asked.

'Something important.'

He looked at her, eyes narrowing but sensing some levity. 'Oh yeah?'

'Yeah. Wanna have dinner with me tonight, before we fly to Italy?'

'You know they have food in Italy, right? Quite nice food, in fact.'

'Max!'

'Consider it a date.'

11

Amy stamped on the accelerator pedal and forced the automatic gearbox to change down a gear. The George Washington Memorial Parkway was quiet tonight so she pushed it as much as she could, exceeding the fifty miles per hour speed limit by a long way and raising a curious eyebrow on Hunter's face.

'You always drive like this?' he asked.

She shot him a glance, then turned back to the road. The sun was setting through the trees on their right and flashing like a strobe on her face. 'Like what?'

'Like your arse is on fire and the only water's at the end of this road?'

She left a long pause for effect. 'There's nothing wrong with my driving.'

'You're doing seventy in a fifty.'

'It's an emergency. Besides, I'm checking my mirrors and I haven't seen a traffic cop since Crystal City.'

'You mean a dinner emergency?'

Amy said nothing. The BMW coupé's engine purred like a lioness as the gears changed up again and the revs dropped. Hunter glanced up through the windshield and tracked the path of a passenger jet on a glide slope descent into Ronald Reagan International Airport. The sun flashed orange on its silver hull as they left Potomac Yard and cruised into Alexandria.

As Amy stepped on the brake and slowed the car, he leaned over and checked the speed gauge. 'Thank heaven for small mercies.'

'Huh?'

'The last thing we need tonight is a speeding ticket.'

She grinned and pulled off Washington Street onto Queen Street.

'What?' he asked.

'Nothing.'

'What?' he said with more emphasis.

'You're worse than Quinn.'

He was looking out at the historic red-brick homes and trying hard not to respond to her. It failed. 'I am not worse than Quinn.'

'Sure you are, Max. Who cares if we get a ticket?'

'It would have slowed us down.'

She laughed. 'Didn't you steal a car in Paris with Jodie?'

'It was an essential part of the mission.'

'Take it easy, Mr Morality,' she said. 'We never got a ticket.'

'There's always a next time, and if you ask me—' Before he could finish, Amy cut him off and pointed off to the left. 'That's the place right there. The parking lot looks full. Don't worry, we can park here. It's residential parking and we don't have a permit, so this is a real illicit thrill for me, Max. We could get caught at any moment.'

He rolled his eyes. 'Can we just get on and eat?'

She pulled in and cut the engine.

* * *

Still smiling from her little joke, Amy blipped the BMW's locks and walked over to the restaurant in the last of the day's light. As she walked into the building, a tall, lanky man saw her and smiled.

'Special Agent Fox!'

'How many times, Eduardo! Please, call me Amy.'

They shook hands with a friendly smile and Amy turned to Hunter with a look urging him to restrain his sense of humour. 'This is Eduardo, the maître d'.'

'Pleased to meet you,' Eduardo said.

'Pleasure is all mine.'

'Please, Amy,' Eduardo said. 'Follow me. I have saved your favourite table.'

* * *

When Hunter saw the menu, he almost fainted. Being more of a burger and fries man, the long list of exquisite meals involving beau oysters, Hamachi Crudo, bouillabaisse, and Skate Grenobloise was a tad intimidating. Peering over the top of the daunting carte du jour, he saw Amy was having an entirely different experience.

'Check out the trout amandine,' she purred, eyes widening with hunger. 'And the duck à l'orange looks pretty tempting, too. What do you think?'

Hunter checked around the table to see if anyone else was listening. Lowering his voice, he said, 'I just found the Burger Américain down the bottom, so I think let's do it.'

She rolled her eyes, but couldn't resist a smile. 'Really? You have all these amazing meals to choose from and that's your pick? Come on, Max – my treat.'

'I'll stick with the burger, thanks, and I bet they think calling chips pommes frites means they can charge about ten times more for them as well.'

'Fries.'

'Chips.'

She gave him a withering glance. 'The price is on the right of the menu.'

Hunter's eyes stared at the figure. 'Wait, is that in American dollars?'

'Sure is. What did you think it was?'

'I thought it was the chef's waist measurement! And check out the price of the roasted scallops!'

'I'll roast your scallops if you don't keep your voice down. I know people in here.'

'Don't make promises you can't keep.'

She sighed. 'I'll order.'

When the food arrived, Hunter picked up his burger and took a large bite. After savouring the high quality of the beef, he said, 'What about Jim's theory on the Creed maybe being involved?'

She shrugged. 'Jim leans toward the wilder explanation. Always has done. If there's one thing Mr

Gates loves, it's a good old-fashioned conspiracy theory.'

'The Creed is no conspiracy, Amy. You know that better than anyone.'

'That's not exactly what I meant.' She took a sip of some wine, her eyes lighting up as the deep blackcurrant flavour rolled over her tongue. 'The Creed is real, of course. What I mean is that Jim has never been a big fan of Occam's Razor.'

'The belief that the simplest explanation for something is usually the most accurate?'

'You got it. Most people would look at what happened on board the *Goa Express* and look at the intel on Neverov and accept it, but not Jim. His mind goes straight to the sons of the Illuminati and Occam's Razor goes right out the window. Man, this is a great wine. You should try some.'

She lifted the glass to his lips but he held up his hand. 'I'll stick with the beer, thanks.'

'Have it your way.' She took another sip and giggled. 'Great wine.'

'I take it I'm driving back tonight then?'

'Huh?'

'If I didn't know you any better, I'd say you were getting a little tipsy, Special Agent Fox.'

Sharp eyes darted up to him and the faintest of

scowls appeared on her face. 'Who says you know me at all, Dr Hunter?'

'I thought our brave stand together against the Creed in the Arctic wastelands had put us on first-name terms.'

Another shrug. 'You started it with that Special Agent crap.'

'How strong is that wine?'

'How should I know?'

After a pause, Hunter checked no one could hear them and lowered his voice. 'I hesitate to bring this up, but has Director Gates said anything to you about the Creed's castle back in Bavaria?'

She paused and set down her fork. Asking him to clarify what he meant was unnecessary – ever since Gates's debriefing at the end of the Atlantis mission, one detail had played on all their minds.

The pit that was full of broken, gnawed human bones found inside the castle's dungeon.

She gently shook her head, partly in answer to his question, and partly to try to rid her mind of the terrifying visions his words had evoked.

'Nothing, no.'

A long silence. Then Hunter asked, quietly, 'What do you think was down there?'

'I have absolutely no idea, Max. It gives me chills

just to think about it.' She saw his expression change. 'You have a theory, don't you?'

He took a drink and leaned back in his chair. 'As a matter of fact, I do.'

She sighed. 'Wanna tell me about it?'

'Oh yeah, sure.'

He took another bite of the burger and looked right into her eyes. 'You look beautiful tonight, by the way.'

'By the way of talking about the discovery of something that eats humans. Thanks.'

'Sorry. Timing never was my strong suit.'

She chuckled.

'What?'

'Nothing.'

'No, what?'

'Suits aren't your strong suit, either. Or ties.' She peered over the table at his tie with a grimace. 'For crimes against fashion, I find you guilty on all counts.'

'What's wrong with my tie?'

'Forget about it.'

He drank some beer and started to relax. 'I'm sorry, all right?'

'You're forgiven, and thanks, by the way. Now, wanna give me the lowdown on your little theory?'

'I'll get straight to the point.'

She muttered under her breath. 'I wish you would.'

'Have you ever read any Homer?'

'Not a word. I never read any classics at college. Not my thing.'

'No problem, here's the bluffer's guide. Homer's most famous work is probably the "Iliad", an epic poem written around three thousand years ago.'

'Topical, then.'

He gave her a look. She really was beautiful.

'You can laugh, but I think the ancient texts are just as relevant to us today as they ever were. In fact, I think they contain truths we have long ago forgotten.'

'I can believe it.'

'Anyway, in the "Iliad" is a reference to something I think might explain what they found in the castle's dungeon. We think maybe it's the earliest reference in the world to what I'm talking about.'

'I'm not liking the sound of this, Max.'

'Hear me out. The "Iliad" charts the fortunes of King Agamemnon and Achilles during the closing phases of the Trojan War and involves lots of exciting sieges and fighting, but that's not what we're interested in.'

'We're not?' She took another sip of wine.

'No, we're interested in what is to be found lurking in the sixth scroll, line one hundred and two.'

'Whoa, that's specific.'

'Hey, I read that thing all over again just so I could brief you on this. That's above and beyond the call of duty.'

'You read the "Iliad" just to tell me that?'

'It's called historical research, Special Agent Fox.'

'Tell me, do you have the scrolls tonight?'

'No, I always walk like this.'

She shook her head and tried to hide her smile behind the wine glass. 'You may continue, Dr Hunter.'

'Gee, thanks. So, twenty-four scrolls make up the poem, and in the sixth one, Homer describes how Bellerophon, a famous hero in ancient Greek literature, arrived in Lycia and must destroy a goddess – that's the word Homer uses. He describes a fire-breathing monster with the head of a lion, the tail of a serpent, and the body of a goat. Guided by signs from heaven, Bellerophon destroyed her. Homer names this monster as the Chimaera.'

The smile faded from her face. 'As in Chimera?'

'Exactly. This meal really is first class.'

'Max! How can you think about your stomach at a time like this?'

'At a time like what?'

'You just sat right there and told me you think the Creed is feeding people to some sort of mythical beast from the ancient world!'

'Oh yeah, that.'

She waved it away. 'Ridiculous.'

'Why?'

'For one thing, how do you keep a thing like that secret for thousands of years?'

'How did they keep Atlantis secret for thousands of years?'

'Come on, Max.'

'Maybe it's not thousands of years old. Maybe they have some sort of genetic engineering nightmare going on in a secret lab somewhere?'

'No way. This is crazy.'

'Is it, though? We know whatever killed those people in the castle doesn't fit the description of any known animal, and we also know that as far as secret societies go, the Creed is about as ancient as you get. Maybe those myths and legends are not so fictional after all. Maybe Homer was describing a real event.'

'Ha! You said that Bellefonte guy killed it!'

'I know I did, but how many lions are there in the world? Maybe this chimera creature the Creed are keeping alive with human chum is just one of many, or perhaps the last survivor of an ancient breed of creatures now gone from our world.'

'Human chum?'

'It just sort of popped into my head.'

'Can we change the subject?'

'Sure. Any news on the fire lance that Jim Gates made disappear into thin air?'

'He didn't make it disappear into thin air, Max. It was transferred to a secure location for comprehensive analysis. We both know it could potentially be the most powerful weapon on earth, or at least somewhere right up at the top of the league of destruction. It's important to keep it locked up.'

'I can't argue with that, but what about the Atlantis site?'

'Not this again.'

'It should be a UNESCO site and any excavation work there should be supervised by UNESCO archaeologists.'

'Don't tell me, led by Dr Max Hunter?'

'I'm the most qualified person to do it, so why not?'

'Because the US government has decreed otherwise and sent a military special ops team to protect the site.'

Hunter sighed. 'It's the most important discovery

in world history, Amy, and apart from a handful of senior people at UNESCO and the US government, no one knows about it.'

'And that's the way it's going to stay, at least for now. You want other nations up there, getting hold of weapons like the fire lance? You want terrorists up there?'

'Fine. We can agree to disagree.'

'No,' she said flatly. 'You're wrong.'

'You're a tough woman, Amy Fox.'

Amy finished her wine and gave him the vaguest hint of a smile. 'C'mon. Let's get back to the city. We have a flight first thing tomorrow morning.'

Vladimir Neverov didn't take his eyes off the old man. The professor of Greek antiquity had been studying the ancient ox statue for an hour, carefully scratching away layers of the chipped black glazing and muttering to himself as he scratched down notes on his pad.

Neverov sighed, but he knew these things took time. The former KGB officer was a man of great experience, a man who had spent three decades searching for what was now in his grasp. No point rushing the last few critical moments that would finally lead him to his destiny.

'Are you sure this is the right one?'

He turned and saw his old friend and colleague

Lugovoy at his side. The big man from Volgograd had led a tough life and had the hard, leathery face to prove it. Two tired, angry eyes stared out at the world from a battered face, crisscrossed with knife-fight scars and other legacies from a life of bad luck and even worse choices.

'It's the right one, Vasya. I would know it any-where. Don't you remember?'

Lugovoy's eyes momentarily flicked to Gubenko, over in the corner. He was eating an apple with a flick knife, stopping for a second to spit some chewy skin on the floor. Disgusting, he knew, but that was Gubenko. Turning back to Neverov, he shrugged. 'Time travels at different speeds for different people, Vova.'

Neverov gave a shallow, absent-minded nod and drank some vodka; looking at Lugovoy's face, he guessed his old friend's theory was right. 'I remem-ber,' he said quietly, still staring at the statue in the professor's experienced hands.

And he did. That terrifying night all those years ago. He'd still been a young man, back then, driving through the Egyptian night to Mount Sinai. If he closed his eyes it was almost as good as being there all over again. Old Colonel Grudinin sat beside him, moaning about the mission and arguing with the

Greek archaeologist he later shot dead in cold blood.

Grudinin was long gone now, of course. He died in the early nineties not long after the collapse of the Soviet Union. Drank himself to death in his dacha out in Peredelkino and found face-down on the carpet with an empty bottle of vodka in his hand.

And a note in his pocket.

A note addressed to Vladimir Neverov, sealed tight and marked confidential.

A note that changed the entire course of young Vova's life.

But that was a long time ago, Neverov thought with a sigh. Nearly thirty years, and he had changed from a young man full of optimism to an old, bitter wreck determined to find what Grudinin had told him about in the note, no matter what the cost.

'All I remember was the uncomfortable drive,' Medinsky said, knocking him from his thoughts.

Two of the Spetsnaz men, Turgenev and Yahontov, grumbled something about old-timers and walked outside for a smoke.

'All I remember were the explosions,' said Gubenko. 'I like explosions. You should have let me blow up the *Goa Express* when we raided it. Imagine it sinking in the bay.'

Neverov ignored him and he went back to his apple. He sighed again and checked his watch. It had already taken too long to track down a specialist prepared to work in such unorthodox circumstances, which in this case meant a cheap motel on the Belt Parkway just north of JFK International Airport. Most archaeologists, even retired ones, it turned out, had been reluctant to meet a group of anonymous Russians and authenticate a relic of dubious provenance, as one professor from Connecticut had put it. But the money they were paying had bought someone with gambling debts, and that someone was Dr Earl Crozer.

'Well?' Neverov said. 'You've been looking at it for hours.'

The old man from New Haven paused a beat, blinked, and turned to him. 'You want me to get this right?'

'How much longer?'

An old KGB habit he couldn't break – always answer a question with another question.

'Ten minutes and you will have the entire translation.'

'And what about your man in the FSB?' Neverov asked Lugovoy. 'Do we have the name of the smuggler in Beirut?'

'Nearly. Like the statue, these things take time. Wheels have to be greased.'

Neverov drummed his fingers on the arm of the chair and stood up without warning. He paced over to the window and looked out at all the cars racing along the parkway. Memories of traffic crawling around Moscow's Garden Ring flooded back into his mind. Kutuzovsky Avenue and the Moskva River and Gorky Park. A long time ago and a long life lived in pursuit of Patrushev's terrifying treasure.

That was what Grudinin had written about in the note.

General Patrushev, who had headed up the Wolf Pack, had been a mysterious figure, even for the old men who'd run the Lubyanka all those years ago. Aloof and distant and dangerous, Dmitry Patrushev was part of the old guard. In his seventies back when Neverov was a young man, the old general had worked alongside Molotov and Kaganovich and even Stalin himself and knew more state secrets than most. But it was one in particular that had interested his protégé Colonel Grudinin, and it involved the night they had been ordered to travel out to Mount Sinai and retrieve a dusty, chipped old statue.

The statue was created two thousand years earlier by John the Apostle and was believed to contain a hidden code pointing to some unknown text he had written for *Revelation*. A verse he was too terrified to include in the final manuscript, for fear others would consider him out of his mind.

What had he written about all those years ago? What had scared him out of his mind? Rumour among Patrushev's old Soviet esoteric researchers was that it had something to do with Revelation 8... The third angel sounded his trumpet, and a great star, blazing like a torch, fell from the sky... Fogged by the vodka, Neverov's mind strained to make sense of it all. Verse 8. The third trumpet of *Revelation*. Chernobyl. End times.

Apocalypse.

More vodka.

Where had John the Apostle hidden the manuscript? Could there really be a Revelation 23 like Grudinin had told him about in his suicide note?

Neverov slopped another slug of vodka in the shot glass and raised it to his mouth.

'*Za zda-ró-vye*,' he mumbled.

To your health.

He would find more than good health at the end of this trail, or at least die trying.

13

Jodie Priest bit the bullet and took the call. She was leaning on the east wall of Dulles Airport's Jet Linx private jet terminal at the time, just out of the rain and watching a Pepsi truck driving along the airport's northern access road. Just off to her right, the rest of the HARPA team were climbing up the airstair of a Gulfstream jet. It was ready to fly to Europe, flight checks done and dusted and engines idling.

She sighed. This, she knew, had been a long time coming.

'Hey, Tyler. How's it going?'

'Not good, Jo.'

She bit her lip and swept her rain-wet hair away from her face. 'What happened now, Tyler?'

'Got mixed up with some guys and we robbed a bank in San Jose. Someone got shot. This time they're going to throw away the key.'

She said nothing.

'They gotta find me first, right?'

Silence.

Tyler got the hint and changed the subject. 'What about you? When am I going to see you again, Jo?'

She paused. Hunter was standing back to let Quinn go up the jet's stairs and get out of the rain first. He looked taller from where she was standing. Taller and stronger.

'I'm doing something new now, Tyler.'

'Something new? What does that mean?'

'It means I moved on. They're good people. We do good work.'

'And what can someone like you offer people like that?'

'Thanks, man.'

'C'mon, Jo! Me and you are like two drops in the same bucket. We come from the same streets.'

After a long pause, she said, 'I'm not coming back, Tyler.'

'But we got so much history!'

'Even so...'

She heard him punch something and curse. A wall, she hoped.

'You're really not coming back to California?'

'No. Not ever. I think I have a chance of making something good for myself. We can't go back, Tyler – we can't be young again. We can't be those people any more. We have to look forward now. I hope you can understand that.'

'I don't get it.'

She wanted to say, *I know you don't*. Instead, she said, 'I hope you find a way to get someplace better.'

'Listen, if you walk away from me I'll—'

She cut the call and slipped the phone into her pocket. Took a second out. Amy had emerged from the plane's door and was waving at her, beckoning her. She waved back and walked over to the Gulfstream. She was stronger than she used to be. No tears this time. Tyler was knocking off banks in San Jose and she was climbing into a seventy-five-million-dollar private jet to be with her new family.

'All good?' Amy asked.

Jodie wrapped her fingers around the wet metal airstair rail and skipped up into the plane.

'All good, boss.'

'Then let's get going.'

* * *

Amy knew Jodie was lying, and she knew why. Everyone on the team except Hunter knew about the young Californian's history with Tyler and all he had put her through before she joined the team. She had been working for him when she broke into Amy's apartment in Washington and got caught, changing her life forever.

Amy decided against bringing any of this up. Jodie was smart but she could lose focus. The worst thing she could do now was talk to her and drag it all up to the surface. She would watch her and make sure she stayed on point. The mission was already looking significantly more dangerous, and perhaps more historically important, than even the Atlantis mission. No one could afford any mistakes.

When the aircraft was at altitude and heading out over the Atlantic on its way to Europe, she unbuckled her seatbelt and called the rest of the team to attention. Blanco stopped her and stepped over to the small galley.

'Nothing is happening until coffee.'
'Good call, Sal.'
When Hunter asked for tea, the gentle hum of the

twin Rolls Royce turbofans was the only sound in the cabin.

'Is that just to be difficult?' Quinn asked.

'No, it's because it's a superior drink.'

Blanco laughed as he handed him the cup. 'Sorry, Max. There's tea, but no bone china cups.'

'I'll overlook it just this once,' the Englishman said. 'But get Quinn here to make a note for future reference.'

'Make it yourself,' she said. 'I'm not your personal assistant.'

Hunter gave an affable shrug. 'You couldn't afford the suit.'

Amy raised her hand and silenced Quinn's reply. 'Ahem, we're still all getting used to Max being on the team and we all have to adapt.'

Quinn turned to Hunter, blowing him a kiss. 'Love you, Max.'

'And I like you too.'

Lewis chuckled. Quinn's eyes narrowed and Amy stepped in once again.

'Okay, so moving on. As you are all aware, we're flying to Italy to acquire a lion statue which we hope will provide a further clue to something we believe John the Apostle hid from the world.'

Lewis popped open his buckle and shifted in his seat. 'When you say acquire, you mean steal, right?'

'Why do you think I'm here?' Jodie said.

Amy gave him a sweet smile. 'We have ascertained that the third Revelation statue is stored in a private museum in Rome. The first is in the HARPA vault in the basement of the FBI building back in DC. The second is with Neverov and his team, but we have what we need from it. We know from translations of the verses on these statues that they contain concerning references to some sort of apocalypse. It's fair to assume the third one will provide the missing key to the puzzle and let us know just what John was trying to hide from the world.'

Lewis shrugged. 'Still stealing.'

'As such,' Amy said, ignoring him, 'the United States government has sanctioned the use of the HARPA team to retrieve the lion statue. It's considered a matter of vital national security. We have been chosen because we don't officially exist and any mission we undertake can be totally denied. If we get caught, we get disavowed.'

'That's fine with me,' Hunter said. 'I still officially work for UNESCO anyway and my boss Juliette is very accommodating.'

'I'm sure she is,' Jodie said.

Hunter smiled wistfully. 'She can't resist my masculine charms.'

'Moving back to the mission,' Amy said patiently. 'Our orders are to remove the statue from Gallo's private museum as fast and silently as possible. Everything I have said is, of course, Top Secret, and it's also what I like to call the good news.'

Blanco finished a long glug of coffee and sucked his teeth. 'And the bad news?'

'The bad news is that Neverov and his unit could well be ahead of us by now. By the time we get to the museum they might already have raided it.'

'And then we're playing catch-up,' Lewis said.

'Right.'

'And there's more bad news. As we have speculated, Giuseppe Gallo may be a high-ranking member of the Creed.'

'Last I heard, crossing them was not a good idea,' Quinn said. 'We're already up against a bunch of former KGB and Spetsnaz, Amy. You think it's a good idea to make an enemy out of Gallo, too? This could make things much more dangerous for us.'

'Only if we screw up big time,' she said. 'If Gallo doesn't find out who took his little statue, then he can't come after us.'

'I wish I shared your optimism.'

'We'll be fine,' Blanco said. 'If we can handle the Creed once, we handle them twice.'

'Sal's right,' Hunter said. 'We all know that the Creed is descended from the Illuminati and that's scary, but we survived them before. Besides – we don't even know Gallo is a part of them. For all we know, the Creed could be controlling Neverov. It's all just speculation.'

'Okay, then,' Lewis said. 'That's reassuring.'

'In the meantime,' Amy said, 'we use the rest of the flight to acquaint ourselves with the schematics of Gallo's palazzo where he houses his museum. Time to get to work, everyone.'

14

The Palazzo Giuseppe Gallo sat near the east bank of the River Tiber, housed inside a traditional Rome building built in the 1560s. Just a few hundred yards from the world-famous Pantheon, access to the palazzo was granted to the public during very restricted hours for tax purposes. Most of the time, like tonight, the building was used only by the Marquis Giuseppe Gallo.

The team was studying the palazzo from a short distance away, enjoying espressos at a café table in the Piazza Navona. As they chatted and pointed things out, Jodie was smoking a cigarette in silence, her eyes crawling studiously along the roofline of the five-hundred-year-old building. Shuttered windows,

honey-coloured plaster crumbling from the architrave, and red terracotta tiles running along the
raking cornice at the very top.

She sucked on the cigarette, not hearing the
others as she searched for the building's weaknesses.
Considered escape routes. Controlled the thrill she
felt at the prospect of breaking in and taking something that belonged to someone else.

The art of burglary.

'It's a beautiful building,' Lewis said. 'I love Italian
architecture.'

Quinn laughed. 'What the hell do you know
about it?'

'As a matter of fact, Meg and I came here a couple
of years ago, not long before we found out she was
pregnant.'

'And that makes you an expert on architecture?'

He shrugged. 'At least I can appreciate something
that isn't made of pixels. No offence.'

'None taken, douchebucket.'

'That's pretty juvenile, Quinn,' Lewis said.
'Calling someone a name like that.'

Blanco shook his head and smirked. Turning to
Quinn, he said, 'What the hell is a douchebucket?'

She shrugged and pointed at Lewis. 'That right
there, I guess.'

Jodie ignored the banter. Hunter had authenticated the statues and translated them from ancient Greek. Lewis had figured out the biblical context of the verses. Quinn would hack the security. Now, it was all on her to find out how to get inside the palazzo. A Vespa raced across the Ponte Palatino, horn blaring as it undertook a taxi and flashed into the backstreets of Borgo.

Jodie's concentration was unbroken. She blew out a column of smoke and spoke in barely a whisper. 'The easiest way in is gonna be one of the skylights.'

'What skylights?' Lewis asked.

'There are six,' she said. 'You can't see them from here.'

'How the hell do you know they're there?' he asked, craning his neck up and trying to get a better view of the palazzo's roof.

'Because I looked on Google Earth on the flight, douchebucket. It's called prep.'

'Got it.'

'And look inside one of the windows on the top floor. Look carefully, and what do you see?'

'Just a wall.'

'Wrong, you see a wall with some light in the wrong place. That's because the light from above is pitching down through the skylight and projecting on the wall. See the way there's a trapezium of lighter paint on the wall?'

'Uh-huh.'

'Skylight.'

Lewis laughed. 'Pure genius. And how might we get to the skylights?'

'There's a pizza restaurant on the first floor of the building at the end of this road. As you can see, it's connected. We go into the restaurant and go out the back and use their fire escape to get to the roof.'

'Fire escape?'

'I checked their website. They have pictures of the terrace around the back.'

Hunter grinned. 'She doesn't miss a trick, this girl.'

'This girl has broken into more places than you've made bad jokes, Hunter,' she said. 'If you don't plan, you get caught.'

Amy checked her watch. 'Good work, Jodie. Let's kill some time before nightfall.'

Waiting for darkness to fall, they left their table and strolled slowly through the quiet streets of Tor di Nona until they reached the ancient river. Here, lovers walked hand in hand on ancient cobblestones and the setting sun sparkled on the Tiber. Up on the Lungotevere Tor di Nona, more Vespas flashed past them and street vendors stepped forward to try to hustle them into buying cheap jewellery and tourist trinkets.

As they walked to the pizza restaurant, they spent a few more moments studying the palazzo – glancing through the front windows and up on the roof. It looked empty, but there would be rooms around the back. They had to proceed with caution and be ready for anything.

'Here we are,' Amy said, pushing open the restaurant's door.

'Yep, this is the ground floor,' Hunter said.

'First floor,' Amy said.

'Ground floor.'

Blanco scratched his chin. 'Whatever you want to call it, we're in the right place.'

'Exactly,' Amy said. 'I guess I'll order a couple of pizzas and grab a table.'

'Nice,' Lewis said, slapping his hands together. 'Make them extra-large and make sure one of them is loaded with anchovies.'

Quinn rolled her eyes. 'We're not actually going to eat them, fool. They're cover.'

'Speak for yourself,' Lewis said. 'I'm starving.'

'I'll buy you a pizza as soon as we're out of here,' Amy said. 'I promise. Now we go to work.'

As they gathered around a table near the back of the restaurant, Amy ordered the pizzas and Quinn took out her GDP Pocket laptop and started tapping away on the keyboard. Only fractionally larger than a smartphone, the compact computer packed a high-speed Intel CPU and offered the sort of real keyboard preferred by hackers.

'All right,' the pale young goth said coolly. 'I already see the museum's Wi-Fi. Give me a second.'

'How long?' Amy asked.

'Not long. Exploiting any weaknesses in Wi-Fi security implementations isn't the hardest thing in the world, and I doubt Gallo has anything special set up. We're well within the transmission radius of their network access point, so now it's just me and Mr Linux and Miss Aircrack.'

'Please,' Hunter drawled. 'There's no need for vulgarity.'

Quinn ignored him and carried on tapping away. She felt the pressure of the moment resting heavily on her shoulders. Was she up to it? Sometimes, her confidence faltered. She didn't exactly hate herself, but she had what a college psychotherapist had once called low self-esteem. She guessed that was about right, and she knew why. She knew when it started but she didn't like to think about it. Talking about it was impossible. Maybe, even after several dumpster fire relationships, she would one day find someone who could listen in the right way. For now, the guard stayed up.

Guard was better than an act. She didn't like to think of it as an act. That meant deceiving the people around her. The stupid young woman in the Nirvana t-shirt playing games, guarding her true emotions against the world. The big hacker with a serious attitude who hacked NASA, downloaded two million dollars' worth of top-secret source code and used it to hack into the International Space Station.

Yeah, that stupid young woman.

The stupid young woman who got bored on her nineteenth birthday and hacked into the Bank of America and stole over a hundred million ATM card numbers and pins. And yet, she was in her early twenties now but still thought of herself as a stupid kid.

'So you can do it, then?'

It was Amy. She was getting impatient.

'I got into Bank of America in fifteen minutes,' she said, still looking down at her computer screen. 'Something tells me Signor Gallo's private museum will be much easier.'

Lewis craned his neck over Blanco and looked up

at the open kitchen. Steam billowed up into the air and rolled along the ceiling as one of the chefs slid another pizza into the wood oven. The smell of garlic and sun-dried tomatoes and basil drifted out across the restaurant. 'Man, do you smell that prosciutto? That smells great. You think they can get our pizzas here before Quinn shuts down the museum's security?'

'Doubtful,' Jodie said.

'Damn it!'

'Let's make a bet,' Hunter said. 'I'll buy drinks after the raid if the pizzas get here first.'

A groan went up around the table. Quinn was first to speak, looking over her screen at the Englishman. 'You're betting against me?'

'Why not?'

'Dangerous,' Jodie said.

'Just trying to make things interesting.'

Lewis was still watching the action in the kitchen. 'Turns out watching fresh pizzas being made is not good if you're hungry. I'm about ready to eat one of the table legs.'

Blanco's broad chest moved up and down as he chuckled. 'Without any sauce?'

'You watch me.'

'Any progress, Quinn?' Amy asked.

'It's password-protected, as I thought it would be. I'm just getting hold of that now.'

'That takes time?' Hunter asked with a smirk.

'A little,' Quinn said, the corner of her mouth turning up slightly. 'When you're buying drinks tonight, I want something expensive.'

'You haven't won yet.'

Quinn was still tapping away. 'Anyone know the most expensive drink a girl can buy?'

Jodie said, 'I read about a vodka cocktail that comes with a real eighteen-karat diamond. Cost like twenty thousand bucks.'

Quinn stopped tapping. 'Ooh, really? You think they serve those around here?'

Hunter shifted in his seat. 'Steady on...'

'Sadly no,' Jodie said. 'It was in Tokyo.'

'This offer is not transferrable,' Hunter said. 'And it ends at midnight.'

'Here they come!' Lewis said. 'Two golden beauties of pure cheese delight.'

Across the room, one of the waiters was sliding the freshly baked pizzas onto a serving board and lifting the counter flap.

'That's too bad,' Quinn said, 'because I just brought down their security.' She snapped the computer shut and slid it into her pocket. 'Sorry.'

Hunter's mouth fell open. 'Bloody hell...'

The waiter delivered the pizzas to the table. 'Enjoy!'

Quinn took a slice and bit off a big chunk. 'Yummy – and I just sent you a copy of the palazzo's schematics from city hall's archives. You're welcome.'

'Then we're going,' Amy said. 'Quinn, stay here and keep an eye on the street for any trouble.'

'Will do. I'll save you some pizza, Ben. Promise.'

'Thanks,' he said with a sad, lingering glance at the delicious food.

'We're all good to go?' Blanco said, looking at the goth.

'Sure. I used a technique called active-cracking, which is much harder to detect. After that, I located and disabled the alarms. You're good to go. Man, this pizza is the best I ever ate in my entire life.'

'Stop, please,' Lewis said.

'C'mon, Ben,' Amy said. 'You already had pizza on this mission. It's time to take this party right through the night.'

15

With the sun down and darkness slowly gathering around them, the team made their way up the fire escape at the rear of the building. Some of the diners below looked up and commented, but there was no trouble. It was just a slow, warm evening in Rome and everyone was just starting to enjoy themselves.

Jodie led the way up, casually walking to the top floor. 'This is the riskiest part,' she said. 'Any of those guys down there get suspicious and it's game over.'

'I'm more worried about what happens if someone's in,' Amy said. 'What are we going to say?'

'You never broke into a place before?' Jodie asked, almost disappointed in her mentor.

'No!' Amy said. 'Of course not. I wouldn't know where to start.'

'You start by knocking.' Jodie raised her hand and knocked three times. 'Then I have a little secret.'

Amy crossed her arms. 'And what if someone answers?'

'You ask them if they've seen your dog and then leave.'

'On the third floor?' Hunter said.

Jodie shrugged. 'Improvise.'

Amy sighed. 'And how does that help us in this case?'

'In this case,' Jodie replied sassily, 'we're not going to do that.'

'You're not in one of your uncooperative moods, are you?' Hunter asked.

Jodie didn't take the bait. 'In this case, Sal and Ben are going to push past whoever's inside. After that, we'll close the door and take it from there.'

'Doesn't look like that's gonna be necessary,' Blanco said. 'Knock again just to be sure, Jo.'

'No,' she said flatly. 'There's no one in here. Let's go.'

'You want me to break the door down?' Hunter said.

'Remember that little secret I said I had?' she said.

'Sure.'

'Sorry to burst your ego bubble, Hunter, but it wasn't my secret love for you.' She fished around in her pocket and pulled out a small metal key. 'It was this.'

'A skeleton key?'

'I'm going to say passkey, but yeah.'

'And you know how to use it?'

'I've been using passkeys since I was a kid, Hunter,' she said, gently wiggling the small key inside the lock. When it popped open, she pushed down the handle and opened the door. Then she turned and winked at him. 'See?'

Carefully, they stepped inside, but Blanco was still outside when one of the diners called up to him in Italian. He called back in the same language and gave the man a cheery wave before stepping inside the room and closing the door.

'What did he want?' Amy asked.

'He asked how Sergio was doing.'

'And what did you say back?'

He shrugged. 'I said I owed him a hundred euros, so he was doing okay.'

'I guess from his laugh we got away with it.'

'I guess we did.'

'Then let's move on,' Amy said. 'Jodie?'

Jodie was already way ahead of them, across the other side of the room. She was shifting a chair from the corner and placing it beneath one of the skylights. 'We go up this way.'

She popped the skylight up and pushed it open. Taking a Swiss Army knife from her pocket, she selected one of the screwdrivers and began to unscrew the frame. 'A hand, somebody.'

Lewis was there, underneath her, and helping her pull the entire skylight out of the roof. They twisted it at an angle and brought it down through the hole and set it up against the wall.

'Now we can get up there,' Jodie said.

'What about Sal's tummy?' Hunter said.

'Don't say mean things about my friend, Hunter,' Jodie said coolly.

'It was just a joke.'

'You don't know us well enough to make jokes like that.'

Blanco chuckled. 'Take it easy, Jodie.'

But she was gone, up through the hole in the ceiling and just two boots disappearing from view. A second later, her upside-down head appeared above them. 'Are you guys coming or not?'

They joined her on the roof, and Hunter took a second to survey the ancient city by night. Gallo had created a private roof terrace blocked from public view by a neatly trimmed box-hedge running around the top of the building. It wasn't unique to the city, but it was still pretty special. Safely out of view from the tourists and diners below, he stopped to take in the scene. 'That moon really is something else.'

'It sure is,' said Jodie. She had already walked along to the palazzo's roof and was kicking some of the step flashing away from one of its skylights. Removing a slim metal pry bar from her bag and burying the chisel point between the wood frame and the exterior cladding, she said, 'But maybe we could write a poem about it later and get on with the job now, huh?'

'That's a date.'

Amy had watched Jodie mature and grow since first joining the team and felt a little like the mother she'd never really had when she was a teenager. She didn't have any kids of her own, but she guessed Jodie was just about at the ready-to-leave-home phase. Sharing a knowing smile with Hunter, she pulled out her phone and made the call. 'We still good to go, Quinn?'

'Sure,' she said, her mouth full of pizza. 'Security system is still down and nothing is going on in the street.'

'Great. How's the pizza?'

'The best, and the waiter's pretty damned hot, too.'

Amy's eyebrows rose an inch. She wasn't used to hearing Quinn talk like this. Maybe she was growing up and spreading her wings too. 'Oh, really?'

'Sure. His name's Sergio. He's just finished his shift. Asked me out.'

'Holy crap, that's bad news.'

'Hey, I'm not that bad!'

'No, you don't understand,' Amy said. 'When we were breaking into the apartment at the top of the building, one of the people eating in the outside courtyard asked us how Sergio was. I think we just broke into the apartment of your new hottie.'

'Ah, not good.'

'You have to stop him getting to the apartment, Quinn. If he sees it's been broken into then he's going to call the police. From there, it's downhill all the way. We haven't even got inside the palazzo yet!'

'Leave it with me, boss.'

Amy slipped the phone into her pocket and explained it to the others.

'In that case, we have to work fast,' Hunter said.

'We have to work fast in any case,' said Jodie. 'We're breaking and entering.'

'Sorry, I'm not used to the criminal underworld. I work for UNESCO.'

'You used to,' Amy said. 'Now you work for the US government.'

'Not sure that makes it any easier to break into other people's property.'

'Get over yourself, Hunter,' Jodie said. 'You know what's riding on us getting hold of the statue inside this building. You want those Russian terrorists getting their hands on some sort of doomsday weapon and starting the apocalypse or what?'

'Of course not. You're quite right.'

'I'm always right,' she said, her wild eyes fixed on his. 'Now, get your ass inside that skylight and start your life of crime with pride, damn it.'

'I started my life of crime when I stole a car with you in Paris.'

'Then you should be good to go.'

Quinn threw her bag over her shoulder and pushed back from the table. Still chewing a mouthful of pizza, she ran out the back and stumbled into the courtyard. Looking up, she saw Sergio slowly climbing the steps to his apartment at the top of the building.

Yeah, not good. Not good at all.

'Sergio!'

He stopped and looked down through the metal mesh steps. 'Quinn! I thought we said we would meet later?'

Yeah, that was a lie, she thought. *I'm going to be speeding away from the scene of a museum robbery later, not drinking with you in a bar.*

'I need to talk.'

'Then come up to my apartment.'

'No... out here. We could walk along the river.'

He shrugged. 'Fine, but first I must change my clothes. I've been waiting tables all evening.'

'But...'

He turned and started making his way up the steps. 'Give me five minutes.'

'Oh shit,' she muttered.

* * *

Amy lowered herself through the skylight and touched down on the floorboards with the grace of a cat. Blanco crashed down after her with the grace of a refrigerator. Hunter and Lewis were already down, and Jodie was ahead of all of them, making her way to an internal door.

The HARPA deputy director had never seen anything like the Palazzo Giuseppe Gallo in her whole life. High-ceilings and ornate plaster cornices, silk wallpaper and parquet floors, velvet couches, and renaissance frescoes of the crusades were everywhere she looked. As they made their way along the corridor, she peered inside one of the rooms and saw a stunning canopy bed with cream-coloured fabric draped over a polished mahogany frame.

'Empty,' Blanco said.

Amy sighed. 'Thank heavens for small mercies.'

They walked along a frayed, antique carpet runner stretching down the middle of the hall, occasionally stepping on a squeaky floorboard. On her iPhone, she looked down at the schematics Quinn had got for them from the internet and saw they were nearing their destination.

'It's through here,' Amy said. 'This is where Gallo stores his collection.'

Stopping in front of mirrored double doors decorated in an ornate black and gold pattern of what looked like intertwined dragons, the woman from Connecticut calmed her nerves and took a breath. 'Here it is.'

Hunter shrugged. 'I don't hear anyone in there, so I guess the only way to get in is—'

'Wait!' Amy said.

It was too late. Hunter pushed open both doors and revealed an enormous room filled with antique display cases and sculptures. The cabinets stood on acres of polished parquet tiles, and high above them, a white plaster ceiling boasted three intricate chandeliers.

'You think this is the collection room?' Lewis asked.

Amy turned and saw he was joking. 'Ah, yeah.'

'Over here,' Hunter said. 'I see it.'

Blanco peered back outside in the corridor and drew his gun. 'Are you sure?'

'That's it,' Hunter said. 'That's the lion statue we're looking for, without a doubt.'

'I hope you're right,' Amy said, squinting. 'These things all look the same to me.'

Hunter shook his head. 'Bureaucrat.'

'I'll take that as a compliment. Just get the statue and let's get out of here.'

Behind them, Jodie swept her flashlight over the plaster wall and onto a giant renaissance tapestry hanging on the far wall. 'Er, guys...'

Amy was first to look. 'What is it, Jodie?'

'I think you should see this.'

'It's freaky.'

'It's weird.'

'It's a chimera,' Hunter sighed. 'It's Creed.'

* * *

Quinn moved fast, jogging up the steps and entering the apartment. She saw no sign of the young waiter and called out to him. 'Sergio!'

No response.

Odd.

'Sergio?'

She took a few more steps inside the apartment and peered down the hall.

'Going somewhere?'

Her skin prickled when she heard the voice, a low, gravelly Russian rumble. Turning on the spot, she saw a man with a shaved head in the hall. He was wearing black combat fatigues like she had seen soldiers wearing in the movies, and was holding a large, nasty-looking submachine gun.

Leaning into a radio on his shoulder, he thumbed a button and spoke in Russian. She didn't know a word of the language and had no idea what he had just said.

'Don't you touch me!' she said, taking a step back. She felt strange now, like never before. A fear stronger than any she had experienced before. This was what it felt like to be trapped and threatened when your team was somewhere else, when you were all alone.

'Put your hands up in the air where I can see them, and throw me the bag.'

Not her bag! Her laptop was in there, and the laptop was her life. 'I'm not armed,' she said, pathetically stalling for time.

He swung the weapon around off his shoulder and pointed it at her. 'Put your bag on the floor and kick it over to me.' He moved something on the side of the gun and it made a metallic clunking noise. She didn't like that one bit. 'Now.'

She dipped her shoulder and let the bag slide off onto the floor. She kicked it gently over to him along the polished wooden floorboards. Then she saw it and was almost struck dumb with terror. The Italian waiter was dead. Slumped over the chair behind the Russian. Bullet hole in his temple and wild eyes staring at eternity.

'What have you done?'

'Shhh,' he said quietly. More words into the radio. 'Hands up.'

'I told you I'm not armed.'

The man had picked up the bag and was rummaging around in it. 'These days a computer can be more dangerous than a gun. I will take your computer.'

'No! It's just personal. There's nothing on there of any interest to you.'

'I remember you from the *Goa Express*,' he said. 'And now I find you in an apartment next door to the Gallo Museum. I'm guessing there is a lot on your computer of interest to my boss. Your little game to play the lost, innocent lamb will not work with me.'

She stared at the barrel of the submachine gun. He was standing too close to her, and the hole in the weapon's muzzle seemed ferociously big and dangerous. 'So, what now?'

'Now we go see your friends.'

16

Hunter's words hung in the air like poison gas. All eyes turned to him in the gloom, but Amy spoke first. 'You think this confirms that Gallo is Creed?'

He nodded. 'Sure, look at that thing! No prizes for working out we were right. The Marquis is in the Creed.'

'You don't know that,' Jodie said.

'You have a better explanation?'

After a long silence, he said, 'I didn't think so.'

'Hey, just because I don't say much doesn't mean what I do have to say is worthless. Better to have the world think you're an idiot than open your yap and prove it. That advice is for you, Hunter. Take it.'

'It's Creed,' Hunter said again, more firmly. 'I just know it in my heart.'

'Then you should listen to your heart more often.'

Hunter spun around, angling his flashlight over onto the man standing behind them. Tall, thin, and tanned and wearing an expensive dinner suit, he was standing with one hand in his tuxedo pocket. He looked like he hadn't a care in the world.

'Gallo!' Hunter said.

The aristocrat nodded once, dwarfed by his shadow projected up on the wall by the multiple flashlights. With his slim, aquiline nose and slicked-back raven-black hair, he reminded Hunter of some sort of bird of prey. '*Sì*, I am the Marquis Giuseppe Francisco Patrizi Gallo, and *sì*, I am a high-ranking member of the Creed's Italian chapter.'

He gave the giant tapestry an admiring glance as he walked over to the light switch. When he flicked it up, a giant electric candelabra spilled bright yellow light all over the room. 'Perhaps this will allow you to appreciate my artwork better.'

'We need to talk about the elephant in the room,' Hunter said. 'Or in this case, the chimera.'

'Ah, you like this piece? This is one of the finest in my house.'

'House...' Jodie muttered. 'At least he's got a sense of humour.'

'All of this, including this tapestry, was carefully collected and curated over hundreds of years by papal treasurers,' he said smoothly. 'My ancestors were always very close to the papacy. Even today, we are a very powerful family with many important connections and lots of influence. It is not wise to cross a man like me.'

'We need the lion statue,' Amy said.

'I know what you want,' he said. 'I know why you're here.' He wheeled in a tight circle and glanced away from them and up at the tapestry. 'They're magnificent beasts, and you will now step away from the display case containing the statue you are trying to steal.'

Blanco was still holding the gun on him. 'The way I see it, you don't have a hell of a lot of bargaining power right now, Mr Gallo.'

Gallo smiled. 'I suppose you are right, but do you think stealing from the Creed is a wise thing to do? We know who you are. We know what you did in Germany. What you did in Atlantis. You are under constant observation. Perhaps this is your chance to redeem yourselves. Maybe if you tell me why you need the statue I will let you live.'

'And if you believe that you'll believe anything,' said Lewis.

Amy said, 'I thought the Creed knew everything?'

Gallo shrugged. 'Different factions know different things. Why do you want this lion?'

'That's not something I'm prepared to—'

A short burst of gunfire made everyone jump.

'Throw down your guns!'

Gallo turned and looked behind him. He saw several men in black combat fatigues and balaclava masks stomping into the exhibition room. 'What the hell is this?'

Amy saw one of the men was dragging Quinn behind him. 'Quinn!'

Gubenko spun around, aimed his Steyr at Gallo, and opened fire. The muzzle flashed and roared as the rounds exploded in the Italian's chest and head, blasting blood mist and brain matter all over the tapestry.

Quinn screamed.

'My God!' Amy said. 'You bastards!'

Neverov was in the centre of the room, submachine gun gripped in his hands as he scanned the cases. 'That one!' he yelled at one of the men. 'Get it. Don't damage it.'

Lugovoy stomped over to the case and smashed

the glass with the stock of his compact machine pistol. He stepped forward, his boots crunching on the shards of glass, and reached into the case to extract the statue. 'It's ours.'

Medinsky violently pushed Quinn towards Amy. She tripped over Gallo's dead body and fell to the floor, landing in some of the smashed glass. Jodie ran to her and picked her up, bringing her back over to the rest of the team.

'All of you!' Neverov said. 'Get up against the wall and lower your guns.'

Hunter unshouldered his weapon. 'We know who you are.'

'You know nothing.'

'You have old weapons,' Hunter said, looking at the base model gun in the other man's hands. 'I know that much. That Steyr must be twenty years old.'

'They beat your handguns.'

Neverov was walking backward now, never once taking the barrel of his weapon off the team. The rest of his men scrambled into position and streamed out of the door back onto the corridor. When Neverov reached the door, he opened fire, wildly sweeping the Steyr from side to side and spraying everything in sight with lead.

'Down!' Hunter yelled.

The team moved like greased lightning, throwing themselves behind display cases and hitting the deck with seconds to spare. With her hands clamped over her ears, Amy winced in fear as the bullets ripped and drilled and raked into the wall behind her. Plaster burst into clouds of dust and flakes drifted down onto her as Neverov lowered his barrel and shredded part of the display case she was hiding behind.

'No!' she screamed, tucking her head down and shielding her eyes from the wood splinters and glass fragments. 'He's going to kill us all!'

'No, he's not.'

She looked up and saw Blanco standing over her. He was offering her his hand. She took it and he pulled her up. 'They've gone?'

The Brooklynite nodded. His expression was grave. 'They've gone.'

'And they have the lion statue!' Jodie said.

Hunter was upon his feet, dusting himself off. 'We have to go after them.'

'Are you nuts?' Quinn said. 'Their guns are way bigger than our guns!'

'Doesn't matter,' Amy said. 'Max is right. We can't let them get away with the statue. We haven't even had time to study it yet. If we lose them, we lose the mission.'

'Then let's rock and roll,' Lewis said. 'They can't have gotten too far away.'

Hunter led the way out of the room and then they followed the trail of broken glass, wood splinters, and gun smoke along the corridor until they found a shredded panel of torn and smoking wood.

'Looks like this used to be a door,' Quinn said. 'What happened?'

Blanco leaned closer. 'I'd say nine-mil rounds and a muzzle velocity of around nine hundred rounds per minute is what happened. They blew the door down with their guns.'

'They must know something we don't about how to get out of here then.' Amy looked through the blasted door and peered down a narrow flight of steps. 'It goes down to some sort of basement.'

'Our schematics never said anything about a basement.' Jodie gave Quinn a look. 'Were they up to date?'

'Yes, they were up to date,' Quinn said. 'Get off my back.'

'Let's get on with it,' Hunter said. 'We're losing time.'

'Wait,' Quinn said. 'You want me to go into a dark

basement owned by a member of the Creed with a chimera tapestry on his wall?'

'Problem?'

'Do German castle dungeons and broken human bones mean anything to you? What if he's got the same thing down there?'

'Only one way to find out, Quinn,' Hunter said. 'Anyone coming with me?'

17

Unarmed and on edge, Hunter led the way, stepping carefully down the wooden steps until he reached the basement. He angled his flashlight around the space and saw nothing but old tea chests and yet more oil paintings covered with old, frayed hessian sacks.

'No ancient beasts,' Blanco said, relieved.

'But there is another door.' Hunter moved across the room cautiously. 'Call me crazy, but I've developed a serious fear of angry armed Russians jumping out of the dark at me.'

He reached the door and pushed it open with his boot.

'Anything?' Amy asked.

'Only if you think a wall made of human skulls is something.'

Jodie gasped. 'Holy shit.'

'It's the catacombs,' Lewis said. 'I should have known.'

'What are the catacombs, Ben?' Amy asked.

'It's where the early Christians of Rome buried their dead. Basically, they're an extensive network of tunnels and crypts under the city, full of the dead. They had to do it this way because they were persecuted and not allowed to build churches until around AD 300.'

'Great,' Jodie said. 'We have to chase insane armed Russians through a giant underground graveyard. And they say birthday wishes never come true.'

'You know what I'm wishing for right now?' Hunter said. 'That lion statue.'

'Max is right,' Amy said. 'Let's get after them before they get too far ahead of us.'

Hunter led them along the narrow stone tunnels. The air was damp and close and everywhere they looked, the skulls of thousands of ancient dead Romans stared back at them with empty black eye sockets.

'I see them!' Hunter called out. 'And they see us... Get down!'

Gubenko was at the rear of the Russian team and now he turned and fired. Yahontov and Turgenev turned and added to the fusillade. They threw themselves down into the dirt just as the Russians' rounds tore into the skulls all around them and blasted an explosion of splintered bone fragments all over them.

Quinn screamed again, but Gubenko was louder, howling like a crazed maniac as he raked the walls full of bullets. Then he and the other men turned and fled back along the tunnel after the rest of his unit.

'Damn it!' Amy said. 'Are they trying to kill us or what?'

Jodie crawled up out of the dirt. 'Funny.'

Upon their feet, they ran forward again, keeping their heads low and trying to stay safe while not letting the Russians out of their sight. Then they turned a corner and saw Neverov leading his men up a flight of stone steps.

'They're leaving the catacombs!' Amy said.

Hunter was first up the steps, carefully peering around as he poked his head up through a manhole and scanned the street for any sign of them.

'They up there, Max?' Blanco called up.

'Now we know why they used the catacombs.'

'Huh?'

The roar of several powerful motorbike engines drowned out his reply, and when Amy got up to street level, she was just in time to see the taillights of a black Ducati Diavel cruiser bike tearing around a corner up ahead. The low roar of its engine echoed in the night streets all around them.

'There were four of them,' said Hunter. 'All part of the plan.'

'Damn it again!'

'I'll give them one thing,' he said. 'They know how to plan an operation. In and out of the palazzo in minutes, an underground egress route and four high-speed bikes as the getaway vehicles.'

'Maybe if you think they're so great you could ask to join them, Hunter.'

He looked over to Jodie. 'Depends on their pension plan.'

She shook her head. 'The only funny thing about you is how funny you think you are.'

'We need to get after them, Max!' said Amy.

'Unfortunately, Colonel Neverov neglected to include some extra bikes in his escape plan, so we're shit out of luck.'

'No, wait,' Jodie said. 'I think I have the answer.'

Amy followed her pointing arm to what she had seen. 'What the hell is that thing?'

'It's an Estrima Biro,' Lewis said. 'A two-seater electric city car. Meg and I hired one when we came here before. They're for rent all over the city.'

Amy regarded the tiny doorless vehicle. It was no bigger than a golf cart, and its occupants were pro-tected only by two roll bars supporting a reinforced glass roof. Leaning forward, she peered through the open vehicle at Lewis, who was on the side. 'There aren't even any doors on it. It's ridiculous.'

Quinn shrugged. 'It's whimsical.'

'It's our only hope,' Jodie said. 'I can get this thing fired up in seconds and it's the only vehicle in sight.'

'It's a metre wide!' Hunter said.

Jodie looked at him, waiting for him to catch up. 'And that's a good thing because...'

'Ah.'

'Exactly.' Jodie climbed into the Biro and broke open the ignition panel. 'We're chasing bikes.'

'She's right,' Amy said. 'And they're getting away fast, so get in, Max!'

'Me? I'm not getting in that thing. I have my repu-tation to think of.'

Quinn pushed a stick of chewing gum in her mouth. 'You sure you're not a blue blood, too?'

'C'mon, Max!' Amy said with a reassuring pat on his shoulder. 'You're our best shot.'

'What about the rest of you?' he asked.

'Don't worry about us,' Amy said. 'Just get the lion statue back and call us when you're safe. We'll meet up and jet out of here as soon as we can.'

'But it looks even more dangerous than the bikes!' Hunter looked at the rest of the team but found no support to his objections. Behind them, the sound of the Ducatis roared as Neverov and his team made their escape.

'Max?' Amy's eyes widened. 'For me.'

When Jodie touched the ignition wires together, the Biro came to life. She moved fast, strapping herself in and taking no credit for the successful hotwiring. Blowing the horn, she leaned her head outside of the roll cage. 'Hey, Hunter! You want another minute to do your makeup?'

Hunter sighed and climbed into the tiny electric car, pausing to make the sign of the cross. 'God help me.'

'I don't know about the big guy upstairs,' Jodie said, 'but I might be able to help you. Buckle up, cupcake.'

18

Hunter grabbed the side of his seat, trying desperately to hold on for dear life as Jodie stamped on the throttle and sent the tiny electric car swerving around the corner into the Piazza della Rotonda. The Pantheon loomed into view ahead of them, its enormous Corinthian column portico bearing down on them like a mouth full of teeth.

The granite and marble marvel was an impressive sight, but not tonight. Not for Jodie Priest and Max Hunter. She was focused on weaving the Biro around the famous fountain and obelisk in the centre of the square and not hitting any of the tourists milling around with cameras. He was scanning for any sign of the fleeing bikers.

'There!' he called out. 'To the east!'

'Huh?'

'Left! They're going down the road to the left of the Pantheon.'

'If they're going left then just say so, Hunter.'

She spun the wheel and jerked the Biro violently to the left, spinning the wheels on the ancient cobblestones. Only the seatbelt stopped Hunter from flying out the side of the car. Tourists shook fists and swore at them.

'I nearly fell out, Jodie!'

'Oh yeah,' she said sarcastically. 'Hang on.'

He shook his head, reached into his jacket, and pulled out his Glock. Now, the angry tourists turned on their heels and started screaming. When safely out of the way, some reached for their phones and began calling the police while others filmed them as they raced across the piazza in pursuit of the Ducatis.

'Where do you think they're heading?' she asked. 'Airport?'

'Maybe, but I doubt it.'

'Why?'

'Neverov is too good. This whole operation is just too slick. In and out of the palazzo in minutes and bikes all set up waiting for the escape. Even a private airfield has security protocols that are really going to slow him down. I'd say keep an eye out for another escape. Chopper, most likely.'

Jodie said nothing. She had the answer she wanted and now dumped her foot down on the throttle and sent the Biro lurching around the left-hand side of the Pantheon.

'Doesn't this thing go any faster?' Hunter said. 'What gear are you in?'

She rolled her eyes. 'There are no gears in this, Hunter. Can you even drive?'

The Ducatis weaved around passers-by and roared down into the next square, the Piazza della Minerva. By the time Jodie got there, the bikes were already vanishing into a side street to the left. One of the men riding pillion on the rearmost Diavel casually rotated his upper body around and pointed a Steyr compact machine pistol at them.

'Incoming!' Hunter yelled.

The gun rattled and clicked in the hot night. The muzzle flashed. Pedestrians screamed and dived for cover as Jodie spun the wheel to the right and sent the Biro skidding across the piazza into another side street.

'That was close!' she said.

'And we lost them.'

'Never,' she said with a smile. She spun the wheel

to her left, and the tyres squealed on more cobble-stones as she drove the little car into a tight skid and down another narrow lane lined with traditional Roman townhouses. 'This road runs east–west, so we should be able to cut them off.'

He gave her a look. 'Shouldn't that be this road runs left to right?'

Jodie fought her smile back and quickly flashed him her middle finger. 'Bite me, Hunter.'

His response was cut short when he saw the Ducatis burst out of a street directly ahead of them. They were only in sight for a second, crossing the end of the road, but at least they knew where they were again.

Jodie got there fast. Tapping the brakes and spinning the wheel to the right, she was once again right on their tails. At the front, Neverov turned in his seat and saw them gaining speed. He made a hand signal and the three rearmost riders peeled away from the pack and turned in formation like jet fighters.

They flashed past the Biro, one on each side. Hunter fired on one of them but missed and buried his rounds into the plasterwork of a restaurant. Then they heard a roar of engines and falling revs, and then rising revs and an even louder roar.

'They've turned around and are on our tail, Hunter!'

Hunter turned and saw Neverov give them more orders with another hand signal. Each bike accelerated while the men riding pillion raised their machine pistols and rotated their upper bodies to aim at the Biro.

Then they were alongside them.

'Do something, Hunter!'

'Hit the brakes!'

'Huh?'

'I might be bloody amazing, but not even I can shoot in two different directions at the same time with one gun. Hit the brakes!'

The men fired.

Jodie hit the brakes and the two pillion riders raked each other and their riders with nine-mil rounds. As the rounds exploded in their chests and blasted the four men from their seats, the Biro juddered and jerked and shook. Cursing loudly, the Californian woman struggled to keep it under control.

In their wake, the men tumbled and turned and rolled over the cobblestones. They came to a stop at the end of long streaks of blood stretching all over the road. Off to their left and right, the riderless Ducatis howled and swerved out of control. The one on their left smashed into a café window and set off an alarm. Now, flashing lights and sirens filled the night as the second one crunched into a parked BMW. The Ducati crumpled the front wing, rotated over on its front wheel axis, and revved wildly before coming down in a smoking, buckled heap on the car's hood.

'Nice work, Jodie.'

'Thanks, but the others are getting away!'

She hit the gas and spun the wheels, leaving the chaos of blood-soaked streets and smashed glass behind them. Swerving around the corner, the other riders were in sight again now, driving down the middle of a broader road lined with cars. Jodie pulled the Biro out into the centre and gave chase as fast as she could.

Hunter leaned out of the car and fired on the riders just as they swerved across the Piazza D'Aracoeli and headed across a park in the middle of a busy roundabout. The shot missed, and now there were too many other cars to fire again safely.

'Nice shooting, Hunter. Maybe I should have brought Quinn instead.'

'It's not as easy as it looks, and it might be a tad easier if you could get this ridiculous roller skate within a thousand yards of them.'

'Whatever.'

Hunter saw an enormous white marble monument looming ahead of them.

'What the hell is that?' Jodie said. 'It's amazing.'

'It's the Vittoriano,' he said. 'A monument dedicated to the first King of Italy when it unified in the nineteenth century.'

'Monument would have sufficed.'

'Eh?'

'Just remember for next time. Less is more.'

'What the—'

Another burst of rounds from the rear rider. Hunter instinctively ducked and Jodie swerved to avoid the bullets. It worked. They chewed into the roundabout's asphalt but missed the Biro, giving Jodie just enough time to straighten the wheel.

Ahead, Neverov was ahead of Gubenko as they ripped out of the park and crossed the far lane of the roundabout. To the Englishman's disbelief, the Russian colonel drove the Ducati towards the massive marble steps on the monument's famous front terrace.

'What does he think he's doing?' he asked. 'There's an iron fence blocking vehicles from getting into the Vittoriano!'

Gubenko clearly didn't see the problem and now pulled a tiny olive-green tube from his backpack.

'What's that?' Jodie said, seeing it instantly.

Hunter squinted. 'Looked like a Bur.'

'A what?'

'It's one of the smallest grenade launchers in the world,' he said. 'Made for and used by the Russian special forces.'

'Dangerous, huh?'

He gave her a look. 'What do you think?'

'What's it fire?'

'One of three projectiles. There's a thermobaric warhead for soft targets, a smoke grenade, and an incendiary. We'll find out what Neverov's packing in about five seconds.'

Gubenko fired the launcher and sent the rocket-propelled grenade across the road and into the metal barrier fence. The fireball exploded in an instant, blasting a good section of the iron barrier into a thousand pieces of burnt, bent metal shards.

Black smoke bloomed up into the night sky, lit by orange streetlights. A man who had been selling chestnuts from a small cart not far from the bottom of the steps was knocked off his feet and sent flying into the air. He landed with a smack on the asphalt and only just managed to scramble out of the way of his cart as it crashed down two seconds after him.

'Holy crap, this is chaos, Hunter!'

'And they still have the lion statue.'

Neverov ripped his Ducati through the smoke and rammed it up the giant marble steps. Gubenko followed in his wake on the other bike and headed up to the colonnade at the top.

'He seems pretty keen on getting away, Hunter. You going to take another shot or what?'

'There are tourists here,' he said. 'You want me to blow one of their heads off by accident?'

She spun the wheel, stamped on the throttle, and aimed the Biro for the steps. 'With your aim, I'd say it's better to take the cautious approach.'

'You're not planning on driving up there after them?' he asked.

'Sure, why not?'

'I'll give you a list by next Thursday, starting with it's one of the most famous monuments in the country and we'll attract the attention of about half the city's police force!'

'That's right – I forgot about your morbid fear of getting arrested.'

'Believe it or not, not everyone has a long list of arrests behind them, Jodie.'

'Stop, you're embarrassing me with all these compliments.'

'Reason two,' he said, ignoring her, 'is how is this roller skate getting up those steps? I doubt it could climb a curb, let alone—'

'Watch and learn, Dr Hunter.'

An improvement on plain old Hunter, he thought.

She hit the bottom step and powered the tiny car up towards the colonnade. The suspension crunched up and down as she ploughed the vehicle up the steps with merciless determination in her eyes.

Neverov was already at the top and was turning his bike to drive along the back of the monument just in front of the colonnade. He crossed the seventy-yard-wide terrace of the Altar of the Fatherland and turned his bike up more steps leading inside it. Gubenko followed his leader inside the colonnade.

'He's going inside!' Hunter yelled.

Jodie reached the top of the steps, spun the wheel to the left, and aimed in the same direction.

'Brace for impact, Hunter! We're going in.'

The Wolves had other ideas. The same man who had fired on them back at the Pantheon turned and opened fire a second time with his Steyr. This time his aim was better. Rounds raked up the Biro's rear panel and shattered the glass roof. Jodie screamed and turned away from the gunfire, sending the electric car into a violent, uncontrolled skid towards the stone balustrade running around the top of the terrace.

'Hold on!' she yelled.

The engine growled as she turned into the skid and hit the brakes. The car spun around one-eighty degrees but was a second too late to avoid an impact, and now the back end of the Biro smashed through the stone balustrade. As it came to a stop with its rear-end hanging over the top of the terrace, Jodie peered outside the roll cage and looked over the side.

'You're not going to like this, Hunter.'

The angle at which the car had come to a halt meant Hunter's side was facing in towards the terrace and he was unable to see what she had seen.

'What am I not going to like?'

'Right now, half this vehicle is hanging over the edge of the terrace and it's a sixty-foot drop to the ground.'

Then, Hunter heard engines revving. 'And you're not going to like my news, either. Gubenko and his Steyr-wielding pillion rider are on their way back to finish the job off and put us over the side.'

19

Hunter didn't wait for a response. Above him at the top of the steps, the black Ducati burst through the portico and shot out into the air before crashing back to earth halfway down the marble steps. Bouncing up and down on the suspension, Gubenko struggled to control the bike while his pillion rider raised the Steyr and tried to get some more shots off.

Hunter leaped out of the Biro and saw only one of the rear tyres was hanging over the edge of the terrace. 'Hit the gas!' he yelled out, grabbing hold of the front of the roll cage bar and pulling on it with all his might.

'That's never going to work!'

'Yes, it will,' he called back, ducking his head as

bullets chewed into the marble all around him. 'It's lightweight to start with and rear-wheel drive, so just do it!'

Jodie hit the pedal and the rear wheels spun around fast. The one hanging in the air raced and whined but could do nothing else. The one on the marble screeched and sent thick, bubbling plumes of rubber smoke up into the air all around them. The car surged forward like a bolt of lightning, leaving Hunter coughing and spluttering in the smoke.

Jodie checked her mirror and saw him running to the car. Ahead of her just off to the right, Gubenko's bike skidded off the bottom step and crunched down on the terrace. He pulled the handlebars hard to the left and turned the bike in a tight arc. Both riders extended their legs for balance and the pillion rider raised the Steyr and unleashed another burst of fire.

Jodie saw the muzzle flash in the smoke and slammed the car into reverse. The last few rounds nipped up off the marble terrace and ricocheted into the car's windshield, punching three neat spider-web fractures in the glass inches from her face. She screamed but carried on reversing, screeching to a smoky halt beside Hunter, who was now less than twenty metres behind her.

The Englishman aimed his weapon at Gubenko

and loosed a few rounds across the night, striking the pillion rider in the chest. He grunted in shock and tumbled off the back of the Ducati, dying in the fall before he hit the deck. Hunter fired another burst at Gubenko and then jumped inside the Biro.

Jodie stamped on the throttle. 'What happened to the shooter?'

'He came to a dead stop, now go!'

'Huh?'

'Neverov is getting away!' he said. 'I saw him leave when I was back at the balustrade. Gubenko was a diversion.'

Jodie got it loud and clear and spun the wheel hard to the right, cutting across Gubenko's path and clipping him on the rear tyre. The Russian lost control of the bike and after a few seconds of uncontrolled swerving, the Ducati crashed over on its side and slid across the marble terrace in a shower of sparks.

She checked her mirror. 'It won't take him long to get back up and running.'

'Pull up!'

'Are you crazy?'

'Do it!'

She hit the brakes and the Biro juddered to a violent stop in another screech of tyres and smoke.

Hunter leaped out and ran over to the dead pillion rider. Snatching up his Steyr, he clambered back inside the Biro, making it rock heavily up and down on its suspension.

'If Gubenko's going to be behind us, I'd rather he didn't have this. Now go.'

She dipped her head and hit the gas. 'I can't argue with that.'

At the eastern end of the terrace, they once again passed the portico where Neverov had driven inside the monument.

'I see them!' she said. 'Looks like they're trying to get off the monument.'

Following them, she drove past the portico steps and swung a tight left, skidding the car around a sharp corner. Straightening the wheel, she drove along a narrow side terrace before smashing through another balustrade in a shower of marble splinters and dust. With Hunter swearing loudly to her right, she swerved down another long flight of marble steps in front of the Museo Centrale and got off the monument.

'Probably only a million euros worth of damage,' Hunter said. 'Not bad for you.'

She said nothing. Eyes fixed on Neverov, she turned another tight left and almost tipped the car over. Hunter held on to the roll cage and gasped in horror as she turned into the swerve and brought the other two wheels crashing down onto the ground.

'What?' she said.

'At least you brought it back under control.'

She grinned. 'It was never out of control, Hunter.'

'Just get me close enough for another shot,' he said, checking the Steyr's mag. 'There's still enough hell in this thing to ruin their night.'

Then they heard the sirens.

'Cops,' she said with a sigh. 'Now there's a way to ruin a good night.'

Hunter darted his head outside the Biro and Jodie rammed the tiny electric car up the smooth flagstone slope leading up to Michelangelo's famous hilltop square, the Campidoglio. Ahead of them, Neverov was skidding into a sharp left turn in front of the Palazzo Senatorio, a large Renaissance-style building used as Rome's City Hall. Hunter knew from previous trips to the city that the building had been constructed on the site of the Tabularium, inside which the ancient Romans had stored all of their archives, but somehow he didn't think Jodie would be all that interested to know.

They reached the palazzo and swung left after the Ducati just in time to see it burning around the back of the building. The pillion rider fired a short round of warning shots from his machine pistol as they turned out of sight once again, and in her rearview mirror, Jodie saw Gubenko reach the end of the Campidoglio behind them.

'Look who's back in the saddle,' she said.

Hunter turned and peered over his shoulder through the Biro's trashed rear window. 'And even more angry than usual, I'd bet.'

Neverov made a sharp turn away from a brick wall and raced around a hairpin bend on the Via Monte Tarpeo to their left.

'What's he doing now?' Jodie said.

'Heading into the Forum!'

'But it's all walled off!'

'Not to Colonel Vladimir Neverov.'

They watched in astonishment as the Russian pillion rider fired another RPG at the wall surrounding the famous centre of everyday life in ancient Rome. Seconds later, Neverov ripped his Ducati through the freshly blasted hole and disappeared inside among the ruins.

'This dude really is serious about shaking us off, Hunter! I've never been in a chase anything like this before.'

'And it's about to get a whole lot worse,' he said,

pointing the barrel of the Steyr at the top of the wind-shield. 'Judging by those flashing blue lights bouncing off the Temple of Saturn's portico columns, I'd say the cops are almost on top of us.'

'Damn it.' She smacked the steering wheel with the heel of her hand. 'And just when I was having fun, too.'

'Fun? Are you insane?'

The car rocked up and down on the rocky ground as she weaved in and out of broken temples and crumbling pillars. 'I'm going to pretend I never heard that.'

'Look out!' he yelled as they flashed past three giant Corinthian columns. 'That was all that remains of the Temple of Castor and Pollux!'

'Are you for real? We're trying to get the statue back, Hunter. We don't care about the architecture.'

'But Canaletto painted it!'

She glanced in her mirror. 'Looks like it needs a second coat.'

He rolled his eyes. 'I give up, and by the way, something that looked important just flew off the back of this car.'

She glanced at him and then back to the ruins. 'Hunter, I hate to be the one to break this to you, but I think this car is toast.'

Another round of fire from the rear pillion rider missed them but tore into the temple's marble columns behind them. Jodie swerved and by the time the car was back under control, Neverov was heading towards the eastern end of the Forum. Now, Gubenko flashed past them and pulled up alongside his leader ahead of them. The Wolves were reunited.

Hunter scanned either side of the speeding Biro and saw police cars swerving to a halt all around the ancient Roman site, but none were coming inside. 'They figure we have to come out eventually, I guess.'

Jodie gasped. 'Yeah, but not like that!'

Hunter looked ahead and saw what she had seen. Neverov and Gubenko had driven under the archway of the famous first-century Arco di Tito and were bearing down on a metal security barrier. Neverov's pillion rider fired another RPG and obliterated the fence in seconds, leaving a clear path for the Wolves. The Russians raced out of the Forum and made their escape from both HARPA and the local carabinieri now racing towards them from stations all over the city.

'Oh, no...' Hunter said.

'What?' said Jodie. 'We can get this through that hole they just blasted, so just relax.'

'No, look where they're going! We're all going to die.'

Jodie watched the Ducatis steering out of view inside a large, darkened archway, but she was typically relaxed. 'We can do that.'

'No, we're going to die. There are cops everywhere and they're going in there!'

'Nah, just watch and learn, Hunter.'

20

Hunter said a silent prayer as Jodie ripped past Constantine's Arch and followed the Wolf Pack into the Colosseum. As soon as he had seen the Russians heading inside the two-thousand-year-old amphitheatre, he knew his evening was about to take a turn for the worse. Seconds later, this was confirmed when Jodie skidded around a narrow stone archway and burst out into the open part of the iconic monument.

Here, Hunter's nightmares became real. Instantly, Neverov and Gubenko peeled off in two directions. Gubenko drove anti-clockwise around the first tier while Neverov was already driving up a flight of the cramped stone steps and was moving clockwise around the third tier high above them.

Jodie hit the brakes and the Biro screeched to a halt. 'Who's got the goodies, Hunter? They're all wearing backpacks.'

'Neverov. He wouldn't trust the lion ágalma in anyone else's hands.'

'Statue.' She turned the wheel, but he stopped her.

'Wait, he'd know I'd think that and give it to Gubenko.'

She sighed and turned the wheel the other way, but he stopped her again.

'What now?' she asked.

'No, he'd know I'd think that, too, so he'd keep it on himself. We need to get up to the third tier.'

'Damn it, Hunter!'

He ignored her and peered up at the bikes as they roared and revved around the ancient building. 'Can we get up there?'

'Not in this,' she said. 'The bikes could get up there but the ancient Romans overlooked the need for electric cars to get around inside here, even one as narrow and small as this.'

'Then we're on foot,' he said. 'Here, take this.'

He gave her his Glock. 'And I've got the Steyr. Between us, we have to stop them from getting back outside the Colosseum. If that happens they either get the statue away or it goes into custody when the cops arrest them.'

'Then let's get on with it.'

'I think that decision just got made for us, Jodie!'

'Huh?'

'Incoming!'

Jodie followed Hunter's pointing hand and registered with nauseating horror the sight of Neverov's pillion rider firing an RPG from a shoulder launcher. He was aiming it directly at them and with a bright flash and a puff of smoke, the lethal projectile was in the air.

'Out!' Hunter said. 'Out, out, out!'

Jodie was already on her way, hitting the ground at the same time as Hunter. Each of them rolled away in opposite directions into narrow brickwork corridors as the rocket-propelled incendiary grenade ripped into the Biro's hood.

A deep thump sounded and for a few seconds, their world lit up like a summer's day as a fireball exploded inside the tiny electric car. Then the shockwave hit them and blackened tubular steel, burning plastic and fuel sprayed everywhere. Thick smoke spewed out of the car's bent, twisted carcass as Hunter turned his head around to scan for Jodie. She was lying motionless in the corridor on the other side of the burning wreckage.

'Are you okay?'

No reply.

Overhead, the roar of the Ducatis stirred him further from his dazed condition. He got to his feet, snatched up the Steyr, and staggered around the wreck over to Jodie. She was unconscious but slowly coming around. Shouldering the Steyr, he pulled her gently away from the chaos.

'Jodie, are you okay?'

'I think so... I feel dizzy.'

'It's a concussion. I want you to stay here, sitting up against this wall. Stay in the dark and keep out of sight until you feel better. Have you got your phone?'

She nodded. 'Sure.'

'Call Amy and tell her what's happened. Tell her we're going to need a vehicle to get out of the city in a hurry and the cops are on our tail. Tell her we'll come to her when it's safe, just like the original plan.'

'Got it.'

'And keep the gun in your hand and use it if you have to. You do know how to use it, right?'

Through one of the giant open arches to her right, the blue flashing lights of the police cars outside strobed on her soot-smeared, grazed cheek. 'Are you kidding?'

'Good.'

'What are you going to do?'

'I'm getting that damned lion back before those bastards get away.' He scrambled to his feet, boots scuffing on the floor.

She coughed and blew out a long, stressed breath. 'Look after yourself, Hunter.'

'I'll be fine.'

'And Hunter?'

'What?'

'I'm glad you came with me and not Quinn as I said before.'

Hunter smiled. 'Easy, girl. Next thing you know, you'll be calling me Max.'

'Don't count on it.'

She never saw his smile. He had turned and was running out of the covered walkway into the main open-air part of the Colosseum. He could hear the Ducatis but not see them. He searched again and saw one of them racing along the third tier on the far side of the amphitheatre. It was hard to track against the wall behind it, but when it drove in front of one of the arches, he saw there was only one rider.

Gubenko.

So where were Neverov and the statue?

He searched again, but the engines of both bikes were echoing so much in the dark amphitheatre that isolating either one was hard work. Then he saw it, on his three o'clock as it raced west on the southern wall. This time there were two riders, and that meant Neverov and the statue.

And a pillion rider with a Steyr.

He could hear the police more clearly now. They were shouting in Italian and one of them was talking through a megaphone. Somewhere overhead, he heard the sound of helicopter rotors and for the first time since New York, he thought the mission might be about to come to a rapid and inglorious end.

With the Steyr over his shoulder, he vaulted over a wrought iron fence and headed up a flight of stone steps to the second tier. Gubenko was where he had first seen Neverov, and the old Russian colonel and his heavily armed pillion rider were rounding a bend on the third tier and turning into the shadows of an obscured stairwell. The pillion rider was holding his Steyr with one hand and talking into a palm mic on the other.

Hunter knew there were more men in the full Wolf Pack than had come out on tonight's raid, and now it looked like they were calling them in for backup.

Time to get John the Apostle's old statue was running out fast, so he turned to his left and sprinted to the bottom of the stairwell he had seen Neverov steer towards. He whipped the Steyr off his shoulder and stepped back into the shadows. The Ducati's 1.2-litre engine revved as Neverov squeezed the clutch lever and dropped down into a lower gear for better torque. Then he drove down the ancient stone steps.

Hunter was ready, lifting his gun to tyre height. He could easily kill them both as they drove past, but gunning down men in a tunnel without warning wasn't his style. The bike's headlight spilled down on the stone at his feet and the engine reverberated loudly as they drew nearer. He heard the sound of the machine bouncing up and down on its suspension as the tyres banged on the steps, and then they flashed into view.

He fired a short burst, but the bike was travelling faster than he thought. His rounds missed the first tyre and tore the rear one to pieces. The back end of the bike smashed down on the aluminium alloy wheel rim and sprayed orange sparks out into the stairwell. A startled Neverov struggled to control his Ducati as it swerved all over the walkway. At the base of the stairs, the pillion rider tumbled off and rolled to a stop against a wall.

Hunter fired again and took out the front tyre. Centrifugal force spun shredded rubber all over the passageway and then the bike went over on its side. Neverov leaped to safety with seconds to spare and the Ducati skidded along the ground before finally bursting outside onto the open walkway. There, it tipped over the edge of the second tier and smashed into the ground with a deep metallic thud and a wild roar of revs.

Neverov scrambled to his feet and called out to the other man. 'Lugovoy, get the bag!'

Hunter hadn't noticed, but when Neverov had fallen off the bike, the strap of the bag containing the lion statue had snapped and sent the bag rolling towards the edge of the walkway near where the bike had gone over.

Lugovoy responded fast, racing over to the bag as Neverov covered him. Hunter had to act fast. The matte black housing of Neverov's Steyr glinted dully in the low moonlight like a warning, but Hunter was armed with the same weapon. He turned it on Lugovoy and fired a burst of rounds at his boots. The Russian scrambled back into the shadows and Neverov ducked behind one of the arches.

Hunter had seconds. Only yards from the bag, he made a dash for it knowing Neverov would fire at him. Skidding to a halt inches from its broken strap, he reached down and snatched it up just as Neverov opened fire on him. Bullets ripped and spit and chewed into the stone flooring all around him as he grabbed the bag and turned to run, but then Neverov stopped firing.

And Hunter saw something that froze the blood in his veins.

21

Down in the centre of the moonlit Colosseum, Gubenko was on foot and dragging Jodie out of the dead man's exit gate and into the main arena. He was holding a pistol to her head and pulling her roughly around the northern section of the amphitheatre towards the emperor's box. Still clutching the bag to his chest, Hunter knew it was over.

'Drop the gun!' Neverov shouted. 'Now!'

Hunter obeyed and Neverov stepped forward. 'The bag, Dr Hunter. Give it to me now or the woman dies.'

Hunter stared across the amphitheatre at the car thief from California. Standing alongside the Russian, she looked smaller than usual. He knew what he had to do and that meant taking at least one look at the lion statue. As he peered down inside the bag, his eyes crawled over the soft sheen of the ancient statue's glazed surface, and instantly he was struck by something – something that made his stomach turn with fear.

'Now, Dr Hunter!'

Slowly, Hunter lifted the bag out towards the former KGB colonel.

Neverov walked closer to him, but then everything changed. Both men heard a pained grunt echo across the amphitheatre and turned to see Jodie moving like lightning, powering a tiger punch into Gubenko's throat and knocking him off his feet. She snatched his pistol up off the ground and fired it in the air.

He scrambled to his feet and for a moment froze like a frightened rabbit. Eyes wide with fear as he took in the look of hate on the woman's face – the woman training a loaded gun on him. Would she kill him?

The distant whomp whomp whomp of helicopter rotors grew louder and deeper and now they all looked up and watched a black Sikorsky appear over the top of the Colosseum's highest northern wall and descend down inside the arena.

Hunter saw with horror a chin-mounted machine gun fitted to the chopper's nose and knew what would come next. Calling out across the giant amphitheatre, he told Jodie to get the hell out of Dodge, and with the bag still clutched to his chest, he threw himself into a roll and grabbed the Steyr Neverov had ordered him to drop.

The Russian moved fast, opening fire and ripping rounds into the ground all around him, but it was too late. Hunter was out of sight and sprinting into the labyrinth of darkened stone passageways inside the Colosseum. He ran past Neverov's trashed bike and down the next flight of steps to the bottom tier where Jodie was already waiting for him.

'You got it?' she asked.

He patted the bag. 'You bet. Where's Gubenko?'

'Inside the chopper. It's picking Neverov and Lugovoy up now.'

'Medinsky must be at the controls,' Hunter said, recalling the briefing notes back in Washington DC. 'We need to get out of here, and in a hurry. Any ideas?'

She nodded, her young face streaked with moonlight spilling down through one of the arches beside her. 'Sure. Before Gubenko took me hostage, he dumped his bike back near the Biro. I saw it when he dragged me out in the arena.'

'Question asked, question answered,' he said, grinning. 'Shall we?'

'I thought you'd never ask. I've wanted to take one of those babies for a spin since the second I saw them back outside the Palazzo Gallo!'

They sprinted back towards the main entrance until they reached the Ducati. Jodie climbed on first and fired it up while Hunter rode pillion, Steyr and lion statue in his grasp. 'Go!'

She twisted the throttle and the Ducati Diavel surged forward like a panther roaring in the Roman night. Reverberations from its titanium Akrapovic exhaust rattled and shook the ancient walls as she ripped back out into the Piazza del Colosseo, blew past dozens of astonished policemen, and headed west. Turning on the Via Celio Vibenna, she roared past Palatine Hill and whooped with delight as the bike passed one hundred miles per hour.

Hunter felt less jubilant. With one life-saving hand wrapped around her waist and the Steyr over his shoulder, he held on to the bag with his other hand and mumbled a silent prayer. Her hair was whipping up behind her like a wild mare's, flicking in his face and blocking his view. He turned to get it out of his eyes when he saw the Sikorsky rising above the Colosseum's southern outer wall like a monster scanning for prey.

He leaned forward and shouted in her ear, 'We're in trouble, Jodie.'

'The chopper?'

'Uh-huh. Please tell me you spoke to Amy and got us a way out of here.'

'Sure I did! You think I'm an idiot?'

'Not when you're taking a ninety-degree bend at seventy miles an hour. Absolutely not.'

She dropped a gear and revved, speeding back up along the Via dei Cerchi. To their left, they were skirting the Circus Maximus where a quarter of a million Romans would watch chariot races. Tonight, its ruins were empty and silent and no more than a shortcut for Jodie, who swerved into it and ploughed the Ducati down the grass slope leading to the main site.

'Are you crazy?' he said.

'I thought we had established that I was not to be criticised while driving at high speeds?'

'How silly of me to forget!' he called back. 'And by the way, at least a dozen police cars are now behind the chopper.'

'Fear not, Hunter.'

Reaching the other side of the open field, she revved the Ducati and piled it up to the top of the slope on the far side. When they reached the crest, the Ducati jumped through the air and crashed back down with a crunching smack on a broad three-laned road lined with umbrella pines and poplars. Skidding to the right, she speeded up again and raced along the road.

'We're almost there, Hunter.'

'Where?'

'Our way out of this nightmare. Hang on!'

Hunter thought the advice was good. Turning, he glimpsed some movement in the sky above the chopper. At first, it looked just like a star, but then it started to grow larger and brighter and move towards them. What the hell was that? He had other concerns, namely the mad, armed Russians racing up behind them in the Sikorsky. Someone inside, probably Gubenko given his past experience of the Wolf Pack, was preparing to fire the machine gun.

'By the way,' he said sarcastically, 'did I mention there's a gun on it? A chin-mounted machine gun?'

Jodie flicked her head around and looked over her shoulder. She couldn't believe her eyes. A dark, sick feeling seemed to fill her up from the bottom of her stomach. 'No way, they wouldn't open fire with a weapon like that in the middle of Rome. It's just too risky. It would cause too much damage, kill dozens or even hundreds of innocent people.'

Hunter stared up at the helicopter. 'I'm not sure the people who want this statue are too concerned with collateral damage, Jodie. Incoming!'

Jodie took evasive action, swerving the bike to the left and right and letting the heavy-duty rounds snake up the road beside them, obliterating the asphalt and flinging chunks of crumbled tarmac up into the air. As they peeled off onto another road and weaved in and out of traffic, Hunter again looked back up at the star.

'I think we just moved up into a whole new level of trouble.'

Jodie turned to him. 'What are you talking about?'

He frowned, pulling the bag tighter to his chest and clutching hold of it like a life preserver. 'It's a second chopper. Police, probably.'

'We need to get under some cover or we're dead.'

She steered hard to the left and skidded off the road. She was aiming for the cover of some trees she had seen in a park and her aim was good. Ripping across the Rome Rose Garden, she flew along a narrow side street lined with pencil pines and parked cars before extending her right foot and turning in a tight arc to their right.

'Gate!'

'What?'

'Gate!'

Hunter looked ahead and saw a metal gate embedded in a high red-brick wall. It was bearing down on them with unsettling speed, but he knew what to do.

'Slow down!' he said.

'Are you nuts?'

'Again, I might be an amazing man, but not even I can hold on to you, hold this bag and fire a compact machine pistol at a locked gate at the same time.'

She said nothing, but dropped some revs and slowed down while he raised the Steyr into the aim and fired at the lock. The rounds ripped into the lock's metal housing and blew it to pieces in an explosion of ricochets and sparks and blasted it clean off the gate. Seeing the way was clear, she speeded up the Ducati and smashed through the unlocked gate at high speed, smacking both of the metal doors back against the inside wall with a sharp, scraping clang.

Safely inside the Giardino degli Aranci, she weaved the bike along a series of neatly manicured footpaths as the Sikorsky and police chopper closed in on them. The famous Orange Garden was an impressive affair hidden from the city behind high brick walls and for a few seconds, it offered them sanctuary.

'But what do we do when he gets out of here?' Hunter asked.

'Then the cavalry's waiting for us. Have some faith, man.'

She drove along the crunchy gravelled path and left the cover of the orange trees behind them. Turning down another narrow pathway ending in a hairpin bend, she slowly made her way back down the slope towards ground level and the main road running just above the Tiber.

'We're too exposed!' Hunter yelled.

'Not for long.'

Without warning, she swerved the bike to a stop and killed the engine.

'What are you doing?' Hunter asked in horror as the Sikorsky opened fire on them again.

Jodie leaped off the bike and let it fall to the sidewalk. Hopping over a low stone wall, she turned to him and winked. 'C'mon, Hunter!'

He shook his head, and with the bag and Steyr still in his arms, he climbed over the wall and saw her running down a narrow flight of graffitied stone steps leading down to the west bank of Rome's famous river. When he reached the bottom, she was climbing on board a modest river cruiser. Lewis was welcoming her aboard and Blanco was revving the engines.

'Ahoy there, sailor!' Amy said.

Hunter had never been so grateful to see anyone in all his life, and quickly raced across the weedy bank and climbed on board. 'We're in deep shit, Amy,' he said. 'Chopper with a chin-mounted machine gun full of angry Russians right behind us and cops all over the place, including airborne.'

'But we have the lion statue,' Jodie said.

Amy turned to Blanco. 'Get us out of here, Sal!'

Lewis loosed the mooring line and Blanco rammed the throttles forward. The cruiser surged out into the centre of the wide river and headed south as fast as its engine could power them. Hunter reloaded the Steyr and Lewis and Amy loaded up two pistols. Behind them, the Sikorsky wheeled in the sky and made a tight arc before swooping down over the Ponte Palatino and turning the gun in their direction once again.

'Uh-oh,' Quinn said. 'There was nothing about this in the Rough Guide.'

Hovering above the River Tiber with its rotor

downwash beating the surface of the river into a wild spitting froth, the Wolves opened fire with the heavy machine gun. Bullets streaked across the surface of the water on their way to the cruiser, forcing Blanco to steer from side to side. Upon the bank, Hunter saw at least twenty police cars racing alongside them trying to keep up with the cruiser. Behind them, above the Orange Garden, the police helicopter flew into view.

'Oh my God!' he said.

Amy turned. 'What is it?'

'Look!'

The Sikorsky rotated in the air and fired on the police chopper, blasting it to pieces and sending it plummeting to earth in a giant fireball. Mayhem exploded all over the place. Hunter watched with some relief as most of the police cars peeled away and headed back towards the wreckage of the police helicopter.

'What's the Sikorsky doing now?' Jodie asked.

'Making me very unhappy,' Hunter said.

Amy leaned forward and looked behind her at the threat. With a sense of dread, she watched the chopper's tail boom swing around to the west as the pilot brought the aircraft's nose around to face them.

Then it started spitting fire.

'They're firing again!'

Blanco pushed the throttle levers forward and spun the wheel hard to the right, sending the cruiser racing between the stone piers of the Ponte Sublicio. They raced under the ancient bridge and turned to the left as the river meandered around the Ripa Grande. The heavy-duty rounds from the airborne machine gun ripped into the boats around them, blasting out windows and obliterating chunks of wood in their wake.

'They nearly got us!'

'Holy crap,' Quinn said. 'If I had a home, I'd want to go there right now.'

Hunter lowered the bag down to the deck and walked to the stern. Raising the Steyr into the aim, he fired on the chopper, specifically aiming for the tail boom. His rounds snaked along the boom and eventually hit the rudder. Swaying with the motion of the speeding cruiser, and flecked with foamy water from the boat's wake, the former army officer kept up a sustained fusillade until his rounds drilled into the tail rotor.

With the job done, he turned to Amy with a smile. 'For Colonel Neverov, it's all downhill from this point.'

Without the tail rotor, the chopper was uncontrol-

lable. Medinsky attempted to bring the crippled aircraft down safely, but it was impossible; all he could
do was delay the inevitable. Then the Sikorsky
smashed down into the Tiber and lurched forward
until its main rotors hit the surface. The speeding rotors whipped arcs of water up into the air for a few
seconds and were then overcome, snapping into fragments and spinning off onto the banks at high speed
as the chopper bobbed about on the surface for a few
seconds.

Then it started to sink.

Amy watched the wreckage of the crumpled helicopter slowly sinking into the middle of the Tiber. It
was hard to see in the darkness, but in the soft amber
glow of the streetlights, she could just make out
movement as Neverov and his men climbed out of
the stricken chopper and began to make their way
slowly back to the bank.

'I kind of expected that thing to blow up,' she said
quietly, her hands wrapped tightly around the bag
containing the lion statue. 'To go up in a big fireball
like in the movies.'

'Sometimes they do,' Hunter said. 'Sometimes
they do not. I've seen it happen both ways.'

Blanco pushed the throttles forward and steered
the sightseeing boat around another bend out of

sight of both the Russians and the Italian authorities. 'They were lucky. When Max shot out their tail rotor, he ended any hopes they had of stable flight, but a skilled pilot, like this guy obviously is, can bring a wounded bird like that down to earth if he knows what he's doing. Plus this guy had a water landing. As I said, they were lucky.'

'And that means we were unlucky.' Hunter leaned against the port gunwale, crossed his arms, and sighed. 'Because they're still alive, we have what they want and now they're even angrier – and that's the good news.'

Amy was opposite him, leaning against the starboard gunwale, arms also crossed over her chest. 'I hesitate to ask, but what's the bad news, Max?'

'Back in the Colosseum, I took a quick look at the lion.'

On hearing the word, everyone in the team turned to face him, each waiting for him to deliver the rest of the sentence.

'And?' Amy asked.

'And it's inscribed with letters I've never seen before.'

Amy raised her hands to her temples in a show of despair. 'What sort of letters?'

'I just can't tell you. They're sort of Koine Greek,

but not. I have no idea what they mean but they could be some kind of code. Sorry, but it looks like we're back to square one. I can't translate the third line of John's verse.'

'You know anyone who might be able to help?' Blanco asked.

Hunter shook his head. 'Not off the top of my head.'

'Ben?' Quinn asked.

'Don't look at me,' said the former Marine. 'I'm strictly history and theology and a smattering of Latin and Greek. No symbols and codes.'

Then, with moonlight lighting her face, they all saw an expression of hope appear on Amy's face.

'You have an idea, Amy?' Jodie asked.

'I sure do,' she said. 'Anyone want to come with me to Greece?'

22

Thirty-six thousand feet in the air, Lewis took another quick look at the picture of his wife and new-born baby and slipped his wallet back in his jacket. Below, the rolling hills of Umbria stretched out like a velvet quilt. Pencil pines, tobacco fields, olive groves, and vineyards coloured an ancient landscape once walked by Etruscans.

Behind them, a burning, shattered Rome was still reeling from the effects of what local news stations were describing as a terrorist act. He knew they were lucky to be alive, and he was grateful Max Hunter was such a good shot. After taking the Sikorsky down, they had sailed the cruiser to a quiet stretch of the river and moored up at Portuense. There, Jodie stole an Iveco Dual Cab work truck and they drove in silence across the city to the airport.

He checked his watch and then looked up at the flight display on the bulkhead wall at the front of the aircraft. The little screen to the left of the galley was showing a picture of the Mediterranean. The thin yellow line between Rome and Athens was where he would spend the next hour and a quarter, much of it high above the Adriatic Sea.

He glanced around the cabin; the rest of the team was getting some sleep. Jodie and Quinn at the back and Blanco stretched out on the couch. In the seat opposite his, just across the aisle, Amy's head was slumped forward against her chest. The new guy had crashed out with an academic paper over his face.

He liked the new guy. Maybe he was a bit cocky but he seemed to know his stuff. Thing was, he didn't mind everyone else knowing it. Not one little bit. Dr Ben Lewis was the opposite. An officer in the US Marines for many years, he had left the Corps when two forces came together in his life and pushed him right back into civilian life.

Those two forces were the news of Meg's pregnancy and one hell of a tough tour in Afghanistan's Helmand River Valley. He got through it. He never talked about it. He tried not to think about it, but he

knew he'd had enough. He didn't want his kid
growing up without a father, so he moved on, returning to college as a postgrad and writing his doctorate in history. The rest was... well, history.

He wasn't quite sure how he ended up working
for James Gates in the HARPA team alongside these
crazy people, but he never wanted it to end. Not that
he had ever said that to anyone; he tried to keep his
thoughts to himself. Hearing Amy mumbling something, he turned and saw her jerking awake. She had
drifted off after their departure from Rome Urbe Airport but was wide awake again.

'Have a nice trip?' he asked with a smile.

'Not really,' she said. 'I just dreamed I was falling
off a cliff.'

'You think that was some kind of omen?' he asked
mischievously.

'Well, now I do, Ben. Thanks.'

'I'm just kidding. Happens to me all the time.'

'What about you? You get any sleep?'

'I'm not tired. I can stay awake for unnervingly
long periods. You know that.'

'I always forget.'

'I was just thinking about the verses on the...' He
glanced over at Hunter. 'On the *ágalmas*.'

She smiled. 'Don't you think that sounds somewhat crass, Dr Lewis? I'd stick to the proper Greek plural if I were you. *Agálmata*. Say it after me.'

He chuckled. 'He sure has one hell of a personality, I'll give him that.'

'He's a pain.'

He looked at her sideways and smirked.

'What?'

'You know what.'

She paused, unsure what to say. 'Oh, give me a break.'

He shrugged. 'Just saying, Amy. How long has it been since Matt?'

Her smile was fading. 'I...'

'I'm sorry. I shouldn't have brought it up.'

'That's okay, really. And yeah, it's been a long time – but Hunter, really?'

'You've gone out together. You already told me that.'

'Yeah, but as friends.'

'I've seen the way you look at him.'

'And how's that?'

'How Meg looks at me sometimes even after all these years.'

Amy's smile was returning, but reluctantly. 'Yeah, right.'

'You deserve to be happy, and I think an arrogant

asshole like Max Hunter could be the man to give you that happiness.'

'Thanks a lot, Ben. Maybe you should stick to being a husband, father, and historian and get out of the matchmaking business while you still can.'

'Is that a threat against my person, Agent Fox?'

'It's a threat against part of your person, sure.'

'Ouch.'

* * *

Behind them, Hunter unbuckled his seatbelt and settled into the soft leather chair. Below him, amber streetlights illuminating Italy's ancient, twisting roads sparkled like newly cut diamonds. He turned away from the private jet's porthole and closed his eyes, his head still spinning with the chaos of the car chase.

And where the hell did Jodie Priest learn to drive like that? Her performance in Paris during the Atlantis mission was shocking enough, but this was something else altogether – not that he would ever tell her.

Eyes closed again, he reached out with his right hand and felt the rim of the ancient ágalma in the canvas bag on the seat beside him. Only moments ago, he reflected, it had been in the possession of

Colonel Neverov and the Wolf Pack, and now it belonged to the HARPA team alongside the eagle. That was the good news. The bad news was that he still had no idea what the symbols on its side meant, and without knowing their meaning, the terracotta lion offered no answers.

That was where Amy's old friend Kostas Venizelos came in.

Hunter had never met Amy's Greek linguistic specialist, and he had never even heard of him. According to HARPA's deputy director, Venizelos had worked for Jim Gates before on more than one investigation, so he was considered a trusted consultant. But Hunter believed the proof of the pudding was in the tasting, so trust was a long way off. Perhaps he was a member of the secretive Creed? Maybe, when they turned up at his Athens villa, they would be met by armed disciples who would take them prisoner and steal the statue? His mind was tortured by the agonies of doubt and suspicion.

'Hey, you asleep, Hunter?'

He twisted his head to the right and opened one eye. It was Jodie, but then he already knew that; she was the only one on the team who refused to use his first name. She was holding two cups of coffee, and now she held one out to him. 'I got you some coffee.'

He shuffled up in his seat and took the cup, surprised that of all people, she would take the time out to think of him and get him a hot drink. 'Thanks, that's thoughtful.'

She shrugged. 'It's just a cup of coffee. You don't owe me anything.'

'No,' he mumbled into the cup. 'I guess not.'

'You get anywhere on the statue yet?'

A simple shake of his head gave the answer, but he added, 'We're doing the right thing going to Venizelos.'

'Unless he's Creed.'

'Yeah, that thought had crossed my mind, too, but I trust Amy's judgement. She says both she and Jim have worked with him before.'

He sipped the coffee; she had added just the right amount of milk.

Without an invitation, she moved the canvas bag to the seat behind them and slumped down next to him with a heavy sigh. 'This apocalypse stuff is freaking me out, Hunter. I'm not going to lie to you.'

He thought about how to reply. To say Jodie was the strong but silent type was an understatement, but lately, she had started to say a little more to him, to make occasional small talk. The truth was, he didn't want to blow it. He liked her.

'I think we're all a bit freaked out by it,' he said. 'But after what we saw in Atlantis and the way Brodie McCabe and the Creed carried on, it takes a lot less to worry me these days. Now we have a band of insane Russian terrorists chasing after us, too. Happy days, right?'

She stifled a laugh, probably not wanting to let him see he had amused her. Instead, she took a long sip of her coffee and pushed back into the seat. Closing her eyes, she said, 'It still beats being out in the world on your own. It's a big, dark, shitty place without good friends or family.'

'Maybe, but I was always more of a loner.'

'Not me,' she said with conviction. 'This team is my family.'

'There's no one special out there?'

This time she laughed, but it was a quiet, bitter laugh. 'Not any more. He was bad news anyway. Dragging me down.'

'I'm sorry to hear that.'

'Yeah, except you're not.'

He didn't rise to it. 'Just being polite.'

More coffee and a sigh. 'I'm sorry.'

There was a long pause filled only by the sound of the engines' hum. Then she said, 'I don't want to talk about it.'

Hunter didn't know what to say, or even if he should say anything. He was saved by Lewis, who broke the silence with an innocent question. 'How long till we land?'

Amy checked her watch. 'Less than two hours. We arrive just after dawn but Kostas can't see us until the evening. He's usually to be found curating Byzantine glazed pottery at the National Archaeological Museum in Athens, but recently he's been away on a dig in Meteora and isn't getting in until later. He came back early just to see us.'

'Meteora's monastery complex is a UNESCO-listed site. I know it well,' Hunter said. 'Sounds like Dr Venizelos is an interesting guy.'

'You have no idea.'

No, Hunter had no idea, and that was what was bothering him. He turned back to Jodie, but she was gone. Back to her own seat and eyes closed. A good idea, and with enough time for some quality sleep before landing, he settled back in his reclining seat and closed his eyes, too. If today was like going to hell in a handcart, he didn't even want to think about what tomorrow might bring.

23

On the road again. This time, cruising north out of Athens International Airport in a hired Dodge Nitro. Here, olive fields stretched to the horizon either side of the three-lane highway, and the Hymettus mountain range loomed to their left, peaking at the craggy summit of Evzonas at nearly three and half thousand feet. On these dusty slopes, the ancients built a sacred sanctuary for their rain god, Zeus, but today tourists hiked its forested slopes. Part of it was even used as a landfill.

Progress... Hunter thought. After a day spent sitting around in an airport hotel waiting for Venizelos, it felt good to finally be moving again.

They skirted around the foothills at the northern

reaches of the range and turned west to head into the city. Dense, grinding traffic slowed their progress to a crawl as they hacked their way through the city centre to the neighbourhood of Monastiraki. Situated immediately to the north of the Acropolis, the area was expensive, upmarket, and relaxed. They parked a road away on Jodie's advice and when they stepped out into the warm Greek evening sunshine, they might have been forgiven for thinking all was right with the world.

Hunter blipped the locks shut and ran his eyes over the luxurious villa. Shaded by a lemon tree planted in the centre of the sidewalk outside the front door, the building was warm and inviting. Salmon-pink stucco plaster and a traditional overlapping clay tile roof were all lit by the low evening sun.

Directly behind them, a wrought-iron fence marked the boundary between the residential area and the Acropolis site. Hunter turned and saw its Doric columns lit orange in the sunlight. Partially obscured by pine trees, the ancient site was as breath-taking as he remembered it from years ago when he had visited with his fiancée, Avril. They had walked all over Athens that week, but a month later they had broken up.

'Earth to Hunter.'

Jodie's voice. He turned to see her beckoning him towards the villa. 'You want to stand around staring at that all night or come in and have a good time?'

He laughed. 'Sorry, just got caught up with some old memories.'

'Avril?' Amy asked.

He nodded. 'But it doesn't matter now. Tell me, what's this Venezuela bloke really like?'

A coy smile spread on Amy's face. 'You'll find out – and it's Venizelos. I know you know it's Venizelos, Max.'

He returned her smile. 'Can't tell me now?'

She winked and pushed past him, skipping up the stone steps leading to the front door. 'I like to keep a man guessing.'

Hunter couldn't think of anything to say. Then Lewis brushed past him on his way to the steps and slapped him on the back. 'True story, man.'

Jodie gave him a look of sympathy and held up her hand and extended her smallest finger. 'She has you wrapped around her pinky, Hunter.'

'Little finger,' he said. 'And no, she doesn't.'

'Pinky,' Amy called out over her shoulder. 'And yes, she does.'

Hunter looked at Blanco. 'You're not going to do that thing where you say whatever it's called?'

The man from Brooklyn gave him a look of gentle camaraderie. Two old guys against the girls. 'Not this time, Max.' He turned and watched Amy reach the top of the steps and ring the bell. 'You got enough problems, friend.'

'Yeah,' Quinn said. 'This time the sentiment is more important than the semantics.'

Amy was now standing at the top of the steps, hands on her hips. 'Are we going to talk to Kostas or not?'

* * *

Sitting on the Hill of the Muses, the Acropolis had dominated Athens since the fifth century BC. Today, the breathtaking view north from the terrace just below the ancient citadel filled Kostas Venizelos's apartment window and struck Jodie Priest with awe. As she stared at the hazy sunset slopes of Mount Parnitha away in the distance, a good part of her never wanted to leave this place.

'I never saw anything like this before in my whole life.'

Blanco was pleased she was impressed by it. 'It's beautiful, isn't it?'

Amy put down her bag and gave a long sigh of

relief to finally be somewhere safe. Turning to her old friend, she said, 'Sorry it's been such a long time, Kostas.'

Venizelos walked over to her. He was holding a bottle of champagne in one hand and waved away her apology with the other as he gave her a long, close hug. 'It's been a long time since we saw each other, Amy. When was it, exactly?'

'I think it was during the Bonetti trial,' she said, her face scrunching up in the sunset as she tried to remember. Her memories of the Manhattan art dealer's smuggling trial came flooding back, including the raid on the Queens warehouse that had led to his arrest. 'You gave evidence relating to some ancient Greek bronzes he was trying to get into the US.'

'But that was years ago! Either no one is smuggling Greek antiquities into your country or you've been using another expert.' He untwirled the champagne cork and pulled the muselet free of the bottle. 'Be honest, Amy. Are you seeing another expert behind my back?'

She slapped his arm. 'Stop being silly, Kostas.'

'At least you are safe now,' he said. 'From what you told me in your call, you are all lucky to be alive.'

'We were lucky to get away with nothing more than a few cuts and bruises,' she replied.

'Too right,' Hunter said. 'When that helicopter turned up I thought we were finished.'

'A helicopter?' the Greek man asked. 'In the middle of Rome?'

Amy nodded. 'Right bang smack in the heart of the old town.'

'But how could such a thing get past air traffic control?' he asked, staggered.

'Perhaps Neverov has friends in high places,' Quinn said.

'Maybe,' Amy said. 'But considering what he did to Giuseppe Gallo, it sure ain't the Creed.'

'The Creed?' Venizelos asked.

Amy frowned. 'Another time.'

'Sounds interesting, but now come with me out to the patio.'

Venizelos led them outside, twisted the bottle, and popped the cork, arresting its flight with his left palm. Bubbles flowed from the top of the green bottle as he set the cork down on the table and began to pour a glass for everyone. Handing them around, he made sure everyone had one in their hand before he put the bottle down and raised his own glass.

'To my old friend Amy Fox, and the brand-new HARPA team.'

They repeated the toast and drank a sip. Hunter

enjoyed the taste of the quality wine and turned his face to the setting sun. It was still hovering over the city, but not for much longer. He took another sip and blew out a deep breath. Turning, he watched with some amusement as Venizelos crawled around on his hands and knees beneath a large gas-fired barbecue. Their host cursed in Greek as he tried to fit a new canister to the valve.

Hunter looked at Amy. 'When does he get to the *agálmata*?'

'Statues,' said Jodie.

Amy smiled. 'Nothing is more important to Kostas than a good dinner, Max. He'll get to it after we eat.'

'I can hardly wait.'

Moments later, Hunter found himself wielding a metal spatula like a weapon. Carefully turning meat on the barbecue's chunky, solid plate, he felt the tension melt from his shoulders. 'I can't wait to get stuck into these things.'

'You took the words right out of my mouth, Hunter.'

Jodie was beside him now, staring at the vast array of cooking meats with wide, glazed-over eyes.

'Not long now.'

'I'll say one thing for you.' She took a deep breath

and sighed. 'You sure know how to cook barbecue.
This smells perfectly goddam delightful.'

A short while later, the HARPA team were all
seated around Venizelos's large, nine-piece cast aluminium patio table, watching their host take generous quantities of fragrant lamb from the hot plate
and heap it onto a large terracotta serving dish. With
a theatrical flourish, he placed it in the centre of a
cornucopia of local cuisine – throubes olives straight
from the tree, delicious vegetable-stuffed vine leaves,
or dolmades, and calamari fresh from the sea driz-
zled in olive oil and lemon.

Quinn pointed at some of the delights. 'What are
these, Kostas?'

'They are baklava,' he said proudly. 'Honey, nuts,
and olive oil wrapped up in flaky filo pastry.'

'Goodness me,' she said, taking two off the plate.

Venizelos laughed. *'Kalí óreksi!'*

'Or bon appetit, as we say in English,' Hunter
said.

Only Amy laughed, and then Venizelos encouraged everyone to help themselves. No one on the team
needed to be told twice, and soon they were all piling
into the delicious spread of food and drink their host
had kindly provided for them. After dinner, Venizelos

started work on the lion statue while Hunter helped Amy clear away the empty plates, glasses, and bottles from the table. Blanco cleaned the barbecue ready for whenever Venizelos would need it again.

Jodie was with Quinn, leaning on the wall with her elbows and looking out over the city as she enjoyed one of the Greek professor's cigarettes. Mount Parnitha was darker now, almost impossible to see. 'This city is beautiful. You're lucky to have such an amazing view, Kostas.'

Venizelos looked up from the statue and shrugged. 'So I am told but I see it every day, which means I never see it. Besides, I am too preoccupied with my work to care.'

'Talking of which,' Quinn said. 'You worked it out yet, Professor?'

He sighed wearily. 'These things take time.'

'It's not Koine, is it?' Hunter asked.

'Actually it is, but it's been altered to create a sort of code. The shapes of the letters have been moved around to change their meaning. I have seen it once before on a theatre mask found among the ruins of a Dionysian temple.'

Jodie stepped up and gave Hunter a consolatory pat on the back. 'Don't worry about your screw-up when you said the script wasn't Koine, Hunter. No one here even remembers, do they?'

'No,' the team said at the same time.

'Thanks, guys,' Hunter said.

Venizelos huffed out a low laugh. 'Really, it's a very good code. I wouldn't hold it against Dr Hunter if I were you. Either way, the script is very badly degraded, and the lettering is ambiguous. You know what would speed things up?'

'If I stopped asking stupid questions?'

'You said it.'

Jodie stifled a laugh as Quinn pouted and stomped across the room. She fell down on the professor's couch and pulled her laptop out of her bag.

'That's her Do Not Disturb face,' Lewis said. 'I'd take the advice.'

Venizelos muttered in Greek. 'Are you absolutely sure these *agálmata* are authentic?' he asked Amy. 'I know in my heart they are and yet I wish they weren't.'

She turned to Hunter. 'Max?'

'Yes, these *agálmata* are authentic,' he said, emphasising the Greek plural with a glance over at Amy. 'Why?'

'Because I think I have a translation of the script. It's fragmentary and I do not like what I'm seeing.'

'And what are you seeing?' Jodie asked.

Venizelos took off his glasses, rubbed his eyes, and sank into his chair. 'Maybe I'm going crazy, but it says, "I am the man between the town and the stairs, and I say to those who seek Heaven's Falling Star..."'

'Why don't you like it?' Hunter asked.

'It's another reference to the Apocalypse,' said Lewis. 'The falling star.'

'Exactly!' Venizelos said.

'But what about the first part of the verse?' Amy asked. 'That sounded even more cryptic.'

Venizelos smiled. 'You mean the part about the man between the town and the stairs?'

'Yeah.'

'That is not cryptic at all,' he said. 'Not to me. I know exactly what it means!'

24

'Care to enlighten the rest of us?' Amy asked.

'It's obviously a reference to the Cave of the Apocalypse.'

Jodie laughed and lit another cigarette. 'Yeah, obviously.'

'How so, Kostas?' asked Blanco.

'The Cave of the Apocalypse is on the island of Patmos. On that island are two towns. The first is Chora, which means town, and the second is Skala, which means stairs. The Cave of the Apocalypse is between the two of them.'

'Ah,' Amy said. 'Got it – and the man statue is the "man" he refers to!'

'Or perhaps John of Patmos himself,' Kostas said.

Lewis took another spoonful of the homemade tzatziki and put it on the side of his plate next to the lamb. The setting sun was warm on his neck, but all of a sudden he felt a cold chill go down his spine. 'The Cave of the Apocalypse. This gets heavier.'

'Wait,' Jodie said. 'You're all telling me there's a real place called the Cave of the Apocalypse?'

'Sure is,' said Lewis. 'It's where John had his vision from God, and it looks like we might be going there to look for the final statue – the one of the man.'

'Did you know about this place, Hunter?' Amy asked.

'Of course,' he said. 'The Cave of the Apocalypse was declared a UNESCO World Heritage Site over twenty years ago.'

'Know all,' Jodie said.

'Back in 1999,' Hunter said, turning to her. 'When you were in a nappy.'

'Hey!' Jodie said.

'Diaper,' Lewis corrected.

'Nappy,' Hunter repeated. 'And before anyone asks – no, I have not been there.'

Quinn broke up the banter. 'What can you tell us about the island, Kostas?'

'First, Patmos is not a big place.' Venizelos spoke quietly, his voice soft and mellow among the chirping cicadas on the dry bark of the surrounding fig trees. 'As Greek islands go, it is rather small and much closer to Turkey than Greece. But this is not un-common for Greek islands. Anyway, it is most famous for being the location of the Cave of the Apocalypse. As Ben here says, this is where the Disciple John had his vision concerning the *Book of Revelation*, and of course where he wrote it. This is its significance. Well – this and the secret tunnel.'

'A secret tunnel?' Amy asked.

He shrugged. Having delivered the shocking epiphany, he now backed away from it. 'Maybe, maybe not. Some of my research on this subject has hinted at a tunnel hidden in the cave. I am sceptical. I have been there several times and never found anything.'

'This whole thing sort of freaks me out,' Quinn said.

Venizelos laughed. 'There really is no need. The island today is popular with tourists, both religious pilgrims and non-religious people simply seeking peace and warm weather.'

'I'm with Quinn,' said Jodie. 'The men who are chasing us are no damned tourists. They're risking everything to get hold of something hidden in that cave, and that's what's freaking me out. Who wants to find an apocalypse, right?'

'Vladimir Neverov,' Hunter said flatly.

'So, now we have three of the Four Living Beings of the Revelation,' Amy said. 'And three verses. On the lion, "I am the man between the town and the stars, and I say to those who seek Heaven's Falling Star..."'

Hunter said, 'And on the ox, "They must ask the Lion, the Ox, the Man, and the Eagle."'

'Which we're trying to do,' said Quinn.

'The eagle says,' said Blanco, '"And the last word of God will unleash the Apocalypse and strike terror into Man."'

'So we're missing the third verse,' Lewis said. 'The order of the Four Living Beings is usually the lion, the ox, the man, and then the eagle. We need the statue of the man and the third verse.'

'Yes, the man will give you the final location,' Venizelos said thoughtfully. 'But you must go to the Cave of the Apocalypse to ask him.' He sighed and turned the statue over in his hands one more time, carefully. 'Yes, this is a very beautiful piece of work, but its value lies in the message hidden here in the inscription.'

'Hidden in plain sight,' Amy said.

'Hidden is hidden if you do not know how to decode it,' replied Venizelos.

Amy raised her glass to chink it against Venizelos's. 'Then lucky you did know, Kostas.'

He raised his glass. 'Indeed, it is!'

In a split second, everything changed. From out of nowhere, a bullet shattered the wine glass and buried itself in the Greek academic's chest.

Amy screamed as the impact of the shot blasted Venizelos back in his chair and sent him smacking into the deck. As the blood bloomed on his white shirt, he coughed and spluttered and died right in front of them.

Hunter and Blanco were already on their feet, guns drawn and scanning for the shooter. They didn't have to search for long. Seconds after the fatal shot that had killed their friend, half a dozen men armed with Heckler & Koch MP5 submachine guns leaped from the single-storey garage roof at the end of the patio and sprayed everywhere with rounds.

Hunter and the rest of the HARPA team were already inside the villa. The English archaeologist led the way through the house while Blanco stayed at the rear and fired a series of cover shots at the attackers.

'That was fast!' Amy said.

Jodie was confused. 'Huh?'

'The Russians,' she said. 'They got out of the Tiber pretty fast!'

Hunter booted open the kitchen door and led them down the corridor to the front door. 'They're not Russians.'

'Then who?' Lewis said, gun in hand.

'Did you see the tattoos on their necks?' Quinn said. 'They all had... Shit!' A bullet shattered the pane of glass in the front door and made her scream out loud. 'Damn it!'

'They're out the front, too,' Hunter said. 'Pincer movement.'

'We're boxed in?' Quinn said.

'No,' Amy said. 'You can get to the garage from inside the house. It's just down this flight of stairs because it's on a slightly lower level than the rest of the villa. Grab that damned lion and follow me!'

Hunter let her move to the front. The focus and determination on her face were masking the pain she must have been feeling over the murder of her friend, but if he had learned one thing about Special Agent Amy Fox, it was her endless capacity to surprise him.

'In here!' she said. 'We can take his car.'

'Is it big enough?' Quinn called out.

Bullets raked up the wall behind them as Blanco ran into view. 'Couldn't hold them any longer, sorry.'

'You got us this far, Sal,' Jodie said.

'Bad news about the car.' Amy was standing just inside the door leading down to the garage.

'What bad news?' Lewis asked.

'They already shot it up.'

Hunter twisted around as Blanco reached where they were standing. Behind him, shafts of light streamed in through the kitchen window and lit up the men as they charged up behind them.

'Into the street!' Hunter yelled. 'If we stay in here, we're dead.'

'Front door?'

Hunter shook his head. 'No way. A crew like that will have the front door covered. What else is at the front?'

'Kostas's bedroom,' Amy said. 'There's a balcony in it we can use to drop down to the front yard.'

Hunter gave her a look. 'How do you know that?'

She returned the look and threw in a wink for good measure. 'I'll take questions at the end of the lecture, Dr Hunter.'

A bright, savage muzzle flash strobed in the hallway behind them. Bullets traced over their heads and bit into the plaster wall in the stairwell. Blanco returned fire, planting two rounds in one of the men and dropping him to the deck, but the others kept coming without a glance at their fallen comrade. Firing controlled bursts at the tattooed men, Blanco yelled at everyone to get moving.

Hunter turned and saw Amy already halfway up the villa's grand spiral staircase.

'Get a move on, Hunter!' Jodie said, rushing past him. 'I don't know about you, but this girl's too young to die!'

'Kill them all!' screamed the man at the front. Hunter saw his face clearer now, the tattoo streaking up from his neck and onto his cheek like a vine. 'They must be killed!'

Something told Hunter he needed to get the hell out of here, so he sprinted up the staircase, gun in his hand. Glancing over his shoulder, he saw the men were already at the bottom of the stairs. They fired, drilling the wooden steps with rounds and blasting them to splinters as they skipped up each step, ever closer to him. He returned fire, burying two rounds in a double-tap in the centre of another man's head. The man dropped like a lead weight, falling back into his associates and knocking them over.

Hunter turned and sprinted as the men climbed over the corpse. *Two down, four to go,* he thought. He burst into the bedroom and found the team exiting through the window just as Amy had suggested. With glass everywhere and the smell of gunfire in the air, he guessed Blanco or Lewis had blasted the window out to make the job easier.

He was wrong. Amy had done it, as he saw when he found her on the balcony with a smoking gun in her hand. She was making sure her team got safely down onto the sidewalk. Blanco was with her, covering the room with a pistol gripped in his hand.

'Over you go, Max.'

He looked at Amy. 'Ladies first.'

'Last time I checked, I was the boss. Get your ass over the balcony, soldier.'

This was no time to challenge her authority, and she was right. 'Yeah, but I'm a gentleman.'

'A gentleman on my team. Ass. Over. Balcony.'

Blanco fired three shots. 'Mag nearly out, boss,' he called out. 'I can't keep them back for much longer.'

Seeing the look on Amy's face, Hunter reluctantly vaulted over the balcony but was relieved when she climbed down after him. Blanco then heaved himself over the iron balustrade and crashed down on the fountain grass lawn and rolled in a perfect parachute landing fall. Upon his feet and dusting himself off, he grinned. 'Feel like I'm eighteen again.'

'Really?' Quinn said.

He shrugged. 'Well, maybe thirty-five.'

Muzzles flashed above them as the men reached the balcony. Stray bullets traced all around them, ripping into the grass and spitting up chunks of dirt. Blanco scrambled over the lawn and caught up with the others, who were now in the street.

'Both ways blocked!' Amy said.

Hunter scanned the narrow street. Whoever the men were, they had parked SUVs sideways in the centre of the street on either side of Venizelos's villa. Looking past one of them into the next street, he saw they had also blown out all of the tyres on their Nitro. 'They're good,' he said.

'And we're dead if we don't get going!' said Quinn.

'What do we do?' asked Jodie.

'Follow me,' said Hunter. 'Once again, the ancient world has the answer.'

25

A sustained burst of submachine gunfire rattled behind them as they vaulted over the iron fence dividing the road from the Acropolis site and scrambled up the dry, scrubby slope towards the ancient monument. With the road blocked off, they had few other choices, and Hunter knew the site was large and offered lots of cover plus several escape routes back down into the city.

'Over here!' he called as they weaved up the tree-lined hill. 'If we can get up to the site, we can run across to the Parthenon and use it for cover. From there we should be able to reach the Propylaea...'

'The what?' Jodie said.

'The ancient gateway to the site,' he said. 'Once

we're through there we can run down the hill and we're pretty much back in the city. They'll never find us there.'

Another peel of automatic gunfire echoed in the night and then more screams for their blood. They never looked back but clambered up the rocks all the way to the top. The climb was hard, almost impossible in some places, but moving silently in the darkness of the night they soon reached the top. Below them on the road winding around the site, they heard the men shouting to each other as they searched the area below.

Pulling himself up over a crumbling stone wall, Blanco was last up top. 'What the hell kind of language is that, Max?'

'I'm not familiar with it,' he said. 'Sounds sort of like Hebrew or maybe Arabic.'

'Aramaic, then,' Lewis said, cocking his head in the moonlight to hear the shouting better. 'It sounds like it could be old Aramaic, but as far as I know, no one has spoken that for centuries.'

'This gets weirder,' Quinn said.

'At least we got away,' said Amy, turning to see the breathtaking sight of the Parthenon. The ancient monument was standing silent sentinel beneath a wild grove of sparkling stars, its white marble columns bathed in the sharp moonlight. 'This mission has its compensations.'

'Yeah,' Quinn said. 'If you count almost getting your head blown off a compensation!'

On cue, a round traced inches from her head and took a pound of stone off the side of a Doric column. She gasped in terror and dived down behind it for cover.

'You were saying?' Lewis said, crashing down beside her.

Hunter moved behind the shaft of the immense column as more rounds chipped at the architrave above his head. Marble splinters rained down as he reloaded his weapon and returned fire at the approaching men. Another barrage of bullets smacked into the ancient stonework he was using for cover, and beside him, Blanco and Lewis scrambled in opposite directions. They were fanning out to make a stronger defensive line.

The tattooed men tucked themselves down behind the wall running to the north of the Parthenon and unleashed another sustained fusillade of automatic gunfire.

'They're good!' Hunter yelled.

'And brave,' said Blanco.

'And persistent,' said Jodie. 'Very persistent.'

Amy smacked a new mag into the grip of her pistol. 'And ruthless.'

'But nobody's perfect,' Lewis said. 'One of them has broken cover.'

The former Marine fired on the man in the darkness. His controlled bursts drove the man back to his original position, but it was too late. As he vaulted over the wall, Lewis's last few rounds drilled into his back and blasted out of his chest in a savage display of accurate shooting.

'Whoa!' Quinn said. 'Wish I had not seen that.'

As the man stumbled forward, his boots caught on the top of the wall and forced him to pivot over into the stony ground on the other side. The sound of his dead body crunching to a bloody stop on the far side of the wall was drowned out by his associates screaming for revenge.

'How far to the gatehouse, Max?' Amy asked.

'Unless we take these guys out – too far.'

'They're breaking ranks again!' Blanco called out.

'Give up your search, Agent Fox!' one of the men shouted. 'Give it up, or you will surely die. You have no idea of the terrible, awesome power you are meddling with! If you find what you seek, your soul will be crushed!'

Blanco looked at Quinn. 'Is he talking about the IRS?'

It raised a nervous smile. 'I know what you're doing, Sal.'

'Oh yeah?'

'Trying to calm me down with humour.'

'Is it working?'

'Not really.'

Another wave of gunshots. Hunter looked around the side of the column's bullet-chipped shaft and saw the remaining men break cover and run screaming towards the Parthenon. They had reloaded their weapons and the assault was serious. One of the men was holding two submachine guns – one in each hand – and Hunter guessed the second belonged to the man Lewis had shot dead moments earlier. Their faces were contorted with rage as they ran towards them, muzzles flashing in the moonlight.

'Are they crazy?' Amy asked.

'Questions about mental health later,' Hunter said. 'For now, shoot!'

The HARPA team opened fire on the men and tore them to pieces. Quinn was the only one without a gun. She was sitting on the ground behind a column, her legs hiked up, and she was burying her face down in her knees as the battle raged around her.

When the firing stopped, she pulled her head up out of the darkness and looked at Amy with fear in her eyes.

'It's over?'

'Yes and no,' Amy said. 'One of them got away.'

'And the others?'

'Well and truly ventilated,' Hunter said.

Quinn winced. 'Can't you just say dead?'

'Sorry.'

They holstered their weapons and Amy shouldered Venizelos's canvas bag containing the statue. Wandering over to the dead men, Blanco and Lewis checked pulses while Jodie and Quinn scanned the area for any further sign of trouble.

Nothing, Quinn thought. That noise over by the gatehouse was an owl. She saw it fly away into the night. They were safe.

'C'mon,' Amy said. 'We need to get out of here and report this to the authorities.'

'Are you mad?' Hunter said.

'No,' she said. 'And you mean crazy. Mad is angry.'

'Not where I'm from, and you must be mad if you want to go to the police! They'll take us into custody and give Neverov and the Wolves the opportunity they need to get back out in front of us!'

'We're going to inform the authorities about what

happened here, Max,' she said, firmer this time. 'But I'm taking on board your point. We'll go to the US Embassy and do it from there. We can't just leave these dead men up here for someone else to find. Kids come up here with their parents, Max. Use your head.'

Behind Amy's back, Jodie gave Max a smug look. 'Yeah, Hunter. Use your head.'

In the shimmering moonlight, they turned away from the carnage and made their way towards the ancient gatehouse at the western edge of the Acropolis.

'That was too close for comfort,' Lewis said.

'I don't know about comfort,' said Jodie. 'But it was too damn close for me.'

Blanco laughed. 'Me too, Jo.'

'Who the hell were those guys?' Quinn said.

'People who wanted us dead in a hurry,' said Hunter. 'And who weren't in any way bothered about destroying the only clue we have – the statue.'

'Which is odd,' said Lewis. 'I thought that, too. They murdered the only man who could have translated the statue and then opened fire on us when we were holding it. Whoever they were, they don't seem interested in finding John's missing codex.'

On their way, they stopped beside the corpse of

one of the dead men. Staring down at his silent face, white in the moonlight, Amy felt a shiver run up her spine.

'And what is this tattoo they all have?' she asked, leaning in a little closer. 'Anyone recognise it?'

Jodie shrugged. 'Looks a bit like some of the tattoos I saw on gang members back in California, but different.'

Blanco frowned. 'A gang?'

'A cult, more like,' Lewis said.

'Quinn?' Amy asked.

'Search me,' she said. 'I left my computer in the Nitro.'

Hunter mulled the question over as he studied the dead man's tattoo. 'I think they have something to do with the Byzantine Empire.'

'You mean the Byzantine Empire that dissolved nearly six hundred years ago?' said Lewis.

Hunter said, 'I know it sounds insane, but yes. The double-headed eagle was one of the symbols of the Eastern Roman Empire.'

'Eastern Roman Empire?' Jodie asked.

'Byzantine,' he said. 'Same thing as Byzantine. In the ancient Byzantine culture, the most important aristocratic families each had a specific symbol that represented them, a bit like the use of coats of arms and heraldry in Western culture. They were usually a mix of double-headed eagles, Byzantine crosses, or monograms, often intertwined with one another. Ciphers were also common, but none of them were exactly like the tattoos on these men.'

'Not at all?' Amy asked.

He shook his head. 'The double-headed eagles common to the Byzantine era are similar but not as simple or stylised as these tattoos. Plus, I'm not aware the ancient symbols had this same strange writing associated with them.'

'It looks like Hebrew to me,' Blanco said.

'It's not Hebrew,' Lewis said. 'It's Biblical Aramaic. I just can't understand why they'd be tattooed with a language no one has spoken for thousands of years.'

A long silence as his words sunk in.

Leading the team away from the dead man and towards the gatehouse, Amy said, 'You think they're the Creed?'

'I don't think so,' Lewis said. 'There was no sign of Byzantine symbolism or Aramaic in the reports from the search of their headquarters in Germany.'

'And they weren't dressed like any of the Creed we ran into on the Atlantis mission,' said Blanco. 'I hate to say it, but I think this is another outfit – not the Russians or the Creed.'

'Oh my God,' Amy said. 'This just gets better and better.'

'Freeze!'

She spun around and saw several men dressed in black combat fatigues, riot helmets, and gas masks. They moved out of the shadows of the Propylaea with submachine guns in their hands and grenades hanging off their belts. Heart beating hard in her chest, she saw a badge on the arm of the man leading them towards her team. It read EKAM. She knew this was the Greek acronym for their Special Suppressive Antiterrorist Unit, and by the way they moved, she knew they meant business.

'Hands in the air!'

Amy felt the tension in her neck and shoulder ratchet up to a level she had never felt before and knew she had to give up. Ordering her team to drop their weapons and do as the men were telling them, she raised her hands in the air. The game was up.

One of them was in front of her now. He removed his mask and took some handcuffs off his belt. 'What is your name?'

'I'm Special Agent Fox with the American FBI. This is my team and we're here to—'

'You're under arrest for the murders of Kostas

Venizelos, Giuseppe Gallo, and all these other men you have shot and killed here tonight!'

The man roughly spun her around and wrenched her hands behind her back. As he slapped on the cuffs and tightened them, pinching her skin, she felt the mission slowly slip away from her. It was all over now. The HARPA team had failed to secure the final Living Being statue and would probably be facing either jail or deportation. Colonel Neverov would find whatever John of Patmos's mysterious Revelation relic was and use it for his own ends, and there was nothing any of them could do about it.

The police officer wheeled her away from the site and towards one of the police vehicles. She was aware that the rest of her team were also in cuffs and being led away. 'Whatever you think you're doing here in Greece,' the man snapped, 'is now over.'

26

The Acropolis Police Station was situated just to the south of the famous landmark. Nestled in the cramped, busy backstreets of the Koykaki district, it was a plain, functional building built of concrete that hid its inhabitants from the world behind tinted glass.

Hidden down in the basement was Interview Room 3F and tonight, their host was Captain Yanis Papademos of the Athens police force. He was a big man with a thick black moustache and bushy eyebrows. Suspicious, searching eyes were framed by an otherwise friendly face and when he sat down, he let out a long sigh of relief.

Blanco felt his pain, but the rigors of old age went straight over Jodie's head.

'Can't you take these damned cuffs off?' she said. 'We've been in here forever and as much as I love this man, I don't want to be cuffed to him for the rest of my life.'

Blanco pretended to choke back the tears. 'I can't say that doesn't hurt, Jo...'

'Sorry, but no,' Papademos said, businesslike and without emotion. 'Standard policy during interviews. You're lucky you're still all together. You will be split up momentarily.'

'But how can we take tea like this?' Hunter said, raising his cuffed hand in the air and pulling up Quinn's hand as well.

Papademos was unimpressed. 'You are under arrest for the brutal murders of Kostas Venizelos of the National Archaeological Museum, the Marquis Giuseppe Gallo, an Italian aristocrat based in Rome, and at least six other as yet unidentified men, Dr Hunter. Do you think this is a time for levity?'

'I find it makes my load lighter.'

'You murdered these men in cold blood!'

Amy sighed and rolled her eyes. 'We did no such thing and you know it.'

'I know nothing,' Papademos said sharply. 'You

were found at the scene of the murders with armed weapons!'

'No court would convict us for any of these deaths! The men we shot at the Acropolis were trying to kill us – it was self-defence! And they're the ones who killed Kostas.'

Papademos shook his head. 'Nevertheless, I think the court will look dimly on your case.'

'All the time you keep us in here, the real killers are on the loose,' Hunter said. 'Is that what you want?'

Papademos waved a dismissive hand. 'I have heard it all before. I want to know why you killed them. Let's start with Mr Venizelos. Was it to silence him for some reason, or simply a bungled robbery? It will make a difference to your sentencing.'

Amy sighed wearily. 'For the last time, if you contact the US Embassy here in Athens they will confirm our identity.'

'So you have told me, but even if they do, this does not make you innocent of the murders of these men. Not even FBI agents are allowed to kill people in Greece and get away with it.'

'Look,' Amy said. 'We were going to tell the authorities about what happened.'

'Yes,' Papademos said with a heavy dose of sarcasm. 'Of course you were.'

'It's true!' she said.

'You are in enough trouble without adding to it with these pathetic lies. Save yourself the effort, Agent Fox.'

Papademos sighed and shook his head. He looked tired but not particularly disappointed. A life spent interviewing criminals with strong incentives to lie must have left him permanently cynical, Hunter thought.

The police captain glanced at his watch and turned to a guard. After speaking in rapid, hushed Greek, the guard snapped to attention and Papademos left the small room, slamming the door behind him.

'Well, that was rude,' Quinn said. 'He never even gave so much as a cheerio.'

Hunter watched the guard. He was young – maybe mid-twenties – and looked like he was serious about his career in the Hellenic Police. At least he had a career, he thought glumly. After tonight, he guessed HARPA was about to come to an ignominious end and there was little chance of Juliette Bonnaire hiring him back into UNESCO. He knew her better than almost anyone and not even a sustained and sincere schedule of begging would move her if she did not want to be moved.

A few moments later, the door opened a crack and they heard a man whispering something in Greek. The guard turned his head to his right to face the whispering man. He looked torn for a moment, but then the scent of fresh coffee wafting through the open door explained everything.

'So what now?' Jodie said.

'Now we wait,' Amy said. 'I've called Jim and he'll pull strings at the embassy.'

Hope flooded into Hunter's eyes. 'He can do that?'

'Jim?' Jodie said. 'He can pull more strings than a banjo band. We'll be out of here in minutes.'

When Papademos returned it was for the briefest of moments. 'I'm sorry to tell you that the US Embassy cannot help you. Their role here tonight is to ensure your civil liberties and rights are not broken, and they will not be. Beyond that, they have little influence. At the end of the day, you have been arrested for murder and we have the eyewitness testimony of several highly trusted counter-terrorist officers. The Italian authorities also want to speak with you. The Marquis was a very powerful and important man.'

'You have no idea,' Amy mumbled.

'I'm sorry?' said Papademos.

'Nothing.'

'And it was self-defence!' Quinn said.

He looked unfazed. 'This is why we have courts, Agent Mosley. You will make your defence in the courts, not here and not tonight.'

'So much for Jim Gates and his Banjo Band,' Hunter said.

'Give him time, Max,' Blanco said. 'These things can be sensitive.'

'And in the meantime, we're screwed,' Jodie said. 'Damn, I wish I had a smoke. Hey, Mr Papademos, you got a cigarette?'

He looked down at her, his face shaded by shock mixed with grudging respect at her bravery. 'Yes, but not for you, Agent Priest.'

'So what now?' Amy asked. 'What happens to us now?'

'Tonight you will be transferred to Korydallos Prison where you will await trial for your crimes. You will, of course, have access to legal advice.'

'Is that a men's prison?' Quinn asked. 'I don't think I like the sound of that.'

'Korydallos houses men and women, Agent Mosley. It's on the western outskirts of the city, not far from here.' He checked his watch. 'You will be there in less than an hour, after processing at both ends.'

Papademos left the team behind, firmly clicking the door behind him. Moments later, the young guard skipped out to grab his coffee.

Quinn was first to speak. 'This is what they call a bad development, Amy.'

'I get that, Quinn,' she said impatiently. 'But what else can we do? Besides, he's right. Yes, it was self-defence, but we still shot those men. That means a trial. Damn it all!'

Hunter shook his head, a look of disappointment on his face. 'O, ye of little faith.'

Amy felt her heart quicken. 'What is it, Max? What's in that devious mind of yours?'

'Matthew 8:26 by the sound of it,' Lewis said with a shrug.

'What's on my mind is that in a few minutes, we're getting processed out of here. Korydallos might be a prison for men and women but obviously, it's going to have a men's section and a women's section. When we get there, we get split by sex. Then we'll get split up again individually and given separate cells.'

'You are so damned good at lifting my mood, Hunter,' Jodie said. 'Please, go on.'

He ignored her, but couldn't resist a smile. 'None of that has happened yet and we're in here on our own.'

'Yeah,' Quinn said. 'Here being an underground interview room in an Athens police station, surrounded by armed guards.'

'Underground, but not completely.' Without turning away from them, he raised his hand above his head and pointed to a grille on the ceiling behind him. A broad smile appeared on his face. 'See that? That's a ventilation shaft. All subterranean spaces must have them. It's basic civil engineering.'

'An airshaft!' Quinn said. 'We can get out in the airshaft! I think I love you, Max.'

'Not so fast,' Amy said. 'We're not doing any of your crazy Indiana Jones stunts that end up with us getting trapped in an aircon duct, Max. This is my team, and we're not winding up in tomorrow's headlines.'

'I can see it now,' Quinn said. 'Acropolis Killers Shot Dead in Bungled Vent Shaft Escape Attempt.'

'Thanks, Quinn!' Amy said. 'The image really enhances my fears.'

'Welcome.'

Amy wasn't placated. 'And another thing. If we do this then we're outlaws, at least in Greece.'

'So?' Jodie said.

'Think it through, Jodie. First, our line of work makes Greece somewhere we might need to visit again. Second, it's not going to take Captain Papademos very long to have our flight cancelled, and third, he has our passports.'

Jodie shrugged. 'So get Jim to issue new passports and we'll pick them up someplace on the way.'

'We could do that,' Amy said, thinking things through more carefully now. 'And the second we get out of here, we need to have him contact the pilots of the Gulfstream and change the flight plan – get us off the manifest. That way when Papademos finds out how we entered the country, there won't be any reason to impound the jet. It's US government property anyway. He'll never go there.'

'We're still not getting into an airport without passports,' Quinn said. 'Think that through.'

'So how the hell do we get to Patmos?' Lewis asked. 'Quinn's right – we can't exactly shoot our way into Athens International Airport and burn out of here in a jet. That's terrorist stuff. They'd probably send fighters up to shoot us down or something. Without the jet, we're screwed.'

'Not necessarily,' Blanco said. 'There's a ferry that sails to Patmos.' All heads swivelled to him, and he gave a self-effacing shrug in response. 'I looked it up on my phone when Kostas told us about the Cave of the Apocalypse. Hell of a lot easier sneaking onboard a ferry than getting into an airport, especially with our skillset.'

Jodie nodded with approval. 'Why didn't you think of that, Hunter?'

'We don't have time for this, is what I think,' said the Englishman. 'We need to get these cuffs off.'

'Easy,' Jodie said, removing a hairpin. 'I wear these for a reason.'

The team watched in amazement as the young thief bent the pin into a hook and carefully picked open the cuffs with nimble, fast-working fingers.

'That was incredible,' Lewis said, rubbing his wrist.

'Not my first time,' she said with a wink. 'What about you, Hunter? Aren't you going to thank me?'

Hunter said nothing. He was already scraping the table over the floor and positioning it beneath the plastic grille embedded in the ceiling tiles.

'Didn't think so,' she said, shrugging and re-placing the hairpin.

He wasn't listening. He had already climbed onto the table, gently punched the grille out of the ceiling tiles, and was manipulating it out of the way. He pulled himself up into the shaft, holding himself up with some considerable arm strength for a few seconds, and then returned with a smile on his face. 'We can get through here. Sal, take one of the chairs and wedge it under the door handle. That should buy us a few more seconds when they try to get in here.'

'Sure thing, Max.'

Amy heard a noise at the door. She spun around and saw the handle move down. Someone was opening the door. She lowered her voice to an urgent whisper. 'Sal!'

Blanco was already at the door, hand curled into a meaty fist. It opened to reveal the face of one of the younger guards. He looked tired and bored, forced to deal with a bunch of foreigners on the midnight shift. Blanco didn't care. He piled his fist into the young man's face and sent him tumbling back outside into the corridor.

Quinn screamed.

Amy gasped and slammed the door shut.

Blanco slid the chair's top rail under the handle and dusted his hands off. 'I might be wrong, but I think we just crossed a line.'

'What are we working with up there, Max?' Amy asked.

'It's big enough to crawl in,' he called back. 'Horizontal for a few metres and then a bigger vertical shaft with a ladder fixed to the wall. Probably some sort of utility shaft to access any problems with the air-conditioning system, by the looks of it. Must go up to the roof.'

'It'll do,' she said.

Then they all heard someone hammering on the door. Loud, aggressive shouting in Greek was followed by the sound of someone kicking the door. Then it went quiet.

'Maybe they got bored and gave up?' Quinn asked.

A gunshot ripped through the door's top panel and buried itself in the clock on the wall. Amy stared up at the shattered face and felt her stomach turn. 'Yeah, I don't think so, Quinn.' Turning to see Hunter's legs disappearing up into the shaft, she ran over to the table and looked up as his head appeared upside down in the vent.

'Are you coming with me, or are you just going to leave me hanging around?'

27

'Quinn first,' Amy said.

Hunter's hand now appeared. 'C'mon, Quinn!'

He helped her up and with no more room in the shaft, they crawled out of sight towards the bigger vertical shaft.

'You next, Jodie,' Amy said.

Behind them, Lewis and Blanco were holding the chair up against the door with their boots while keeping their heads out of the line of fire. Another round burst through the door, showering them with a misty cloud of wood dust and splinters.

'You want to draw straws for who goes up next?' Lewis said.

'No,' said Blanco. 'Amy goes up next, and then you do.'

Amy knew there was no point in arguing, and she pulled herself up into the shaft.

Blanco squinted as another round blasted what was left of the top panel into powdery matchwood. The chair they had wedged up under the handle was too heavy and in too tight. The more they pushed against the door, the more they pushed its legs into the floor and strengthened it, but both men knew it would eventually give way. 'We need something else,' Blanco said, pointing to a spare table beside the door. He and Lewis muscled the table over and wedged it up against the chair blocking the door. 'That should help. Time to go, Ben.'

'You're not going to change your mind, are you?'

'How well you know me, young man.'

Lewis scrambled onto the other table and climbed up into the shaft.

On his own in the interview room, Blanco leaned his head around the obliterated door panel and counted three guards. Turning, he saw the angle was too acute for them to get a clear shot at the vent. From the way the chair was still wedged under the handle, it looked like he had maybe twenty seconds to get to the end of the room and up into the shaft before they could get a lethal shot off.

Away he went, sprinting across the room and vaulting up onto the interview table. He heard the door crash open and men shouting in Greek. Arms up into the shaft and fingers gripping the wooden beams running around the vent opening, he heaved himself up into the conduit. Bullets traced past his vanishing boots, but he was already inside and crawling along the metal shaft.

'How's it going, Sal?'

He craned his head up and saw Amy at the end of the shaft. She was clinging to the metal ladder Hunter had described. There was no sign of the others. 'Get going, Amy! They're right behind me.'

She took the hint and climbed up out of sight on the ladder. Blanco was right behind her, pulling himself out of the horizontal shaft and swinging up onto the ladder. Behind him, one of the Greek police officers was scrambling along the tunnel.

'Hurry, Sal!'

He was just out of sight of the police now, with his boots just above the level of the horizontal shaft. 'Keep going! I have an idea.'

As Hunter led the rest of the team up out of sight towards the roof, Blanco waited for the Greek man's head to appear. Then he booted him in the face and knocked him out. 'Sorry,' he said, and he meant it. 'But that stops any of your buddies coming through the shaft until they can drag you back out of the way.'

He reached down and took his gun, an eight-shot Ruger GP100 revolver. He smelled it and knew it had been recently fired. No surprises there. Popping open the cylinder, he counted six shots. Looking up, he saw Lewis reach the top of the ladder and step out of sight. After a few moments climbing, he reached the top of the ladder and found himself standing inside a concrete bulkhead. The small, boxlike utility room gave access to the roof via a fire door, which Lewis was holding open.

'Nice of you to join us,' Amy said. 'What happened?'

'I needed a kickstart.'

She frowned. 'On second thoughts, I don't want to know.'

He turned and slammed the door shut. 'Won't take them long to get through and open it,' he said. 'And they'll know the shaft leads up here anyway, so they'll be all over us in seconds.'

With the sights and sounds of downtown Athens buzzing around the police station, Hunter was scouting the outer edge of the roof to find an escape route. Then they all heard someone pounding on the bulkhead door.

'Faster than I thought,' Blanco said.

'We need a way out of here, Max!' Amy shouted. 'And fast.'

The police in the bulkhead tried to shoulder-barge the door, but Blanco and Lewis were leaning hard against it.

'Metal door,' Blanco said. 'Not shooting through this one.'

'It's not going to be long before they get up here another way,' Amy muttered.

'The only way is over the roof,' Jodie said. She had been quietly studying the layout of the buildings and now she knew what to do. 'The police station is part of a long terrace of buildings running along the road below us to our left. We go over the roofs to the end of the terrace and climb down. It's a nightclub with a balcony halfway down. I remember from the drive.'

'Only a thief remembers things like that,' Quinn said.

Jodie turned to her. 'Then it's a good job I'm here, egghead.'

They heard several police officers out in the street below them. They were shouting at them, probably orders to give themselves up, Amy thought. 'Arguments later,' she said. 'We do what Jodie says – get going!'

'And stay down!' Jodie said, turning away from them.

She and Hunter led the way, climbing up over a concrete wall and then jumping down onto the roof of the next building along. The rest of the team followed below them, with Blanco at the rear. Running up a gable, the big man from Brooklyn heard a bullet trace past him and vanish in the night. He dropped into a crouch and turned, firing over the heads of the police. It was a deliberate warning shot and it worked, driving the men back inside the building to regroup and think again.

'We don't have long,' Blanco called out. 'And when they come back they're going to be armed like a SWAT team.'

Jodie was already climbing down the nightclub's façade. Quinn, Lewis, and Amy joined her on the second-floor balcony. When Hunter and Blanco swung down onto it, they found the others mingling with dozens of people holding drinks. Red and purple lighting from inside the building strobed over their faces in rhythm with a deep bass beat.

Wrapping his arms around Amy's waist, Hunter said, 'Can we stay for just one song?'

She rolled her eyes. 'Go down!'

'All I wanted was a dance!' he said.

'To the next balcony, Max!'

But he was already leaning over the wrought-iron balustrade and scanning for the next way down to the sidewalk. Finding a solid iron drainpipe bolted to the wall beside the balcony, he found what he was looking for and started climbing. Jodie, Quinn, and Lewis followed him and then Amy and Blanco were at the rear. Reacquainted with terra firma, the HARPA team searched for a vehicle.

Jodie spied a BMW SUV parked up over the road, but Quinn had a better idea. Seeing a seven-seater taxi outside the nightclub, she hailed it over to them, and then they were away, driving nice and slowly. Lost in the traffic and with no sign of the police behind them, Amy finally breathed a sigh of relief.

'Where do you need to go?' the driver asked.

'The Acropolis,' Amy said.

The driver turned, making the vinyl seat squeak. 'It will be closed.'

'We need to go to a house nearby.'

Jodie looked at her. 'Huh?'

'I need to get my bag,' Quinn said. 'I left it in the

Nitro before we went into Kostas' villa. No bag, no computer.'

They swung by Venizelos's place, grateful for Jodie's advice to leave the SUV parked in the street behind the villa. Police had cordoned off the road leading to the dead professor's house and there was a marked car parked up outside it, but the next road along was untouched. The cab driver cruised past and pulled up at Amy's instructions some distance from the Nitro. Far enough away not to see the blown-out tyres.

'I'll just be a minute,' Quinn said.

When she returned, she had her bag over her shoulder. Hopping back into the Mercedes, she buckled her seatbelt and blew a lock of hair away from her eyes. 'We can go.'

'But where?' asked the driver.

'Head out of town,' Blanco said. 'West.'

'This is...' The driver searched for the right English word. 'Vague.'

'West,' Blanco repeated.

They drove out of the city, using the quiet, subdued half hour to get their thoughts back together. Deep in the labyrinth of backstreets in Neo Faliro, Blanco put the policeman's revolver to the driver's head. 'Pull over and get out.'

Genuine shock flashed over the man's face as he complied with the order. Blanco didn't enjoy doing it, but there was no other way. Sooner or later, the driver would work out he had shuttled foreign fugitives to the ferry port and would give the information to the police. Then they would go through CCTV and if they found them on the ferry, they would make the next step: that they had gone to Patmos – and as Venizelos had told them before his murder, it was not a big place.

Blanco took the wheel and burned away from the driver, deliberately driving in the wrong direction until he was out of sight and then turning and heading west once again. As they cruised west, Quinn said, 'Did any of that just happen?'

'Sure did,' Jodie said. 'Life moves pretty fast, right?'

Her words melted into a long, soft silence as Blanco drove the car safely to Piraeus. When they pulled up at the terminal, Amy spoke first. 'What time does the ferry go, Quinn?'

The goth had been busy on her computer for most of the drive and she replied instantly. 'Next one is at midday tomorrow.'

'We have to be careful,' Hunter said. 'Papademos will be putting out an all ports warning as we speak and when the taxi driver identifies us, he'll locate us not too far from the ferry terminal.'

'So when are we boarding the ferry?' Jodie asked.

'Now, while it's dark,' Blanco said.

Quinn looked confused. 'But how do we get on board?'

Blanco put a fatherly arm around her shoulder, his mind full of memories of how he boarded Raul Vazquez's yacht for the Atlantis mission. 'Ever climb up an anchor chain?'

She turned sharply and frowned at him. 'What?'

'Because I have, and it can actually be very liberating.'

28

The former KGB colonel lit his Ziganov cigarette and clipped shut his old Soviet lighter. Blowing the smoke out slowly through his nose, he felt the tension slowly flood out of him like poison drained from a snakebite. They had lost Gallo's lion statue to the hands of Hunter and Fox and the rest of the meddling HARPA team, but all was not lost.

'Vasya, let me see the images you took back in the palazzo,' Neverov said.

Lugovoy tossed the colonel the compact camera he had used to photograph it after the Gallo raid. 'They're on this.'

Gubenko knocked back a shot of vodka. 'You want to see the pretty pictures of the little statue, boss?'

Medinsky gave him a bitter look. 'It's an *ágalma*, ignoramus.'

Gubenko leaped to his feet and drew his knife. 'You want to call me that again?'

The other man squared up to him and drew his own combat knife, a hideously savage weapon with a high carbon steel serrated blade. Its black epoxy coating reflected the room's light in a quick dull flash as he waved it in Gubenko's face. 'If you think I'm scared of you, you're crazy. But then, you are crazy!'

Gubenko's lip curled. 'I'll gut you like a pig, *zasranets*!'

Medinsky bristled at the insult. 'If you think I'm such a shitass why not come over here and teach me a lesson I'll never forget?'

'Enough!' Neverov yelled, smacking the knife from Medinsky's hand and then pushing Gubenko roughly back down onto his chair. He stuffed the photos of the statue inside his tactical vest and sighed wearily. 'Enough of this bullshit! We have a job to do and we must stay focused.'

'I am focused!' Gubenko snarled.

'Focused? You were disarmed by a common thief, and a woman at that!'

The other Wolves laughed as Gubenko slunk back over to his vodka, mumbling under his breath.

Neverov's mind had already moved on. Like the others, he had to retain focus.

Focus and determination. He took another shot of vodka straight from the bottle and a second, much deeper drag on the Ziganov. The look of betrayal and horror on Professor Samaras's face still haunted him even after all these years.

Old man Grudinin had gunned him down in the cave inside Mount Sinai over thirty years ago, but if he thought about it hard enough, it all came flooding back. The crack of the nine-mil round leaving the Tokarev's barrel. The way it split the cave's grim silence as it ripped through the damp air towards the Greek scholar. The rancid sulphur smell of the gun smoke. The noise Samaras made when he saw the blood blooming on his dusty shirt.

The way he felt when he knew he was party to murder.

Professor Samaras was the first man he had seen killed, but he was not the last. It pained him to think how after Sinai, he had moved on from witness to killer. If he could seek redemption for his crimes, he knew he would. His beloved parents, Mikhail and Daria, back in their plain, sad khrushchyovka apartment in Omsk, would have been disgusted if they had ever discovered what he had become – the monster the KGB had turned him into – Colonel Vladimir Mikhailovich Neverov, decorated hero and common murderer.

Redemption.

But from where could he seek it? He was steeped in the old Communist Party and conformed to all its doctrines. He had learned lots from old Grudinin, chiefly that there was certainly no God in this world. *What a ridiculous idea!* he thought. No, God was for men like Samaras. If Neverov sought redemption, then he must do it for himself. More Ziganov smoke burned down into his lungs, leaving its sickly trail of tar on everything it touched.

Lugovoy snapped his phone shut and sniffed. 'That was Sergei, my contact in the FSB.'

'What did he say?'

'He said that after Rome, the HARPA team travelled to Greece and came under attack in Athens.'

'Greece?'

'He tracked their transponder.'

Neverov's eyes swivelled to his old comrade. 'But they came under attack? Who?'

A shrug. 'He does not know, but whoever they are, they killed their Greek contact Venizelos and then exchanged fire with the HARPA team at the Acropolis. Special Agent Fox and the rest of the team were taken into custody by the Greek authorities afterwards. That is all he has.'

Neverov thought carefully about what he had just heard. 'Who else is on the trail of our little relic, Vasya?'

'I don't know, but they were well-armed.'

The ex-KGB colonel gave a resigned nod. Whoever was involved in these things was always well-armed. 'Did Sergei manage to get the tracking device onto the HARPA team as I ordered?'

'He did. It's inside the geek's computer. He put it there during the skirmish at the Acropolis.'

'And where are they now?'

'You're not going to believe this,' Lugovoy said, aware that his words had silenced Gubenko and Medinsky's conversation and got the interest of even the Spetsnaz men. 'But they are on board a ferry in Piraeus.'

Neverov stubbed out his cigarette and took one final vodka. 'Where and when does this ferry go?'

'The island of Patmos, midday tomorrow.'

Neverov grinned. 'Transfer the money to Sergei and send my thanks.'

'Yes, sir.'

'But where are they going on the island?' Medinsky asked.

'It has to be the Cave of the Apocalypse,' Neverov muttered.

Lugovoy said, 'Should I call the authorities and have them arrest the HARPA team in Piraeus?'

'No, not at all. Let them go. We will fly to the island and get there before them. Make all necessary preparations, Vasya. I want fresh weapons and ammunition.'

'I'll ask Sergei when I pay him.'

'Good work,' said Neverov. 'It looks like we are back in the game.'

29

The Blue Star ferry crossing had been a welcome break for the team. With seven hours of gentle sailing across the Aegean Sea with the sun slowly setting at its stern, the nineteen-thousand-ton passenger ship had made good time and given the HARPA members time to patch themselves up and get some sleep. Now, as it weaved its way around the south coast of Ikaria, Amy, Hunter, and the others were gathered at an outside bar on the starboard deck.

'I still can't believe what happened to Kostas,' Amy said, taking the top off a cold beer. 'I've worked with him for years and to see him murdered like that...'

As her words trailed away, Blanco stepped up to the plate. 'He was a great guy who worked hard to get relic smugglers behind bars. He made a real difference to the world and I'm sure as hell going to miss him, too.'

He and Amy chinked glasses. No one else on the team had met Venizelos before, but it was easy to see how much he had meant to Amy and Blanco. As the ship rolled slightly in a gentle swell, Hunter sipped some beer and set it down on a coaster. 'We'll be in Patmos in less than two hours, and I don't know about the rest of the team but my theology could do with a brush-up. Ben?'

Lewis finished some beer and smiled. 'But where to start?'

'At the beginning?' Quinn said.

'It was a rhetorical question,' he said, broadening his toothy smile even further. 'And the answer is with some basic facts. First, let's talk some more about the *Book of Revelation*. If John really did write an extra chapter and hide it from the world, you need to know more about this whole subject.'

'Should I take notes?' Hunter asked.

Jodie said, 'How about shutting your yap and listening?'

'I can do that.'

Lewis sipped his beer. 'First, the oldest copy of the Bible's New Testament is what we call the *Codex Vaticanus*. It's safely locked up in the Vatican and composed of nearly eight hundred pages of vellum. It's been dated with special palaeographic techniques to the fourth century.'

'Old,' Jodie said.

'Yes, very old,' said Lewis.

Finally unable to hide her interest, Quinn set her laptop down on the chair and turned to face Lewis. 'What was your PhD thesis on again?'

'Concepts of death in the *Book of Revelation*.'

'So, right now you're feeling kinda smug and important.'

'Pretty much, yeah. And before you ask, the *Codex Vaticanus* might be old, but it's not complete. There are several books not included in the original version of the codex – mostly from the gospels – but also, and importantly for us, the *Book of Revelation*.'

'So if they're not in the codex, they could be in the cave with the final statue,' Jodie said. 'Which is sort of our current theory, right?'

Lewis sighed. 'Maybe. Look, we believe there are over three hundred separate manuscripts of *Revela-*

tion, all in Greek, and most of them turn up in other uncial codices.'

Jodie frowned and lowered the beer bottle from her lips. 'Huh?'

'It's a type of script common to Europe in the early dark ages,' Lewis said. 'Don't worry about it. The point is these manuscripts have mostly made it into the other codices and from this, we have formed our knowledge of the *Book of Revelation*. But just imagine if when John had his vision of the ascended Jesus Christ, he was told other things about the end of the world. Imagine if he was told other things, which he wrote down onto a manuscript, which never made it to any of these codices.'

Quinn shuddered. 'Getting chills over here.'

'All of this over a pile of vellum scrolls,' said Jodie.

'Not just any old pile of vellum scrolls,' Lewis said. He sipped more beer, clearly enjoying his moment in the spotlight. 'Like I just said – the *Book of Revelation* is clear about the end of the world and the picture it paints ain't pretty, but what if there's more? What if Jesus told John something else in his vision?'

Quinn arched an eyebrow. 'Like maybe stop taking psychotropic drugs before walking in the hills?'

'You're so cynical, Quinn,' Lewis said.

'Am I?' she said. 'I read that the entire Bible story was nothing more than the result of some crazy mushroom-taking fertility cult. Imagine the entire West being built on that. Give me a break.'

Lewis sighed and shook his head. 'You're talking about a theory ascribing the taking of the amanita muscaria mushroom to the development of ancient Sumerian cults, from which some claim the Christian Bible descends. It's just another theory. I'm talking about the *Book of Revelation*, and for the purposes of what we're talking about, its provenance is irrelevant.'

'You're full of fancy big words tonight,' Jodie said.

Amy and Hunter exchanged an amused glance as Lewis blew out a deep breath and started again. 'So, as I was saying, the final book in the New Testament, the *Book of Revelation*, is of central importance to Christian eschatology.'

'Eschatology?' Jodie asked.

'It's the part of theology that deals with the end of the world, and the judgement of the soul in the afterlife.'

'Ah,' Blanco said. 'The scary stuff.'

'One of the central ideas that John was trying to discuss in the *Book of Revelation* was the afterlife, especially in Revelation 20, and I think he genuinely believed what he was writing about. Remember, he lived in the first century AD back when the existence of God simply wasn't challenged. He wouldn't have fooled around on the subject.'

Jodie lit a cigarette and kicked back on the soft chair. 'Maybe we should take a leaf out of his book, so to speak.'

'Why, afraid?' Quinn said.

'Bite me, dorkette.'

'Ouch,' Quinn said. 'The kitten has claws.'

'I ain't no kitten, dude.'

'As fascinating as it is, watching you two trade barbs,' Hunter said, 'perhaps our time would be better spent if we got back to the briefing? I might be a bloody amazing archaeologist but I know next to nothing about Biblical scholarship.'

'But you're too modest,' Quinn said.

Amy cracked a smile. 'He has much to be modest about. Right, Maximilian?'

'Anything you say, Amadea.'

Lewis and Blanco laughed and shared a high five.

'I knew he knew about that,' Lewis said, taking another sip of his beer. 'Knew it.'

Hunter held in his laugh and broke away from the banter at the table to look over at the sun as it set down on the sea. Behind him, he heard Amy's voice grow more serious.

'Changing subject for a second, anyone think there's a link between Neverov and the men who killed Kostas?' she asked.

Lewis shrugged. 'We have no evidence to suggest there's any connection, but I think we're all making that assumption in our hearts.'

Blanco gave a solemn nod. 'That's what I was thinking, and if so then I think we all know what that means – we're up against much more than we thought.'

The chatter at the table fell silent.

'It means this time it's personal,' Amy said. 'After what they did to Kostas Venizelos, we have a big score to settle.'

'Before we all get carried away,' said Jodie, 'let's not forget what Amy just said – there's zero evidence linking the Wolf Pack to the men who attacked us in Athens. Not an ounce.'

'She's right,' Lewis said. 'Maybe the tattooed men are pulling Neverov's strings, maybe it's the other way around. Maybe they're not connected at all. We can't let our fears cloud our judgement. This is just too important.'

Hunter nodded. 'It certainly is as far as archaeological discoveries are concerned. Not to mention the threat to world peace and stability if they get their hands on whatever John of Patmos was trying to hide in the lost scroll.'

Amy sighed. 'I see the ferry terminal. C'mon, everyone – let's get back to the hotel and get some food.'

'Good idea.' Blanco groaned as he heaved himself up out of his chair. 'I've had enough hell-raising for one day.'

'You and me both, brother,' Lewis said. 'We don't know when we'll get another chance to get some decent food, and it's on Jim, right?'

* * *

At the hotel, they organised rooms and met downstairs in the restaurant. After they ordered drinks, they picked up their menus and took in the wide range of excellent meals on offer. Blanco and Quinn chose the marinated seabass with avocado and bottarga, while Lewis went with a beef fillet with beetroot leaves and cream cheese. Amy selected the roasted carré of pork with celeriac and quince and a fig-walnut sauce.

'Blue blood food,' Quinn said.

Amy ignored her. 'What are you having, Jodie?'

'Nothing on here,' she said. 'Is there a burger place anywhere close?'

'I hear that,' Hunter said.

Amy sighed and closed her menu. 'You can't be serious.'

Hunter also closed his menu. 'You think I'm the kind of person who eats smoked aubergine salad with pine honey and quail eggs?'

'It wouldn't hurt you to try something slightly more elevated from your usual diet.'

Blanco laughed. 'You're casting pearls before swine, boss.'

'This is what I call frou-frou food,' Hunter said. 'All hat and no cattle.'

'Yeah,' Jodie said. 'All sizzle and no steak.'

'Exactly,' said Hunter. 'All fur coat and no knickers.'

Jodie stifled a laugh. 'That's what I think, too.'

The Londoner caught the young thief's eye. 'You want to go and find a burger together?'

Jodie hesitated, and the table quietened. Everyone on the team knew how long it took for her to open up to strangers, so when she tossed her menu down and pushed her chair back, they all hid their surprise well.

'Let's do it,' she said. 'If the Apocalypse is immi-
nent, what the hell, right?'

Hunter gave Amy a shrug. 'See you frou-frou guys
later.'

He got up from his chair and walked out of the
hotel. Jodie was behind him, and now she turned and
winked at the team. 'Don't wait up, kids.'

30

The sun was bright and hot before breakfast. Inside the whitewashed Skala Hotel, the team was nursing some sore heads thanks to a few too many ouzos the night before. Everyone except Hunter and Jodie. They hadn't returned from the burger bar until well after midnight, causing much drunken speculation about what had happened.

Up in her room, a shower had never felt so good to Amy Fox. She stood beneath the large chrome shower rose and let the hot water run over her. It splashed on her forehead, rushed through her hair, and massaged her neck and shoulders. Blowing out a deep breath, she felt the stress of Athens flowing out of her and disappearing down the drain with the used water.

Never had she been so scared in all her life, and a good part of her wanted to give Jim Gates a resignation letter, or at the very least a transfer out of the HARPA team and back to the safety of a comfortable desk job. After the shower, she got dressed and with a cup of fresh coffee in her hand, she stepped out of her room and found the rest of her team gathered on the patio beside the pool.

Behind them, the sun was rising over a distant peninsula, casting sparkling rays of golden light over the surface of the sea and the pool. To the east, it lit up the rugged coast of Arki island and turned its rocks a rich orange colour. This place, she thought, might just be the paradise she had always dreamed of. Then, in the breaking waves of the Aegean, she caught a glimpse of three dolphins. They were visible for only a second and then gone again with barely a splash. She gasped, the morning suddenly filled with the hoarse cry of a levant sparrowhawk.

And Blanco's fat, contagious laugh.

She turned and saw him almost in tears. By the looks of it, Lewis had laid down another of his notorious jokes and got an excellent result. Even Quinn was smirking.

'Care to let me in on the gag?' she asked.

Before Lewis could reply, Hunter and Jodie stepped out on the patio.

'What time did you two get back last night?' Amy asked.

No reply.

'Jodie?'

'Sorry, what?'

'I asked what time you got back to the hotel.'

'One, maybe.'

Amy arched an eyebrow. 'Late.'

'I guess.'

The sharp shrieking of gulls wheeling in the blue sky split the awkward silence around the breakfast table. Hunter's eyes were closed.

'And did you enjoy your burgers?'

'Uh-huh. Delicious, thanks.'

Amy and Blanco shared a look. Lewis raised his eyebrows and returned to his theological research with a 'don't look at me' expression on his face.

'They must have been big,' Amy continued.

'Not that big.'

'But they took you four hours to eat them.'

Jodie furrowed her brow. After a confused pause, she said, 'Oh, yeah, right. No, we went out after. Hunter has a lot of energy for such an old guy.'

Quinn turned her head slowly until she was looking around the side of her seat at Amy. 'Interesting.'

'I'm not old,' Hunter said.

'Oh, you're not asleep then?' asked Amy.

'Just dozing.'

'I see.'

He opened one eye. 'Look, I know what's on your mind.'

'You do?'

'Sure. You've been dying to ask us since we stepped out here.'

'Oh, really?'

'Yeah,' he said, closing his eye again. 'Were the burgers vegetarian or regular beef. The answer is they were just normal beef.'

Amy shook her head. 'Fine, be like that. You know what? I don't care what the hell happened between you two last night, just so long as it doesn't affect the team.'

'It might,' Hunter said. 'I nearly put my back out.'

Amy's gasp was louder than Lewis's chuckle.

'What the hell?'

Blanco cast a protective, fatherly eye over Jodie but instantly saw from her face that they were having some fun at Amy's expense. He shut his eyes and sat back to enjoy.

Quinn's smile faded. Listening to Jodie and Hunter teasing the boss was amusing as far as it went, but the truth was, nothing much ever lifted her spirits for longer than a few seconds. Much like Dr Jekyll and Mr Hyde, Quinn Mosley and Ghost were two very different sides of the same coin.

Quinn was quiet, shy, and introverted. Ghost was wilder. Much wilder. When she got online and started doing her thing, she became outspoken, gregarious, and ruthless. There was no counting the damage she had caused as Ghost, and she had no problem with any of it; she just didn't care.

But in the quieter moments when the darkness fell, Quinn felt guilt. She never showed it. Regret was weak. She enjoyed her hard-won reputation as the team's enigma, so showing any sign of weakness was out of the question.

Her worst fear was making a mistake and letting the team down. She hated that feeling and looked back on the Atlantis mission with a shudder. Amy had asked her to retrieve her bag with the satphone from the back of the truck they were in before it crashed. She had failed and the phone had been crushed.

She sighed and lowered her sunglasses. Looked out across the bay. The translucent turquoise waters of the Aegean Sea were still today. Littered with countless islands like jewels strewn on electric blue velvet, this was the original home of the word archipelago, once used to describe only this place. This was a glittering landscape of gulfs and bays and calderas, heated in the summer by the hot, dry Etesian winds and the cradle of two ancient civilisations – Minoan and Mycenaean. This was somewhere Quinn Mosley might just be able to find happiness.

Her thoughts were interrupted by a ringing telephone and when she turned, she saw the banter was over and Jodie was walking away from the table with her cell phone in her hand.

* * *

On the other side of the patio, away from her team, Jodie Priest read and then quietly deleted Tyler's newest text. Then she glanced up from her phone and slipped her sunglasses on. For a while, she stood still, silently admiring the clear, sparkling waters of the yacht marina, and thought about how different things must be here compared with the life she knew back in California, back with the Tylers of this world.

She watched a red and white fishing boat sail into the marina and moor up alongside a sun-bleached jetty. Once it was safely roped into place, the fisherman walked back to the stern and began coiling up a length of bright blue rope, working in the hot sun as his small boat bobbed gently up and down on the smooth water.

'All good?'

She turned and saw Blanco at her side. He had a big, goofy smile on his face and was clearly enjoying the sights of the amazing little harbour.

'It will be.'

He nodded and said nothing, his eyes concealed behind his shades. Amy walked over and joined them, concern all over her face. 'What's up?'

'She's tight-lipped,' Blanco said. 'But I think it's man trouble.'

Jodie rolled her eyes. 'Please...'

Amy's sigh was heavy and long. 'Is that what the cloak-and-dagger routine with the phone has been about?'

Jodie looked embarrassed. 'Sorry, I thought I was more subtle than that. I should have known I couldn't get one past you.'

'Yeah, you should have. Is it Tyler again?'

Jodie nodded, face staring down at her boots. 'Yeah.'

Hunter had strolled over. He looked at Amy. 'Tyler?'

'Tyler is...' Amy paused.

'My ex,' said Jodie. 'He's my ex. And he's trouble with a capital T.'

'Come on,' Amy said. 'Let's go back to the table and finish breakfast. We have a big day ahead of us.'

Sitting down, Blanco reached forward to pull another slice of mizithra pie off the large stone serving plate in the centre of the table. 'I didn't know Tyler was bothering you again, Jo.'

Her look of embarrassment worsened. 'Sorry, Sal. I should have told you.'

The smile on Blanco's cheery face faded. 'You can tell me when you need my help, that's all you need to know.'

'What's this guy all about?' Hunter asked.

Jodie said, 'We met in juvie and spent some time together on and off. I was young when we met, just sixteen. He stood up to the system. Didn't let anyone push him around, not even the cops. To me, back then he was a real hero. I just wanted to run away with him and go on the road. It seemed kinda romantic. I was just a kid.'

'And now you've moved on,' Amy said. 'Which is good.'

She nodded. 'Sure, but Tyler hasn't.'

'Which is bad.'

'Right. He keeps calling me. Trying to get back with me. Talking about the good times we had and trying to reel me back in. I know what he's doing.'

'Have you told him you've moved on with your life?' Blanco said.

'Yes, but he's a very persistent guy. As I said, he stands up for himself, fights for what he believes in. Fights for what he wants – and he wants me.'

'But you don't want to go back?' Amy asked.

'Of course not, Amy. Back then, you saved my life. You think I want to go back to Tyler and a life of crime?'

'Sorry. I'm just being protective, I guess.'

Blanco rubbed his eyes and yawned. Checked his old, scratched watch. 'Just tell him no, Jo.'

Jodie lit a cigarette and leaned forward, elbows on her knees and head slumped forward, eyes staring down at the ground between her shoes. 'Thing is, he's not taking no for an answer, Sal, and I think he might start getting dangerous. He's already started making threats.'

Amy was shocked. 'He's threatening you?'

A sad, broken nod. 'Maybe I should just give in to him. He threatened me and what's left of my family.'

Blanco's face reddened. 'You want me to fix this? You know I can fix this.'

She blew out some smoke and looked up at him, a sad smile forming at the corner of her mouth. 'I think maybe that might be cracking a peanut shell with a sledgehammer, Sal. But thanks.'

Quinn finished her breakfast and wiped her hand on her black jeans. 'If you give me his last name and date of birth, I'll totally destroy his entire life. It'll take less than an hour. What crimes do you want him to have committed? I'll get them on his record like that.'

She snapped her fingers to show how fast Tyler's life could get turned upside down, but Jodie shook her head. 'Thanks, Quinn, but it's not necessary. Besides, the son of a bitch already has a record as long as your arm.'

'I could make it longer. Much longer. Next time he gets picked up for a misdemeanour, the cops could find an international arrest warrant for murder.' She shrugged. 'Just let me know and I'll tie the bastard up for years.'

Hunter laughed. 'That's just fantastic. Totally unethical, by the way, but still magical.'

'There's really no need, Quinn,' Jodie said. 'This is a battle I have to fight for myself.'

'So what are you going to do?' Lewis asked.

'I don't know, but it's my problem and not anyone else's.'

Hunter broke into the conversation, his face suddenly much more serious. 'All right, everyone. It's time to leave. The cave opens in less than thirty minutes and we need to be there before the crowds.'

31

A white disc sun in the middle of a cobalt-blue sky dazzled the team as they made the short walk through Skala and up into the olive-covered slopes in the middle of the island. As they reached the end of the meandering historic trail, they saw a priest setting up a stall of tourist souvenirs and preparing for a day of profitable trading.

'Looks like we're here.' Hunter took in the small, whitewashed stone building which had been con-structed around the entrance of the cave. 'And we seem to be the first.'

'Then let's get on with it,' Amy said, checking her watch. 'With any luck, we can get what we need here and be right back out again without any trouble.'

Hunter heard what she said but kept his mouth shut. With a man like Neverov on their tail, and now the added pressures of the mysterious tattooed men and, almost certainly, an international arrest warrant, something told him they wouldn't be alone for long.

He followed Amy into the shade, walking down some steps into the temple. Off to his right, he saw the famous cave for the first time and was surprised by its size. The sacred cave was bigger than he had appreciated from photos back at UNESCO, and it had been incorporated into a special, purpose-built chapel.

The chapel looked like most others belonging to the Greek Orthodox Church and was decorated with brass candlesticks, icons, and colourful frescoes. The cave was also full of golden frescoes and in the corner was a small metal cage, fencing off the section where John had heard the voice of God. An open Bible rested on a natural pedestal in the cave wall, and two smooth wooden benches offered rest to weary pilgrims.

'This is incredible,' Lewis said. 'Think about this for a minute. Where we're standing right now is the last place on Earth where God spoke to a human, at least directly. This is a big deal. I wish Meg could be here.'

'Wait a minute,' Hunter said. 'Something's up.'

Amy turned. 'What's wrong?'

He walked away from them over to the other side of the cave. 'There's no draft over in this part of the chapel,' he said. 'That's what's wrong.'

Blanco wandered over to him. 'Say again?'

'This section of the chapel is well out of the way of the entrance and there's no moving air over here at all, and yet look at the flames on those candles.'

'Maybe it's coming from behind that screen,' Jodie said, pointing at a wooden screen covered in golden murals.

'In Eastern Orthodox religions it's called an iconostasis,' Lewis said. 'It's how they separate the nave and sanctuary in their churches. As you can see, they're usually decorated with religious iconography.'

'Pretty,' Jodie said.

'Yeah,' said Quinn. 'Pretty boring.'

'Heathen.'

Hunter took another step forward and peered cautiously around the edge of the painted wooden screen. 'Whatever you call it, there's a breeze coming from behind it.'

'Be careful, Max!' Amy said. 'I don't like this.'

Blanco walked up beside Hunter. 'You're not going in there alone, brother.'

Hunter nodded and gave him a nervous smile. 'I won't be alone, Sal – take a look behind the screen.'

The English archaeologist watched Blanco poke his head forward into the small sanctuary behind the iconostasis. A second later, the man from Brooklyn shook his head. 'Damn it, we're too late.'

Amy stepped across the chapel. 'Too late for what?'

'To save this priest,' Hunter said. 'He's been shot through the head, stripped of his robes and hat, and dumped here.'

Amy gasped and took a step back.

'And that's a cassock, not a robe, and a kalimavkion, not a hat,' Lewis said.

'Thanks for the update,' Jodie said. 'I'll make sure to make a note when we get home.'

'By the looks of it, whoever murdered this man did it to gain access to that.' Hunter pointed to a large fissure in the cave wall and then down to a large life-size mosaic of Christ laying on its side beside the crack. 'Seems the good Lord has been hiding a secret tunnel all these years.'

'The passageway Kostas told us about!' Amy said. 'We found it.'

'No,' said Hunter grimly. 'Someone else found it.'

'Wait a minute,' Jodie said cautiously. 'There must

have been a struggle in here and then a gunshot, right?'

'I guess,' Amy said. 'What are you getting at?'

'How long has he been dead?'

Hunter sighed. 'No more than thirty minutes. I'm no doctor but some of the blood still hasn't congealed.'

'In which case, he was shot after the place opened,' Jodie said. 'There's nowhere else up here to store that stall we saw out the front, guys.'

'Oh, shit!' Amy said. 'The man we saw out the front wasn't a priest. He was a—'

The bullet smacked into the top of the iconostasis and blasted its top panel to dust.

'He was the man who killed the priest,' Hunter said. 'And we're out of here.'

Another gunshot rang out. Hunter turned and saw the man more clearly now. It was Gubenko, his identity obscured by the black hat and robes of the man he had murdered moments earlier. In his hand, he was gripping a nine-mil Makarov pistol and his face told a simple story of revenge and murder. He raised the weapon again and screamed in Russian as he fired the third shot. The round zipped past Amy's head and ricocheted off the rock at the side of the tunnel.

'Go!' she cried out.

Hunter bolted like a stallion and hurriedly led them into the fissure at the back of the sanctuary. It was a tight space and pitch black, so he pulled his flashlight from the bag over his shoulder and switched it on just as the passageway twisted around a tight turn to the right.

'Did I tell you guys I think I might be claustrophobic?' Quinn called out.

'Tell me later,' Amy said.

'At least we have some rock between us and that psycho,' Hunter said. 'Keep running!'

They followed Hunter down the tunnel a few hundred feet until reaching a hand-built arch in the passageway. As they ran through it, Hunter noticed a slab of hand-hewn rock held in place above the arch by two guides carved into the bedrock.

'Amazing. It's a guillotine door,' he said. 'Held up there above the arch by a rope tied to a counterweight, in this case, that boulder.'

'And it's coming down.' Blanco pulled a combat knife from his pack and sliced the rope in one swift slashing movement. The rope tore apart with a snap and the heavy rock slab plummeted down into the sand, shutting off the arch.

'*Do svidaniya,*' he said with a shrug. Seeing their

faces, he explained. 'I dated a girl from Omsk once. She made great pirogi.'

Hunter laughed. 'Beautiful.'

Relieved that the threat of Gubenko was on the other side of a ton of volcanic rock, the team took a second to catch their breath.

'And now what?' Quinn asked.

'Now we keep going.' Amy turned and shone her flashlight down the passageway. 'Wherever it may lead us, I guess.'

They started down the passageway, hoping the slab hadn't sealed them inside the mountain, but Hunter stayed where he was, staring at the stone slab.

'Max?' Amy called out.

'This arch is odd,' he said. 'Arches are old. Very old. They started right back in the time of the ancient Sumerians. Romans loved them and made a lot of improvements with them with concrete, but the ancient Greeks weren't big on arches. They found them inefficient and preferred horizontal beams or lintels.'

'The point, Hunter?'

He turned and saw Jodie arching an eyebrow.

'The point is that this doesn't look Roman to me, and if it's not Greek then it must have been built by an older culture.'

'We can worry about that later,' Amy said. 'A

priest is dead and thanks to Agent Gubenko, we know who did it – the Wolf Pack. That means Colonel Neverov and his men are on this island, and probably at the end of this tunnel. We have to stay vigilant and keep moving.'

They moved away from the sealed arch and continued along the passageway until they reached a freshly dug hole in the earth. Staring inside the hole, Amy saw a glowstick twenty feet down, partially covered in dust. Someone had dropped it down a few moments earlier. She sighed. 'Max?'

Hunter curled his fist into a ball and pounded the rock wall with it. 'Looks like Neverov really did get here first. Damn it!'

Blanco said, 'I wonder if he's still down there?'

'There's only one way to know for sure,' said Hunter. 'And that's going down and getting dirty.'

'You make it sound almost romantic,' Amy said.

'No matter what I do or say,' Hunter said, 'I'm just naturally charming like that.'

'Get in the hole, Hunter,' Jodie said.

32

Hunter climbed down the rope. Thanks to his army training and a determination to keep fit in his new career, the descent took little effort and he dropped down the last few feet, landing with a gentle puff on the powdery dust below.

'The Eagle has landed,' he called up, rubbing his hands together to relieve the friction burns.

'And what do you see?' Amy said.

He switched on his flashlight and swept it around in a circle. 'Dome-shape structure carved out of the bedrock. Smooth walls, good workmanship. One tunnel leading off in a northerly direction. Beside it, a very narrow split in the rockface, a rift cave, probably.

There's some Koine Greek carved on the arch above the tunnel.'

'What does it say?'

Hunter stepped closer, angling the beam up at the carved letters. '*Ti stene e pule kai tethlimmene e hodos apagousa...*'

'Wait, we're all coming down,' said Amy, and then she led the rest of the team down the rope until they were standing beside Hunter. Looking at the carved lettering, she put her hands on her hips and frowned. 'English, please.'

'I can read the letters, but I'm not sure of their meaning.'

'It's from the Bible,' Lewis said. 'Matthew 7:14 – "For the gate is small and the way is narrow that leads to life, and there are few who find it."'

Amy looked at the former Marine with admiration. 'What's its meaning in this context, Dr Lewis?'

'Hard to say but in biblical terms, it's usually interpreted as Jesus comparing the way into life as being through a gate. The King James version is different – it reads "Because strait is the gate, and narrow is the way, which leadeth unto life, and few there be that find it."'

'Why is that important?'

'Because when I say strait I'm not saying straight.'

He spelled out the last word. 'Straight means not crooked, but strait is an archaic word for cramped or having a restricted capacity. I think John was using this passage of Matthew to give us some sort of clue, to help us find our way down here.'

'He's telling us to go inside the rift cave,' Hunter said.

Quinn looked at the split in the rock with horror. 'But that's even narrower than the one we just walked through, Max! It's barely wide enough for me, never mind you or Sal or Ben!'

'Quinn's right,' Jodie said. 'That's just crazy. The arch around that tunnel entrance was built for a reason.'

Hunter shone his flashlight inside the stone portico and angled it down the slope. There, in the darkness of the tunnel, he saw a body, crushed to death by a block of stone falling from above. 'Yeah, and that reason is it's booby-trapped.'

'Huh?' she said.

'It's one of Neverov's men,' he said. 'Dead as a doornail because he wasn't lucky enough to have me on his team.'

'It was Ben's translation that gave us the clue,' Jodie said.

'Ah, yes,' Hunter said with a smile. 'But it was my inference that pointed the way to the rift cave.'

'Do you even know what modesty means?' Jodie said, slowly walking away from the portico and towards the rift cave.

'Sure,' he said, coolly walking past her. 'When it comes to being modest, I'm the best in the entire world.' He met her rolling eyes with a wink and turned sideways to go inside the narrow rift cave. The others followed his lead and began to shuffle sideways through the split in the rock. Soon, the small chamber behind them was nothing but a memory.

Hunter was anxious but kept it to himself. The rift cave was inches wide and getting narrower. Doubts about his deciphering of the hidden message back in the chamber rose in his mind. Had he made a mistake? Was he leading his teammates to their deaths? Caving deaths were not uncommon. It was a dangerous business and he knew it.

Now, the cold slimy rock was only an inch from his nose as he shuffled forward, his flashlight pointing the only place he could point it – at the ground and slightly angled off to his right. He heard Quinn sniffing in the dark. Was she crying?

'Hey, Quinn,' he called out.

'What?'

She sounded small.

'You hear about those two guys who found a bat in a cave?'

'No.'

'They decided to play baseball with it.'

Lewis groaned, but only a polite chuckle from Quinn.

'Don't worry,' he said. 'There's always light at the end of the tunnel, and in our case, I mean this literally.'

'We're getting to the end?' Amy said.

He felt a wave of hope ripple through the team. 'Sure are, and the rift's getting wider. We're through!'

He stepped out of the fissure and into a large cavern. Sweeping his flashlight around, he saw a jungle of stalagmites and then the unmistakable outline of a manmade altar. The stone table was just inside an alcove on the far side of the cavern, framed beneath a crumbling stone pediment. Hanging around the altar were dusty sanctuary lamps and ornate candelabra, and above it hung an intricate altar canopy and dossal curtain. In the corner of the cave, four giant pillars towered up to the roof. On the cornice of each one was a different carving matching those on the statues – an eagle, an ox, a man, and a lion.

'Well, we found something,' he said. 'But no sign of John's man statue.'

He walked over to the altar and sighed.

'Max?' said Amy.

'It's as I thought,' he said. 'Looks like Neverov beat us to it. Damn it all to hell!'

'Huh?'

'There's nothing here,' he said. 'Nothing on the altar, nothing behind it. No statue. The Wolf Pack beat us to it, but how? I just don't understand how they got here first! The clue about this cave was on the lion statue. Sure, they had the statue for a few moments in Rome, but only Kostas could translate it.'

'Obviously not,' Amy said. 'They must have photographed it and had someone else decipher John's cryptic message.'

'Or one of us is a traitor,' Lewis said, lifting his flashlight up to his chin and illuminating his face like a ghost. 'But who?'

'Stop it, Ben,' Amy said. 'And don't be so stupid. No one here is a traitor, but Max is right to ask how Neverov got here before us. Whatever we were looking for is gone. Neverov and the Wolves got to it first.'

And then the cave was filled with noise. Russians screaming, automatic weapons roaring. The orange and white strobing of muzzle flashes lit the ghostly stalactites above their heads like snarling fangs.

'Down!' Hunter yelled. 'Everyone, get down!'

33

The team scattered in all directions, seeking cover wherever they could find it. Hunter's new sanctuary was the altar, behind which he now rolled to a stop and reached for his handgun. The Russian terrorists on the other side of the chamber tracked him across to his new cover position with their automatic weapons and opened fire, rounds drilling into the marble walls over his head.

He raised his head above the top of the altar just enough to see the men and returned fire, killing one on the spot and driving the others back out of the chamber. He heard an explosion to his left – a grenade, to be sure – and turned. At the far end of the tomb, Jodie was dragging an unconscious Quinn to the safety of one of the colossal stone support pillars standing in the four corners of the giant cave.

To their left, Amy, Blanco, and Lewis emerged from behind a boulder and ran over to the same pillar for cover. The Brooklynite was firing on some men just out of Hunter's view and giving Amy and Lewis time to get over to Jodie and Quinn. Bullets struck the apex of the pediment and blasted a cloud of rock dust down onto their heads.

'How many more are there?' Hunter yelled.

Blanco squeezed off another three rounds, the powerful recoil jerking the handgun back with each shot. 'Half a dozen.'

Before Hunter could reply, more Russians burst into the chamber, guns blazing. Sweeping their automatic guns across the cave, they made their way across to the altar's enormous marble predella. By the time they reached it, their assault had shredded much of the previously beautiful masonry to ugly rubble and debris. In the crossfire, all of the sanctuary lamps and candelabra had been destroyed, and the altar canopy and dossal curtain were nothing but tattered, smoking rags.

Neverov's army was fast and ruthless. Their provenance in the Russian Special Forces was obvious to Hunter as he watched them fan out into groups. One kept Amy and the others pinned down in the corner while another was keeping him tucked down behind the altar. Every time he tried to get into a good firing position, they opened fire on him with an incandescent rage he had never before encountered. But he had to get a shot at them. Bullets left pockmarks on the wall behind his head as he reached for a handhold, then he swung himself up and fired blindly through the chaos.

They returned fire again, driving him away from the altar and over to one of the columns. It was a retreat but he had no choice. With no one to stop him, Neverov reached the altar, pulled the shredded dossal curtain apart, and stepped inside the back of it. Hunter tried again, crawling to the foot of another column with a better angle and levelling his gun at the terrorists' leader. Squinting down the sights, he lined them up over Neverov's head, but before he could get a single shot off, he was instantly driven back behind the marble pillar.

'Damn it!'

'Must try harder, Hunter.'

Even under the circumstances, he couldn't resist a grin.

'Thanks, Jodie.'

'I thought you guys were on first name terms by now?' Amy asked.

'Whatever gave you that idea?' Jodie said.

Distracted by the conversation and fearing a trap, the Russians unleashed another savage wave of automatic fire on both positions. Hunter tucked his head down away from the flying marble chips and dust as Amy's screams filled the cave.

'How's Quinn?' he called out.

'Still out cold,' Lewis said. 'Probably just as well.'

Hunter knew what he meant. Quinn hated gunfire and battles, especially in a confined space like this. Maybe it really was for the better, but she had been out for a while now and he was starting to get concerned.

'Can you get a shot at them?' he called out.

'Yeah, sure,' Amy said. 'We just thought we'd save our ammo for target practice after the mission. Jeez.'

'Just asking.'

From behind the altar curtain, Neverov called out for his second in command. Lugovoy obeyed instantly, breaking cover and darting through the curtains into the darkness behind the altar curtain.

'Looks like something's got the old boy interested,' Hunter said. 'I'm going in again!'

Medinsky was closest to the curtain, and now he

spun around, unshouldered his Steyr, and screamed as loud as he could while firing all over Hunter's position, driving him back once again. It seemed never to stop, and the English archaeologist wrapped his arms around his head as the air was filled with rounds and marble dust.

'I don't think he likes you very much, Max,' Blanco said.

'No shit.'

'But I think if he just took the time to get to know you a bit better, maybe he might.'

'Funny, Sal.'

'Look out, Max!'

It was Amy's voice. He poked his head out from behind the cover and saw Medinsky running towards him, gun still firing, slung low with the stock up against his hip. He was screaming in Russian and casually sweeping the muzzle from side to side to ensure every inch of his hiding place was covered in as much lead as possible.

Hunter scrambled back and raised his handgun, firing on the Russian, but his bullets went too high, burying themselves in the cave roof above his head. Medinsky's enthusiasm to kill the Londoner had tempered his judgement; the Steyr was out of rounds and now he threw it off to his side with another scream of rage.

'What a shame,' Hunter said. 'I bet you were looking forward to that.'

The Russian said nothing but launched himself at the Englishman with fury in his black, hate-filled eyes. Hunter fired his last shot at him but the bullet went wide; the Russian had already jumped into a rolling-dive, anticipating the shot.

These guys were even better than the Creed.

He fired again but got nothing but a dry click; he was out of ammo. He saw Blanco break cover. He was trying to reach him and help.

'Get back, Sal!'

The advice was unnecessary; the Russians surrounding the altar fired on him and forced him back behind the pillar. Hunter cursed but had no time to worry about the others.

Medinsky came out of the dive and was on his feet. His hand reached out and grabbed at Hunter's throat. He missed, curled his other hand into a fist, and punched it hard into his stomach, just below his ribcage. The strike was good and fast and sent him doubling over in a coughing fit. The Russian seized his chance, driving his knee up into Hunter's face, blasting him back off his feet and crashing to the ground. Hunter felt dizzy and sick and started to lose his vision. He shook his head and took a deep breath, coming back around just in time to see the hulking figure of Medinsky padding over to him with a serrated combat knife gripped in his hand.

'Time to die, Hunter.'

34

The Russian grabbed him by the shirt and pulled him to his feet, pulling his knife hand back ready to strike. Hunter registered the lethal threat and smacked the blade out of his hand. With no weapon, Medinsky simply curled his hand into a fat, meaty fist and drew his arm back like a bowstring. Apparently, a punch would suffice, the Englishman thought.

'I've dreamed of this moment, Hunter.'

'Hey, what you do in your own time...'

Medinsky grunted with rage and unleashed his fist towards Hunter's face. The archaeologist saw it coming and darted his head to the right, allowing the Russian's tight fist to smash into the rockface behind his head. The skin on his knuckles burst apart and sprayed blood over the cave wall, sending him into a convulsion of pain. Grabbing his damaged hand, he spun around, chest heaving up and down as he took another swing at his enemy.

A shot rang out in the gloom. Hunter watched Medinsky come to a thundering stop, bleeding fist mid-air. More blood now, not dripping from his smashed knuckles but from his stomach. The blood bloomed on his camo fatigues and ran down over his tactical belt. Falling to his knees, the big Russian mercenary looked confused.

'Who shot me?' he asked.

Hunter scrambled into the cover of a boulder less than a yard from his foe. 'Not me.' Another shot rang out, louder now, followed by a puff of dust as the bullet ricocheted off the top of the boulder. Hunter ducked down further behind it. 'And not my team, either. Whoever it is, that one was meant for me.'

Medinsky was still on his knees, exposed on the cave floor with blood pumping from the wound in his stomach. He brought his two bleeding hands, encrusted in sand, up to his ashen face and pressed them against his temples. 'He's up on the ledge.'

A third shot exploded with a bright muzzle flash high above them and blew off the top of a stalagmite just in front of their position.

'I know,' Hunter said. 'I can see him. Goatee beard and shaved head. He's moving back into the shadows of that alcove, the bastard. He's definitely not one of ours.'

'Then he must be one of the Brotherhood.'

'Brotherhood?'   Hunter   asked.   'What Brotherhood?'

Medinsky was losing consciousness and if Hunter wanted to know more, he knew what he had to do. He took one more look up at the sniper and then broke cover, scrambling the short distance over to Medinsky and grabbing hold of him by the straps of his chunky tactical vest.

'What are you doing?' the Russian asked.

Hunter said nothing. The shooter had tracked him over to Medinsky and opened fire again. This time, a sustained burst of gunfire chewed into the sandy cave floor all around him as he heaved the dying man's bulk back into the cover of the boulder.

'You saved my life.'

'What's left of it.' Hunter looked at the wound and winced. 'What Brotherhood, Medinsky?'

'Why should I tell you?'

'Because one of them just blew a hole into your stomach and you're dying.'

'I'm not afraid of death.'

'That's not the point.' Hunter ducked as another round pinged off the boulder and flicked up a cloud of dust and rock fragments. 'You tell me who the Brotherhood is, and I promise I'll kill the man who shot you.'

Medinsky laughed. It sounded like someone unblocking a drain. 'Very well. You were a soldier once, like me.' He raised a trembling bloody hand. 'Shake on it.'

Hunter shook his hand. 'Who are they?'

'The Brotherhood of the Falling Star.'

Hunter frowned. 'Never heard of them.'

'I would think not. They are extremely secretive.'

'Then how do you know about them?'

Another gravelly laugh. 'My commanding officer, Colonel Neverov. He has spent thirty years in search of what you seek. On that long, winding road, he has crossed paths with the Brotherhood many times. He was surprised it took them so long to react to the threat this time.'

'The threat?'

'We are the threat, Hunter, at least to the Brotherhood. What you and I seek so badly, they already possess and they are determined to stop us, or anyone else, from getting our hands on it.'

'On what?' Hunter asked. 'What is it they're hiding from the world?'

'First, you should know they have rigged this whole cave to blow up. We found explosives all over the place. They're connected to a tamper-proof timer via a Wi-Fi link.'

Hunter wiped the sweat from his eyes. 'I guess I owe you for that.'

'No, you tried to save my life. Now we are even.'

'Now, tell me what this Brotherhood is so desperate to hide from the world.'

But Medinsky was dead. His blank, glazed eyes turned upward and rolled back into his head, and Hunter knew it was over. 'Damn it.'

Lowering his body to the ground, he relieved the dead Russian of all his ammo and weapons and then saw Lewis sprinting across the cave towards him. He weaved in and out of the stalagmites with the speed and agility of a gazelle and then threw himself down behind the boulder next to Hunter.

'All good, Max?'

'Not really,' he said.

Lewis glanced down at Medinsky. 'You kill the bastard?'

'No, I did not. We have a sniper.' Another shot rang out. 'He's been keeping me pinned down in this position for a while because I ran out of lead. I only just got re-armed.' He waved the Russian's Makarov in the air.

'Good work.'

Lewis ducked down lower under the boulder as another man opened fire on him with a carbine. Bullets ripped out of the muzzle and its flashes strobed the cave's gloomy darkness. Calm and measured, the former Marine took it in his stride, easily reloading his pistol and wiping the dust from his eyes.

Tracked by the sniper, the two men crawled out of the line of fire and bunched up in the shadows behind one of the pillars. Safely out of danger, he returned fire on the Russians. There seemed to be even more of them now than when he had counted them earlier on, but this time they were following the lead of Neverov and firing in controlled bursts instead of raking rounds everywhere. And since the other team turned up, they were now fighting on two fronts.

'Where is everyone?' Hunter said.

'Don't know. I lost Amy and Sal ages ago but I think Quinn is with them. She came around.'

'And Jodie?'

Lewis pointed to their left. 'Check it out.'

He turned and saw Jodie was fighting with one of the tattooed men. Raising his gun, Hunter moved to fire, but Lewis stopped him. 'She can handle it, Hunter. Besides, they're too close. You could hit her. Look – Sal's closer and he's already on his way!'

'But—'

'We move again and the sniper gets us. We have our job to do; let them do theirs, Max.'

Jodie struck the man away with a roundhouse kick and sent him tumbling down into the dirt, but he sprung back up onto his feet like a panther. Reaching for his belt, Hunter saw a flashlight glint on the polished ivory handle of a Damascus pocket knife, which the man now grabbed and threw at Jodie.

She had already seen it and leaped into the air, cresting the flying blade. She watched below her as it flew through the air and smacked against the rockface. The man attacked again, and she lifted her right leg and kicked out, swirling in the glowstick-lit dust and knocking him over into the dirt.

Blanco reached her now and saw she was okay. Sensing movement behind her old friend, Jodie cried out and he turned to see a man climbing up the rocks behind them. He was trying to get up on the ledge. Was it a Russian or one of the tattooed men? He couldn't be sure in the darkness, but it didn't matter. He raised his gun and levelled it at the man, squeezing the trigger gently and barely moving the weapon's barrel a millimetre as he buried a round in his back. He fell in grim silence and hit the cave floor with a meaty squelch.

'They usually make more noise than that,' Jodie said.

Blanco turned serious eyes on her. 'Not when I shoot them, they don't. Let's get moving.'

The team gathered together again behind one of the columns. Amy was in shock. 'What the hell is going on here?'

'It was a trap!' Hunter called out. 'An ambush! The Brotherhood got here first and rigged the entire place to explode. It's supposed to kill Neverov and the Wolf Pack and us, too.'

'The who got here first?' Amy asked.

'They're called the Brotherhood of the Falling Star,' Hunter said. 'And before he died, Medinsky told me they already possess what we're trying to find.'

'Which explains why Neverov has taken after them in such a hurry,' Amy said. 'They're all leaving the cave!'

'Brotherhood of the Falling Star,' Quinn said. 'Finally something that sounds both mysterious and dangerous in equal measure.'

Amy said, 'You said they rigged this place to explode. Can we defuse the timer?'

'Medinsky said it's tamper-proof.'

'It is,' Blanco said. 'It's over here on these rocks. I could do it if I had more time, but not in thirty seconds and with no proper equipment. Eight minutes to blast off, by the way.'

'Does that answer your question?' Hunter asked Amy.

'Yes,' Amy said. 'Which means we need to get out of here right now!'

35

They climbed up the rope and navigated their way through the rift cave as fast as they could, aware of every second ticking away. They were halfway along the first tunnel when the explosives detonated. The blast was savage. A blinding white flash was followed by a deep bass thump and then they all heard Blanco calling out from the back of the tunnel. 'Cloud of dust and smoke racing up behind us!'

'Then keep going!' Amy yelled.

They scrambled out of the tunnel, reaching the chapel just before the smoke and dust overtook them and spewed out into the hot day. Throwing themselves to the hard, rocky ground, the team members rolled down the slope as the smoke and detritus from the cave blasted out into the sky and then rained down on them like ash.

Hunter clawed at the scree and brought himself to a stop. Around him, the rest of the team did the same. When they were all still and getting their breath back, Blanco called out in the dusty air, 'Neverov! He's getting away!'

'Where?' Amy asked.

'Over to the southeast,' he called back, coughing and wiping soot and filth from his face.

'I see them, too,' said Hunter. 'Looks like five of them – Gubenko and Lugovoy and a couple of Spetsnaz guys, I guess. Medinsky is dead. I watched him die.'

'They're going after the Brotherhood,' Amy said. 'And so should we.'

They got to their feet and gave chase, but halfway along the path, the Russians moved out of sight. Seconds later, a chopper rose into the air, turned, and flew quickly away from them towards the bay. When they arrived on the cliffs and looked down, they saw the biggest superyacht any of them had ever seen. Written on its stern, one single word gave them the magnificent vessel's name.

Tiamat.

'What's Tiamat?' Jodie asked.

'Babylonian primordial goddess of the sea,' said Hunter.

'That clears that up.'

The superyacht was at least one hundred and fifty metres in length with a twenty-yard beam, a swimming pool, and two helipads. On each one, there was a helicopter with blades still whirring from having recently landed. One of them was Neverov's.

'The Brotherhood must have flown back to the yacht after snatching the statue,' Amy said, desperately watching the *Tiamat*. It was berthed in the turquoise water between Petra Beach and Tragonisi Island, and thanks to their elevation, Hunter had a clear view of the entire top deck. Hell was being unleashed all over it as Neverov's men poured out of the helicopter and attacked in pursuit of the statue the Brotherhood had removed from the altar.

'What's going on?' Amy asked.

'Looks bad,' Hunter said. 'They're at each other's throats.'

Blanco peered down at the chaos, his calloused hands gripping the rocks in front of them at the edge of the cliff. 'This Brotherhood must want to keep John's codex hidden away pretty damn bad.'

'Not as bad as we want it,' Lewis said.

'And we can't let either of them get their hands on

it,' Amy said. 'We all heard Jim's briefing about Neverov and his men. They're dangerous.'

'And the Brotherhood don't seem too touchy-feely, either,' Jodie said.

'But they seem pretty rich,' added Quinn. 'Check that yacht out.'

Amy agreed. 'A vessel like that has to be funded by serious capital, even if it's just hired.'

'How much do they cost to hire?' Lewis asked.

'A million bucks a week, minimum.'

Hunter looked at her. 'Who knows that?'

'Blue bloods,' Quinn said. 'That's who.'

Amy sighed. 'It's just a case of being informed and briefed, Quinn. You might not have worked it out, but I spend my life dealing with smugglers. I know a thing or two about superyachts.'

Quinn shrugged. 'Meh.'

Jodie looked at the young goth. 'Maybe instead of being such an asshole you could use your little laptop and find out where it's registered? That way we can be sure who owns it.'

'Could be tricky.'

'You mean you might get confused by all the other five hundred-million dollar-superyachts called the *Tiamat* out there?'

'Funny, but not funny,' Quinn said. 'I meant whoever registered that yacht' – she lowered her voice to a conspiratorial whisper – 'just might not have used their real name.'

'Whoever owns it, we have to get on that yacht and find the statue before Neverov,' said Hunter. 'And I think we can use their firefight to our advantage.'

'Agreed,' Blanco said, pushing himself off the rocks and dusting his hands off. 'Those guys busy shooting the crap out of each other is the perfect distraction. We can get in there, grab the statue and be on our way before they know what's happened.'

'Risky,' Amy said. 'There's a lot of guns down there. I don't like it. I see a lot of different ways one of my team ends up taking a bullet. It's a big risk.'

'That's kind of what we do,' Blanco said. 'At least, it is these days.'

'So how do we get on board?' Quinn asked. 'It has some helipads.'

'Except we don't have a helicopter,' Lewis said.

'So how the hell are we going to get over there?' Jodie asked.

'Not swim,' Quinn said. 'No way is anyone getting me in that water.'

Hunter turned back to the yacht. Bobbing about at its starboard stern was an old, battered twin-engine cruiser lashed to the support gantry of the *Tiamat*'s davit crane. He guessed that Neverov and his unit had arrived on Patmos in a Sikorsky helicopter – the same Sikorsky that was now idling on the rear heli-pad. He guessed he had split his team into two sub-units, with one landing on the deck in the chopper while the other stole the boat from one of the many moored up in Grikos Bay so they could attack the Brotherhood on two fronts.

'What's good for the goose is good for the gander.'

Amy glanced at him, bright sunlight brushing her cheek. 'What are you trying to say?'

'Take a look at the rear of the yacht. No way does a ship like the *Tiamat* have a heap like that cruiser as its tender. Some of our Russian friends must have stolen it from the bay and sailed it out there. Maybe even while the Brotherhood was still in the cave.'

'A pincer movement?' Lewis said. 'I like it.'

'And surely they think we're dead after what happened back in the Cave of the Apocalypse,' Quinn said. 'That gives us another advantage.'

Hunter surveyed the mayhem unfolding on the Tiamat's top deck one more time. Because of their distance from the yacht, it was hard to distinguish one side from the other, plus they were all wearing similar black fatigues. Going from the position on the deck, he figured out where Neverov's two units were and watched as they engaged in more ferocious firefights.

The party who had boarded via the cruiser were fighting their way along the quarterdeck. Those who had landed in the Sikorsky were engaging in a skirmish on the sundeck. It looked like Neverov's strategy was to divide the Brotherhood's forces in two and then create a distraction with one unit while getting the other inside the vessel to retrieve the statue. Submachine gunfire crackled in the hot day. Men screamed and yelled orders as they jostled for the superior position.

'So when do we go?' Jodie asked.

Blanco checked his gun. 'There's no time like the present, friends.'

'C'mon,' Hunter said. 'We're wasting time. Anyone like a ride in a nice fishing boat?'

36

The crossing was smooth and thanks to Blanco's careful navigation and the firefight up on the bow deck, they were almost at the *Tiamat*'s stern before anyone in the Brotherhood saw them and opened fire. Amy, Hunter, and Lewis fired back and drove the men into the protection of a covered promenade deck.

Blanco pulled up to the stern and Jodie hopped on board the yacht. Amy and the others provided plenty of cover fire as she lashed a mooring rope to the support gantry of the davit crane and drew her gun.

HARPA was at the party.

Hunter leaped on board and shot at the men on

the deck above them. After a short exchange, he struck one in the throat and sent him tumbling over the rail into the sea. The other men peeled away from the main group and retreated to the superyacht's bow.

'Let's get going,' Amy said. 'I don't want to be around when Neverov and the Brotherhood get bored of shooting at each other and turn on us instead.'

'Which way?' Quinn asked.

'Head to the top deck first,' Hunter said. 'We can access the bridge or most personal quarters from there.'

When they reached the top of the stairs and climbed onto the top deck, the skirmishes they had watched from the top of the cliffs had turned into a full-scale battle for control of the superyacht. Blanco ran over to where half a dozen dead men were sprawled on the deck and took their weapons. Throwing submachine guns and pistols to the rest of the team, he checked his magazine was full.

'Check yours, too,' he told Jodie and Quinn. Amy, Hunter, and Lewis were already checking theirs. 'Good to have some backup weapons.'

Hunter heard more screams and peered down the starboard deck towards the bow. Several black-clad figures were crouch-walking along the bridge deck, submachine guns held tight to their bodies. He guessed this was more of Neverov's men, probably those who had boarded at the stern, making their way towards the yacht's nerve centre. Maybe Yahontov and Turgenev.

When Amy peered down at the foredeck, she couldn't believe what she was seeing. Even before the words left her lips, she already knew the answer. 'Wait a minute, Max. Is that Alexios Kandarian?'

He finished loading his gun and slid the weapon back into his holster. 'Huh?'

'Alexios Kandarian,' she said again. 'As in, the man I arrested back in New York City on a long list of smuggling charges?'

The former army major looked where Amy was pointing. 'Bloody hell, talk about bad pennies turning up everywhere.'

'But how?' Blanco asked. 'It was a ten-million-dollar bail.'

Jodie said, 'Small change for a man like Kandarian.'

'Except you're not allowed to put up your own bail,' Amy said.

Jodie shrugged and didn't even try to look like she

cared about it. 'So he must know lots of people who could put up that sort of money.'

'She's right,' Lewis said. 'I bet his lawyer had a list of people ready to pay up before he even got to the prison.'

'We can worry about that later,' Hunter said. 'Let's get inside the bridge and start looking for the statue. It has to be on board because Neverov chased the Brotherhood straight back here after escaping from the cave.'

'So where do we start?' Lewis said. 'Bridge or quarters?'

'Jodie?' Amy asked.

'Ah, I get it,' she said. 'Ask a thief to think like a thief.'

'Well... yeah, except you're not a thief!'

'Then we try his personal quarters first,' she said. 'If there's a safe or any kind of secure environment, most likely it's going to be somewhere close to where he sleeps.'

A deep thud shook the deck and then a fireball exploded out of the bridge, blasting glass out across the smooth surface of the water.

'And that rules the bridge out...' said Hunter.

'Just what the hell was that?' Quinn said.

'Sounded like a mortar to me.' Hunter peered along the starboard deck towards the bow.

'Me too,' Blanco said. 'Neverov's getting serious about getting that statue.'

'But we're more serious,' said Amy. 'So let's get on it.'

They followed her inside the yacht's top deck, and Lewis paused by a door to study a fire escape plan. 'Kandarian's quarters are this way,' he said, pointing down a long narrow corridor. They made their way along the carpeted passageway, passing several bulkhead doors before reaching their destination.

'This is it,' Lewis said. 'At least, that's what the map said.'

Jodie leaned in closer to the door and squinted. 'Uh-oh.'

Amy looked at her. 'What is it?'

'It's a Weiser Smartkey door lock,' she said. 'And a good one.'

'Can it be opened without a key?' Amy asked.

Jodie grinned. 'Not by your average Joe.'

'And what about you?'

'What do you think? I can get us in here.'

Quinn rolled her eyes. 'And I thought Hunter was arrogant.'

Jodie made no reply. She had already pulled a

screwdriver from her bag and was working on the lock. As she popped off the metal faceplate behind the handle, Blanco and Lewis were standing guard behind her, guns in their hands.

With the cover off, she pulled another small metal tool from her bag.

'What the hell is that thing?' Hunter asked.

'It's a blind hole bearing puller,' she said, taking the puller and working its tip inside the handle. 'I use it to locate the locking pawl and then voila, we're in.'

'Work fast, Jodie,' Quinn said anxiously.

'I always work fast,' she said.

Amy looked nervously down the corridor. 'How fast?'

'Faster if I have quiet,' Jodie said, tinkering with the lock as if she didn't have a care in the world.

'How are we going?' Amy asked, watching her young protégé. She was the picture of calm under pressure.

'I'm just dragging the tip across the actuator – you hear that click right there?'

'Not really. What does it mean?'

'It means we're in.'

The lock popped open with a thin metallic clunk and Jodie pushed down on the handle and swung the door open. 'Let's find the statue!'

They stepped inside an enormous suite of such opulence that for a few seconds, no one knew what to say. Amy found the words first. 'Floor-to-ceiling sliding glass doors, a private solarium, Italian master bathroom with its own luxury whirlpool and spa flotation tub. Whoa.'

'And a walk-in safe,' Jodie said. 'Which could be trouble to break open.'

'Yeah... this place has everything.'

'It even puts the *Oceanus* to shame.' Hunter was referring to the large luxury vessel owned by Raul Vazquez, the Cuban antiquities collector who had taken them prisoner on board his ship during the Atlantis mission.

'I wouldn't say that, exactly,' Amy said, recalling the time she and Hunter spent inside Vazquez's brig.

'But this is one helluva floating penthouse suite,' Quinn said, tracing her hands through a silk voile. 'And wow, by the way.'

They all heard the metallic clicking sound of a hammer being pulled back on a gun.

'When it's on a ship it's called a stateroom.'

They turned around and saw Kandarian standing behind them. He was alone and armed with what Hunter instantly recognised as a vintage single-action colt 38 revolver, complete with a polished ivory handle. In the other hand, he was holding what could only be the one remaining statue created by John the Apostle, except this one was different. The statue of the man was holding a discoloured papyrus scroll to his chest and gazing out on the world with a reproachful stare.

'Fancy meeting you here,' Hunter said. 'Do you come here often?'

Kandarian said nothing. He looked surprised to see them in his inner sanctum and took a step forward with the gun raised in front of him. 'Hands up and drop your weapons. Right now.'

Amy took a step away from the billionaire magnate. 'I don't think so.'

'Do as I say, or die.'

Hunter huffed out a weary laugh. 'You and whose army?'

Kandarian paused. 'You won't get away with this,' he said. 'Look at your situation. You are trapped on my yacht in the middle of the bay, surrounded by dozens of armed Brothers. You have only the most rudimentary knowledge of what you seek. Your search for a truth you can never possibly understand has come to an end. If you beg my forgiveness, I will make sure your deaths are quick and painless.'

'What was John the Apostle hiding when he

made these four statues, Kandarian?' Amy said, ignoring his threat. 'What is it you're so desperate to keep from us... from the world?'

'You are not worthy of the knowledge,' he said coldly.

'Hand over the statue!' Hunter said.

Kandarian's eyes narrowed. 'Aren't you forgetting that I'm armed?'

Hunter stepped closer to the billionaire. 'And aren't you forgetting that so are we? On my last count, we have four guns to your one. And ours are all automatics with fifteen rounds in each mag, while your very beautiful Peacemaker has a six-shot cylinder. Classy, but not up to the fight tonight. Now, toss the gun on the floor and hand over the statue.'

Kandarian seemed to calculate the situation. Then he dropped the Colt and handed the statue of the man over to Hunter, who pushed it in his bag and took a step back. 'What now?'

'Now, you get in there,' Amy said, pointing to his giant walk-in safe.

'Yeah,' Jodie said. 'There's no safer place than a safe.'

Staring down the muzzles of automatic weapons, Kandarian walked into the safe. Amy slammed the door shut and spun the combination dial. 'That should keep him quiet long enough for us to get the heck out of here.'

When they reached the deck, it was like walking into hell. Neverov's Wolf Pack of former KGB men and Spetsnaz operatives had delivered the total carnage the HARPA team had expected. Much of the observation deck was alight, and a gentle sea breeze was blowing the smoke from the burning teak deck in their faces. Up ahead nearer the bow, just below the burning bridge, they heard the chunky rattle of a GPMG.

'Who's firing that?' Quinn asked.

'Not Neverov,' Hunter said, peering along the starboard deck to find the source of the noise. 'It's a Pecheneg – a Russian gas-operated monster and too heavy for his team to be carrying around in any of the packs I've seen them wearing. Must be Kandarian's men.'

'Let them fight it out,' Amy said. 'We have the statue so let's get back to the fishing boat and get out of here.'

No one could argue with that. They followed Amy down a wooden spiral staircase and along the deck back down to the stern where they had moored the boat. 'Almost there,' she said.

'We're not safe until we're back onshore,' Blanco said. 'We're still in danger.'

The sound of gunfire above their heads split the day. Hunter craned his neck up and saw a muzzle flash in the sunlight. The Brotherhood had found them and were giving chase on the deck above them. Then they heard a deep thump and watched helplessly as a rocket-propelled grenade ripped through the air and impacted with their fishing boat.

37

The explosion was wild. Stray pieces of wood burst out of the fireball and showered *Tiamat*'s stern. Hunter screamed for the team to take cover and rolled behind the gunwale as the lethal wood fragments ripped over his head and smashed into the yacht.

Rolling onto his back, he raised his gun into the aim and fired on the men above him through the hole at the top of the stairs. There were two of them, and he struck one in the head and watched him hit the deck, but he missed the man with the RPG launcher. The man now turned the launcher on him and prepared to fire.

'No!' Hunter yelled and tried to roll away, but

then he saw bullets riddling his chest. The man dropped the RPG and tumbled over the side into the bay. The lucky Englishman scrambled to his feet and saw Jodie Priest standing beside him, smoking gun in hand.

'Don't say I never do anything for you, Hunter.'

'I'll try to remember.'

'How the hell are we going to get out of here now they blew up our boat?' Quinn asked.

'By air,' Hunter said. 'This boat has two helicopters up top, remember. We're going to borrow one of them and fly right off this boat.'

More heavy automatic gunfire and the sound of a man screaming in Russian. Quinn turned to Amy, looking for some sanity. 'Sounds even more dangerous up there than before.'

'We have no choice, Quinn,' Amy said. 'We can do this.'

Hunter led them up the steps and over to the body of the man he had killed. Blanco took the RPG launcher from him and the one remaining grenade. Then they ran back along the starboard side of the yacht and took another two flights of steps and a ladder until they finally reached the helipads. Each one was hosting a helicopter – one was obviously

Kandarian's luxury Eurocopter and the other was Neverov's Sikorsky.

Under heavy fire from the GPMG, Neverov was leading his men in a retreat and trying to get back to their chopper. Then Hunter saw the old KGB colonel perform an act of heart-stopping bravery as he broke away from the Wolves and drew the Brotherhood's fire onto himself.

'What is he doing?' Amy said. 'He doesn't stand a chance!'

'He's letting his team get away,' Hunter said.

'Don't ask me to do that for you,' Amy said, horrified. 'It's a suicide mission!'

Neverov sprinted away from the first helipad and vaulted over the rail running around the outside of it. The men behind the GPMG swivelled their gun on him and opened fire. Hunter watched with a strange mix of horror, disgust, and admiration as the old Russian was blasted from the ship and tumbled down dead into the water.

'My God!' Amy said. 'They killed him!'

'But it worked.' Blanco pointed to the Sikorsky. 'The Wolves are on board and taking off!'

The black ex-military helicopter ascended into the air above the helipad and turned to fly away, but it was too late. Neverov's sacrifice had been in vain and the Brotherhood fired on the chopper. It rotated quickly away from the yacht, making a shot on the tail boom too hard to make, so they fired on the control rods. Hunter saw what they were doing and knew it was the best way to bring it down in the circumstances. If they could blow one of them out, the pilot would lose control of the main rotor.

Their rounds ripped into the control rods and blasted them into pieces, instantly breaking their connection to the swashplates and ending cyclic control. The response was predictable, and now he watched as the helicopter spun around wildly, its engine roaring and howling as the machine plummeted into the side of the yacht and exploded in a devastating fireball.

Hunter shielded his eyes from the flash. So did the others. Then the wrecked chopper tipped over the edge of the deck and crashed into the bay.

Quinn arched an eyebrow. 'And you wanted to steal a chopper?'

'Yeah,' Blanco said. 'We're going to need a diversion.'

'I think I already said I'm not doing what Neverov did, right?' Amy said.

'Not that sort of diversion.' Blanco loaded the grenade into the RPG and jogged back along the deck. 'In a minute, you're going to see a good chunk of what's left of the bridge go up in flames. When that happens, all hell will break loose.'

'Memo to Sal,' Jodie said. 'Hell is already loose.'

'Fine, but it's going to get worse. Like when you poke a bees' nest with a stick when you're a kid. When that happens, I want you in that chopper. Max, fire that bird up and meet me at the stern. I'll get on board and away we go.'

'Sounds insane,' Quinn said.

'Sounds risky,' said Lewis.

They heard men yelling in the Brotherhood's strange language once again.

'Sounds like we have no other choice,' Amy said. 'Do it.'

They watched Blanco sprint through the smoke and flames and then waited in the cover of the rear of the bridge house. Less than a minute later, they saw a flash and felt a deep thud and a roar and then men screaming all over again. Submachine guns rattled and automatic pistols crackled in the Aegean heat.

'They're shooting at Sal!' Jodie said.

'He knows what he's doing,' said Amy. 'Everyone, into the chopper!'

They left their cover and sprinted across the rear helipad. Climbing inside, Hunter buckled himself in and instantly felt at home. Much of his life had been spent piloting helicopters for the British Army and he relished any opportunity to get back in the saddle. He checked everyone had their harnesses on and performed a speedy freedom of control test on the tail rotor pedals and then checked the collective and cyclic.

'When do we get into the air?' Jodie said.

'When we've done the pre-flight checks,' Hunter said. 'Because if there's anything wrong with this aircraft, you'll be going into the sea rapidly after getting into the air, okay?'

'Jeez, it was just a question.'

The turboshaft engine roared and the rotor shaft began to turn. As the blades began to whir, Hunter was able to lift the chopper off the helipad and clear the yacht. He flew out wide on the ship's portside and swooped down low almost to sea level. There, hanging off the back of the davit crane, Sal Blanco was waving at them. Hunter pulled in low and tight and the man from Brooklyn leaped into the sea and swam towards the Eurocopter's starboard skid.

Back on the *Tiamat*, Belisarius was leading a team of armed men to the stern where they fanned out. Some opened fire on the man swimming away from them, others on the chopper. Bullets pocked the surface of the sea as Blanco grabbed the skid. 'Go! Go, go, go!'

Hunter rotated the chopper and raced away in a hail of speeding bullets, turning and diving and swooping and evading their fire until they were safely out of range.

'Bloody hell,' he said, finally relaxing. 'That was close.'

'Close?' Blanco said. 'Those crazies nearly blew my ass off!'

'But you got us out of there, Sal,' Amy said. 'We all owe you our lives.'

'No way,' he said. 'We got ourselves out of there, working as a team. No one here owes me anything.'

Amy smiled. 'You can't blame a girl for trying. Max – land this thing somewhere quiet until we can work out what the last statue has to tell us. That's the plan.'

'We have a plan?' Hunter turned to her, a big toothy smile on his face. 'I thought we were just making this up as we went along.'

'Just bring this thing down somewhere safe and drop the smartass attitude.'

Hunter spied one of the many small uninhabited Greek islands off to his right and pulled on the cyclic. 'I'd like to come back at you with some witty repartee,

Amy, but I fear I might be digging myself even deeper into a hole.'

'You're learning, Dr Hunter. Where are we landing?'

'See the small island over there? There's nothing on it. We'll be safe there.'

She arched an eyebrow. 'It seems UNESCO's loss was our gain, after all.'

Hunter said nothing and gently set the helicopter down on a beach on the eastern side of the island. As the blades whirred to a stop, the team climbed out and breathed in the calm hot air for a few moments. Sitting on a rock with his legs dangling over the edge, Ben Lewis was already poring over the discoloured papyrus scroll that they had found on the fourth and final statue.

38

Less than an hour later, the young historian joined the land of the living again. Looking up from his rocky perch, he noticed for the first time that the tide had come in and he was now on his own personal island. Sliding off the rock, he waded through the warm, ankle-high water back to the beach.

'Good news?' Amy said.

He nodded. 'Yes. I think I have something.'

'Great news,' she said. 'What about you, Max – find anything on the actual statue?'

'Not yet,' he said. 'The lettering is coded, as Kostas told us. I need more time.'

'Then it's over to you, Ben.'

The team now gathered around in the shade of

the helicopter. Lewis nodded to himself as if something made sense, and then started his briefing about what he had found on the scroll. 'First, I think I know roughly where we need to go.'

A sigh of relief from everyone. Amy smiled and encouraged him to go on.

'We were right all along. We're searching for Revelation 23, an entire book of the Bible which he hid from the world because of something from the vision. Something he desperately wanted to keep from the world.'

'My God,' Amy said.

'Yeah,' continued Lewis. 'And there's more. John says Book 23 also contains something he calls the Tabula Dei.'

'Map of God?' said Hunter.

Lewis nodded. 'Right.'

'Sounds scary,' Quinn said.

Lewis cleared his throat. 'This scroll is littered with information. If you look here, you'll see a drawing of who I believe to be the son of Domitian, the Roman emperor at the time John of Patmos was a very old man, nearing the end of his life. The child died in infancy and the emperor had him deified. The bit that interests us is right here, around the top of the child.'

'The seven crosses?' Quinn asked.

Lewis shook his head. 'They're stars, not crosses. They're a reference to one of the visions John of Patmos had concerning the Son of Man. As we know, he wrote about it in *Revelation*. In the vision, he saw Jesus risen from the dead with bright fiery eyes, hair as white as snow, and wearing a robe held in place with a shining, golden girdle, or sash. John went further, claiming Jesus was standing amid seven candlesticks and in his right hand were seven stars.'

'Hence the seven stars on the scroll?' Amy asked.

'Exactly, and for this reason, Jesus was often portrayed with the seven stars, as were other deified individuals, like Domitian's dead son. It's a really important piece of writing because believe it or not, it's the only description of what Jesus looks like throughout the entire Bible.'

'But what's the significance of the seven stars?' Jodie asked. 'I still don't get it.'

'It's not hard when you know the full story,' Lewis replied. 'In the vision, Jesus told John that he was alive forevermore and had the keys to hell and death and told John to write down all that he was seeing. He also told him that the seven candlesticks represented the seven churches, and the seven stars were the seven angels of the seven churches.'

'Still not with you, Ben.'

'Wait a minute,' Hunter said. 'Seven churches as in the Seven Churches of Asia?'

Lewis smiled. 'Yes, you know them?'

'Sure, they come up from time to time in the archaeological world.'

Lewis laughed. 'Small world – except they're also called the Seven Churches of Revelation, or the Seven Churches of the Apocalypse.'

Jodie shuddered. 'There's that word again.'

'Indeed there is,' Lewis said, his tone firm and sombre. 'This is serious stuff. As serious as it gets. John says Revelation 23 and the Tabula Dei are hidden in one of the churches.'

'We're getting closer,' Blanco said.

'Maybe,' Lewis said. 'But there's a problem. All Seven Churches of the Apocalypse and their locations are mentioned in *Revelation*, but the problem is I can't work out which specific church John is referring to in this scroll.'

'Which shall henceforth be known to the world as the Patmos Codex,' Hunter said.

'Whatever we call it,' said Lewis, 'I can't crack it.'

'Not yet,' Amy said. 'But you will.'

He sighed, uncertain he could do what she needed him to. 'As I said, I haven't worked out from this exactly which church Book 23 and this Tabula Dei is hidden in, but it's definitely in one of the Seven Churches, and they're all in Turkey.'

'Good work, Ben,' Amy said.

'Just think about that,' said Lewis with his usual wonder. 'Somewhere in one of the Seven Churches of the Revelation is a lost book of the Bible.'

A wave of nervous excitement rippled through the small team as they climbed back inside the helicopter. Hunter fired up the engine and moments later they were flying up into the sky. Amy and Blanco gave each other a look. The man from Brooklyn asked, 'You guys really think we're going to find it?'

Hunter pushed the cyclic to the left and the chopper swung around to the north, a wry smile lighting up his face. 'I guess there's only one way to find out. Let's fly to Turkey.'

Amy got out her phone.

'Who are you calling?' Blanco asked.

'Jim. After what I saw happen to Neverov and the Wolf Pack on that superyacht, we're going to need some backup before we go any further. He has army and air force contacts all over the world. With some luck, he might be able to have someone get a team together.'

* * *

Alexios Kandarian looked out at the devastation on the *Tiamat*'s forward main deck with deep dissatisfaction. Belisarius was down there, and he watched the enormous man padding around, directing Brothers in their efforts to clear away chunks of helicopter machinery and put out burning aviation fuel. Two men were dragging the corpse of one of the Russian soldiers to the portside deck rail. He watched them heave the body over the rail and throw it in the sea.

All this destruction, he thought. So much wickedness. Evil everywhere, as weak men and women sought something they couldn't possibly understand. He turned his thoughts away from the chaos and focused on the True Light that only the Brotherhood of the Falling Star truly knew. On the ancient secret inside the Ark that only the very highest in the Brotherhood knew and understood.

Below, Belisarius turned from his work on the deck and walked up the short flight of steps into the wrecked, smoking bridge house. Seeing his most loyal devotee covered in soot and sweat, he was pleased the Russians who had committed this atrocity were all dead, but there was still revenge to be had on the HARPA team.

'We're almost there, sir.'

'Good.'

'The Brothers are ready for anything.'

Kandarian smiled, his thoughts turning to a small church in rural Turkey. There, inside a hidden sanctuary deep below its foundations, was a high altar. On the high altar was a jewel-encrusted tabernacle, and inside the locked tabernacle was what all these sinners sought so badly. It had already cost the Wolf Pack their lives, and now it would cost HARPA theirs, too. His smile broadened when he thought about such a small, modest thing that could drive so many weak souls to their deaths.

The Tabula Dei.

He turned to Belisarius. 'And the stars of Heaven fell unto Earth, even as a fig tree casteth her untimely figs, when she is shaken of a mighty wind.'

'Are you thinking of any particular star, Eminence?'

Kandarian turned to his disciple. 'They have the fourth statue and the scroll, Belisarius.'

The young giant looked confused. 'But how? My men destroyed Neverov and all his men.'

'We were attacked on two fronts, my loyal servant.'

A frown darkened Belisarius's face. 'Hunter and Fox.'

The billionaire nodded. 'Yes. They raided my stateroom in the middle of the gunfight up on the main deck. They locked me in my safe. Fools didn't know I have a safety release in there, but they were gone by the time I got out.'

'But you have always taught that the Fourth Being will reveal the path to the Ark!'

'This is true. If they are able to decipher the scroll, it will eventually lead them to the Ark.'

'Then we must stop them!' Belisarius said.

'Calm, calm. We will stop them. The place they seek will not give itself up so easily, old friend. We have time to get there first and protect it from their wicked plundering.'

'But the location is known only to you, Eminence!'

Kandarian walked out onto the smoking deck. Loyal Brothers were still putting out spot fires and clearing up the detritus from the battle. 'I know thy works, and where thou dwellest...' he said quietly. 'Even where Satan's seat is.'

Belisarius understood at once. A look of disquiet appeared on his face. 'Your Eminence has told me the location of the Tabula Dei.'

Kandarian was unfazed. 'It is time you knew, Belisarius.'

'But if the HARPA team finds the Tabula Dei, it will certainly lead them to the Ark!'

'Yes, Brother. Yes, it will. That is why we must stop them. Gather the men at once and brief them. We are to return to Leros where we will board the plane and fly immediately. Has the *Tiamat* sustained much serious damage?'

He shook his head. 'Nothing under the waterline or to the engines. We can reach the full seventy knots and be in Leros in less than twenty minutes.'

'Then take us out to sea, Belisarius. When Hunter and Fox reach their destination, we will be waiting for them.'

39

39

Hours later, as an eastern Aegean dusk blushed the sky a deep vermillion, their helicopter touched down in Izmir's Cigli Airport. The Anatolian city was home to over four million people and the third-largest metropolis in Turkey, but tonight its most important feature was the small, dusty statue and its mysterious scroll, sitting on a table in a fast-food restaurant.

Hunched over the scroll with a magnifying glass, Dr Ben Lewis was desperately searching for some kind of clue to refine his earlier work. That had led them this far, to Izmir, but it wasn't enough, and as Amy and Quinn went shopping in the airport for gauze pads, alcohol, and bandages to patch up their wounds, the young historian worked hard, determined to make their stop in the city as fleeting as possible.

When Amy and Quinn returned with the medical supplies, the HARPA deputy director sat next to him and sighed. 'Any luck?'

'Not yet,' he said.

'What about you, Max?'

'Yes,' he said, unwrapping a burger. 'While Ben has been studying the scroll, I've been looking at the inscription on the man statue. Thanks to having Kostas' previous translation in my toolkit, I was able to translate it, and it's fairly straightforward. The inscription on this statue reads, "For only then will they find Satan's throne."'

'So now we have all four verses,' Amy said, referring to her phone. '"I am the man between the town and the stairs, and I say to those who seek Heaven's Falling Star – They must ask the Lion, the Ox, the Man, and the Eagle – For only then will they find Satan's Throne – and the last Word of God will unleash the Apocalypse and strike terror into Man."'

With her words hanging in the air, a grim silence descended on the team.

'Mean anything to you, Ben?' Hunter asked.

Lewis looked up from his work, vaguely annoyed at the distraction. He was met by the sight of Max

Hunter leaning back in a red plastic chair, mouth full of burger.

'As a matter of fact, yes, but I still need to translate the scroll. There's much more information on here.'

'Too bad,' Hunter said.

'I'd probably work faster without any interruptions.'

Hunter took another bite of the burger. 'Makes sense. I know I do.'

Blanco and Jodie returned from the counter with two more trays of food. Cheeseburgers wrapped in greasy paper, little cartons of salty fries, and large cardboard cups of bubbling, ice-cold Coke.

'Here,' Jodie said, placing a burger and a Coke next to Lewis. 'Enjoy.'

The former Marine looked aghast. 'Whoa, not near the scroll, Jodie!'

'Sorry.'

'This could lead us to a missing book of the Bible! It doesn't get any more important than this. Revelation 23 and the Map of God! So here's a rule. We don't put blue raspberry slushies within twelve inches of the Patmos Codex.'

'Sorry, again.'

'Don't worry about it.' He pushed them away and

went back to the dusty, crumbling papyrus and faded ink. 'I just need some more time on this. Quiet time.'

'Maybe a fast-food joint in the middle of an airport wasn't such a good idea,' Blanco said.

'It's all we have,' Amy said. 'Sorry.'

Lewis turned another leaf and moved his magnifying glass up to the top for another search of another page. 'Forget about it.'

'How much more to go?' Hunter asked.

Lewis set down the magnifying glass, sighed, and turned imploring eyes to the English archaeologist. 'Imagine if I asked you a bunch of stupid questions when you were trying to study one of your old pots.'

Hunter scrunched up his burger wrapper and nodded. 'I can see how irritating that would be.'

'Thank you.'

'And I prefer artifacts or relics to "old pots", by the way.'

'Fine.'

Lewis returned to the codex.

Hunter said, 'It's just that it looks like you're nearly finished and time is getting on. Neverov and the Wolf Pack might be dead and out of the picture, but Kandarian and the Brotherhood of the Falling Star are well and truly still in it.'

'I get that,' Lewis said, turning the final page. A

second later, he rolled up the codex, put the magnifying glass down, and took a long drink of Coke. Everyone in the team stared blankly, each waiting for him to say something.

'Well?' Amy said at last. 'Do we know which church, or not?'

Lewis took his time with the Coke. Then he leaned back in his chair and smiled. 'The thing is there's a sequence to the Seven Churches. When they're mentioned in *Revelation*, it's in specific verses, and that gives them an order of precedence.'

'Which is?' Amy asked.

Lewis paused for a moment and looked up to the ceiling, counting something off on his right hand as he muttered to himself. 'Ephesus, Smyrna, Pergamum, Thyatira, Sardis, Philadelphia and Laodicea – one, two, three, four, five, six, seven.'

'And how does that help us?' Quinn asked.

'Don't you see?' Lewis said, beaming. 'On the scroll, one of the seven stars is bigger and brighter than the others.'

'The fifth one along!' Amy said.

'Does that mean we're going to Sardis?' Blanco said. 'That was the fifth church you mentioned.'

'Close, but no cigar,' Lewis said.

'I don't get it,' Amy said. 'I was certain I was right.'

'You are,' Hunter said, turning to Lewis. 'You want to tell her, or should I?'

'You know?' Amy said.

He gave a self-effacing shrug. 'I thought I did, but after what Ben's just said, I know I do.'

Lewis laughed. 'John of Patmos wrote *Revelation* in Koine Greek, which was written from right to left, like Hebrew. This means to him, the burning star isn't the fifth one along but the third one. He's trying to tell us that Revelation 23 and the Tabula Dei is in the third church he wrote about in the *Book of Revelation.*'

'Pergamum,' Blanco said.

'Satan's seat,' Hunter said. 'Another UNESCO site.'

'Whoa,' Quinn said. 'That's some deductive reasoning right there.'

'Max?' Amy asked. 'Have you been to this place?'

He nodded. 'Yes and no. I'm aware of the site in western Turkey. I travelled there once during my doctorate, but I don't know it well.'

'John says there's a passageway beneath the ruins of the theatre there,' said Lewis. 'Under an archway.'

'So how do we get there?' Quinn asked.

Hunter pointed out of the window at the helicopter they had escaped from the *Tiamat* in. 'We will be travelling by Air Kandarian.' As they looked down at Kandarian's luxury helicopter, they saw a Sikorsky UH-60 Black Hawk swoop over the end of the airport and touch down beside their Eurocopter. 'And it looks like Director Gates has come through again – the cavalry has arrived.'

Amy's eyes brightened as she watched the twin-engine military utility chopper powering down on the apron. 'They're from Incirlik Air Base. There's a USAF complement there of over five thousand airmen and a contingent of Special Forces who use the site as a forward base for regional missions.'

'And tonight, that mission is raiding the Third Church of the Apocalypse,' said Quinn.

* * *

They quickly boarded the executive Eurocopter and patched up their wounds while flying north to the town of Bergama, the modern name for Pergamum. Travelling at just under three hundred miles per hour, the chopper made a low pass over the town's terracotta roofs and busy streets before swooping up onto the large hill to the north. They landed next to the famous ancient Ruins of Pergamum, dating back through Roman times all the way to the Byzantine era.

The chopper carrying the Delta Operators landed thirty yards to their right. Franko, Milton, and Schiff were first out, followed by Vranos and Pozniak. Amy spoke with Franko for a few moments and then the five of them fanned out and created a security perimeter around the site at the top of the hill.

Gates had not spoken with the Turkish authorities to clear the flight through their airspace or conduct the search at the site. Relations between Greece and Turkey were strained, and Turkish airstrikes against its Syrian neighbour had also ratcheted up tensions in the region.

The recent decision by the American president to remove Turkey from the F-35 fighter jet programme in response to buying the Russian S-400 air defence system had moved Ankara further away, and no one wanted to be the straw that broke the camel's back. Gates knew the likelihood of giving a covert team with military backup access to the site was next to zero, so he went by one of his favourite sayings.

It's better to ask forgiveness than permission.

In the gathering darkness, Amy pulled a night vision monocular from the bag slung over her shoulder and scanned the ancient ruins ahead of them. She saw no sign of any body warmth or movement, but then Hunter nudged her in the ribs.

'What is it?' she asked.

'Down there.'

The former British Army major pointed down at a line of vehicles. They were snaking into the town in a valley formed by the bottom of the hill and another lower hill to the west. The road came from the north, and driving along it at cruising speed were three black Humvees heading into the town.

'You think it's Kandarian?'

'Maybe. They might have flown into Edremit in the north. That would explain the direction of travel.' The corner of his mouth turned up into a sly grin. 'Know anyone else who drives a fleet of Humvees?'

Blanco walked over to them. 'The Delta Ops are in place, Amy.'

'Good,' she said. 'And it looks like we're going to need them. Look down there.'

Blanco followed her pointing arm to the fleet of black Humvees as they twisted out of sight in the northern reaches of the ancient town. 'The Brotherhood?'

'Gotta be,' she said. 'Although Hunter thinks it might be Madonna on tour.'

Hunter turned to face Blanco's frown. 'I did not say that.'

'Sure you did, champ,' Amy said. 'How long till they get up here?'

'They have to drive less than two miles,' Hunter said. 'They'll be up here in under ten minutes, but then they have the Delta boys to play with. They should buy us the time we need to get in and find Rev 23 and the Map of God. First, we need to blow a large hole in the side of this mountain. Lewis reckons the scroll says there's a passageway located under what's left of the theatre.'

'Isn't that criminal damage?' Quinn asked.

'Yes,' Hunter said, 'but what lurks beneath is much more valuable, don't you think, dear?'

'I'm not your dear, Max.'

'Just an expression, love.'

'Or your love.'

'And I'm not your love, either.'

Hunter and Blanco took explosives from the Special Forces chopper and padded over to the archway at the top of the theatre and set them up. Speaking into a palm mic, Amy briefed the special ops men. 'Three Humvees on the way, I repeat three Humvees. We're probably looking at maybe ten or twelve men. Has to be Kandarian and his Brotherhood.'

'Copy that,' Franko said. 'We'll keep them busy.'

The explosion shook the ground with a deep

thud and sprayed chunks of masonry and rocky ground into the air. Shielding their heads with their arms as the rocks and stones and mud rained down all over them, the team waited until the air had cleared before breaking cover and running over to the theatre's flagstone floor.

Gathered around the newly blasted entrance into the hillside, Hunter spoke first. 'Nice hole.'

'Glad you approve,' Amy said with a smile. 'Shall we?'

Hunter straightened his hat and adjusted the bag over his shoulder. He could see a flight of stone steps descending into darkness. 'I'm game if you are.'

'Lead the way.'

He placed his foot on the first step and checked it was strong enough to take his weight. After so many years, the subsidence beneath its foundations could have played havoc with it, but it was good and now he made his way down into the earth. When his head was at ground level, he stopped and turned to face them.

'Problems?' Amy said.

He reached into his bag with a stupid grin. 'Need a torch.'

'Flashlight.'

'Torch.'

'Whatever you want to call it,' Blanco said, 'we need to hurry things along. I hear the Humvees' engines in the distance. Sounds like they're climbing the hill to the south.'

'Which means fireworks any second now,' Jodie said.

Hunter switched on the flashlight and swept the beam in front of him, angling it down so it lit up the steps as they receded into the darkness below him. 'That's much better. Now, if we can stop standing around yapping, we might make some progress.'

The steps led them down into the hill's interior along a narrow passageway carved out of the bedrock thousands of years ago. The rocky walls were white-washed with lime and reflected the flashlight beams brightly as they made their way along the tunnel.

At the rear of the line, Quinn and Lewis were reading GPS signals off her mini laptop, but they grew weaker by the step and then died out completely. The young goth sighed and put the computer away; now it was back to basics as they made their way along the tunnel. Without technology, it felt to Quinn Mosley like they were operating on a wing and a prayer.

They reached the base of the stone steps and found themselves standing in a large natural cave whose stalactite-spiked ceiling disappeared into a darkness their flashlights were too weak to light. Spying another gaping mouth of a tunnel on the opposite wall, they weaved around waist-high stalagmites and crossed the cave floor.

Inside the new passageway, the terrain was harder with fist-sized rocks littering the dusty ground and roughly hewn tunnel walls full of jagged razor-sharp rocks. Hunter saw this section had given its carvers a much harder time than the tunnel leading up to the surface.

Then the blood-curdling sound of gunfire echoed down the entrance passageway.

'Delta Ops are engaging with the Brotherhood,' he said grimly.

'We must be almost there,' Amy said.

'There's nothing we can do except keep going,' said Blanco.

Jodie, who was standing close by him, nodded. 'They'll be okay. They're tough men.'

Lewis had wandered off into the black void ahead of them through the same sort of stone slab doorway they had encountered back on Patmos. Now, he startled them by calling out, 'I think I found it. Get over here.'

'What have you got, Ben?'

'It's a split in the rock, like back in Patmos. I think they did the same thing in both locations and used natural cave formations as part of the architecture of their sanctuaries.'

'He's right, damn it,' Jodie said. 'This is the entrance to the sanctuary.'

'Adytum,' Hunter said.

'What's the difference again?'

Hunter pointed to the space they had just walked through. 'This is the sanctuary and that is the adytum.' He turned and pointed at the split in the rock. 'It's the innermost and most sacred part of any temple, even more so than the sanctuary.'

'I'm so glad you're on the team,' she said.

'Thanks,' he said. 'And I'm... And you're taking the piss out of me, aren't you?'

'It's true what they say,' she said. 'You're as sharp as a razor blade.'

Blanco pushed past them. 'Are we going in there or not?'

'After you,' Hunter said.

But Blanco was already gone, vanishing into the shadows of the tunnel.

40

When they reached the end of the tunnel, there was no doubt they had found what they were looking for. A vast, natural cave appeared before them, formed from the region's basalts and andesites. Punctuated by boulders and scree and stalagmites, a series of alcoves ran along the far wall. These were manmade and one of them, in the middle, contained a carved stone altar. Even from back in the entrance, they could all see the small, dust-covered box resting on top of it.

Hunter reached it first, carefully picking it up from the high altar and blowing the dust off the top of it. The fine powder had accumulated over centuries, and now it scattered in Blanco's flashlight beam. Behind him, Amy set up a small LED camping lantern for more light.

When Ben Lewis walked over to Hunter, he felt like he was in a dream. The cocky English archaeologist was holding in his hands a carved wooden tabernacle box. On its lid, a beautifully carved Lamb of God stared out at him with reproach in the darkness of the adytum.

Don't open me, it whispered out to him. *Don't look inside.*

But I have to.

He looked at Hunter and took the final step, walking through the flashlight-illuminated dust motes until he was almost face to face with his teammate. 'Mind if I take it from here?'

'Not in any way at all.' Hunter handed him the locked box with a cautious look and raised his hands, palms out. 'I've seen the end of *Raiders of the Lost Ark*. This baby is all yours.'

'That's very good of you, Max,' Amy said. 'Not many archaeologists would turn down the chance of making such a discovery. I'm glad you're in HARPA.'

'Technically, I'm still with UNESCO,' he said. 'I could be planning on taking this for myself and giving them all the glory.'

Jodie shook her head and sighed. 'No, that wouldn't work at all, Hunter.'

'Oh yeah?' he said. 'Why not?'

'Because I'd shoot your balls off for being a traitor.'

Hunter considered the comment. 'I was just joking, of course. I'm completely on this team now.'

Jodie raised an eyebrow as the corner of her mouth turned up. 'That's just what I thought.'

'Good,' Amy said. 'This is a HARPA mission, not a UNESCO one.'

Hunter gave a mock salute. 'Yes, ma'am. Besides, I already tried the lid and it wouldn't come off.'

Quinn laughed. 'That is so you, Max.'

'Wouldn't come off?' Amy said. 'What are we talking about here, some sort of puzzle?'

'Exactly,' Lewis said. He had been fiddling carefully with the lid while the others were talking. Now, he pulled out a Swiss army knife and used the rim of the box as a fulcrum point to try to prise the lid off. 'It reminds me of a Sri Lankan puzzle box, but with some important differences. But I think I can...' The lid popped off in his hands. 'Open it.'

Amy broke the silence. 'What's inside, Ben?'

He peered inside and gasped. 'Another roll of discoloured papyrus! It's Revelation 23.'

'Then we found it,' Amy said, almost in a whisper. 'We actually did it.'

The team gathered around Lewis, flashlights at their sides, except for Blanco's, which he was angling down inside the box. A small, tightly rolled scroll of papyrus sat innocently inside. Lewis reached down and pulled it out. 'If we're right – this book of the Bible has been missing from history since the day John wrote it.' He unrolled it and frowned.

'What's up, Ben?' Amy asked.

'Can't read it, sorry. It's in another language altogether.'

'Damn it all...' said Blanco. 'Was this guy trying to make this hard or what?'

'But look – another scroll!' Lewis said. 'It's the Tabula Dei... The Map of God.'

He set down the box and unfurled the map. Struggling with the Greek for a few moments, his eyes finally lit up. 'It says this map will lead us to the location of the Ark. He says the Revelation relic is inside the Ark.'

'As in Noah's Ark?'

'It doesn't specify.'

'I don't understand,' Blanco said. 'Is he saying there's another relic?'

'Yeah,' Jodie said. 'I thought Revelation 23 was what we were searching for.'

'Apparently not,' Hunter said.

'And he says this "Revelation relic" is inside it?' asked Amy.

Lewis nodded.

Blanco leaned in and pointed at the map. 'What's that mountain, Ben?'

'Mount Ararat.'

'Which is a highly significant biblical location, right?' asked Quinn.

'Of course,' Amy said. 'It's where Noah's Ark landed after the Great Flood. Even I know that! And yet the Tabula Dei says this Revelation relic isn't on Mount Ararat but over to the southeast of it in these other mountains. What gives?'

Lewis smiled. 'You're not exactly right about the Ark's location, Amy.'

'But I also thought the Bible says the Ark landed somewhere on Mount Ararat,' Hunter said.

'No, it really doesn't,' said Lewis. 'The Bible doesn't mention Mount Ararat specifically but instead refers to Urartu, which was an ancient kingdom covering a large area of eastern Turkey and part of modern-day Armenia. People didn't start associating the Ark with Mount Ararat itself until much later in the tenth century. The Tabula Dei isn't wrong. The fact it's pointing us to somewhere other than Mount Ararat is a good thing. The location marked on John's Map of God is where we'll find the Ark, and whatever John says is inside it.'

Quinn reached forward and pulled the map from Lewis's hands. 'Let me see that map again.'

'Hey, be careful with that thing!'

Quinn opened her laptop and started typing. A few seconds later, she spun it around so the rest of the team could see it. 'Guys, you're not going to like this.'

Amy looked at the screen and frowned. A jumble of concrete buildings and what looked like an airport stared back up at her from the flickering laptop. 'What am I seeing here, Quinn?'

'You're looking at a Google Earth image of the place marked on the Tabula Dei as the location of the Ark and the mysterious Revelation relic.'

'So what are all these buildings?' Amy said.

Blanco was also staring at the image. 'Yeah, what are we looking at, Quinn?'

'Kandarian Kargo HQ.'

There was no time to respond to the shocking discovery. They heard movement behind them – the coarse, crunching sound of men's boots on the rocky ground. Blanco spun around, sweeping his flashlight up into the split in the rock they had used as an entrance to the adytum. What he saw horrified them all.

Two tattooed Brothers were dragging a badly beaten Milton into the light. Walking behind them were Alexios Kandarian and Belisarius.

'I'm sorry, Special Agent Fox,' Milton called out. 'We did our best but there were more than we thought. Another two Humvees were already in the town waiting for the Brotherhood. Sixteen of them against the five of us. I'm the only survivor.'

'Shut up!' Belisarius snarled. 'No one wants to hear your sad story of failure.'

'How the hell did you get in here?' Amy asked.

'Silence!' Kandarian shouted. 'Drop your weapons and raise your hands or I will kill the only surviving member of your protection team.'

'Don't do as he says!' Milton called out.

Belisarius thrust the stock of his Steyr into the American's back and sent him crumpling to the ground with a grunt of pain.

Amy stared at the beaten, swollen face of Milton and knew she had no choice but to comply and obey their instructions. She was no killer and letting him execute a teammate for not doing as he said was, to her, the same thing as pulling the trigger herself.

'All right, Kandarian,' she called out in the cold gloom. 'You win. We'll stand down and come away from the adytum.'

She saw Hunter bristle with anger, but he did as she told him and dropped his gun, bag, and flashlight into the dirt. Blanco, Lewis, Jodie, and Quinn all followed him and then they stepped back from the adytum's stone entrance archway.

'Good,' Kandarian said. 'Now walk towards my men.'

Hunter lowered his voice. 'They'll kill us in here in a heartbeat, you realise that?'

'I'm no fool, Max,' she whispered. 'But what choice do I have? They already murdered Franko, Schiff, Vranos, and Pozniak! I won't let them kill anyone else on my team.'

'They're still going to kill Milton, and now us too.'

'I made the call. That's what being the boss' – she paused here and glared at him – 'is all about. If you don't like it you can submit a written report to Director Gates when—'

'When I get us out of his mess?' he interrupted. 'Sure.'

'Enough!' Kandarian yelled, and he turned to Belisarius. 'And kill the protection.'

Belisarius fired into Milton's chest without a

second thought, and Amy watched him crash down dead into the rocky cave floor. The bullet had burst through his chest like a cannon and felled him like a tree. When the big man hit the ground, everyone felt it shake.

'My God!' Amy said. 'You just murdered him in cold blood!'

'Silence!' Kandarian's face was stone. Cold, hard, and emotionless. There was zero emotion or reaction to what he had just ordered and witnessed. 'Or you will be next. Now you are a handful of unarmed amateurs against many more highly trained armed professional mercenaries. I strongly suggest you stay out of our way and let us work and take what we want or you will die down here just like your foolhardy friends.'

'You're just a bunch of insane cultists,' Hunter said. 'How could anyone believe anything you say?'

Kandarian was walking past the prisoners on his way to the adytum, but now he hesitated and turned to face the Englishman. 'Insane cultists? I think you are misinformed, Dr Hunter. I am the enlightened Leader of the Brotherhood of the Falling Star and Keeper of the Revelation Relic.'

41

Hunter and Amy caught each other's eye and shared a knowing glance. The English archaeologist tried hard to look unfazed and shoved his hands into his pockets as casually as he could. 'Is that supposed to impress me?'

Kandarian drew up closer to him now, pulling his pistol from the holster on his hip and pushing the muzzle into his cheek. 'Tell me, Dr Hunter. Why would an enlightened man of religion need to impress a common little soldier and bone-digger such as yourself?'

'Because deep down you know nobody loves you and all you really want is a good friend?'

Kandarian curled his lip and pushed the gun

harder into his cheek. 'A good part of me wants to blow your head off right now.'

Aware the eyes of his teammates were on him, Hunter never flinched. 'Then put your money where your mouth is and do it.'

'No, because the better part of me wants you to die in a much more unpleasant and painful way. This will happen soon enough.'

'I'll look forward to it.'

Kandarian pulled the gun away and thrust it back into the holster. Turning to one of the Brotherhood, he said, 'See to it that their hands are bound behind their backs and keep them out here while I take the Tabula Dei into the adytum and meditate for a moment. Soon, our world will be returned to its original state as it was in the Garden of Eden. No more sinners.'

'Yes, Eminence.'

Tense, anxious minutes passed, then Kandarian returned with Revelation 23 and the Tabula Dei in his hands. He looked calm and peaceful.

Belisarius looked at the papyrus scroll. 'Why are you taking these manuscripts from the High Altar, Eminence? You have always taught that these sacred works must remain where they belong.'

'Yes, but our plans have changed, my loyal follower. Special Agent Fox and her team of amateur adventurers have slowed us down for the last time. They are to die here, now. Have the men lash them to these stalagmites and then set explosives.'

'Explosives, Eminence?' Belisarius was aghast. 'In this most sacred of sites?'

'Are you questioning me?'

'No.' He looked down at his boots. 'Of course not, Eminence.'

'Good. My will is the will of God, Belisarius. It is a divine will.'

Belisarius bowed to his master and then, in his strange language, ordered his men to work. At his side, Kandarian now turned to his prisoners. 'You have fought valiantly for your cause, but because that cause was evil, you have failed. You will die here in this place and there is nothing anyone can do to stop it.'

Amy looked at Hunter and recognised the look she saw in his eyes.

It's now or never.

Turning, she saw Blanco and the others were thinking the same thing.

Blanco moved first. Closest to Kandarian, he lunged forward and attacked him, powering a right hook into his jaw and knocking him off his feet. He cried out for help from Belisarius and the giant spun around and headed towards them.

Hunter made the distance in seconds, responding instantly to the threat posed to his teammate by the Armenian giant. Belisarius saw the ex-soldier charging him down and spun around to face him, bringing his compact machine pistol up into the aim and curling his finger around the trigger.

It was too late. Hunter was already on him and swung a haymaker into his face.

Nothing.

The giant grinned, swept his arm in a wide arc, and knocked Hunter out of his path as if he weighed nothing at all. The Englishman crashed onto the rocky cave floor and rolled over and over with the force of the blow until coming to a stop in front of Quinn and Jodie.

'Hello.'

Jodie rolled her eyes. 'You might want to get back on your feet, soldier. Another one of them wants to use you as a punchbag.'

She was wrong. The man she had warned him about wanted to use him not as a punchbag, but for target practice. He pulled an Uzi from a holster and held it at arm's length. A rooky mistake to be sure, Hunter thought. With Blanco and Lewis now fighting

Belisarius two-on-one, he lunged forward and smacked the weapon's muzzle out of the way, driving the back of his fist up into the young man's face. He grunted in pain and squeezed the Uzi's trigger. A rapid burst of hot nine-mil parabellum rounds raked into the adytum's dusty floor, missing their target by inches.

Hunter rotated on his heel so his back was to the Armenian, placing himself between the man's body and the arm holding the weapon. Then he simultaneously thrust his head back, piling the back of his skull into his nose and twisting the Uzi from his grip. Swivelling back away from him, he brought the wire stock up into his temple.

The Armenian hit the deck like a sack of wet cement. Hunter didn't have to check if he was alive or not. No one survived three pounds of gun piled into the temple, not delivered at that velocity, anyway. He snatched up the man's ammo belt and slung it over his shoulder as chaos erupted in the adytum.

Beside him, Quinn ran for the safety of a stone pillar. Jodie covered her with another Uzi she had snatched up off the floor as Blanco disarmed and knocked out one of the Brothers. Taking his blow-back-operated pistol, he fired on some of the men as they fled for whatever cover they could find.

Scanning the adytum, Blanco saw no sign of Kandarian.

A man rushed Quinn. She pushed him away. Her courage surprised her, but when she heard more shots, she threw herself back down to the ground. She cursed herself for being such a coward, but when the bullets traced across the air only inches above her head, she let it slide. Staring up at the chaos exploding all around her, she decided the safest place to be was up on a ledge she had seen to her right, but before she could get to her knees, the man crashed down on top of her.

She screamed as his hefty weight crushed her into the grit, but then he rolled off and leaped to his feet. He reached for his knife and yanked it from the sheath. Its cold steel blade flashed in the green light of the glowstick. Quinn wanted to cry, but she had been through too much to fall apart at the final hurdle. Whatever happened now, she would not give up and let this man kill her without a fight.

She scrambled to her feet and took a step away, only to feel the rockface at the rear of the alcove bang up against her back. She was trapped and the man was moving closer with evil growing in his narrow eyes.

'Your friends aren't going to save you now.'

'You keep away from me, you son of a bitch!'

When he laughed, the sound of his voice was swallowed up by the chaos of the fight exploding all around them in the cave system. 'Who is going to stop me?'

'Me.'

He paused and stared at the young goth. For a second, he looked almost sorry for her. 'You? Don't make me laugh!'

With her chest heaving up and down with fear, Quinn looked around the alcove and time seemed to freeze. Lewis was hitting another of the men in the face with a hefty punch and knocking him to the floor. Blanco was struggling to pull a hunting knife out of a dead man's ribcage. She wished she hadn't seen that.

Then a loud bang exploded in the cave and the man in front of her froze and dropped the knife. When blood ran from his mouth, she guessed what had happened. He crashed down dead onto his face and she saw Amy standing behind him, smoking gun in her hand.

'You okay?' she asked.

As Quinn looked at her, she saw the shining blade of a knife slip in front of her throat. Behind her, a grinning Belisarius grabbed her by the shoulder and called out, 'Everyone, stop fighting and take a step back, or she dies.'

'Take it easy,' Blanco said, instantly seeing how dangerous the situation had become. 'Just take it easy, fella.'

'Shut your mouth and drop your weapons!'

Kandarian strolled forward out of the shadows and patted his follower on the back. 'You have done well, Belisarius.'

When the HARPA team had laid down their weapons, he ordered them once again to stand in the corner with their hands raised.

Belisarius pushed Amy over towards her friends so hard she nearly fell over. She turned and stared at Hunter. His eyes were fixed on the Leader of the Brotherhood, and if he was frightened he wasn't showing it. Blanco was struggling and kicking out at two men as they forced him to the ground and began lashing him to a sturdy stalagmite. They had already tied Lewis, Jodie, and Quinn down and now they were coming for her and Hunter.

'You can't do this, Kandarian!' Amy cried out as two more men dragged her across the cave to her own personal stalagmite. On the far side of the cave, they were lashing Hunter against another of the rough, upward-growing basalt mineral deposits.

'I can and I have, Agent Fox,' Kandarian said.

Boots crunched on the stony cave floor as the Brotherhood moved in and out of their line of sight. Belisarius oversaw much of the activity, ordering men back and forth as they finished their work and picked up their packs.

Amy controlled her breathing. 'So, you're going back to the Ark then, huh?'

It was desperate, she knew, but it was all she could think of. Her words got the reaction she was looking for when Kandarian turned and stared at her, the ghost of a smile on his face. 'What do you know of the Ark?'

'Enough.'

'You're bluffing.'

'Maybe, maybe not. Why don't you let us out of here and we can talk about it?'

Kandarian sneered. 'What you do or do not know about the Ark does not matter any more, Agent Fox. You and all of your friends will be dead in...' He looked at Belisarius. 'How long is the timer?'

'Five minutes.'

'Five minutes,' Kandarian repeated and turned to the entrance. 'I don't know what it feels like to have thousands of tons of rocks fall on you and crush you to death, but you are about to find out.'

'If I'm going to die,' Amy cried out, 'then you can tell me what this has all been about.'

Kandarian stopped on the spot and turned. She saw from his face he was considering her final, desperate plea.

'Very well, then you shall know.'

Blanco lowered his voice. 'I can't believe that worked...'

'Shh!'

'You already know a great deal about the prophecy.' As Kandarian began speaking, the cave grew deadly silent. 'But not everything. The knowledge is a secret, hidden by John the Apostle two millennia ago and guarded by the Brotherhood ever since the fateful day I discovered the terrible truth. This is why he hid the votive statues, the Four Living Beings of the Apocalypse. He had four of his disciples walk them to different sacred sites, so no one person would ever again find all four. One was sent to Mount Sinai, another to Megiddo. The third went to Petra in the Wadi Musa.'

'The Valley of Moses,' Hunter said.

'Exactly, and the fourth was kept in the Cave of the Apocalypse. Yes, you have found the Tabula Dei, the Map of God. Yes, you have read the map and can see where it is pointing to. Yes, you know the

Ark is there even though this is not what you think it is.'

'Is he supposed to be clearing this up or confusing us even more?' Jodie said.

'And yes,' he continued, 'John of Patmos wrote twenty-three chapters for his *Book of Revelation*, not twenty-two as is universally accepted today. Yes, Revelation 23 contains not prophecy as we find in the previous twenty-two verses, but a historical account of something his vision of the Lord told him. But John the Apostle wrote it in an ancient code only the Brotherhood have deciphered. This is why you could not read it.'

'Tell me something I don't know,' Lewis said.

Kandarian ignored him. 'If you had read it you would already know what I am about to tell you now. The vision told John of Patmos not only what awaits a world of wicked sinners, but that God had already punished us.'

In the grim silence, Amy said, 'And how did he do that?'

'He sent a comet to destroy Sodom and Gomorrah,' Kandarian said casually.

'Tell me,' said Quinn. 'Do you spend a lot of time breathing in cheap incense?'

'It's not as crazy as it sounds,' Hunter said. 'You

remember when we were on the plane flying to Luxor during the Atlantis mission?'

The young goth shrugged. 'Sure. You told us about the Taurus Meteor Shower.'

'Taurid,' he said. 'Our planet orbits through it twice a year. Every June and November we pass through it, and some have argued we got badly smashed up on a pass through it around twelve thousand years ago.'

'I remember,' Amy said. 'Those meteors crashed into Greenland and nearly wiped out Atlantis, just when Plato said their civilisation collapsed. That's why the Atlanteans created the fire lance – to destroy any future meteors.'

'I knew you were listening,' Hunter said. 'The point is that while that happened twelve thousand years ago and wiped out Atlantis, there was another collapse of human civilisation much more recently, around four thousand years ago.'

Belisarius rounded on them, gun in his hand. 'Shut your mouths and listen to His Eminence!'

'No,' Kandarian said. 'Please, Dr Hunter – go on. I'm fascinated. You were saying something about the collapse of civilisation four thousand years ago.'

Hunter stared at his captor for a moment and then resumed. 'For a long time, archaeologists have struggled to explain the almost simultaneous collapses of several great civilisations. The Harrapin culture in the Indus Valley, Sumerians in Mesopotamia, and Egypt's Old Kingdom all fell at around the same time. Over forty cities and their cultures vanished from history at roughly the same point in history.'

'And now you have an explanation?' Kandarian raised an eyebrow.

'Maybe, yes.'

'Enlighten us.'

'Astronomers have calculated that once every two and a half thousand years, our planet is bombarded by even more meteorites than usual, and that this bombardment lasts around two centuries.'

'That's a lot of rocks,' said Jodie.

'It is,' Hunter continued. 'And thanks to the work of French archaeologists who found something at three separate areas in the Middle East – a specific calcite substance only occurring in meteorites – the evidence seems clear. Four thousand years ago, in around 2200 BC, the earth was pounded by an intense meteor shower. That was just around the time that—'

'That is talked about in *Genesis*?' Kandarian said. 'Not quite.'

'And this is what you think happened to Sodom and Gomorrah?' Amy asked.

'Again, not quite.' Kandarian paced up and down in the green light of the glowstick. 'To begin with, everything Dr Hunter has just said is blasphemous. Remember, "Then the Lord rained upon Sodom and Gomorrah brimstone and fire from the Lord out of heaven." You see, those cities were not wiped out by chance or accident, as Dr Hunter has described, but deliberately destroyed by God for their wicked and depraved sins.'

'We're back on that,' Jodie said with an eye roll.

If Kandarian heard her, he didn't show it. 'Sodom and Gomorrah were located near modern-day Al-Lisān in Jordan. Those cities were obliterated by the Lord, but another meteor that was part of the same shower flew over the top of them and crashed into the Armenian Highlands, near Mount Ararat.'

'Ah, slowly it comes together,' Amy said.

Kandarian gave a cold, emotionless smile. 'And that meteorite brought with it a visitor from the heavens.'

'What are you saying?' Lewis said.

Blanco frowned. 'What do you mean when you say a visitor?'

'I mean the relic mentioned in John the Apostle's missing chapter,' Kandarian said quietly.

'I still don't get it,' said Amy.

'He's crazy,' Jodie said.

'No, not crazy,' Kandarian said. 'And now it is time for me to go. I have said too much. There is nothing you can do now. The whole world will feel the wrath of God by midnight and there is nothing you can do about it. It is now time for you to go to the Lord and receive judgement. Goodbye, Special Agent Fox.'

Kandarian raised the pistol and pointed it at Amy. She froze in terror, her eyes fixed on the black hole at the end of the gun's muzzle and certain she was going to die. Then Kandarian lifted the gun above her head and fired at the lantern, plunging the cavern into almost complete darkness.

She watched them leave and when the stone slab crashed down and sealed off the entrance, she felt her stomach drop about a million miles. She looked at her team, whose faces were lit now only by the eerie light of the green glowstick, and knew she had let them down.

'This is all my fault.'

Her words were punctuated by the rhythmic beeping of the digital timer Belisarius had set to detonate the explosives. It was sitting on one of the many packs of C4 the Brotherhood had left positioned all over the cave, each just out of their reach.

'Don't talk like that,' Blanco said. 'We're all in this together, for better or worse.'

'We're not the Three Musketeers,' Quinn said.

'For one thing, there are six of us,' said Jodie.

'Good math, Jodie,' said Quinn. 'I can't understand why you never went to college.'

'I could have gone to college!'

'Sure,' Quinn said. 'I know what you'd have done if you'd gone to college.'

'What?'

'Your professor.'

'Hey!'

'Shut up!' Amy cried out. 'And I know we're all frightened, but we're not going to spend the last few seconds of our lives arguing with each other.'

'Seconded,' Lewis said.

'One minute left until the bang,' Hunter said.

But he was wrong. The bang came seconds after he had spoken. It was a savage flash of blinding light and a deep roar that rocked the cave, and then everywhere was obscured by a thick cloud of black smoke.

42

In the smoke and confusion, Amy was the first to speak. 'What the hell was that?'

'About two C4s, I'd say,' Hunter said.

'Wrong... again.'

In the darkness, Hunter squinted when he heard the voice. It was gravelly, deep.

And Russian.

It spoke again. 'It was four C4s.'

Fifty seconds.

A tall, strong man materialised out of the smoky darkness. Then Hunter felt someone hacking at the rope binding him to the stalagmite. When he turned, he could just make out in the clearing smoke the tall, lean figure of Colonel Vladimir Neverov. His face was covered in soot and dust, but he was unmistakable.

'I'd reach for a gun to defend myself, Colonel,' Hunter said, 'but something tells me you wouldn't be here if you wanted to kill me.'

'A good deduction.'

With his hands freed, Hunter pulled the rope from his body and ran over to Amy. Whether she was still in shock from the explosion or from Neverov rescuing them, he didn't know. It didn't matter. There were less than forty seconds on the timer and there was no time to think. When he had untied her and she was free, they saw that Neverov had already released Jodie and Quinn.

Thirty seconds.

'Don't forget about me!' Lewis said. 'Remember how funny and charming I am?'

Hunter freed Lewis, and Neverov unlashed an astonished Blanco. When they were all ready to go, the Russian colonel led them through the stone slab arch he had obliterated with C4 and back up the sloping tunnel to the main entrance. They were outside on the hill when the explosives detonated and they all felt the low rumble beneath their feet. Part of the ground collapsed down in a shallow basin and then a column of dust and smoke blasted out of the entrance inches from where they were standing.

They dived to the ground and shielded their faces as the rock and dirt and smoke blew past them like a hurricane. When it finally settled back down to earth, they got to their feet just in time to see a line of Humvees cruising away to the south.

'Kandarian...' Neverov pointed to the cars. 'He will die for killing my men.'

Amy took the lead, brushing past her friends until she was standing beside the ragged, bruised Russian. 'What just happened in there, Neverov?'

'I saved your lives.'

'Yes, but why?'

'And how are you still alive?' Hunter asked. 'We saw you die back on the Tiamat.'

'No, you saw what I wanted Kandarian to see.'

'You killed FBI agents,' Amy said coldly.

'No, Gubenko and our Spetsnaz backup killed them. Against my orders, as it happens.'

A long silence.

'And just how did you know to come here?' Jodie asked.

Neverov smiled. 'I think maybe I can tell you now. In Athens when you fled from Kandarian and his men in the Acropolis, I had a contact place a tracker in your computer.'

Quinn was shocked. 'Wait a minute, my computer?'

'Yes, but don't feel bad. It leaves no trace. There was no way you could have known it was in there.'

'That makes me feel a lot better, thanks,' she said sarcastically.

'There is no time for this now,' he said. 'We must go.'

Amy felt torn. Neverov was the enemy, or at least he had been. Now he had saved their lives but she still felt animosity when she looked at him after all he had put them through. She saw from their faces that the rest of the team felt the same.

'We must go, I say!' he repeated.

'But how?' Amy pointed at their chopper, now no more than a burned-out smoking wreck, flames slipping off its bent rotors into the night. The Special Ops helicopter was in the same condition. 'Looks like the Brotherhood took out our ride.'

'But not mine,' Neverov said. 'When I tracked you here, I called an old friend of mine who lives in Istanbul. Ex-VVS.'

Hunter noted the blank look on Amy's face. 'Russian Air Force.'

'His name is Yuri and he works for Chornomornaftogaz. They operate some offshore jackup rigs in the Odeske gas field out in the Black Sea. Tonight, just for me, he stole his company helicopter and is waiting for us on the other side of this hill.'

'What sort of bird is it?' Blanco asked.

'Airbus H15. Why?'

'Because I know that helicopter well,' Hunter said, stepping in. 'And its range is about half what we need to get to Mount Ararat.'

'We're not flying it to Mount Ararat,' said Neverov. 'We're flying it to Izmir Airport, a short distance away from here.'

Amy frowned. It was not easy putting the fate of her team in this man's hands. 'What happens at Izmir Airport?'

Neverov smiled. 'I am not stupid, Agent Fox. I have already made contact with the Kremlin. Three hours ago they ordered pilots at our base in Khmeimim in Syria to fly an Ilyushin to Izmir Airport. After it picks us up it will fly us into eastern Turkey and land at an airport a few miles to the north of Mount Ararat. There, we will pick up an ex-military vehicle and drive to the Ark.'

'You seem to have thought of everything,' Amy said.

'I leave nothing to chance, but with my men dead I need your help.'

Amy looked uncertain. 'I don't know...'

'I saved your lives, Special Agent Fox, and in doing so I risked my own life.'

'Not all of our lives,' Amy said. She turned and stared at the black hole in the hillside. 'I have to make contact with Jim Gates and tell him the men from the airbase died here today... Died defending us. I want their bodies pulled out of this mountain and returned to the States.'

Blanco put his arm around her shoulder and steered her away from the carnage. 'Of course.'

'We can talk on the plane,' Neverov said, glancing at his watch. 'It will already be waiting for us and time is running out faster than you think.'

* * *

A rose-pink ribbon of sky appeared low above the Armenian Highlands. Through its warm dawn light, the Ilyushin roared above an endless ocean of harsh, untamed wilderness. The deep growl of its powerful engines thundered out into the void around them.

Are we too late?

Hunter's thought came to him as he stared out of

the window across the mountains flashing past below them. It was getting a little rockier now, here and there, a little bleaker. He imagined Kandarian and the rest of the Brotherhood already at the site. What were they protecting? Would everyone in HARPA make it out alive?

He recalled a story he had done for an edition of *National Geographic* a few years back when he had gone into the Mayan jungles with a photographer called Ashleigh Reed. He was on a UNESCO-funded expedition sailing up Mexico's Tzendales River to locate a missing city named Sac Balam, or the White Jaguar.

Many had tried to find it but never succeeded. Hunter was making good progress and was convinced the prize was within his grasp when they had stumbled on an illegal coca plantation hidden in the depths of the rainforest. Chiapas State was a big, empty place. Wild, too. He loved it, but drug dealers armed with AR-15s and six-barrelled rotary cannons he could live without.

He made the call to pull back and live to fight another day, but it was too late. The Comitán cartel had other ideas and broke away from their work producing cocaine to track Hunter and Ashleigh down in the jungle. They had become separated and he had escaped, but they had found Reed and killed her, hanging her body up on a makeshift crucifix as a warning to others. Her face haunted him when things got dark, like now.

Hunter pushed the memory away. The four Soloviev turbofans hummed gently in the background as the Russian airlifter cruised at thirty-seven thousand feet. The atmosphere onboard the foreign military plane had been tense, but not threatening. Settled into the flight, Hunter now turned to the old Russian colonel.

'Tell me, Colonel Neverov. How did you get involved in all this?'

'It was a long time ago,' Neverov said. 'The KGB found one of the statues and locked it away from the world in the vaults deep beneath the Lubyanka. After the Cold War, everything changed. Fell apart. Imploded. My life as I had known it ended. The system frayed and crumbled and then the statue was stolen and dumped on the black market. I was fascinated by it and knew from a note there were more of them.'

'A note?'

'From my commanding officer, General Patrushev. He was in a secret society called the Creed and I think he knew things about this world that most of us cannot even imagine.'

Hunter's eyes flicked over to the others. Amy and Blanco had heard the reference to the Creed but were keeping their shock to themselves. Before Hunter could ask more about what Neverov knew of the secret society, the Russian spoke again. 'I spent my life searching for the statues. When they finally resurfaced, I thought I was dreaming.'

'This is more like a nightmare,' Amy said. 'Not a dream.'

Neverov accepted the point. 'Yes, a nightmare which has killed many of my oldest friends.'

'Why the hell did you save us, Neverov?' Hunter asked.

'Because on the yacht, I overheard Kandarian talking to Belisarius about the relic and what they plan to do with it.'

'You know what it is?' Blanco asked.

'No, but he said he intends on wiping out most of humanity with it. That I cannot allow.'

Amy frowned. 'But I thought that's what you wanted to do with it.'

'Then you don't know the first thing about me, Special Agent Fox. I have devoted my life to this quest precisely to stop men like Kandarian from having it, and that includes the US government or any other government. If this really is the doomsday device we all think it is, then I know I have done the right thing with my life. We cannot let Kandarian get away now.'

Amy said quietly, 'No...'

Neverov reached for a hipflask full of vodka from his bag and downed a generous triple measure. As the spirit burned its way deep inside him, he winced at the pain behind his eyes. Another slug of the vodka, another wince. 'We cannot let him destroy mankind... however he plans on doing it.'

In the silence, the pilot's voice crackled through the intercom. 'Landing in ten minutes. Buckle up.'

Amy and Hunter exchanged a glance.

'Looks like this is it, then,' she said. 'It's down to us to stop Kandarian and whatever the hell this Revelation relic really is.'

43

After the Ilyushin touched down at Iğdir Airport in the foothills of the Armenian Highlands, the team and their new Russian addition drove an ex-Turkish Army Otokar Cobra to Mount Ararat.

The winding journey took them through a dusty valley to the west of the famous peak and then south through the town of Doğubeyazit. They skirted the settlement's northern sprawl without drawing attention to themselves and continued on their way, east now and up onto the western slopes of Ararat. From here, they headed down the range to the east as they drew closer to Kandarian Kargo HQ. In the back, Lewis charted their progress against John the Apostle's Tabula Dei.

The military mobility vehicle rumbled and crunched its way up an isolated track, gaining elevation at a steady pace. Blanco was driving, sitting up front with Vladimir Neverov, and the rest of the team were in the back. Hunter peered through the tiny windows in the back panel and studied the incredible sight of dusk settling over eastern Turkey's Ağri Province. *Moments like this*, he thought, *make everything else worth it.*

'We're here.'

It was Neverov, sitting in the Cobra's cockpit. He checked his pistol was loaded and in working order as Blanco pulled the vehicle off the track and cut the engine. The man from Brooklyn raised a pair of chunky field glasses to his eyes and fixed them on a target through the windshield. 'I can see some sort of concrete structure built into the saddle of the mountain on its southwestern slope.'

'Good,' Neverov said flatly. 'Then Kandarian will be dead in an hour.'

'This can't be about revenge, Colonel,' Amy said. 'That's not the goal of this team. HARPA is here to secure the Revelation relic, Revelation 23 and the Tabula Dei and bring Kandarian to justice.'

Neverov stuffed his gun into his tactical vest. 'Don't get in my way, Agent Fox.'

'Hey, best not threaten Amy, mate,' Hunter said. 'Might not turn out how you planned.'

'I threaten no one,' he said. 'But Kandarian is mine.'

'Leave it, Max,' said Amy. 'We need to get on.'

Hunter turned and scanned the desert's craggy, bouldered surface. How this place had supported life all those years ago would be a mystery to most people, but he knew how much the regional climate had changed over so many thousands of years. Like ancient Egypt, this barren landscape had once been very different. After studying the mountain slope, he said, 'All right, everyone here had experience of mountains?'

Everyone except Jodie and Quinn raised their hands.

'Don't worry about it,' he said. 'I've had a look and it's not too bad. Looks like a goat track leads up most of the way and then it gets trickier, but no ropes or anything like that.'

'Damn,' Jodie drawled. 'There goes the foreplay.'

Hunter smirked. 'Hey, just put your hands and feet where I do and don't look down.'

'Sounds fine to me,' Jodie said.

Quinn shuddered. 'Sounds like a recipe for disaster.'

'I'll be right behind you,' Amy said. 'Let's go.'

* * *

When they reached the top, they were on the outer perimeter of Kandarian Kargo HQ. It was a vast complex from where Kandarian ran his empire, nestled on a plain tucked down between craggy peaks in the highlands. A large airfield sprawled out to the complex's west, but Hunter was more interested in a potential ingress route to the south.

Positioning themselves behind a raised concrete drainage channel running to the south of the entrance, they had a bird's eye view of the main entry point. Two box trucks were pulling out of the complex while a large MAN truck pulling a nondescript, filthy curtainsider had finished groaning up the steep gradient leading to the complex. Men in some kind of gatehouse were ambling about and talking to the driver. They shared cigarettes and smoked and laughed as the darkness of night gathered around them.

'I say we kill them and go right in.'

Hunter turned to Neverov. 'Too many CCTV cameras, Colonel. By the time their bodies hit the tarmac there'll be dozens of armed men out here, guns blazing.'

'But we are running out of time!' he said.

'He's right,' Lewis said. 'Don't you remember what he said back in the adytum at Pergamum? He said by midnight it would be too late to stop his plan. We have less than two hours!'

The men walked to the back of the trailer and checked inside. Then they walked back to the cab and lit more cigarettes.

Hunter wiped the sweat from his forehead and waved a fly away with the same hand. Even now up at this elevation, well after sunset, the summer night was hot and close. 'We've got plenty of time, but only if we stay alive.'

'So you have a better idea?' Neverov said.

'As a matter of fact, I do. Watch this.'

Without warning, Hunter scrambled back from the drainage ditch and moved slowly down the slope towards the flat asphalt area outside the large concrete entrance. With her heart in her mouth, Amy watched as the Englishman broke cover and crouch-walked through the darkness to the back of the trailer. He was out of sight for a few seconds and then appeared again, waving them down.

'Here we go again,' Amy said, her voice uncertain as she led her team away from the entrance and down the slope towards Hunter. 'What's the plan, Max?'

'Anyone like an apple?' He tossed a bright red apple at Lewis.

The ex-Marine darted a hand out and caught it. 'Thanks.'

'There's a lot more where that came from,' Hunter said. 'This truck's carrying about twenty tons of fruit and vegetables. Either Kandarian is going into the grocery trade or he doesn't have a very optimistic view of future food chains. Anyway, all aboard!'

'An apple truck?' Quinn said. 'This is how we're getting inside?'

'Uh-huh,' said Hunter.

'I like it,' Jodie said. 'As break-in ideas go, it's hardcore.'

Hunter smirked. 'I see what you did there, Jodie.'

She hid her smile. 'Move your ass, Hunter.'

He jumped up into the trailer and helped Amy up beside him. Moments later, the whole team was hiding behind crates of fruit, and then they heard the heavy-duty diesel engine fire up. As the truck pulled away and headed inside the complex, Hunter checked his gun.

'All good?' Amy asked the team.

'Ready,' Blanco said.

The truck rumbled deeper inside the compound. 'Are we there yet?' Quinn said.

'No,' Amy said.

'Are we there yet?' Quinn said again.

'Not funny, Quinn.'

'Humour is how I protect myself.'

The truck grumbled on for less than ten minutes and then pulled to a stop. The engine cut and the trailer stopped vibrating. 'We're here.'

'We need to move fast,' Lewis said.

'Ordinarily I would agree with you, but not this time.' Hunter got to his feet and moved to the back of the trailer. 'This time, we wait.'

'For what?' Neverov said.

The trailer's locking gear clunked and then the rear door swung open. A man in a dark blue boiler suit and baseball cap emblazoned with the Kandarian Kargo logo looked up and saw Hunter. A look of confusion registered on his face but then Hunter swung his leg back and kicked him in the head, knocking him out cold. Hunter leaped out of the truck and dragged him back up to the trailer.

'Some help, please.'

Blanco was there, grabbing the man's legs. When

they had the unconscious man tucked away in the curtainsider, Hunter closed the door again and looked down at him. 'He's about my size, I'd say – wouldn't you?'

Amy was horrified. 'You're not seriously going to do what I think you're going to do?'

'And I'd like some privacy to change, please,' he said by way of reply. 'I'm a very modest man.'

Jodie nearly choked on her apple. 'Now I've heard it all.'

* * *

Hunter adjusted the boiler suit, stuffed his Glock in the pocket, and pulled the man's baseball cap down low over his face. Hopping from the trailer, he found himself in a busy delivery area. Another half dozen full-size rigs were being unloaded by men dressed in the same outfits. More food – dried goods, pasta, and rice. Thousands of bags of flour. Thousands of boxes of water. Endless sacks of wheat and potatoes and sugar.

Standing at the rear of the truck, he whistled and got the attention of the men unloading the next truck in the bay. He beckoned them over with a generous wave of his arm and then glanced up into the trailer. 'Ready for some action?'

'How many?' Lewis said.

'Five.'

'We need six more uniforms,' Amy said.

Hunter saw the problem and called out at another man. He joined the others and strolled over to the rear of the fruit truck. Whatever language these men spoke, Hunter didn't know it, so before they got to the truck, he made a big show of swinging open the doors and climbing up inside the trailer. The rest of the team was already hidden down behind the crates.

Hunter moved through to the front of the trailer and waved the men forward. When they climbed up into the truck, the HARPA team swung into action. Jodie and Quinn broke cover and slammed the doors shut. Under the cover of Amy's gun, Blanco, Lewis, and Neverov leaped out from behind their crates and attacked the men.

The battle was not hard. Whoever these men were, they were no match for a crew who counted British and US Army, US Marines, FBI, and ex-KGB among their number. They went down like the sacks of potatoes they had been unloading from the next

truck and then the HARPA team stripped their unconscious bodies of the boiler suits. After changing
into the Kandarian Kargo uniforms, they tied and
gagged their prisoners and stacked crates of fruit
around them.

'That should keep them hidden from any casual
observation,' Hunter said. 'But it won't take long for
someone to notice they're missing and start a search.
We haven't got long.'

'So let's get on it, cowboy,' Amy said.

As they walked away from the delivery bay, they
entered a tunnel carved into the bedrock of the
mountain. The floor was smooth, polished concrete
but the sides were roughly hewn. Minutes passed.
When they reached the end, they emerged onto an
elevated platform looking out across a vast cavernous
hangar. 'This place is like some kind of bunker,'
Quinn said. 'I find that appeals very much to the
prepper in me.'

'You're not far off,' Hunter said. 'I think this place
is exactly like a bunker. I think it was built to survive
the New Apocalypse that only Kandarian and a
handful of his closest initiates and disciples know
about.'

'You really think so?' Quinn said.

Hunter glared out into the cavernous space. 'Absolutely! Just take a look around! Everything here suggests that the Brotherhood created this place to hunker down and protect themselves in.'

'Something so terrible it required a bunker carved out of granite two hundred feet inside a mountain...' Jodie said.

Hunter turned. 'Basalt, but yeah.'

'Whatever,' she said. 'It still gives me the shivers.'

'Me too,' Lewis said. 'And I'm a tough former Marine.'

Amy stared up at the ceiling and whistled. 'Just what the hell are Kandarian and his followers planning that is so bad he had to create this place?'

'That's what we're here to find out,' Hunter said.

Blanco took the weight off, leaned on a rail, and looked out over the bustling scene. 'My brother's pizza parlour seems very far away right now. I'm not so sure I want to know what this psycho has in store for the world.'

'Too bad, Salvatore,' Amy said. 'Let's get moving.'

'Not so fast!'

Amy turned and saw Belisarius standing with three other men in boiler suits. Armed with submachine guns, the men stood fast as the giant padded forward and ripped the Glock from Hunter's hand.

He turned to Neverov and scowled. 'I thought you were dead.'

'I was, but I was resurrected just to drag you into hell.'

'Maybe one day,' Belisarius said. 'But not today. You're coming with me.'

44

On the other side of the complex, Kandarian watched the men finish loading his mysterious freight on board the enormous aircraft. With almost the last of the dull metal drums on board what he had called the Angels, he now turned to Alina Jahovic, who was standing at his side.

'Our destiny nears,' he said coolly. 'Are you ready to change the world, my darling?'

Jahovic's electric-blue eyes flashed rapaciously as they crawled over the men toiling down in the hangar. 'I've been ready for this all my life.'

'Good. The final payload is in place. Let us go to Belisarius and see his progress.'

Kandarian turned and walked through the

skeletal hull of Noah's Ark, around which he had built his empire's headquarters. Reaching the end, he climbed into one of the small electric cars alongside Alina. The almost silent vehicle cruised along the smooth concrete as Kandarian drove through his labyrinthine HQ towards its dark heart. When he got out of the car, Alina hung back.

'Come, my dear, let us go together.'

She looked over his shoulder at the tunnel behind him. 'Perhaps I will stay here in the car.'

'There is nothing to fear. Come.'

The tone of his words told her she had no choice. She swung her legs out of the car and walked with the leader of the Brotherhood down a narrow passageway until they reached a vast canyon ripped out of the mountain by a savage comet impact thousands of years ago.

She felt scared and in danger, but Kandarian's face was a study of calm, peaceful control. He looked down into the canyon and saw various pits dug out over the last year or so. Some were failed attempts to reach the falling star, others had been more successful. The entire scarred place looked like the burned-out devastation of a lignite strip mining operation, and down at the very bottom of it all was a murky subterranean lake.

'We're almost ready!'

It was one of his men, calling up from the channel. He stopped work and swung his pickaxe down into the ground, pausing to wipe sweat from his forehead. Leaning his elbow on the wooden handle, he looked up to Kandarian and Jahovic and spoke again.

'The explosives are all in place just as you ordered, Eminence.'

'And they'll only destroy the lake, leaving the rest of the complex unharmed?'

'Yes, Eminence.'

'Good work.' Kandarian looked out over the water, as smooth and black as polished onyx, and nodded his head. 'Then get the men out of this cave system and back up into the complex. The planes take off in less than thirty minutes and I want this lake and its precious gift buried forever under millions of tons of rock.'

'Yes, Eminence.'

Then, his radio crackled. 'What is it?' he snapped.

'We have some visitors, Eminence,' said the deep voice of Belisarius.

Kandarian looked from the man up to Alina. 'HARPA.'

* * *

Amy Fox was contemplating how she had let her team down yet again. She was standing on the polished concrete floor of the complex's nerve centre when a rich, smooth voice interrupted her thoughts.

'I am the Alpha and the Omega, the beginning and the end.'

She turned her head and saw a man's silhouette up on the gantry. As he stepped out into the light and revealed his face, they all heard the loud rasping noise of a klaxon sounding somewhere on the other side of the hangar.

Amy's shoulders tensed. 'Kandarian.'

'The one and only,' he said.

'What the hell is all this about?' Hunter asked.

'This is prophecy made real, Dr Hunter. This is the righting of a terrible wrong. This is the salvation of the human race!'

As the klaxon continued to roar, a dozen enormous hydraulic hangar doors began to slide slowly open. When Hunter saw what they had been concealing, he had to hide his shock from Kandarian. Twelve Antonov AN-225 Mriya aircraft were parked up in a neat line on the other side of the doors. The name Mriya was Ukrainian for 'dream', but Hunter was looking at no dream. As he stared at the dozen planes, each a brilliant white with KANDARIAN

KARGO emblazoned on their tails in bright red, he knew this was a very real nightmare.

'What the hell are they?' Quinn asked.

'AN-225s,' Hunter said. 'The world's largest planes. My question is, just what the hell does Dr Strangelove up there on the gantry want with them?'

'What are you planning, Kandarian?' Amy called up.

Kandarian smiled. 'The Lord led me here and now my work is done. We came here to search for something so very precious and we found it. Inside this cave system at the bottom of this canyon is Wormwood.'

Amy's eyes narrowed. 'What the hell are you talking about?'

Wormwood.

The word made Amy's blood run cold. 'What is Wormwood?'

'My God,' Lewis said quietly. 'You can't mean...'

'I do indeed mean precisely what you fear, Dr Lewis.' Kandarian spoke into his radio and ordered the pilots to the aircraft.

'What's going on here?' Hunter said.

Lewis had turned white, his mind suddenly full of images of his beloved wife and newborn son in mortal danger. 'Wormwood… It's another Bible reference. John wrote it.'

'He did indeed!' said Kandarian. '"And the third angel sounded, and there fell a great star from heaven, burning as if it were a lamp, and it fell upon the third part of the rivers, and upon the fountains of waters, and the name of the star is called Wormwood; and the third part of the waters became wormwood; and many men died of the waters, because they were made bitter."'

'What the hell is he going on about?' Jodie said.

'He's quoting Revelation again,' said Lewis.

'Yes, I am. If you're interested, the great star that fell from heaven was the comet I spoke of before, which cut a gorge into this very mountain range thousands of years ago. The rivers he describes, which the comet poisoned, are all gone now. All that remains of them is a single underground lake.'

'Poisoned?' Amy asked.

'The comet brought with it another lifeform, Agent Fox,' Kandarian said. 'A visitor from the heavens.'

'Bacteria!' Lewis said.

'Not quite,' said Kandarian. 'But similar. I spent my life searching for the Ark and when I found it, I also found the gorge created by the meteor. A gorge with a lake deep inside its black belly. Only when my men started falling ill and dying did I start researching what was happening. What I found changed my life. I found Wormwood, a totally alien form of microscopic life – a polyextremophile capable of withstanding the harsh realities of space.'

'The theory of panspermia,' Hunter said. 'The scientific theory that there is life everywhere in the universe.'

'I've read about this,' Amy said to her team. 'What he's saying makes sense.'

'More than sense!' Kandarian snapped. 'It is divine will! When the star fell from heaven, it brought with it the toxic spores. It is more lethal than cholera or typhoid but in a similar family. It induces what we call a blood fever in whoever absorbs it. They die of unstoppable internal bleeding. In Revelation 23, John called it Wormwood because it made the water taste bitter, but he lacked the scientific knowledge to understand what it really was.'

'Am I dreaming this?' Quinn said.

'Sadly, no,' said Hunter.

Kandarian was now walking along the gantry and heading towards the steps leading down to the aircraft hangar. 'When John had his vision of seven seals on a scroll of vellum being slowly removed to reveal mankind's future, including the breaking of the seventh scroll when heaven will fall silent, he had another vision. A vision of the past given to him by God and showing him where the falling star crashed to earth, right on top of the Ark! It was a message from the Lord! Our Lord who was trying to punish sinners... but the meteor carrying Aimatos landed here. Today, I finish his work.'

'Aimatos?' Amy said. 'I thought you said it was called Wormwood.'

'In its natural state, we call it Wormwood, but after... processing, we call it Aimatos.'

'Processing?'

'The microorganism is lethal enough as it is, but at considerable time and expense I have harnessed it and made it even more powerful.'

'You mean you've weaponised it,' Amy said with disgust.

'Whatever you choose to call it, Aimatos is the name of the blood disease it induces in humans when they drink it. None of our test subjects lasts more than twenty-four hours after being injected with it.'

'Good God!' Amy said. 'You tested this nightmare out on people?'

He waved away her horror. 'The Brotherhood believes we will be fulfilling the prophecy of John's Revelation by releasing this toxin into the world's water supply.'

'You're insane!'

'No! I am descended from the ancient Byzantine imperial dynasties and charged by God himself to carry out his divine will.'

'Not with us around,' Amy said. 'We're going to bring this nightmare to an end.'

'I'm afraid not, Agent Fox.' Kandarian spoke calmly, the rich baritone timbre of his voice echoing in the vast space. 'Operation Aimatos is quite unstoppable. As you can see, we have been busy here for many months and our preparations are complete. We have already mined the spores from the comet and weaponised them. All that remains now is for me to implement God's will and disperse them around the world in the water supply.'

Amy took a step back but stopped when she felt the muzzle of a gun between her shoulder blades. Turning, she saw Belisarius standing behind her with an Uzi in his hands. She pulled away from the weapon but he moved closer, pressing the muzzle to her midriff. She moved away again and looked back up to Kandarian on the gantry crane.

'You are out of your mind, Kandarian!'

'I am merely implementing God's will. It is the only purpose of the Brotherhood of the Falling Star. It is *my* only purpose. I have dedicated my life to this moment, Agent Fox. I have studied every ancient manuscript in the biblical canon and I am of clear mind and clean conscience. God sent the comet Wormwood to Earth to cleanse mankind's sins, but something went wrong. The comet smashed into his creation and buried itself into the side of this ancient mountain. That was not supposed to happen.'

Aware he had everyone's attention, he lifted his arms into the air and raised his voice to a crescendo. 'Tonight, I intend to right that wrong!'

Blanco leaned towards Amy and lowered his voice. 'Is this guy for real?'

'I can hardly believe it, but I think so.'

Kandarian walked over to the edge of the gantry and stared down at the fleet of vast Antonov AN-225s. 'Progress report, Belisarius?'

'The iodide flares are almost all loaded, Eminence.'

'Good, then we are nearly ready to leave. Evacuate the complex.'

'Yes, Eminence.'

'Iodide?' Hunter called up. 'Is that how you intend on delivering this insanity? Cloud seeding?'

'That's the easy part,' Kandarian said coolly. 'The silver iodide is loaded into flares which are dispersed into clouds. The delivery vehicle may change. Sometimes, rockets are used and sometimes the flares are dropped from aircraft. We are using a fleet of twelve aircraft because rockets would be too suspicious. The target countries would see them on radar, track them for speed and trajectory and then fire a counterstrike. Perhaps some of them would get through, perhaps others would not.'

'I can't believe how calm he is,' Jodie whispered. 'He's totally nuts.'

'This is why the Brotherhood of the Falling Star is using the Antonovs. Each of these aircraft has a flight plan filed with its target nation. Each nation believes these are just more Kandarian Kargo flights. They have no idea of the deadly freight they are hiding deep inside their metal bellies. As the planes enter their airspace, they will disperse Aimatos into the clouds along with the silver iodide which will trigger the precipitation.'

'Making it rain your poisonous bacteria all over the land,' Hunter said with disgust.

'And into the reservoirs and rivers and other water supplies. The water tables everywhere will be infested with it and everyone will die.' Kandarian broke into a crazed peel of laughter as Belisarius oversaw the last batch of Aimatos into the idling aircraft.

'And what about us, Kandarian?' Amy asked. 'What does your God say should happen to us?'

'Some things God leaves to my personal judgement. In your case, you are to be executed here inside this mountain. When the last plane flies out, the underground lake is rigged to explode to protect us from Wormwood in the New Age. Your bodies will be lost under millions of tons of basaltic lava rock and never seen again.'

He turned to Belisarius. 'Take them down to the lake, and this time make sure they die.'

'Yes, Eminence.'

As the giant grabbed Amy's arm, Hunter reached out and smacked the Uzi from his hand. The open-bolt submachine gun struck the concrete floor with a loud smack and Amy instantly kicked it closer to the Englishman. He snatched it up and spun around, opening fire on Kandarian up on the gantry.

Then all hell broke loose.

45

As Hunter sprayed the gantry with nine-mil rounds, the Brotherhood leaped into action. Kandarian turned and hit a button, which activated a second, louder klaxon. This alerted the entire complex to the emergency. On the lower level, Belisarius sprinted for the cover of a nearby tunnel and pulled a submachine gun from one of the dozens of men sprinting into the hangar.

Enraged by his failure to contain the prisoners, the Armenian giant now turned his new weapon on the HARPA team and opened fire with incandescent rage. The savage fusillade of gunfire spat all over the hangar, chewing into the concrete floor and peppering the side of the nearest Antonov.

Hunter and the rest of the team were already taking cover. Amy landed beside the Englishman, ducking her head as a bullet traced past. She was working hard to suppress a wave of guilt about leading her team into this mess when Hunter elbowed her in the ribs.

'Hey! Take a look!'

She twisted around and watched as Kandarian sprinted along the gantry to another set of stairs further along. As he ran, he barked orders into his radio.

'He's trying to get down to the aircraft,' Hunter said. 'He wants them in the air now!'

All around them, members of the Brotherhood streamed out of tunnels and passageways and along the gantries as they made their way towards the Antonovs. Then Vladimir Neverov caught sight of Kandarian and broke cover. Raising his Steyr and aiming for the Armenian, he shot from the hip. Bullets nipped and pinged at the gantry rail and chased Kandarian all the way to the end, where he slipped out of sight into the shadows. Neverov stopped firing and leaped up the stairs to the gantry, three steps at a time.

The look on his face said a thousand words.

'He's killing Kandarian no matter what happens,' Amy said. 'It's not right.'

'None of this is right, Amy!' Hunter reloaded his gun. 'Our job is to make sure this place is destroyed, and that includes the lake and all the Aimatos canisters inside the aircraft!'

'I know.'

Kandarian made it to the bottom of the steps and sprinted across the concrete to the last Antonov. Belisarius was already there, firing on Neverov and keeping him at bay while his leader ran up the rear cargo ramp. The engines were already humming, and now the pilots were turning the aircraft and heading out of the hangar towards the runway.

'This is getting out of hand!' Amy said.

A low roar emanated from deep inside the mountain in the cave system beyond the Ark, and they all felt the ground shake.

'What was that?' Jodie asked.

'Must have been the C4 Kandarian was talking about,' said Hunter. 'They've detonated some of the explosives and destroyed the lake.'

'Saves us doing it,' Lewis said with a shrug.

'Guys...' Quinn said.

Amy turned and saw the young goth. She was crouched down behind one of the pallets, covering her head with her hands. 'You might like to know that the last of the planes just left the hangar! They're all outside now.'

Amy's heart quickened. Everything was rapidly falling apart. Most of the gantry was on fire now, millions of tons of rock had been blown up and brought down on top of the lake, and now men in boiler suits were racing out of the complex and running up the cargo ramps of Kandarian's fleet of death.

Neverov ran back over and slid down beside them. His filthy hands gripped the Steyr and his face was black with soot. Now, he raised his voice to be heard over the klaxon. 'I lost Kandarian. He got out another way. He's in one of the Antonovs!'

'What's the plan, Amy?' Jodie said.

'I just can't see how we can stop all twelve Antonovs from taking off!'

'There is a way,' Neverov said. 'All of the aircraft are now outside on the apron lined up ready for take-off.'

'And?' Amy said.

'If one of the Antonovs were to take off first and then crash into them, the kerosene aviation fuel would ignite in an uncontrollable fireball. Jet fuel burns at well over a thousand degrees, and yet bacteria die at around one hundred degrees. The fire would kill all of it, forever.'

'There's just one problem with your plan, Colonel,' Amy said. 'It involves someone flying one of these planes and crashing it on purpose.'

Neverov's face hardened. 'This is no problem. I am able to fly it. It is a Ukrainian plane flown by many Russian companies and military units. I have flown one before.'

'What you're talking about is insane! It's suicide!'

'It is my choice, Special Agent Fox!'

Amy lowered her voice. She knew there was no changing his mind. 'This is crazy.'

'I will get inside the first Antonov, kill the crew and seize the aircraft. Then I will fly in a circuit and return to the complex. You will seize the one behind it and stop the others from taking off. When I bring the plane about, do not be within a kilometre of this place.'

Amy looked at Hunter for support, but the Englishman was already reloading the Uzi he had snatched from one of the dead men. 'We're really going to let him do this?' she asked.

Hunter said nothing.

'It's his choice,' Blanco said. 'And he's right. There's no other way to destroy this Aimatos creation of his.'

'Good... we are agreed. Now get out of here!' Neverov said. 'Get as far away as you can!'

As the older Russian man handed her his dog tags, Amy couldn't hide her shock. 'Why would you do this for us?'

'I am not a genocidal tyrant. The Wolf Pack were not psychopaths. We were trained Russian soldiers here to do a job. That job was to retrieve the Aimatos microorganism and return it to private labs in Moscow for analysis and then hide it from the world. We were just trying to do for our country what you were trying to do for yours, but I failed.'

'You mean, my enemy's enemy is my friend?' Hunter said.

Neverov managed a sour smile. 'Something like that, Major Hunter. You were worthy adversaries. Now, take my dog tags and get away before it's too late. I will fly this Antonov into the airfield and make sure this nightmare ends here and now. This is my only chance of redemption and I must seize it while I still can.'

'I still don't know about this,' Amy said. 'We'd have to place a lot of trust in you to do that.'

'We can trust him,' Hunter said, turning to Neverov. 'I know you're a man of your word.'

A sad nod. 'And now it's time to go! Run!'

Hunter wasted no time in implementing the Russian's plan. As Neverov ran ahead of them towards the first Antonov, the Englishman led the rest of the HARPA team out onto the airfield and up the back of the rear cargo door of the second Antonov. Resistance was as fierce as he'd expected. Firing on the men in the back of the giant aircraft, they worked hard to get up inside and make their way along to the cockpit.

Hunter ripped a grenade from his belt and threw it inside. 'Down!'

His team pulled back and took cover.

The cockpit exploded in a blinding burst of white light and electric sparks. The force of the detonation blasted the Perspex windows out into the night air, leaving only their bent and burned frames sticking out like charred ribs.

Flames covered every surface of the flight deck and thick black clouds of smoke spewed from the polyurethane foam chairs and billowed up onto the ceiling. It rolled out of the cockpit and into the main cabin and created a noxious black fog. Seconds later, the sound of gunfire echoed from somewhere back down in the Antonov's cavernous cargo hold.

Hunter sprinted away from the burning cockpit and took the narrow metal stairs leading down from the upper deck three at a time. Leaping the bottom six steps, he landed with a crash on the lower deck and was heading straight for the first exit when he heard an Uzi firing. He turned and saw one of the Brothers shooting at Jodie.

She dived to the riveted plate floor, rolling away from the rounds as they chewed into the metal all around her. She reached out for the gun and grabbed it, swinging it around at arm's length and firing on her opponent. The Brother was exposed and had nowhere to run, and his arrogant confidence in his own ability to hunt her down was the end of him. Jodie fired into the big man's chest and blasted rounds into him.

After the first three had found their mark, she closed her eyes, her finger still squeezing on the trigger. Empty cases flew from the ejector port and the smell of gunfire exploded in the air, but she didn't stop until the whole mag was clear. Then she heard the sound of dry clicks as the hammer struck empty space. She opened her eyes in time to see the man's shredded body crash down onto the floor and sprawl out in a dead heap beside a pallet of Aimatos canisters.

Aware that the aircraft was turning to the right,

Hunter called out to his friends. 'We need to get out of here right now! Neverov won't waste time!'

They sprinted out of the rear cargo door and into the night. The chaos had grown. The long line of Antonovs were trapped behind the one they had just disabled, but the explosion in the cockpit had caused the aircraft to turn to the right. An impact with the third Antonov was inevitable and now Hunter watched as it ploughed into it and exploded.

A fireball blasted out into the night, lighting everything as bright as day for a few seconds and then fading back to black. The rest of the crew were abandoning the third Antonov now, streaming out of any exit they could find and making a break from the burning aircraft. With well over seventy thousand gallons of highly flammable kerosene in the wings rapidly approaching its flashpoint, Hunter couldn't disagree with their strategy. Then he saw the first Antonov roaring along the runway, its six monstrous turbofans growling as they lifted the one-and-a-half-million-pound aircraft up off the airfield and into the night.

'There goes Neverov. We need to be far away from here, guys!'

Through the carnage, they saw an airplane push-back tractor rumbling through the smoke towards them. Standing on top of it, Belisarius was holding an Uzi in each hand and cursing in his ancient language. With the tractor still driving along the runway beside one of the Antonovs, he was aiming both guns at Hunter and Amy and the rest of the team as he cried out in rage and fired.

But the tractor got too close to the Antonov's number six engine, which was still at full throttle and making the plane spin around. With the turbofan's blades spinning at nearly twenty thousand revolutions per minute, Hunter knew what would come next. He grabbed Amy and turned her away from the scene a second before Belisarius got sucked through the rapidly spinning blades and blasted into the axial flow compressor into a thousand pieces.

As his body parts were sprayed out the back of the jet in a bloody mist, Quinn doubled over and vomited, but time had run out. Blanco was pointing into the sky at the ominous sight of Neverov's Antonov as it wheeled in the night and aimed directly for where they were standing.

The team went quiet for a split second.

'Go, go, go!' Hunter yelled. 'Now!'

They sprinted off the apron, running through the burning oil smoke, away into the scrub surrounding the complex. They made it to Neverov's kilometre just in time to see Kandarian stumble out of the back of the last Antonov and register with terrified horror what was about to happen to him. Then Neverov was true to his word, and he ploughed the giant strategic airlift cargo plane into the apron, directly striking the head of the line and exploding everything in the most ferocious fireball any of them had ever seen.

The momentum of the speeding Antonov caused a domino effect, smashing each aircraft into the next and triggering fireball after fireball after fireball. A wild conflagration exploded and lit the night for miles, spraying burning jet fuel and twisted metal debris across the airfield. The heat scorched their faces as they watched, and in the middle of it all, Alexios Kandarian had been incinerated along with his Aimatos nightmare. Turning from the carnage, the team made their way back along the goat track until they reached the Otokar Cobra. On the short walk, none of them spoke a word.

Then Blanco swung open the Cobra's driver's door. 'C'mon. Let's get the hell out of this place.'

46

Back at the airport a few miles to the north, dawn rose over the Turkish horizon. Hunter walked across the warm asphalt apron and wearily climbed up inside the HARPA jet. He was grateful it was here; James Gates had ordered the pilots to fly out to Iğdir as soon as Amy had told him where they were going, and they had taken off from Athens immediately.

The first flight of the day, the Russian Ilyushin that had delivered them to this place, roared off the runway and gradually disappeared into the southern sky as it flew back to its base in Syria. Hunter paused on the Gulfstream's top step and took one last look at the airport before stepping inside the private plane.

'Any sign of the Brotherhood out there, Hunter?' Jodie asked.

He shook his head and crashed down into one of the leather seats. 'Not that I could see – and when are you going to start calling me Max instead of Hunter?'

'When I know you better,' she said.

'You mean like when we've been through something serious and life-changing together?'

'Sure.'

He shook his head but said nothing. They were all too shaken up by what they had seen back in the mountains. Neverov's resurrection, the truth about what the Revelation relic really was, Kandarian's insane weaponisation of it into Aimatos, and then the sight of twelve Antonov An-225s exploding in the night in the heart of the Armenian Highlands. It was a week none of them would ever forget.

Stretching out in his seat, Hunter breathed a long sigh of relief. Beside him, Amy was pulling a blanket from a bag. She looked exhausted.

'Getting ready for a good day's sleep?' he said.

'And then some.'

Jodie laughed. 'Me too.'

'Looks like we're not alone,' said Amy.

Hunter glanced down the aisle, and sure enough,

she was right. Lewis and Blanco were settling down at the back, each too tired to talk. Quinn was already asleep. Then the pilot spoke to them over the cabin speaker. Hunter presumed it was a message to prepare them for take-off, but he was wrong.

'This is a message for Special Agent Fox,' he said. 'We have an incoming communication from Director Gates. It's on the plasma screen.'

The announcement woke Quinn, who grumbled and begrudgingly opened her eyes. Amy was already staring wide-eyed at the screen up on the cabin wall when Jim Gates's familiar face appeared. It was odd seeing the rain of Washington DC on the window behind him. It all looked so normal and safe compared with what they had just been through.

'I hear congratulations are in order,' Gates said.

Amy huffed out what might have been a very cynical laugh. 'I'm not seeing it quite that way, but thanks all the same.'

'You had a mission and you succeeded. Good work.'

'Thanks,' Hunter said. 'It was a piece of cake.'

The sound of Blanco chuckling from the back made Gates frown. 'Some sort of in-joke?'

'You could say that,' Hunter said.

'It's good you're settling in, Dr Hunter. Amy, you look like you could use a shower and a few days off.'

Amy managed a weary laugh. 'Try a month off.'

'That's too bad,' Gates said. 'All I can offer you is twenty-four hours.'

The team members turned and stared at each other. Blanco said, 'I don't know whether to laugh or cry.'

'Yeah, you do,' Jodie said.

'If this call is about the mission debriefing, Jim,' Amy said, 'it's going to have to wait.'

'It's not, but the mission debriefing is going to have to wait, all the same.'

Amy's tired eyes narrowed. 'Why?' she asked cautiously.

'We have a problem. A big problem.'

'Another one?' Quinn said.

'Yes,' Gates said. 'And this one might just make your last few days seem like a Sunday school picnic.'

'That I find hard to believe,' Lewis said.

Amy sighed. 'What's it about this time, Jim?'

Gates stared into the camera and as usual, his face was giving away nothing. 'Tell me, Team HARPA, what do you guys know about the Titanic?'

* * *

MORE FROM ROB JONES

Another book from Rob Jones, *The Titanic Legacy*, is available to order now here:
https://mybook.to/TitanicLegacyBackAd

ABOUT THE AUTHOR

Rob Jones has published over forty books in the genres of action-adventure, action-thriller and crime. Many of his chart-topping titles have enjoyed number-one rankings and his Joe Hawke and Jed Mason series have been international bestsellers. Originally from England, today he lives in Australia with his wife and children.

Sign up to Rob's mailing list for news, competitions and updates on future books.

Follow Rob on social media here:

facebook.com/RobJonesNovels

x.com/AuthorRobJones

ALSO BY ROB JONES

The Hunter Files

The Atlantis Covenant

The Revelation Relic

The Titanic Legacy

The Excalibur Code

THE *Hit* LIST

Every crime has a story...

THE HIT LIST IS A NEWSLETTER DEDICATED TO PULSE-POUNDING, HIGH-OCTANE ACTION THRILLERS!

SIGN UP TO MAKE SURE YOU'RE ON OUR HIT LIST FOR EXCLUSIVE DEALS, AUTHOR CONTENT, AND COMPETITIONS.

SIGN UP TO OUR NEWSLETTER

BIT.LY/THEHITLISTNEWS

Boldwood

Boldwood Books is an award-winning fiction publishing company seeking out the best stories from around the world.

Find out more at www.boldwoodbooks.com

Join our reader community for brilliant books, competitions and offers!

Follow us
@BoldwoodBooks
@TheBoldBookClub

Sign up to our weekly deals newsletter

https://bit.ly/BoldwoodBNewsletter